Marionette
The Zombie Series
Season 1

Includes

Copyright © 2018-2022 SB Poe
All rights reserved.
ISBN: 9798598016237

Marionette
Book 1
S.B. Poe

When the Black Death hit it decimated nearly a fourth of all mankind. They were sure it was the end times. They were wrong but while it was happening, when people were dying all around and cries for help went unanswered, they had only one word for it, Apocalypse.

**

"AP Report: The outbreak of rabies in Madagascar has spread to Africa. This current outbreak was recognized by the World Health Organization just 48 hours ago. The rapid spread of this outbreak has prompted US State Department officials to impose a strict NO/FLY policy for US citizens intending on traveling to or from Africa, Australia and Madagascar. The State Department letter says this restriction is temporary and that airlines will hopefully work with customers to reschedule flights. We advise US Citizens within affected areas to reach out to their nearest consulate with questions."

Whispers

The weather was starting out just fine. A cold snap was rolling through at midday and the winds were picking up. The temps were already falling and JW Toles was looking forward to the afternoon. He was headed to his little 180/acre piece of Alabama timberland. Complete isolation. JW likes to have that at times. Kate, his wife, knows that, and it's why she encouraged him to buy the land in the middle of nowhere. The boys enjoy it during hunting season but this wasn't hunting season, so he would be alone. JW had spent about ten years in the Army on the shiny part of the spear before he had to quit. Kate knew why he needed to be alone sometimes. She knew he was a really good man with some terrible demons. He never drank, rarely yelled, never hit, never abused, but he was hard. He was not diplomatic. It made for awkward social interactions so he didn't interact socially. Kate made excuses early in their marriage but as time wore on she would just say, "JW doesn't get out much" and leave it at that.

For his part, JW knew it made things hard for Kate, and that is why he agreed to go to the VA. He found a good doc who helped. He was a mostly normal dad at his kids' soccer games when they were younger and as they went into high school, he went to their football games and baseball games. Most dads went to practice too but JW didn't enjoy standing around and talking. Well, mainly talking.

But today wasn't about any of that, today was about being alone and JW was excited. It was fall break and Kate, being a teacher, was out of school. Josh and Scott, being a junior and freshman respectively, were out too. Josh was going to leave tomorrow to head to a friends house on the lake for a few days and Scott and Kate were going to spend the week pulling out all the Christmas boxes including the lights that JW would be stringing up around the house in a few weeks. Everybody had his or her plans.

They were having an early lunch. Josh was filling his backpack with Vienna sausage cans and long john underwear. He had his sleeping bag and fishing gear. Kate was mainly looking forward to having the house mostly empty. Kate enjoyed reading in the quiet, which was rare with a house full of boys (JW included, she would joke).

"Hey Dad," Scott called from his room, "Can you come in here for a sec?"

JW walked into Scott's room. He was leaned back in an ergonomic computer chair in front of what looked to JW like some kind of multiscreen CIA spying display. Scott's workstation was slightly impressive. Scott was a gamer. He enjoyed coding and met some game creators online helping beta test games for them. He didn't make much money doing it but they paid for all his gear and his Internet bill. Kate didn't really love it but JW convinced her that if Scott could make a living playing video games, more power to him.

"Have you been watching this stuff out of Madagascar and the rabies thing?" Scott asked.

"Not really, just heard some stuff on the news, sounds bad but they have dealt with this kind of stuff there for a while with plague outbreaks."

"Not this kind, Dad. Look,"

Scott pulled up a YouTube video and hit play. A cellphone video started playing. There was a crowd of people walking down the street. Not marching, or chanting or holding signs but just walking all together. The video is shot over the shoulders of soldiers or policemen; they are pointing rifles at the crowd. They open fire and the first lines of people go down. They fire again and most of the rest hit the ground.

"Watch this" Scott says.

They all start to get up. Each one stands and starts shuffling towards the camera again. The police fire again. This is repeated at least two more times before the cameraman and the police break off running.

Scott opened another video; this one is of a man standing on a dirt street in Africa. He is walking in the same aimless gait as the crowd in the other video. It looks like some kind of aid camp because you can see a white tent with a red cross on the hill. The person filming is speaking English.

"This man died less than one hour ago. I saw him die. He came back and attacked a nurse. This is real. We need help." The video ends.

"If you have to say it's real, it probably isn't." JW smirked

"No Dad, I think this may be bad."

"It's bad Scott, but this isn't real. You know that. Rabies doesn't do this. I am sure there are some incidents of attacks but that (pointing at the monitor) isn't what rabies does. Ok?"

"Not really" Scott says as he turns back towards the large screen in the middle.

JW walked back into the living room with a little smile on his face.

"What is that look for?" asked Kate

"Oh nothing, Scott just thinks zombies are on the loose."

"Is that all?" Kate smiled.

Scott was incredibly smart. He thought about things in ways that made JW and Kate wonder if he made more sense than they were capable of understanding. JW said he thought logistically. He planned ahead. That was what made him a good game tester. He knew if getting from point A to point B made sense in the game and if it was worth the effort. But zombies? Kate smiled again.

JW went out to his truck to make sure everything was ready to go. He had packed for a few days of camping. He always carried his pistol and on this trip he was carrying his little civilian version M4 style rifle so he could maybe shoot some wild hogs. They had recently been seen in the area and JW had read an article about how this rifle was almost perfect for pig hunting because it just was. So JW, not really needing an excuse but wanting to have one, used that as the justification to buy one. He loved it. It felt familiar. Anyway he was looking forward to the week ahead.

Kate had picked out three books to read and Josh was completely ready to get going, although he would have to wait till tomorrow because his buddy had to work today. He was going to spend the day relining his fishing reels. Kate also planned to take advantage of Josh and have him help bring everything down, so after he leaves she can just kick back and relax.

JW came through the kitchen door just as Kate was informing Josh of his coming servitude. Josh didn't seem surprised.

"Well, guess I'll be heading out" JW said.

"Well, guess you need to give us a hug" Kate replied. He did

JW went out to his truck and turned the key. He pulled out of the driveway and looked back through the rearview mirror. He caught Kate, Josh and Scott all standing in the big bay window of the kitchen waving at him.

"Wish I could take a picture" JW thought as his eyes returned towards the street in front of him.

In 76 miles, over one river and one lake and around a bunch of bends in the road and one 2.5 miles drive down an old dirt road he would be alone. He turned on the radio to his favorite station. It was talk radio and news. No music. Music put him in moods. Sometimes good moods, sometimes bad, so no music.

All the way there he listened to the news. Between coverage of the latest political crises there was Madagascar. The virus had hit epidemic levels, and the government was having difficulty responding. The UN and WHO had declared an emergency, and the US was teaming with Britain to send a couple thousand troops to help with security. JW couldn't help but keep thinking about Scott's videos. He smiled as he turned down the dirt road. He stopped. He always stopped at this spot. The creek he stopped over marked the southern boundary of his property and he had spent a tiny fortune putting this bridge and road in. The gate was just across the bridge. JW liked to stop on the bridge. He looked at the creek running below and smiled. He moved on. He pulled up to the gate. He got out, unlocked it and drove the truck through. He got out again and locked it behind him.

***

"The disease that has been ravaging Madagascar and Africa has spread to Europe and there are possible reports of cases in the West Coast, more to follow"

***

The radio played as he drove towards the wide spot that served as his campground. Another 1/4 mile. His phone rang.

"Hey honey" It was Kate "Just wanted to let you know we got all the lights down and they went straight into the trash. Only one strand lit up and we couldn't trace anything out"

"Ok, kind of random reason to call, but Ok" JW said

"Well, also, I have been watching TV and talking to Scott"

"Oh this is gonna be good"

"Stop it, John, I am more than a little nervous and now they say it has reached the US"

"Yeah, I just heard that too. What do you want me to do?"

"I want you to stop your truck before you get too far out for cell service and start calling anyone you know from your army days or your dad's army days and find out what the hell is going on. I want you to do that right now and I want you to have an answer to me as quickly as you can. And I want you to consider coming home." Kate's voice rising through the phone.

"Slow down, let me stop and" a deer crossed the road and JW slammed on the brakes, phone flying out of his hand and straight against the windshield.

"Shit" reaching for the phone. 'Hey, you still there"

"Yes, what the hell just happened?"

"A damn deer run across the road. I'm fine. Did you say you wanted me to come home?"

"Yes"

"Are you serious?"

"Yes"

"Let me call you back, I will stop and call a guy or two who may know something and call you back"

"Ok, hurry" Kate said

"Love you bye" and JW hung up the phone. He opened his contacts and found Bridger Preston. Bridger had eaten the same dirt as JW in the Army and had parlayed that into a part-time analyst role on a major news network. He and JW had been tight but not in a while. They still exchanged phone numbers and Christmas cards. He called the number.

" Hey, JW, is that you?"

"Yeah, it's me Bridge. How you doing?'

"Ok under the circumstances"

"What does that mean Bridger?"

"Well first of all my damn spot today got pushed to 5 am tomorrow, because of the damn news reports of this virus thing hitting the West Coast. It's fake news, and the government is about to make a formal statement on that and they are also going to tell folks that this is completely overblown"

"And is it?" JW asked

"I don't know. Right now I am buying a couple of cans of beans to ride it out." Bridger said half jokingly

"But the virus, I have seen some videos"

"Yeah, I saw em too. Don't know what to make of them. I mean come on. That looks like a zombie movie."

"That's what my youngest said just a few hours ago."

"Well, I can't argue with him. The only question is, was it real?"

"Was it?" JW asked

"JW, are you asking me if there are zombies in Madagascar?"

He could hear the smirk on the other end of the phone.

"Alright, I get ya. Be safe and thanks."

"Don't get bit." JW could hear Bridger's laugh even after he hung up the phone.

JW sat there processing what he had just been told. His buddy was as skeptical as he was but it was becoming more and more apparent that this virus might become a problem. Ok, that is not unreasonable. The next step, reanimated corpses, was unreasonable. And reason wins.

"Hey honey, I just got off the phone with Bridger Preston."

"And?"

"Well he says the virus has not spread to the US, and the government is about to say that and that the government will also say that everything is under control."

"We're screwed"

"KATE, I'm shocked"

"Yeah right, anyway, what did Bridger say?"

"He said it's a virus, they spread, we find a cure or something, life goes on. I know you said you wanted me to come home, and I will but I am going to stay up here tonight. I won't make camp, I'll just build a fire and sleep in the bed of the truck."

"What about Josh leaving tomorrow?" she asked

"Let me sleep on it. I'll keep my phone charged with the truck and keep tabs on the news but you can try to have him stay home."

"What do you mean try, I will just tell him," Kate sounded exasperated

"He's seventeen and even if you tell him you can't physically make him. Catching flies requires honey"

"Who the hell would want to catch a fly?" Kate said

They said their goodnights and JW assured Kate he would be home before noon. He parked and plugged his phone into the truck. He kept the key in the radio position to give juice to his phone and he turned up the volume to hear the news. He got out in the wide spot of the road and started to build a campfire. He had brought along several larger logs that he had chopped and stacked for these occasions last spring. He had enough for the week. He needed all the little stuff to get the fire going and the woods can provide plenty. He had gathered an armful and was turning to head back when he lost his footing. He had managed to step right into a small rodent hole that he hadn't seen and it was just enough that when he turned his weight shifted the wrong way and he fell. He was laughing at himself on the way down, right until the moment his head made contact with the rock he also hadn't seen.

"Reports of the virus outbreak in US were in error. US government spokesman says the virus is being monitored. The spokesman also says the US government is confident in its abilities to combat this through educational efforts and expects the public to understand the mild threat and to take appropriate precautions should that become necessary"

***

The news played through the entire night across the wide spot on the road. JW slept.

When JW finally woke it was quiet. And dark. He looked at his watch. 4:15. He assumed it was morning. Damn his head hurt. And he was cold. And dressed.

"What the hell happened?" he thought.

Then he started to remember. He remembered tripping. He remembered gathering wood. It was like his memory was coming back in pieces. Then he remembered his conversation with Kate.

Kate, oh shit. He thought

He stumbled towards the truck and reached up to touch what was causing his head to hurt and he saw the blood on his hand. Not much but definitely blood. He wondered if he had a concussion. He didn't feel sick, but he was a little wobbly. When he got to the truck, he opened the door expecting to hear the bong bong bong of the door chime but instead only silence. He saw his phone with the charger cable attached and realized the radio was no longer playing.

"Great" he thought, knowing a dead battery meant he would have to get someone to come rescue him.

He hated that. He picked up the phone to call his family and realized it was still 4:30 in the morning. He could wait. Instead he opened up his newsfeed and started reading about Madagascar.

Morning

Kate was lying awake. She had drifted off for a little while, nervously. Now she was awake again, and the clock said 4:20 so she knew she hadn't slept much. She turned the TV back on and saw test bars. She panicked a little and realized it was local and flipped the channel to national news. Madagascar.

***

"AP sources are reporting widespread power outages throughout Australia and Eastern Africa. The UAE and Saudi Arabia are reporting cases of the rabies virus, now being dubbed the Marionette virus. Reports of multiple attacks by mobs of infected wreaking havoc throughout some parts of Madagascar have yet to be confirmed. US officials are monitoring the situation and as of now there are still no confirmed reports of the Marionette virus in the US despite earlier reports from West Coast news sources. Those sources have not been able to confirm any treatment at any hospitals. We will continue to monitor the situation. In other news, President Wilson canceled a planned trip to Texas and instead will fly to Camp David to start a long holiday weekend."

***

Kate relaxed a little. After listening to Scott last night and watching his "news" videos she had expected to awaken to the trumpets sounding and some kind of dragon thing crawling out of the ocean with a tattoo of some numbers on its head or hand. The details on that part had escaped her, apparently. But presidents don't go on long weekend trips if the end times are upon us. Or do they? She was pretty sure they didn't, so she felt a bit more relaxed. She climbed out of bed and made her way into the bathroom to do her morning business. She walked into the kitchen and flipped on her single serve coffee maker. It always took it a minute to warm up, so she picked up her phone to check her e-mail. 47 new messages. As she was performing the ritual of cleaning out her inbox, one of the subjects caught her eye. "Family Preparedness Plan" She opened it up. It was some kind of survival/canning device as best she could tell. It looked like a camo pressure cooker and Kate giggled a little. She was pretty sure that if things got so bad that you needed to camouflage your kitchen ware, there wasn't any coming back.

"Mom, mom, come in here quick" Scott called from his room, surprising Kate that he was up this early.

She went to Scott's room, and he had a feed from BBC on his main screen. The scroll said ***"Marionette arrives in Spain"*** and the images were unbelievable. It was a feed from a traffic camera and it wasn't showing traffic. It was showing hundreds of people just ambling around in the middle of an intersection that should be filled with cars and buses. The cars and buses were there, but the cars had their doors open and the buses were empty. Every person in the images was ambling the same way she had in at least a dozen other feeds Scott had shown her throughout the previous evening.

"Scott, this can't be real. It just can't be" said Kate

"Mom, I am connected to the whole gaming world. These folks tend to not spend too much time giving out personal information because they don't want to get doxxed if they pissed the wrong guy off. I am seeing folks putting pictures, phone numbers and addresses all over the place begging for help. And then they just go dark. This is bad."

"Ok, I'll call your father, go wake up Josh."

"Josh left about an hour ago."

"What?"

"Yeah, he said he was gonna get a head start and just meet Bill there."

"Shit."

Her phone lit up in her hand.

Her 5:00 a.m. alarm.

"Shit shit double shit" Kate said out loud, thinking it wasn't, as she turned off her alarm.

She called Josh.

"Josh, where are you?" Kate asked

"I just pulled up to the lake house, and I am gonna sit here and wait for Bill."

"No, you are going to come home right now."

"Excuse me?"

"Josh, I want you home right now. This Marie Antoinette virus has me very worried and..."

"Wait wait wait, the Marie Antoinette virus? Do you mean the Marionette virus?"

"I don't give a damn what it's called, I want you to come home."

"Mom I just got here."

"Now, home."

"Yes, mama" Josh surrendered on the phone. But he figured he was at the lake, he had snuck a six-pack of beer and dammit he was going to walk down to the water and drink a beer. Five A.M. is still five o'clock. Mom would just have to wait a few minutes more.

Kate called JW.

"Good morning honey, what time you heading home?" Kate asked. Surprised at how quickly JW answered the phone.

"About that" JW responded a bit sheepishly.

"About what?" Kate asked. Relieved to hear his voice as though she just needed to make some kind of connection with him, which reminded her again of just how nervous she was.

"Well, genius here managed to fall asleep and let the truck battery run down. It's no big deal, I will just walk back out to the main road and flag someone down to give me a jump" JW was making it up as he went now but he was hoping she didn't notice. She noticed.

"Really, John, you are going to flag someone down and say, Hey my truck is broke down back here in these woods and I need you to let me get in your car and ride with you back into these woods off the road where nobody can see you so you can help with my truck. Really? That doesn't sound axe murdery at all. Now tell me what happened and what we need to do."

"The battery is dead. That's it. I left the key on but I don't want you to come get me. Just send Josh."

"Josh isn't here, he went to the lake, but I called him and he should be on his way home now."

"Well call him back and tell him to come get me. He's halfway here already if he is at Bill McFarland's place."

"Why can't you call him?"

"I think I may need to start conserving my phone battery."

Kate hung up the phone with Josh, slightly angry that he had not already left the lake but glad he was still up that way so he could go get JW.

She turned to the big bay window and looked out into the front yard. The Alabama sky was that gray October color that usually meant football championships and pumpkin patches.

"Please, bring my boys home." Kate said to no one in particular.

Bridger Preston walked into the local affiliate in Nashville at 4:30 for his satellite spot about the latest arms deal between Israel and the UK, which really wasn't that big of a deal but someone decided to give it 3 minutes. He was still amazed that he worked in a news business that prided itself on being 24 hr. news but never seemed to manage to give any story more than 3 minutes. If you have 24hrs you should be able to devote some time to serious discussion and not just soundbite journalism. But what the hell did he know. He was just an analyst, paid to analyze things. He didn't want to steer too far out of his lane.

As he entered the control room, the first thing he noticed was the quiet. Admittedly it was 5 in the morning but usually there were still folks shuffling around and talking. This morning everybody was just watching the feeds coming on the banks of televisions in the back. BBC, CNN, FOX, Al Jazeera and his network all carrying, in one form or another, stories about the Marionette virus. A scene from a street camera in Spain, a dusty road somewhere in East Africa and other odd scenes, streamed across the back wall. The one that caught Bridger's attention was the same one that had drawn the control room from their duties. In larger than normal type across the bottom of feed from Spain,

"FIRST CASE OF MARIONETTE VIRUS CONFIRMED IN NYC.
WHITE HOUSE TO MAKE STATEMENT SOON"

Bridger read it again. And again. His mind was working through all the ramifications. He had spent his life trying to explain to people what the outcomes of any particular decision could mean in the long run. By working through the ramifications you could reasonably predict different scenarios playing out. If you could see all the outcomes that put you ahead of the game, if you can see all the outcomes, reduce it down to one and be right? Well that's why they pay Bridger Preston the big bucks.

Bridger thought about the strange conversation from the previous evening. JW Toles. Damn he hadn't talked to JW in a year or two and except for getting a Christmas card last week he hadn't thought about him in a few months. He was thinking about him now. JW had been a good soldier and Bridger respected him. When he first got to JW's unit JW had only been there about six months, which made him the next newest guy. Bridger's arrival got the FNG label off of JW and for that reason alone JW was always kind of grateful for Bridger's arrival: their friendship came later.

Bridger kept playing it through his head. If JW Toles had come out from his little world to contact him, there was something to be concerned about. JW was not the kind of guy to just pick up the phone and call for a chat about some virus in Madagascar. He was beginning to wonder how JW always seemed to have his "spidey-senses" tuned to just the right thing. When they were in the big ashtray JW had always seemed to sense which buildings to pay more attention to than others. It seemed Madagascar had been the right "building".

He decided he needed more information, so for now he was just like everybody else who was waking up on the east coast of the US, watching the TV and wondering what the hell was happening?

JW decided to walk back to the gate so he could meet Josh. He figured by the time he walked the half-mile back he wouldn't have to wait very long. He grabbed his backpack without thinking and slung it over his shoulders. As soon as it was on his back, he realized he would be coming right back when Josh got here but something told him just to carry it with him, it would be good exercise. He shut the door of the truck and started walking. He got about ten feet from the truck and turned back to grab his rifle. He just couldn't bring himself to leave it unattended in his truck, even in the middle of nowhere. It was habit. Loaded down with his backpack and rifle carried in his right hand, JW had a brief moment and laughed. He did his best to ignore the fact that the thing that screwed with his head the most was how much he missed doing the shit that screwed his head up.

He started down the road. He was wearing a pair of GI issue pants that he had bought on his last visit to the VA Commissary, with a pair of long johns underneath. He had on two long sleeve t-shirts and a fleece camo top with a frogtog jacket. All of his clothes had that slept in feel and nothing really felt like it was on right. He stopped. He dropped his pack and laid his rifle across it. He unbuttoned his pants and re-tucked his shirts in so nothing was all bunched up. He got everything buttoned back up and slung his pack back on. As he turned, he thought he saw someone walk across the road around the next corner. He did a double take but didn't see anything.

"Probably just another deer." He thought, as he unconsciously chambered a round into the rifle.

He started down the road again. A little more comfortable and a lot more alert. He walked to the point where he thought he had seen something (someone?) and stopped. He didn't see any sign of anything and no obvious tracks in the road. He looked at the honeysuckle growing just off the road and decided it had just been a deer standing here feeding. He had about another quarter mile to go and decided to stop and call Josh.

He pulled up Josh in his contacts and hit send. No service. It was spotty all along this road. He kept walking.

Josh was about three miles from the turn off to the bridge road. He called it the bridge road. His dad and brother called it the creek road. But they were wrong. He was rounding a bend when he saw the truck on the side of the road. He slowed down. As he passed he noticed the passenger door was open but nobody was in the truck and nobody was standing by the truck. As a matter of fact he didn't see anybody, anywhere. Both sides of the road give way to fields that run to the woods 100 yards away, so he could see a pretty good area. No one. Odd

He rounded the bend and started down the last stretch of paved road. His turn was about 2 miles down. Even though he would probably get fussed at for using his phone while driving, he called his dad.

JW could see the gate and was halfway hoping to see Josh waiting. He knew it shouldn't be too long. His pocket vibrated.
"Dad, I'll be there in about five minutes," Josh said.
"Can I assume you pulled over and put the vehicle in park to make this phone call?" JW said in his most "sound like a father." voice.
"Nope, bye" Josh said, and the line went dead.

JW smiled. He and Josh had a strange relationship. They both grew into who they were together. JW was trying to piece a life together from a bunch of fragments when Josh came along. They bonded over things that had been therapy for JW, fishing, hunting and just being outdoors. They had been as much comrades as father and son when Josh was young and they had fun. As Josh got older, JW kind of withdrew from him. Josh had rebelled a little in middle school as kids in middle school do and JW wasn't quite sure how to handle it so he didn't. He watched Kate step up and help guide Josh through those years.

Ever since then there had been this strange space between them. They still had fun and laughed but it had changed. JW couldn't quite figure it out.   As he was thinking about this, he saw Josh coming down the road to the creek. He walked up to the gate and unlocked it. Just as he did two very low, very fast and very loud military aircraft raced over his head. JW instinctively ducked to his knees and looked up. Josh heard the roar and slammed on the brakes because that's what teenagers do when they panic. The rear of the SUV decided this was the perfect moment to see what was going on up front.

JW watched as Josh lost control and spun completely around in the middle of the road looking straight back where had he just traveled. He stopped, put the SUV in park and opened the door.
"Well, that was fun" he said, seeing his father hustling across the bridge towards him.
"You, ok?"
"Yeah, just a little shaky. What happened to you?" Josh said making a motion towards his own forehead.

JW reached up mirroring Josh's motion and touched the spot on his head that hurt. He had almost forgotten about it.

"Oh, I just bumped it gathering wood. No biggie" JW said.

"Well, ok, let's get the truck" Josh said starting to get back in his SUV

"I think I am just gonna leave it here. We can come back and get it in a day or two. You can just bring me up here when you come back up to the lake and we can get it then." JW said without really knowing why.

"I locked the gate already. Let's go home."

Josh, not even trying to figure out his Dad's logic anymore, just shut the door and started the engine. JW loaded his pack and rifle into the back seat and climbed into the passenger side.

"Maybe we can grab a bite on the way home," JW said, and they started back down the dirt road again.

Kate stood staring at the pantry. It was pretty well stocked. Her and JW had struggled when they first got married. They would scrape together 75 cents to go buy a roll of toilet paper when things got really tight. They had worked hard through JW's problems but it was a full time effort. JW had held several jobs since they got married but he never held any job more than a few years. Most jobs no more than a few months, and one famously for about an hour and a half. It created a lot of uncertainty about the future when you're buying toilet paper by the roll.

JW finally got some help from the VA and had settled into a good job checking gas lines for the state. He spent most of the time monitoring data from his computer but occasionally he would have to go and ride the gas lines to check them. He enjoyed that part enough. It didn't pay great, but he got a check from the VA too and with Kate's income things had stabilized. After being that broke, their combined income now felt like winning the lottery. They had enough money to pay all the bills on the first of the month. They could keep the pantry stocked and go out to eat occasionally. That was the wish list they made twenty-five years ago when they used to lay in their bed and listen to the couple in the apartment above them beat their head against the headboard.

As she looked in the pantry, she made a meal plan in her head. She decided to make chili for supper. She had the beans and the tomatoes and knew she had the sausage and beef in the freezer. She had crackers but not oyster crackers. JW really liked oyster crackers and Kate wished she had some to make up for being a nervous Nellie asking him to come home. She needed oyster crackers.

"Scott, come with me to the store, I need to get something."

"What do you need?" Scott called from his room

"I *need* you to come out here and go with me to the store, now."

Scott reluctantly emerged from his room.

"Can I drive?"

"Grab the keys" Kate said.

She didn't know if letting Scott drive was a great idea, but she was trying to hide her underlying nervousness and letting him drive would be completely normal since he was about a month away from graduating from a learner's permit to his drivers license.

They pulled out of the garage in Kate's big SUV. All her friends had these mid-sized SUV's that can't decide if they are an all-purpose vehicle or a station wagon. Kate liked the height of her full size SUV, she felt like she could see everything. Actually it was a real pain in the ass to see anything that wasn't right in front of you but Kate had all the lane warning and parking features you could pack onto it. Kate will be the first on the block to buy a self-driving full size SUV. She tells JW that it would be like having an on demand chauffeur that drives you wherever you want to go, whenever you want to get there. Think about it, you could get in your big old SUV tell Jeeves to head to Dallas, go to sleep in the back and wake up in Dallas. How freaking cool would that be? JW says it would take Jeeves about two weeks to figure out that he doesn't need these useless, fleshy bags of water around and it would be sayonara. JW doesn't get it.

The grocery store was only about a two miles from their house, as the crow flies, but it took about ten minutes to get there navigating through their neighborhood. The neighborhood had one entrance. It wasn't gated, but it had a security camera that monitored who came in and out so if something happened they had a good chance of finding a vehicle that was out of place. The Toles lived on a cul-de-sac at the back of the neighborhood. Their backyard was against an area of woods that ran almost five miles deep before it reached railroad tracks and just beyond, the river.

Construction of the neighborhood had stopped during the last recession. The original plans supposedly had the neighborhood extending deeper, but they ran out of money. JW and Kate had bought the last house in the neighborhood for a steal. Truly. They paid a fourth of what the market value was prior to the crash. They were lucky. They had been getting their finances straight just before the crash and since they didn't own anything, the crash was more of a news event for them. Kate was a teacher and JW was 'flexible'. JW used his VA loan, and they bought themselves a house. Kate made it a home.

As they reached the neighborhood entrance, they noticed a sheriff's deputy parked beside the road. It wasn't unusual to see them there because they would watch for people running the stop sign at the four-way stop at the entrance. The crossroad had once been the main road between north of the river and south of the river about fifty years ago. The town had grown, and the route was moved east with a highway that crossed the river on the big beautiful six-lane bridge. The route at Kate's neighborhood was now mostly local traffic. If you go straight you end up at the new highway. Turn left and you head down to the river and the old bridge and beautiful little elementary school where Kate teaches fourth grade. Turn right and go about a mile and on your left is Magix. Known around the Toles house as simply *the store*. They turned right.

As they turned into the parking lot Kate was surprised that it wasn't full. She had been so nervous earlier she had half expected it to a shopping frenzy. They parked and went inside.

She guided the cart straight to aisle 7. That was where they kept the bread. She got halfway down the aisle before she realized that while they kept bread on aisle 7, they did not keep oyster crackers on aisle 7. She walked back down the aisle and scanned the overhead signs for crackers. Aisle 4. Away she went. She found oyster crackers and threw two bags into her cart.
"Really? That's what we came for? Oyster crackers." Scott asked
"Your father likes them with chili. So yes." Kate defiantly stated.

She walked down the aisle absently adding cans that were on sale to her cart.

"Does dad really like this stuff too?" Scott asked sarcastically

"No, I just wanted to pick up a few things while we are here." Kate said.

Her mind was starting to tick off a list of things that for some reason Kate felt like she really needed. She went to the water aisle and grabbed two cases, ignoring her strong urge to grab more. She grabbed some rice and dry beans. She had grabbed a decent stock of canned goods but she wanted to add to it. As she turned down the aisle, she saw an older woman. Their eyes met and Kate realized that the woman had the same sort of list running through her head. Kate stopped and looked around.

"We need to leave now." Kate whispered to Scott.

"Yeah, there is a weird vibe in here." Scott agreed.

They casually went to the registers and starting checking out. Kate looked at the young man checking her out and smiled. He smiled back. She could see it in his eyes too. Everybody is wondering if they should just panic and hoping someone doesn't step over the edge first. Kate and Scott pushed their cart, now all bagged up, out to their SUV. As they pulled away, Kate noticed the parking lot had filled up.

As they turned back into their neighborhood, she noticed that the deputy was gone. They drove home. They walked into the kitchen and unloaded their stuff. Kate started getting things together for making the chili and reached over and flipped on the TV so she could hear the news.

JW reached down and started changing the radio in Josh's SUV.

"What are you doing, I like that song." Josh said.

"Just gonna try to catch a bit of news." JW said landing on the station he wanted.

***

"The White House briefing is expected to begin in just a few minutes. We expect them to address the confirmed case of Marionette virus in New York and also address the level of concern coming out of other parts of the world as this strange infection spreads. There are reports of almost unbelievable atrocities coming out of Africa and Australia. Mr. Martin, the White House Spokesperson is briefing now.
'Good morning, today we are going to try to answer your questions. The Surgeon General will be speaking here in a moment and will bring you up to speed with what is happening and the latest information about the virus from the CDC. But first let me start with a statement from the White House.

President Wilson has been fully apprised of the situation in Madagascar and has directed the NSC to gather as much human intelligence as possible in Africa and Australia. We are at this moment putting eyes on the ground. President Wilson was forced to dismiss the head of the CIA and the Secretary of Defense this morning because of their failure to have proper oversight of intelligence sources during this outbreak. He views that lack of control as a dereliction of duty on the part of those entrusted to provide our security. President Wilson has named Asst SecDef Johnson as acting SecDef and has nominated Senator Umbridge from Tennessee as the next head of the CIA. Since congress is not in session President Wilson has used his executive authority to appoint Umbridge as acting director effective immediately. The President has entrusted the Surgeon General as coordinating authority in all efforts related to the containment of the Marionette virus. The President has great faith in Surgeon General Camer to ensure that the American people remain safe from harm.' That concludes the statement. Surgeon General Camer" he motions to a uniformed man standing next to him.

***

Camer was a former doctor at Walter Reed. He had been the right doctor to the right people. He wasn't a bad doctor. He was actually pretty good, but this position was supposed to be mostly ceremonial without any real authority. The President had just changed that and now the nation was waiting hear what the man who was now supposed to fix this had to say.

***

"Good morning. Let me begin with New York City. Yesterday afternoon there was a reported case of Marionette virus in an apartment complex on Long Island. The supposed infected patient was a newly arrived visitor from France here with his wife to visit their daughter and grandchild. They arrived yesterday, and he began showing symptoms this morning. His family had found him unresponsive and called 911 assuming he had suffered a heart attack. When paramedics arrived, they reported that the patient had resumed respiration but was unresponsive to stimuli. That was the last report from the paramedic unit. The apartment complex has been quarantined and the residents are being told to shelter in place. We are attempting to gather more information about the travels of the couple prior to their arrival and we are also attempting to contact anyone who was on their flight from France. Thus far those contacted have shown no sign of infection. We are classifying this as a potential pandemic as we expect this to become more widespread. We do not have mortality rates yet but we believe they are higher than we would like to see. We are continuing to develop information about this virus and we will continue to update the American people. At this time we are advising all businesses to consider skeleton crews and for most people to remain close to their homes unless immediate needs arise. The US government will remain staffed but we are declaring that all non-essential personnel to be furloughed until further notice. We will remain vigilante. Questions?"

***

"Shit" JW said under his breath turning down the radio. "I think we need to skip the burger and head on home." He called Kate.

Kate had just started browning the meat when her phone rang.

"Where are you?" Kate sounded strained.

"We should be there in about thirty minutes. I left my truck, I'll tell you all about it when we get home. How are you doing?"

"I am better now, I just wish you were here" Kate did not sound relaxed.

"Be there soon, love ya" JW hit the end button and started flipping through his contacts again.

Kate walked into the living room and turned the sound down on the TV. The images were jumping between street cameras and phone video interrupted briefly by one talking head after another.

Bridger was stubbing out his fourth cigarette and lighting his fifth. He had spent the last twenty minutes on the phone with the newly promoted deputy post commander at Ft. Bragg, who just happened to be his last commanding officer in the 82nd Airborne when Bridger was finishing out his contract. Colonel Eckerd, oops, General Eckerd had told him just about the same thing he heard in the last three calls he placed. Nobody knew anything for sure except that there were places they were talking to a few hours ago that they couldn't talk to now. There are whole parts of nations just going dark. They are trying to figure out if they are having communications issues or lost power or just what the hell was going on. The conversations all told him one thing for sure. There was a lot of confusion about exactly what was happening.

He stood there smoking and thinking. Downtown Nashville is a beautiful place. It invites people to stroll the streets and wander down by the river. He was about a block from Broadway and he wondered if going into a bar at 9:30 in the morning and having a couple of shots would raise any eyebrows. He started walking.

The morning was in full swing and some folks were standing outside out their workplaces enjoying the morning sun. The day was warming up nicely from a cool start. It was the first really cool morning that had a good north wind with it. The blustery air made folks stand a little closer to the buildings, and he was able to navigate the sidewalks without too much interference. He made a right-hand turn away from the river he had been strolling beside and started up Broadway. He turned right again into *The Oasis*. The guy behind the bar looked back over his shoulder away from the TV that he and the rest of the folks in the bar were watching and asked Bridger,

"What can I get for ya?"

"Too early for tequila?"

"Hell no man, according to the TV, right now seems like the perfect time for tequila!"

"Serve it up." He said as he sat down at the bar.

The other folks there appeared to be the live act that played the day shift. A guy from Georgia, another from South Carolina and the singer trekked all the way from California and looked like he wanted to be the new Garth Owens or somebody, Bridger didn't really get country music. He was listening to them discuss the news. One said he read online that if you get infected, you start trying to eat other people. Another one said the brain shuts down and people just wonder around. What was obvious to Bridger was that nobody here really knew what was going on. He wondered if that was true everywhere. He looked up at the newscast. His phone rang.

"JW, I am amazed at your timing," he said

"What do you mean?" JW said as he sat in the passenger seat of Josh's SUV.

"Well I was just wondering if anybody knew what was going on, and you call."

"You have got to be kidding, tell me you know something about this. How bad is this going to be?" JW starred out the window, beginning to get a nervous feeling in his gut.

"JW, I have talked to several people including Mike Eckerd, he's deputy Post CO at Bragg now, and they all tell me the same thing. They don't know shit, but they all paint the same picture. Area reports infection, area urgently calls for help, and area goes dark. And it all happens within hours. I don't KNOW what this is, but it doesn't matter at this point. If this thing gets going, it doesn't stop. I am about one drink away from getting in my car and coming down to hook up with you." Bridger was almost sure he had made that decision already.

"We'll have that drink together, when you get here," JW said, wishing the drive from Nashville to South Springs was a lot less than five hours.

"JW, I am serious. I am about to get in my car, stop by my house, get my big bag of guns, my bulk box of ramen and my secret spy compass I got in my cereal box and head your way." Now Bridger knew he had the makings of a plan.

"I'll keep the beer cold." JW said.

"Brother I am on my way" Bridger downed his drink and stood up.

"Fellas, y'all have a great day" he exited the bar and headed back the way he came.

When he got to his townhouse he changed out of his suit and put on some jeans and a shirt. He headed to the kitchen to see what kind of supplies he had because he did not intend to stop on his trip. Was he really going to do this? Load up and head south to see a guy he hadn't spoken to in years just because they happen to be both nervous about the same thing. If it were anybody other than JW Toles the answer would be obvious. Since it was JW, the answer was pretty obvious too. He started pulling cans off the shelf.

Josh and JW had about five miles to go, they came to the main intersection on 44. If they turned left, they would find themselves headed to the highway and the big bridge over the river. Continuing straight would take them across the river on the old two-lane bridge and on down 44 to the turn into their neighborhood. Josh went straight. When they crossed the bridge JW briefly came out of his thoughts to notice Kate's school. It looked all nice and neat. The buses parked in the parking lot all lined up just waiting to bring the kids back. All the playground equipment stood perfectly still, anticipating the end of the fall break. JW went back to thinking.

Kate opened the pantry and grabbed the beans. She was headed to the fridge to get the tomatoes when Scott yelled out.
"Mom, come in here, now!"
Kate went into Scott's room and he had a live stream running on his main viewer. It was chaos. People running. There were people down on the ground and people leaning over them, a lot of people leaning over them.
"I don't want to see anymore of this stuff from Spain, Scott." Kate said turning back
"Mom, that's Atlanta!"
Kate stopped.

JW and Josh turned into the driveway. As they pulled into the garage JW got out and looked back down the driveway. Standing on the front porch across the street was Evelyn Collins. Evelyn was the only other person still living in the cul-de-sac that was here when JW and Kate moved in. There were five houses in the cul-de-sac and four of them had been bought during the downturn. One was JW's but the other three had been speculators who sold them at the first chance they got to make a profit. Since then they had been bought and sold a few more times. Evelyn and Max Collins had been living here when JW and Kate moved in. Right now two houses were for sale and empty, the latest just two weeks ago when Ray and Margie Dockery moved out and headed to Ray's new job in Huntsville. The other one, Joe Strong's house, had been empty for about three years. Which leads back to Evelyn Collins, sort of. Evelyn was a year or two younger than JW but she carried herself like she was much older. She was a widow. A young widow by most standards. Her husband, Max, had died in a freak hunting accident. He and Joe Strong had gone duck hunting with a few other guys. Somehow Max fell out of the boat and his waders filled up with water. He drowned. Joe had told JW once that when Max went in the water his waders got so heavy they couldn't pull him out. Joe said they got him within an inch of the surface and he could see Max desperately trying to reach his neck out to get his mouth above water, but he couldn't. Joe said he watched the light go out right there one inch below the surface. Joe had moved out about three months later and his house still sat empty. JW wondered if Evelyn had ever heard that part. It wasn't something you brought up on a casual hello at the mailbox. The only other neighbor on the street was Carlos and Rosita Menendez. They had been living here about three years. Carlos was a professor at the University and

Rosita was a pediatric nurse. They had left two days earlier heading to Disney with their son and his family. So for right now Evelyn and the Toles were the only people in the cul-de-sac.

Bridger was a firm believer in the 2nd Amendment. He actually had a big bag of guns. He decided in his mind that he was going to fully commit to this being a full-blown Armageddon event and he was going to be armed to the teeth. If it turned out to be a false alarm, oh well. It was always fun to get all his guns out. He loaded the bag into the trunk of his car. He carried his Glock 19 on his hip and he had a Sig stuffed into the glove box. He loaded a backpack with a days worth of food and water into the passenger seat and he put a box with more supplies in the back seat. He knew he would stop and get gas at the station right down from the house. He was ready to go. He walked back inside to see if there was anything else he needed. Bridger never married. Never had kids. Never wanted to. For times just like this.
"Nope, got everything I need." He locked the door, chuckled, and got in his car.

He pulled into the gas station. There were several cars getting gas, and he put his credit card in the terminal to start his pump. As he stood there pumping he looked around. He made eye contact with a few of the other patrons and he saw a look he had seen before. Whenever they were in some shithole village in some shithole country and the bad guys were planning an attack, word would begin to spread through the town. Usually the moments before an attack, the locals would have this look. Anticipation of annihilation is what JW had called it. Bridger was seeing that look right now.

An explosion broke through the sky. It wasn't close enough for him to fear the effects but it was close enough that he felt them. His body vibrated and his ears registered the pressure change. He brought his shoulder up around his neck and bent his knees. The sky darkened with a smoke cloud to his north towards the river. He had put 11 gallons into his tank. Bridger decided that was exactly enough. He dropped the nozzle back into the slot and pulled away without getting a receipt. He processed the quickest route south and turned left then right then left again. He was trying not to act like he was running for his life, but there was a nagging feeling up the back of his neck that he needed to go faster. He made a right and headed for the on-ramp to I-65 south. He didn't see the man until he had made contact with him. The guy just (fell?) walked right in front of him as he went under the bridge. He slammed on the brakes. He jumped out. What he expected to see was someone broken to bits with bones sticking out everywhere, which is what he saw. What he didn't expect was to see him trying to get back up. "Hey, hey stop. Sit back down. Let me help." Bridger said, "I am so sorry, I didn't see you."

But the man just continued to try to stand. Both his legs were broken below the knee, typical in a car strike. The right leg had broken cleanly and was only partially attached; the bones were sticking out, just like the bones of his wrist. He kept trying to swing his leg back under him and every time he did the foot and ankle swung awkwardly away. He would fall forward bracing himself on the bones sticking out of his wrist. He never cried out in pain or said a word. The asphalt had torn his face and his nose was gone. A flap of skin that had torn off his forehead covered one eye and the whole right side of his face was a streak of blood and skin. His left eye settled on Bridger. He was dumbstruck. The good eye, well better eye, was opaque. He could tell that it was looking at him. He saw the expression of the man's face change when the eye settled on him. It turned angry. The man (thing) doubled his effort to stand. Bridger stopped. He stood there for a second processing what he was seeing. He squinted and turned his head sideways.

"Was this it? Is this Marionette? Here, right here." He decided he would get in his car and dial 911 and wait for an ambulance. He hit send. No service. He hit send again. No service. The man outside was now unable to do anything more than just drag himself on his stumps and was dragging as hard as he could, blood trailing behind. His better eye never leaving Bridger.

"Screw it, if it's not zombies, they'll just have to get me for hit and run." he said, putting the car in reverse and backing away. He pulled back out into the road and watched as the man he had hit, broken legs and arms and all, desperately tried to crawl down the street after him.

He jumped up on the interstate and set off at 83 miles per hour. In his rear-view mirror were the tops of tall buildings in the distance peaking from behind the trees. Bridger turned his attention forward. The sign said Birmingham 188 miles. The traffic going south was a little heavier than normal for a lunchtime rush but not much. It was just past 1:30 and he went faster. He decided the state troopers would have better things to do in the apocalypse than give him a speeding ticket. He pressed the accelerator further. He was faster than most of the traffic but again, not by much. He passed a few minivans and SUV's that looked like they were headed camping or to the beach but when he looked at the driver, he saw confusion. He felt like he was trying to outrun something. As though all the bad stuff was behind him but gaining. He had no way of knowing that Mahmoud Ibrahim had landed in Birmingham earlier this morning after a vacation to Paris which ended on a flight yesterday to New York with a lovely French couple who were coming to America to visit their daughter.

Together

When JW and Josh walked through the back door, Kate for the first time since JW left yesterday, felt a little better. They had been through a lot together. It was hard to make a marriage work. They loved each other desperately and had since the first moment they met. It made the difficult parts that much harder. Sometimes love isn't enough. They had crossed that bridge a time or two but every time they decided that whatever they had to do, they had to be together. It was that unyielding desire to be together that made them do the hard work. She hugged him tight.

"I am glad you're home, what happened to your head?" Kate asked

"Nothing, it isn't important anymore. We have to talk. SCOTT get in here." Yelling towards the bedroom.

Scott came in and sat down at the kitchen table. They all sat.

"I talked to Bridger again, he is headed this way." JW said.

The look on Kate's face told JW that she understood immediately the seriousness of what he had just said. If Bridger Preston is dropping whatever a 45-year-old single straight bachelor has to drop and coming down here to see him, it means Bridger is worried. Kate started to worry again.

"It should take Bridger about five or six hours to get here. That puts us after dark." JW said. "Scott I need you to give me a breakdown of what you know so far." "Well we just saw some video out of Atlanta and it looks bad. I have seen video from New York, Boston, Washington DC, Philadelphia, Raleigh, Cleveland and Minneapolis. I have seen images and read stories from all over the West Coast and Canada. It's all the same. People are attacking other people. The military and police can't seem to stop it and it is spreading fast. It started showing up yesterday morning on some gamer YouTube channels out of Australia and Madagascar. It looked like the same thing only shot from different angles so everybody started calling bullshit. Sorry." He continued "Yesterday when I called you into my room it had started showing up again, only this time it was on more "newsy" type channels with a LOT more footage. In a little over 24 hours it went from a few random places in Madagascar to all over the world. What are the next 24 hours going to be like?" Scott asked, not because he expected an answer but because started doing the math in his head.

JW was looking down while Scott was talking; he had started to do the math too, he just kept looking at a little scratch on the top of the kitchen table, he spoke.

"Listen guys," hardly believing what he was about to say. "We need to make a decision and make it now. We know whatever this is it spreads fast and brings bad things with it. From what we have seen, and I am not saying it is 100% true, the 'infected' are not in control of their own actions. That makes them dangerous. We don't know how this is spread but we have to make a couple of assumptions. Contact with the 'infected' is bad. People are going to panic. We are going to protect ourselves and we are not going to lose our heads. The next few days we'll see what happens but I think we need to be a little more proactive."

They were all nodding.

"Ok, Josh, you and Scott start emptying some of those plastic totes we keep the Christmas stuff in and start putting canned goods in them, if we have to leave we need to have some things ready to go." JW said.

"What do you want us to do with the Christmas stuff?" Josh asked.

"Just dump it out in the storage building, I don't think we are going to be decorating this year." JW said.

Up until this very moment Josh had not contemplated what was really happening. He knew this was serious but really, how serious is some virus. Yes everybody gets all nervous, then they get their shots, and everybody moves on. He looked around the table and the faces of his parents told him, this was not going to be easy or short or over soon. For the first time he could remember, he felt unprepared. He was seventeen, invincible and had everything in front of him. He realized now that the future he always envisioned for himself may not turn out that way.

"Kate, we need to go have a conversation with Evelyn Collins." JW said starting to get up from the table.

Kate stood joining him as they started towards the front door.

"Y'all boys get that stuff packed up, we'll be right back. Then you and I, Josh, may have an errand to run. Maybe you too Scott." JW said walking out the door. Kate and JW walked out the front door and JW started down the sidewalk when Kate touched his arm. He paused, turning back to look.

"Why do we need to see Evelyn?" Kate asked

"I have an idea about making this place just a little more secure and I want to make sure she would be ok with it. And if she isn't, to let her know that I am doing it anyway. If I can figure out how." JW turned and started walking. Kate followed.

When JW and Kate returned, Josh noticed his mother had this odd look of shock and humor on her face. When his father started explaining his plan, Josh had the same look.

"We are going to steal two school buses from your mother's school" JW said.

Scott was the only one to laugh out loud. Josh wanted to at first but when he looked at his father, he knew it was not a joke. Not even close.

"I can get into the school and get the keys out of the office." Kate volunteered because she had heard the whole plan across the street at Evelyn Collins house.

"Ok, I think we should plan ongoing as soon as possible. I also think would all should go to the school together. Well, not Evelyn, but all four of us. I am going to drive one of the buses and your mother will drive the other. But first let's head out into my room." JW said.

JW had a small four by four room in the garage that was mainly for the hot water heater but he had wedged his gun safe into it when they first moved in. He wasn't a gun nut or a prepper so he didn't have an arsenal. The gun safe did hold several handguns, 9mm mostly, which is what he really enjoyed shooting. He had his new rifle and three pump shotguns. He also had his deer rifle and a couple of old 30/30 lever action rifles from his grandfather. He grabbed the lever actions. He also grabbed a box of shells and one of his 9MM pistols. He turned and handed the rifles to Josh. "Load some rounds into these two." JW passed that ammunition.

"Kate, I want you to carry this." He handed Kate the 9MM, it was in a holster with a clip on it so she could just slide the clip inside her waistband. She knew how to use the gun too.

"Scott, you and Josh will carry these rifles but they will stay in your mother's vehicle. As will you. When we get there your mother and I will get two buses started and I will lead us back in one bus, you (nodding to Josh) and your brother will follow in your mother's car. Your mother brings up the rear in the other bus."

They all loaded up into Kate's SUV and started to pull out. JW hit the button on the garage door. As they headed out the long road through their neighborhood, JW continued the plan.

"Once we are moving, I really don't want to stop. There are three stop signs and one traffic light between the school and here. They are all suggestions at this point. If I don't stop, you don't stop. Stay tucked in tight. As long as we stay tight we should be fine." He continued. "Once we get back to the neighborhood we are going to park them at the entrance to the cul-de-sac. If we pull both of them back into the wood off the curb on either side they should cover the entrance. It won't keep anyone out on foot that really wants to get in, but it may discourage folks who aren't looking to put in any effort. And it will definitely keep other vehicles from getting all the way back here before realizing there is only one way out of the neighborhood."

The way the cul-de-sac was positioned was an afterthought. The original plan had houses rounding each corner coming out of the cul-de-sac but they never got built. The main road ends and the cul-de-sac is simply a street that goes slightly down hill off to the right at a 45-degree angle from the dead end. Trees line the entrance two lots deep on both sides. The pseudo isolation is what drove JW's interest in the first place.

When they arrived at Kate's school they pulled around behind the buses.
Kate and JW got out quickly entered the school to retrieve the keys. They chose two buses from the rear line. JW got into the first bus and started it. He went back out. Kate had started the other bus and joined him. They all four stood together at the back of the two running school buses and realized they were about to commit grand theft auto of government property. If it wasn't the zombie apocalypse, they were going to have some very serious explaining to do.
"Stay tight. I will back out, then Josh you get behind me. I will wait until your mother flashes her headlights and then we go. Stay tight." JW said. "If something happens and we get separated. Get back home."

They froze. The approaching sound of sirens made them think their heist was over before it got started. But four police cars, a fire truck and two more ambulances raced by headed towards the highway. They looked at each other again. It was time to go. JW backed his bus out and Josh fell in behind him as he pulled towards the exit of the parking lot. He waited for Kate to fall in behind Josh. She flashed her headlights. Off they went. As he went through the first stop sign without stopping, he saw a few folks gathered in their yards talking to each other. At the next non-stop sign, he saw another group of folks standing outside the church on the corner. Nobody seemed to notice the two school buses rolling down the street. Why would they? The light was green and they went right through. The next intersection was the four-way where they would turn right into their neighborhood. As JW turned in his heart leapt into his throat. There was a sheriff's car parked at the intersection. The driver's door was open but JW didn't see anyone. He didn't hang around and look. He headed towards the back of the neighborhood. The rest of the caravan followed.

Bridger was about 30 miles north of Birmingham and traffic had definitely picked up. The northbound lane out of Birmingham was packed with cars leaving town and Bridger began to think he might need to bypass the city. He took the next exit and pulled into a gas station to check the map on his phone. No service. He looked up at the service station and wondered if they still sold maps. They did. He got back in his car and opened up the map. He found the road he was currently on and traced it to where it intersected another county road that headed south. He pulled away. Twelve miles down the road he came to County Rd 6. He turned south. He knew he could stay on 6 until he crossed County Rd 81. He could stay on 6 to Northview and get back on the main highway to South Springs or he could turn onto 81 for a few miles and hit 44 and head straight to JW's house. He would take 44. He turned on the radio and was surprised the XM station he usually tuned to, Rock Plaza Central, was broadcasting news.

***

'The Federal Emergency Management under the Direction of the Surgeon General has issued a shelter-in-place warning for all citizens East of the Mississippi River to include the entire Ohio River Valley. A state of emergency now exists in all major metropolitan areas and the President has activated ALL National Guard personnel to respond to the crises. The governors of the individual states are now entrusted with plenary powers from the federal government to oversee coordinated efforts related directed to their states. FEMA stands by to offer any assistance to the governors'

***

Bridger thought that had been a long-winded way of saying you're on your own. And he finally decided that whatever *this* was, it was going to get worse before it gets better. He picked up the pace.

He had just turned south onto 44 when he saw the wreck. A log-truck had spilled its load right on top of a car. The cab of the truck had detached from the hauler and was off the road slammed into a tree. He stopped the car and got out. The vehicle under the logs was crushed. He looked in through what he thought was the drivers window. He heard shuffling in the dark opening. Suddenly a young woman appeared in the window.

"Help me, my husband and I are trapped and he is knocked out or something."

"Ok, ok, let me see what I can do." He said.

He surveyed the situation and figured he could use his car to push the log blocking the window off and maybe get a space big enough for them to crawl out. He pulled his car up and started nudging the end of the log and finally got it to move the right way. He pushed it off and got out of his car. By the time he got back over to her car the woman was already crawling out. She put her feet on the ground and reached back in.

"Here let me help", Bridger said arriving by her side.

The young man was now awake but very disoriented. They coaxed him through the window. Bridger helped them over to the side of the road as another car pulled up. The old man got out and walked up to Bridger.

"Damn, what happened here?" he asked

"Don't know, just got here myself and helped these two out of the car." Bridger replied.

"Anybody check on the driver yet?" the man asked. It was the first time Bridger had thought about it.

"Not yet."

"Well y'all stay here and let me go check on him and we'll see if we can't get some help coming. My phone isn't working, can't get a signal but we'll figure it out." The old man started up the slope towards the cab of the truck. Bridger looked at his phone. It had been doing the tail chase emblem most of the way down. He was...

"Aahhhhhhhhahhhhhh" came a scream from the direction of the cab.

Bridger and the young woman ran up the little slope and stepped over to the driver's side. They were not prepared for what they saw.

The old man was on the ground, his face frozen in a scream that was no longer making any sound because the driver was currently ripping his throat out with his teeth. Blood was spraying everywhere and the driver was making guttural animal sounds as he slurped and chewed. The girl screamed. The driver raised his head slowly and turned to face them. His left arm had been deboned. All the skin and muscle was in a ball around his wrist and his arm was a collection of bone and sinew hanging down by his side since there was no muscle to move it any more. His face had been smashed against the steering wheel and one of his eyes was hanging out of its socket. One side of his mouth had been ripped open and his lower jaw was exposed. It was full of blood and flesh from the old man. He slowly tried to stand, as if trying to detect which way gravity was pulling him down and counteracting it. He was having difficulty getting up because he couldn't use his left arm.

"Stop dude" Bridger said. The young lady was in shock and froze. The driver stood.

"Stop now" Bridger summoned his most don't screw with me voice.

The driver started walking towards the girl. Bridger saw the same gait he had witnessed at the TV station on the bank of TVs. It was here. Now. He slid his pistol out of his hip holster and thumbed the safety. He raised it at the driver.

"Stop now or I WILL shoot you."

The driver never stopped. He was just a few feet from the girl. She had finally snapped too and was backpedaling away.

"Stop" He didn't stop.

Bridger fired one round into the man's right shoulder. He flinched from the impact but his gait never broke. Bridger fired again. Left shoulder. Same result.

He fired a third round. Center mass. He knew he had just blown this mans heart to pieces and yet the gait never changed. He was still moving when Bridger fired the fourth shot. Just over the right eye. The man went down.

"Shit" Bridger stood with his gun pointed at the heap on the ground, fully expecting it to get back up again.

When he was sure it wasn't moving, he holstered his weapon and turned to look at the girl. She had gone to her knees. She had her hands over her ears and her mouth was agape. Her eyes met Bridger's.

"Holy fucking shit mister what the fuck was that"

Bridger liked her instantly.

"I don't know. I think he had Marionette. I think that was what that was." motioning towards the lump on ground.

"Oh, shit, oh shit oh shit, what the fuck I mean what the literal fuck."

Bridger knew she was still in shock and she was starting to meltdown.

"Hey, hey we're ok. It's ok" He tried.

"OK? YOU JUST FUCKING SHOT A FUCKING MAN WHO WOULDN'T QUIT FUCKING TRYING TO FUCKING ATTACK, EAT, RAPE, I DON'T KNOW WHAT THE FUCK HE WAS DOING BUT YOU KEPT FUCKING SHOOTING HIM AND HE KEPT FUCKING MOVING EVEN AFTER YOU FUCKING SHOT HIM, AND YOU THINK IT'S OK?"

"Well when you put it like that." Bridger said.

He just stood there looking at her waiting for the next flurry of "fuck" but she actually laughed a little.

"Hey, what the hell is going on?" Bridger and the girl looked back towards the road to see her husband stumbling up towards them.

She stood and walked towards him motioning for him to stay where he was. He stopped. Bridger took one more look at the scene in front of him. Two people had died right here. Apparently one of them, twice. He turned to join the couple by the road.

JW stood with his back to the cul-de-sac watching Kate get out of the bus she had just parked. It was parked nose to tail from the one JW had just parked. JW had pulled his into the woods just a little and Kate had parallel parked between the end of JW's bus and the woods behind her. She had to run over a few of the smaller pine trees to wedge it in tight.

"OK, I think that will do what we need." JW said.

Josh and Scott were already back inside the house and had gone to Scott's room to try to see if there was any more information. Scott clicked on the FEMA website. The normal splash page had been changed.

■■
***

A SHELTER IN PLACE ORDER IS IN EFFECT

"FEMA is now being directed at the state level. The Federal Emergency System has been fully activated. All coordination for assistance and evacuations should be directed to the respective state emergency management systems.

***

He clicked on the CNN link and it was completely down. As he started looking through all the news links, he would find some down, probably overwhelmed, and some had quit updating their content. Information, it seemed, was becoming the latest victim of Marionette. He began looking at social media. There was a lot more information, but he had always viewed it as mostly made up crap. He decided that under the circumstances he would be more open-minded. He found a lot of videos of folks seemingly infected by Marionette, and he also found a lot of conspiracy theories. Some said it was an attack by aliens, some by Bigfoot and an interesting one about global warming releasing ancient bacteria. The one video that got his attention showed a girl on the ground with someone biting her leg. She was screaming and when they finally got the biter off her, she scrambled back away. As the camera turned from the biter, lying on the ground dead after being hit in the head with a shovel, to the girl it shows her face and as you watch, her eyes go opaque and she bites the arm of the guy who is carrying her. The person operating the camera screams and takes off but as they put the phone to their side to run, you can see the girl continuing to bite (eat) the guy's arm.

Josh looked away from the monitor briefly to see JW standing in the doorway.

His mouth was open and Josh thought he saw, for the first time, fear wash over his Dad's face. It was almost immediately replaced with a face Josh had seen all his life. The face he had seen when he and Josh were on the way to the hospital when Josh broke his leg. The face he had seen when Scott had that incident with the butcher knife that cost Scott the tip of his pinky. The face he had seen his dad make to his mother when they were struggling with money. The face that said, don't worry, I will take care of it. Josh began to wonder if that face he had always seen as reassuring was just a mask. In that moment, he looked just a little smaller to Josh.

Scott turned around and asked.
"What do you think, Josh?" he asked, seeing his father standing in the doorway.
"Hey Dad, did you see that?" Scott asked.
JW answered.
"I saw it, I think we need to start thinking about what we do next." he said.
"JOHN get out here now." Kate yelled.

All three ran out the front door, half expecting to see her down on the ground being attacked just like the girl in the video. Instead, Kate was standing in the street pointing back up towards the top of the hill where they had just parked the buses.
"There is someone up there walking around the buses." Kate said.

From their angle looking back up towards the buses, which were about 100 yards away, they could see a set of legs walking on the other side. It looked like dark pants with dark shoes.

"I bet it's the deputy. I better go up there." JW started walking. Josh fell in beside him.

Kate and Scott waited. JW and Josh wedged themselves between the buses but when they got through they didn't see anyone at first, then they saw the deputy standing up the road. They walked a few steps towards the deputy and called out but the deputy was focused on the house up the road and had started walking towards it. Josh ran on ahead a few steps. JW thought to himself that the deputy was being really cautious about where he was looking. The deputy was bent over a little as he walked forward and JW thought it made the deputy looked like he was shuffling. Josh was reaching out to get the deputies attention.

Shuffling, shuffling. JW quit thinking. The gun was out and the round had already slammed into the back of the deputy's head before Josh ever touched him. JW stood there, wisps of smoke coming from the end of the Ruger, and started shaking. He managed to thumb the safety back on and holster the gun before he threw up. Barely.

"Jesus Dad, Jesus. You just killed him. You just killed a cop. Are you out of your mind?" Josh was screaming at JW. JW, for his part, was doubled over trying to figure out why lunch came before breakfast. Josh kept yelling and backing up towards the buses. Kate pushed through just as Josh reached the bus.

"What happened, are you ok, where is your father, was that a gunshot?" Kate fired questions at Josh, who was still yelling towards back towards his father. She could see JW up the road a little doubled over.

"He just shot him. He just blew his head off. He's crazy mom. I think he snapped. He just shot him." Josh finally answered her.

Kate started walking towards JW. He glanced up and saw her coming and stood. She raised her arms up slightly, palms down, letting JW know to just calm down. He got the message. She walked up to him and hugged him. She wasn't quite sure what happened, but she had actually seen him snap once. This wasn't what it looked like. At least not the vomit.

"Hey, hey. It's ok. What happened?" she asked.

"I shot him. I think he was one of those things. He wouldn't answer, he just kept walking. Josh was reaching for him. I...I..." he trailed off.

"John, *was* he one of those things? Was he?" she begged

JW looked at her, eyes red rimmed and bloodshot and tears slowly coming down his cheek.

"I don't know" he collapsed to his knees. She went down with him.

Bridger knelt down beside the couple as they sat down on one of the logs scattered across the road. Cars pulled up to the wreck, but they were all hesitant to try to get around it. As they quickly u-turned to find another route Bridger could see the faces in the cars. It was panic.

"Listen, I don't know what is going on, but I don't think any help is coming." He started.

"I think we all are going to be on our own for a while. My name is Bridger, Bridger Preston." He extended his hand towards the couple. The man took his hand off his head and shook it.

"Raj Varma. This is my wife, Tilly." He said. Nodding towards the girl Bridger had just (saved?) helped.

"We were trying to get back to South Carolina." Raj continued.

"And now our car is a fucking pancake." Tilly chimed in.

Bridger didn't know what to do. He wasn't about to turn around and head back north but he didn't want to just leave these folks on the side of the road. "Listen, I can't help you get to Carolina but I have a friend a little ways south of here that will let you stay with him until we can figure it out. I don't know if that would help or not but I am offering to let you go with me to South Springs."

The two looked at each other. Tilly spoke. "Mister"

"Bridger" he interrupted

"Bridger, mister, whatever. After what the fuck I just saw back there, I don't give a rats ass if you are going to Eastbumfuck Egypt, just take us the fuck with you." She said.

"She gets going when she gets nervous." Raj said.

"Yeah, I caught that." He said

"Fuck you both." Tilly stood.

"Are you sure we'll be safe going to South Springs?" He asked

"Raj, I don't know if we'll be safe walking over there and getting your stuff out of your car, but I guess we'll find out." He said.

They all stood and walked over to the crushed car. They could get to the back seat which allowed them to pull some of their things from the trunk. Raj and Tilly were on a belated honeymoon in New Orleans so they had a few suitcases of clothes and not much else. They hadn't exactly planned for the end of the world. They loaded the things they had into the trunk of Bridger's car. Tilly got in the front seat so Raj could lie down in the back. They slowly wound their way around the scattered logs and came out the other side heading south on 44 again. It had started to get dark. Bridger could see the lights from a gas station. Raj was resting across the back seat. As they passed the station, the lights flickered out and back on again. They kept driving. Raj started talking.

"Back there, at the wreck, we had left New Orleans this morning trying to get back home. The interstate was very busy and we got caught in a traffic jam. We got off the interstate and had started going on the back roads. The phones quit working and we had pulled over to try to figure out which way to go. The truck just came around the corner and turned over on us. We were just sitting there." He trailed off.

"Do you know what is happening?" Tilly asked. Bridger was caught off guard because she hadn't used fuck every third word.

"Not sure, but I have seen a lot of the same kind of things from video's of this Marionette virus going around."

"Yeah, you already said that, but I asked if you knew what the fuck is happening" There she was. "I mean why the fuck is the radio only playing that stupid FEMA warning and nothing else? Why don't our phones work? Why are the lights flickering? I mean a fucking virus doesn't make the fucking phones quit working? It's obviously not a fucking computer virus, so I'll ask you again, do you know what the fuck is happening?" she spoke the last line somewhat mockingly for someone who had just been saved by the guy she was mocking, Bridger thought.

"No. I don't know for sure but I can make a guess, that's what I do for a living, make guesses. My guess is that this virus is making people panic, and possibly for good reason, and when people panic accidents happen. If those accidents affect the right power distribution sources, like say, a transmission line to a cell tower or twenty, then you have outages. If the folks who are supposed to fix those power disruptions and outages are also panicking, they aren't working. Things begin to break down. If the crisis passes, things get fixed. We are right now at the finding out if the crisis is going to pass stage. But that is just a guess." Bridger finished.

"Well that's fucking great." Tilly said as they drove into the growing darkness.

Kate had managed to get JW back in the house. He was sitting in the living room leaned forward in his chair, hands crossed against his forehead like he was praying. Kate was trying to finish cooking, even though she knew nobody felt like eating. Josh had gone into Scott's room. Kate walked to the door.

"Josh, can we go outside and talk for a minute?" Just as she said that the lights flickered.

"Crap." Scott said, as his monitors blinked and everything started rebooting.

"Sure, nothing to see here anyway." Josh said and followed her out.

They walked out onto the front porch, the sun was finishing its day and the sky had turned purple, Kate motioned for Josh to sit down in the swing with her. He sat.

"Josh, I don't know what you think happened up there." Kate started

"I know exactly what happened up there, Mom. He freaked. He shot the guy." Josh interrupted.

"He thought he was going to hurt you, he thought he was infected with this virus." Kate said

"So because he thought the guy was infected, he shot him. What if he thinks I am infected or you or Scott, does he just shoot us?" Josh asked.

"That's different Josh, your father did what he did to protect you. Don't you see that?" Kate said.

"No mom, I don't see...what the hell?" Josh was looking past his mother.

There was a woman just squeezing between the buses and as Josh looked past her, he could see someone else trying to follow her. They both stood. The woman fell down. They took off running towards the top of the road. The woman was screaming and trying to get up. The other person had made in through and just as Josh and Kate were approaching he fell on top of the woman. She screamed in pain. Kate and Josh stopped. They could see the man taking bites of skin off the woman's face. Every time its head lifted up a gush of blood would fill the hole it had made with its teeth. The woman was taking deep breaths and screaming and trying to get free but with every move the gnashing jaws of her attacker would clamp down and she would scream again, it's hand digging into the flesh of her stomach and coming up bloody.

Josh looked down at his mother's hip and saw the gun she had been wearing since they stole the buses. He grabbed it out of the holster before Kate could stop him. He thumbed the safety and fired. The round hit it in the back. It looked up. The woman screamed and it went back to biting her in the chest. He fired again and it turned to look at Josh and Kate. They were standing about fifteen feet away. It bit into the woman again. She had stopped moving. Josh fired once more into its back. It stood walked towards them. He fired three more rounds haphazardly at it. The first shot hit its throat. The second shot hit it just under the eye and it went down. The third shot missed entirely. They stood there.

Kate slid past the body on the ground and went to the woman. She was dead. Kate closed the woman's eyes and walked back over to Josh. He was still pointing the gun at the pile in front of him. His eyes were wide.

"Hey, hey. You ok?" Kate asked a stupid question and knew it. "It's ok, honey. Just let me take the gun." He handed it over without a thought.

"Shit, mom. What was that?" Josh was starting to shake a little.

"I don't know son. I don't know" She turned to hug him.

As she did, she could hear...something. She looked back. The woman had raised her head. Kate stepped back, pulling Josh with her. He reached out and steadied her. The woman was now raising herself up onto her elbows, trying to sit up. Her abdomen had been torn and eaten and she didn't have the muscle left to sit up. The signals still went to her legs and they started drawing up and twisting. When she rolled to one side what guts were left inside her spilled out on the road. She managed to get her arms under her as she rolled over and she raised her face to them. Her eyes were opaque and her face was dripping blood out of each bite the thing had made. She looked at Kate and Josh and screeched.

Kate's face had contorted into a mix of fear and pity. The last expression was resolution. She raised the pistol she had taken from Josh. She shot the woman in the forehead. They stumbled back towards the house. Kate stopped.

"What?" Josh sounded exasperated.

"If those two can get through, others can too. We have to move the bus a little. Just a little. Just enough to close that gap." She said.

Her and Josh started back to the buses. They carefully walked around the two bodies now lying in the street. She climbed into the bus and put it in neutral. There was enough downhill slope that it rolled forward on its own until it touched the back of the other bus. She climbed back out. They stood for a second. They were both trying to process what had just happened. Josh was wondering what they were going to do next. Kate was wondering what it was like on the other side of those buses. Evening had given way to the streetlamp. It flickered. They ran back to the house.

The Dying Fire

They had made good time down 44 and they were about forty miles from South Springs. Bridger had noticed that the traffic was starting to get a little heavier coming from the direction they were going. Most of the houses and businesses they passed had no lights. They hadn't passed anything in a while except pine trees and power poles.

"I have to pee." Tilly said, breaking the silence.

"I don't think there are any service stations nearby." Bridger said.

"I don't give a shit. Just stop the car and I can go on the side of the road. I am about to burst." She said.

Bridger saw a mailbox ahead and saw that the mail truck had created a place to pull over. He used it. He couldn't see any lights up the dirt road from the mailbox.

"I think I'll go too while we are stopped." Raj said, sitting up in the back seat now.

They had been listening to the radio in the silence and the reporting had gone from FEMA emergency broadcasts to individuals at local stations reporting about local instances of the virus. They had not picked up any stations from South Springs yet but everything everywhere else was sounding real bad. People attacking people, police and military beginning to be overwhelmed. Shelter location reports and emergency contact information to help find missing people.

Bridger got out and walked out into the road. He scanned both directions and couldn't see any other cars coming. Tilly had stepped out and was crouching down just outside the car with one hand on the handle for support. Raj walked to the nearest tree just off the road. He was looking back over his shoulder.
"How much longer until we get where we are going?" he asked.
"Maybe another hour or so." Bridger replied.

Tilly and Raj were finished with their business and leaned against the back of the car. Tilly pulled a pack of cigarettes out of her pocket. Raj looked at her disapprovingly.
"Oh fuck off." She said, as she lit the smoke.

Bridger walked to the back of the car. Pulled out a cigarette of his own and lit it.
"Where are we going?" Raj asked.

Bridger turned to answer him but his attention was drawn up the dirt road they were currently blocking. Someone was running towards them.
"Help, please. He's sick. Our power went out and we can't get the phones to work." The boy running towards them yelled.
"Who's sick? What's wrong with them?" Bridger asked as he stepped around Raj and met the boy in the dirt road.

"My grandpa, he's sick. He has heart problems and he isn't feeling good. We tried to call the ambulance like before but we can't get through." The boy said, breathlessly

"Who is we?" Raj asked

Bridger looked back over his shoulder at Raj. Raj caught the look of approval.

"My mom and me. We came to check on him and he..." The boy ran out of breath.

"Ok, ok. Settle down. We will get in the car and drive up to the house. I don't know what help we can give but we'll see what we can do." Bridger said.

"Thanks" the boy said. They all got in the car.

"You know, my husband is a doctor." Tilly said.

It just occurred to Bridger that he two people he had been riding with for the last hour were absolute complete strangers. He knew almost nothing about them. He hadn't asked. And they hadn't volunteered. They had spent the majority of their time together in shock. They had just listened to the radio and drove. What little talk they had managed had only been in response to what they had heard on the radio. Small talk had gone away.

"No, I didn't know that." He said.

"Dermatologist." Raj added.

They drove up the dirt road about fifty yards and the house appeared in the moonlight off to the left. They stopped in front of it. Sitting under the carport was an old pickup truck. Behind it was parked a small red SUV. As they stopped, the boy opened the back door and ran towards the house. Bridger, Tilly and Raj got out and walked to the front door. On the porch was a swing with one side on the ground, the chain long broken. There was an old stuffed chair that looked rattier than the swing. Next to the chair was a small bucket filled with sand and cigarette butts. Bridger swung the storm door back and stuck his head in.

"Hey, anybody here?" he yelled.

A woman, who appeared to be in her mid-thirties, came out of the hallway in front of Bridger and motioned them in. She saw his gun on his hip, and flushed.

"Are you a cop?" she asked.

"No, mam but don't worry, it's only for protection." He said in his most calming voice.

"Do I know you?" she asked as she squinted her eyes, trying to see him a little better in the candlelight.

"I don't think so, but you may have seen me on TV." He said.

"That's it, you're Bridger Presley." She said.

"Preston. Yes." He said.

"Preston. Yes Preston. You are the guy who talks about the army stuff. My husband is in the Army reserves and I watch you when I can. He says you know what you're talking about. He watches you too. My name is Sally. Sally Forester." She extended her hand. He took it.

"Nice to meet you Sally, this is Tilly and Raj Varma. Raj is a doctor." Nodding towards the couple coming through the door behind him.

Raj and Tilly made for an odd couple even before the apocalypse. He looked like the Rhodes scholar he was. Buttoned down and neatly pressed. Even now. She had fire red hair cut in what used to be called a pixie cut, Sally didn't know what they called it now. She also had horn-rimmed black glasses with the most striking green eyes and was dressed like a hippie from Sally's childhood. Sally smiled.

They all stood in the living room. Candles lit the house and it cast shadows over the furniture. It was the living room of an old man. One chair pushed against the wall with a table next to it. There were several half-filled glasses sitting on the table and one closed book with a pair of reading glasses sitting on them. One wall had pictures of children and several pictures of one older lady. One of which showed her kissing the bald head of a bearded man. On the other wall was a big flat screen TV. It was dead.

"How is your father doing?" Raj asked.

"Why don't you come and tell me. He is resting now but if you would look at him, I would feel better." Sally said.

She turned back down the hallway. Raj looked at Tilly. She shrugged. He followed the woman down the hallway. Tilly and Bridger waited in the living room. Tilly sat down in the chair. Bridger found a spot on the floor and leaned his back against the wall. He pulled out his phone. Nothing. The power blinked back on.

"Hooray" the boy yelled as he came out of the kitchen. The power blinked off again.

"Shoot" the boy said dejectedly.

Tilly was smiling at the boy when the woman came back down the hallway. Raj came behind her. Tilly saw the look Raj gave to the boy, and she walked him back into the kitchen away from Raj and his mother. He went willingly.

"He's not doing well. His breathing is shallow" Raj said. "I don't know for sure that being in a hospital would do any good, and this isn't a hospital. I don't think he has long."

Sally was crying. She knew, but she didn't want to accept it. She went back into the back room. Raj and Bridger stood looking at each other. Raj walked into the kitchen and brought Tilly and the boy back down the hallway after Sally. Bridger was left alone. He looked outside. He couldn't see shit. Tilly and the boy came back, the boy was crying.

"He said his goodbyes." Tilly said with a tear rolling down her cheek. The boy went into the kitchen.

After a while, Sally and Raj came out of the back and closed the door behind them.

"He's gone." Raj said.

They walked into the living room. Sally sat in the chair and sobbed. Tilly knelt down and hugged her. They all gathered around her with their heads bowed trying to help comfort this stranger. They stood there for a long time. Sally finally spoke.

"He was so stubborn. He wouldn't quit smoking. He said something was going to kill him anyway, he might as well enjoy what time he has." She chuckled through her tears.

"Thank you for being here. I know this is very strange, but today has been a very strange day." Sally said.

"No fucking shit. Sorry. So sorry." Tilly said.

The boy walked from behind Raj and sat down on Sally's lap. He was almost too big for laps but not quite. His mother hugged him.

"Why are you crying momma?" he asked.

"Pawpaw passed Jesse. He's gone." She said.

"Not yet momma, I heard him back there, up and walking plain as day." Jesse said.

"Jesse, that's just the wind. Pawpaw's gone. We watched him go." She said nodding towards Raj.

"He's walking around momma, come look." Jesse said and jumped off his momma's lap and ran towards the back of the house. Sally started after him. Raj was looking confused. He and Tilly made eye contact. Bridger watched as a thought washed over Raj's face, then Tilly's, then his.

"Wait" They yelled in unison. But the boy had already reached the door to the bedroom at the end of the hall.

Sally watched as her son, only nine, opened the bedroom door. The thing inside that had once been his grandfather grabbed him by the back of the head and snatched him up. Before the boy could even scream the thing had bitten his nose completely off and was already taking another bite from the boys face. Sally screamed and ran towards the thing she once called Daddy. As she grabbed for her son, the thing let go of him and grabbed her arms. As she struggled to hold on to her son, the thing spun her around and bit deeply into her shoulder. She screamed in pain. It took another bite further up her neck and the blood came out in violent splashes.

Raj ran down the hallway and into the room. He stopped. The thing was down on the floor eating the woman. Jesse had managed to crawl towards the door. Raj fell backwards when Jesse reached up. Bridger stepped between them. He could see that Jesse was seriously injured but still alive. He grabbed his hand and pulled him towards the hall. The thing had its head down and was focused on what it was currently doing. Bridger didn't know how long that was going to be so he didn't take any chances.

He pulled out his weapon and fired one round. It slammed into the top of the things head. It fell backwards against the bed it had already died on once and died again. Raj had pulled Jesse back into the living room. Bridger checked on Sally. She was dead. He sat down with his back to the door looking over the carnage. He reached into his pocket and produced a cigarette. He lit it and let it hang off his lips. He inhaled through his mouth and out his nose. Once, twice. Sally's eyes opened. Bridger didn't see them open. He only saw her sit up. She was facing away from him. "Sally?" he said, cigarette falling out of his mouth. He was trying to get up when she twisted on her butt and threw herself back at him. He managed to stick a foot out and it caught her in the stomach. His foot sank deep into the opening. She spun and even though her intestines were hanging from his foot down to the floor, she reached out for him. He got his hands up and grabbed her arms just below the shoulder. Her mouth slammed shut inches from his face. She was trying to extend her jaw towards him when he flipped her off him and onto her back. He slammed her down several times banging her head against the hardwood and threw himself back away from her. He produced the firearm again and placed one just below her nose. She fell. The candle fell off the table onto her. It began to burn her hair. Bridger stood and stumbled towards the light in the living room. He found Raj and Tilly standing over Jesse. He was dead. Bridger walked up, still holding the pistol and shot the boy in the head. He walked out the front door. The fire began to catch in the back bedroom.

"What the hell was that?" Tilly asked chasing him out the door. Raj followed her looking back over his shoulder as the storm door shut behind him.

"She came back." Bridger said.

"Who? What the hell do you mean 'came' back?" she said.

"The woman, Sally, she was dead. She came back. Just like the old man. Just like the truck driver. Just like the boy would have. She came back and attacked me." He was still walking towards the car.

"Stop, just stop. What are you saying? That can't..." she trailed off, the truth of what she had seen twice with her own eyes hitting hard.

"And where we are going there is someone who knows how to deal with this?" Raj asked.

"Folks, I don't know if there is anybody anywhere who knows how to deal with *this*." Pointing back at the house. "But if there is one guy in the world who I would want to help me get through *this*, well let me just say. We are on the right road." Bridger started up the car. Raj and Tilly took one more look, flames starting to lick the roof from the back of the house. They got in the car.

JW sat in the living room with the emergency broadcast signal repeating over the TV. He ignored it. The message had been playing for over an hour. It said the same thing. All JW heard was noise. Scott was in his room watching cellphone video being broadcast from all over the country. They all looked the same. It was horrific. The front door slammed open and Josh came into his room. Kate ran into the living room and turned the TV off. JW looked up at her.

"Whatever it is you think you have to deal with, deal with it. We need you here. Now."

She relayed the story of what had just happened to her and Josh. By the time she had finished Josh and Scott had come into the living room.

"Dad, I'm sorry. I didn't get it, I do now." Josh said.

The lights went out. They didn't come back on. Kate found her way into the kitchen and grabbed a flashlight. She came back into the living room and lit candles. JW took the flashlight and walked out into the garage. He came back in with several more flashlights from his hunting bag. He gave one to Josh and one to Scott. He went into the bedroom and brought back the rifles he had given them earlier.

"From this moment forward, nobody leaves this house without being armed." He said flatly.

"Your mother and I are going to go and get Evelyn and bring her over here if she will come."

"What do we do?" Scott asked.

"Absolutely nothing."

JW and Kate walked out the front door. The stars were shining, ignoring the happenings down here. There was a glow off to the East. It wasn't the glow of city lights. It was the glow of fire. The night sky was pierced with the sounds of sirens in the distance. There were helicopters flying off to the North and JW recognized the distinctive percussive signature of detonations. He didn't know if it was munitions or storage tanks but he knew something had just exploded. It sounded like it had come from the river which was a little over five miles away from JW'S house. What they had heard was the sound of the Amtrak derailing as it rounded the bend before it crossed the river, but they didn't know it. They crossed the cul-de-sac. Evelyn was standing on her porch watching.

"Kate, I came outside and saw you and Josh a minute ago. I thought I heard gunshots." Evelyn said.

"You did." JW flatly. "Kate and Josh encountered some infected and they had to defend themselves. We are here to recommend you come over to our house tonight, we can help keep you safe." JW finished.

"Safe? From a virus? How do you propose to keep me safe from a virus? Do you have a cure?"

"Not from the virus Evelyn," Kate said. "From the infected. They attack. That is how it spreads."

"And how do you know that?" Evelyn questioned.

"I saw it." She said.

"Listen, I don't care if you come or not. But I am offering. If you want to stay in your home, stay. We will check on you in the morning." JW turned to walk away. Kate looked at him and started after. She looked back at Evelyn.

"Evelyn, please, if you change your mind. Come." Kate said.

Evelyn drew her jacket up a little tighter as she watched Kate follow JW back across the cul-de-sac. She wasn't sure what to do. If that crazy ass ex-army guy, who never ever speaks to her, came all the way over here to ask her to come stay with them for protection and his wife agreed with him, either they were a psycho-killer husband/wife duo or this might be an offer she needed to seriously consider.

JW and Kate had made it about halfway across the road when JW stopped. He turned and looked up the road to the buses. It was dark but he could make out the darker shapes lying on the ground where Kate and Josh had left them.

"I am sorry, you shouldn't have been out there." JW said.

"Bullshit. Whether I should have or shouldn't have doesn't matter anymore. Not tonight. What I have seen on the TV, on Scott's damn computers and with my own eyes is what matters. What I did was what needed to be done. I have been doing that our whole marriage. And now you need to realize something. That man, that man you keep inside, that man that scares you, that man that allowed you to do whatever you needed to do to come back home to me all those years ago, we need that man. I need you to make peace with it and be what we need you to be. For us."

"Ok." He started back to the house.

"Ok? Just like that?" she said.

"No, not just like that. But ok." He walked up the porch. "We have work to do."

When JW walked back inside Scott and Josh were sitting in the kitchen with a candle. He sat down with them.

"We have to secure this home. All interior doors have to come off so we can use them to cover the windows. We can push the Fridge in front of the kitchen door. We can push the couch against the front door and we can keep the garage door down. We only enter and exit through the front door if we have to go outside." JW rattled off his plan. "Let's get to work."

The next two hours were filled with hammers and nails. They managed to cover all the windows except the half-window over the sink. They used a couple of cookie sheets, screws, and JW's cordless drill to cover it. They were moving the refrigerator in front of the kitchen door when someone knocked on the front door. JW looked out the peephole.

"Come on in Evelyn." He opened the door and let her in. Kate met her and they walked into the living room.

JW and Josh pushed the couch up against the door. JW walked into the garage. The garage door had portholes, too small for anyone to get through but plenty big enough to watch the street. They faced Evelyn's house across the cul-de-sac and JW could see the cul-de-sac. What he couldn't see, because of the trees, was all the way back to the buses. He decided he would make patrols. He broke out the walkie-talkies from his hunting bag. He grabbed some fresh batteries and put them in. He walked into his room in the garage and opened his safe. He grabbed a box of pistol ammo and another magazine for the M4. He slung the rifle over his shoulder and left the safe open. He walked back into the kitchen.

"I can watch the street from the garage." He announced. "But I can't see the buses. I will go out every hour or so and just walk to where I can see up the road. I won't be out long. When I go I will take one of these." He showed them the walkie-talkies. "I want y'all all to rest as best you can. I will need someone to be awake each time I go out. Just in case."

He didn't need to say in case of what.

It was just past 11 when JW made his first walk outside. He woke Kate, who had managed to doze off sitting on the couch with Scott's head in her lap. Josh was asleep in his room and Evelyn was snoring loudly in JW and Kate's bed.

"Be careful." She said as he walked out the door.

She closed the door behind him and dead bolted the door. He walked out into the street and turned his flashlight off. The moon was bright and he could see a good ways up the road but not all the wall to the buses. He walked up the road until he could see them. He just stood there, listening. He could still hear sirens to the north and could still see the glow to his east. The sky was glowing in the direction of the sirens too. The helicopters were gone. He turned and walked back to the house. He made patrols all night long. He would just lie on the couch against the door between patrols. He looked at his watch. 4:30. He headed out again.

As he started up the road something caught his eye. Lights. Headlights. Pulling up to the bus. He crouched down and started moving towards them. The car stopped. He could see one person walk around from the driver's side and step in front of the car. He couldn't tell if there was anyone else. He crept closer. He could see there were two, maybe more. The first one had already climbed up on top of the hood of the bus and was reaching back. He pulled the one up and was reaching for the other one. When the first one jumped down onto the ground JW turned on his flashlight. "Don't take another step." JW said.
"I told y'all we was on the right road." Bridger said, raising his hands and blinking in the light.

Reunion

JW stood there, seeing but not believing. He lowered the rifle. Bridger helped the other person down from the hood of the bus. JW had been so wrapped up in the things that were going on he had forgotten. He looked at Bridger and smiled. They had been through a lot together back during JW's old life. Bridger had covered his ass too many times to count and vice versa. And even though they had fallen out of close contact, and both of them knew why, none of that seemed to matter. He walked up and hugged Bridger.
"Good to see you brother." Bridger said.
"Good to see you too." He said.
"JW, this is Tilly and Raj. He's a doctor and she's a hoot," he laughed.

Tilly shot him a glance but amazingly held her tongue. Her and Raj lowered their hands.
"Is everything ok?" a voice came over the walkie.
"Yep, just fine. Bridger is here"
"Hey Katie" Bridger yelled over JW
"Hey Bridger" she replied.
"Honey, Bridger brought some friends. We've got company for breakfast, heading your way now." JW said.

They walked back to the house. Kate and Scott were up and as they came through the front door, Josh came stumbling out of his room. He stopped and watched as his Dad and Bridger and two strangers walked through the door.

"Hey Uncle Bridger." He called.

"Hey Josh, damn you growed up." He said walking towards him with his arms going out for a hug.

"Yep." Josh said, extending his hand for a handshake. Bridger took it and yanked him in for the hug anyway.

They all went into the living room and sat down. Kate lit more candles and JW went to the kitchen. He turned on the stove. The gas was still on. He lit a burner and started pulling food out of the deep freezer. Kate had put as much as she could in the deep freezer when the power went out and it was still cold. He knew it wouldn't be for long. He started cooking sausage and bacon. He turned on another burner and started frying eggs. The living room grew quiet. The smell of food had made the group of travelers lose interest in recounting their story. Kate had heard enough to know what was happening on the other side of the buses. Chaos. They sat in the candlelight silently.

JW brought the plate of eggs and meat into the living room and had some paper plates tucked under his arm. Kate rose to help him and he asked her to grab the silver ware. They sat around the coffee table eating. He had boiled some water and found some instant coffee in the cabinet that he had forgotten about. He poured out cups. Tilly had finished eating and was lying on the couch. She was soon snoring. Raj lie down on the floor next to her and fell asleep. JW and Bridger leaned against the back wall.

"We need to bring my car inside your little compound." Bridger said. Smiling.

"Why?" JW asked.

"Because all my shit is in it and all their shit's in it." He said, nodding towards Tilly and Raj.

"Who are they?"

"Hell if I know, I came on them at a wreck. They were hurt. I helped them. Their car was crushed." He said.

"Yeah but why are they with you?" JW asked.

"Because I couldn't just leave them after what we saw."

"Why not?" JW asked.

"Because we're the good guys." Bridger smiled.

"Good answer." JW smiled too.

They had this conversation before. In a different time, in a different place, facing a decidedly different enemy. But they knew that it was a necessary conversation. They stood, JW nodded to Kate as they walked out the door. Kate nodded back. They walked outside up the road towards the buses.

"So what made you think to do this? With these?" Bridger said reaching out and touching the bus. The sun was beginning to come up. Everything had turned that gray color of early morning. Shapes took form.

"I just wanted to..." He broke off.

They became aware of someone walking on the road on the other side of the bus and knelt down to see. They could see bare feet and bare legs walking. JW stood up and opened the bus door. Bridger jumped up.

"JW, get your ass up here, you are not going to believe this."

JW climbed on the bus and looked out the window. In the street next to Bridger's car was an elderly woman. She was naked and wet. She had a shower cap on. She was just shuffling along. The bus driver's window was facing up the street so Bridger opened it.

"Hey" he called.

The woman stopped and without turning her body, turned her head towards Bridger's voice. Her shoulder turned and her arms swung with them. Then her legs finally started to pivot with her hips.

"Well shit, I guess I know why they call it Marionette now. She looks like a fucking puppet on a string." Bridger observed.

JW turned his flashlight on the woman and they could see the opaque eyes and the slack skin. She screeched at the light and started towards it. JW handed the light to Bridger and shouldered his rifle. One shot. She fell. Bridger turned the light off.

"Well, I guess I don't really need to know where you stand on taking out these puppets." Bridger said.

"Puppet?" he asked

"Gotta call em something." Bridger said.

"Keep working on it." He continued, "I have seen enough to know they are dangerous and right now anything I think is dangerous to my family is dead. Period." He said.

"That's what I am counting on. Brother." Bridger smiled.

They started to get off the bus, JW turned to look back up the road. What had been an empty street one minute ago now had three or four people shuffling down it, in the direction of the bus.

"Damn." JW said.

Bridger looked back. He could see them too. He watched as another came out of the driveway just up the street. It turned towards the bus.

"You think they heard the shot?" Bridger asked.

"Maybe. Maybe they come to sound." He said.

They watched as the infected made their way down the street towards them. Each one made the same stuttered move as they walked. They would throw their upper body forward and their legs would shuffle under them. They repeated it over and over.

JW sat down in the driver's seat and Bridger was looking out the window behind him. JW reached his hand out of the window and banged one time against the side of the bus. The reaction was instantaneous. They all jerked forward towards the sound. They weren't exactly running but continually falling forward with their legs moving just enough to keep them from falling down. They were a few yards from the bus and JW raised the rifle again. He dispatched each one until the street was empty again. They watched. Ten minutes passed and they didn't see anything else coming down the street.

"We need to get my stuff out of my car." Bridger said.

"I think I can spare a pair of clean socks if you need them." JW said.

"Thanks, I do, I didn't pack any. What I did pack was my bag of guns and I am pretty sure we are going to need those." He said.

JW cranked the bus and moved it so that Bridger could pull his car through. He parked the bus back, making sure there were no gaps someone could easily walk through. What he had seen in the last hour had made him realize that even though he could keep a vehicle from coming in, these things didn't drive. He would have to figure this out.

"What's it like out there?" JW asked nodding towards the buses.

"What do you mean?" Bridger asked.

"I haven't been a hundred yards outside those buses since we parked them." Yesterday he thought to himself. "My guess is that since these things are wandering the woods, things got worse since then."

"No shit, Sherlock. They have. I don't know what this is, but it is everywhere. If it's a virus, it's airborne. We encountered a family, isolated as hell, and one of them died of old age. He came back. No contact with anybody. Nothing. Just died and came back. I don't know if we are all just ticking time bombs or what but yeah, it got worse. Why?"

"I think we may have to go back out there." JW said, looking at the buses again.

On a String

This was a people problem. The more people, the more chance to become infected if this was a virus, and the more chance to encounter dead ones too. They needed to be away from people and not by just a few blocks and a bus. They needed to be miles away from folks. And JW had the perfect place. They just needed to figure out how to get there. They had figured out how to get out of a lot of tight spots. Some were bar fights in Fayetteville; others were gunfights not in Fayetteville. This was going to be basically the same thing. Just a simple forced march under fire. Except they weren't firing at you, they were trying to eat you. Bridger smiled.

"Basically the same." He mumbled.

"What?" JW said.

"Nothing" He smiled at JW.

JW looked at him turning his head sideways. He was glad Bridger was here. He was still having a hard time processing what happened with the deputy but he was beginning to put it in that place he keeps those things. That place was getting full and it took a little longer. Bridger had seen some of those things JW put away. That helped in a strange way.

"So you think this is the best move?" Bridger asked.

"Nope, but I have to go out there and see. Just a little recon job. I need to check out to the main road. I have to at least see that far. After that, well."

"Well?"

"Well nothing. One step at a time. Right now, you say nothing. You just tell them I am doing a walk. Not anything else. Ok?" JW said.

"Yeah, I got that but why are you walking. Just use my car." Bridger said.

"No, I walk. I can see more. I need to be deliberate."

"Ok, your plan. I will be on the other end of that." pointing to the walkie in JW's pocket.

"You call if you need the cavalry."

"Will do, you just get back there and make sure everybody gets a present from your Santa bag." JW said.

"Ho, Ho, Ho" he smiled.

JW dropped to his belly and rolled under the bus. He had the rifle and his pistol. He stood and looked down the street. He had a little over a mile to the entrance where the four-way stop was. And probably a deputy's car. He glanced at the body just up the road. He started walking. The sun was up over the trees now and he could see down the road. He didn't see any cars or people. As he reached the first house on the left, he glanced down at the deputy lying face down in the road. He reached down and rolled him over.

"I'm sorry". He said.

He reached into the deputy's pocket and grabbed his keys. He took the gun belt off him and put it on. Glock. Four mags. Flashlight, two pair of handcuffs and Taser. JW inventoried in his head. He started walking again. He moved slowly but deliberately. Had covered about half the distance to the main road without seeing anything. He had stopped a few times to listen to the sounds of helicopters off in the distance. None had approached.

"Hey, hey you." JW heard a voice to his right. He shouldered the rifle.

"Hey don't shoot." A man about JW's age was peaking out a side door of the house.

JW knew the house. He didn't know the man who lived here but Kate had told him the guy worked for the state too. He was a geologist or chemist or something.

"Please just don't shoot, I am not infected." He said.

"How do I know that?" JW asked

"Well, I am not trying to eat you."

"Fair enough" JW lowered the rifle.

"What are you doing out here?" He asked.

"I am walking to the main road to see what it looks like." JW said.

"It looks like a road. I know who you are. I saw you come rolling by yesterday in those buses. You're that," he hesitated "that guy that lives at the end of the road."

JW realized something. If you really want people to leave you alone, move into a neighborhood with a bunch of gossipy neighbors and don't take part in their gossip.

"I am just seeing what options are available. Choices." JW said. "How many folks are left?"

"I don't know about anything other than just these few houses right here." He waved his hand over about six houses up and down the street. He started pointing at each one.

"That one is gone. Dead. The next two are in the second house together, an elderly gentleman and a family of four. Except for the mom. She is in the other house. Dead but not dead. You know?" He raised his eyebrow at JW. JW nodded. "The rest on that side are dead or gone away. Some left this morning with the folks to my right. The couple to the left is inside my house with my daughter and her friend. We had a sleepover and we haven't been able to reach her parents. So 8, no 9, counting me."

"How do you know?"

"Know what?"

"About the house across the street, when was the last time you talked to them?"

"Well, it's been a few hours but there hasn't been any of those things out there."

"What news have you heard?" JW asked, less formally "I mean, besides the obvious."

"Well the only thing I have heard lately is on a battery powered police scanner. It was some police and some civilian talking. The lady was telling the cop that people were eating people and that blood was everywhere. There was no help. The cop was telling the lady to get to the shelter at the fairgrounds on the east side of town. She said she was at the fairgrounds."

"OK. Listen, I am going to walk to the main road. If you want me to I can stop by on my way back. I am going to see if it's safe to leave." JW said.

"And go where?"

"Away from town. At least for a while." He said.

"Do you think it matters?"

"I don't know, but at least there will be less of those things."

"I don't know your name," he said.

"JW. JW Toles."

"Charlie. Charlie Fair." They shook hands.

"I'll stop by on my way back."

JW walked back out in the street. He walked on without encountering living or dead. He heard a few sirens and an occasional helicopter in the distance. Most of the cars were gone from driveways. A dog crossed the street in front of him. He could see the entrance to the neighborhood. He saw the deputy's car. He opened the trunk. There was a shotgun and another rifle in a built in case. There was also a big first aid kit and some road flares. He grabbed the shotgun and opened the driver's door. He mounted the shotgun in the rest and used the deputy's keys to crank the car. He turned out of the neighborhood slowly heading north towards the river and the bridge. He could see Kate's school ahead. It looked like folks had tried to gather there. Cars filled the parking lot. He thought about turning in but the windows in the building made him keep going. Every window was smeared in blood and handprints. Whatever had happened, it had been bad. He drove to the bridge and stopped. There was one car parked in the middle of the bridge with its door open. He knew he could get across the bridge. That was what he needed to know. He started to turn the car around and looked down the street towards town. He could see more vehicles. He had no reason to go towards town. He went anyway. He needed to know.

Charlie closed the door and his daughter looked at him.
"Who was that?" she asked.
"That was JW Toles. He lives at the end of the road." He said.
"You mean that weird guy." She said, turning to her friend. "I heard he was like tortured and stuff when he was in the CIA and they messed with his brain."
"Jennifer, please. He is just a retired veteran who likes his privacy." He looked at her. She raised her eyebrows.
"OK he's a little weird." He said.

"Listen, he is talking about trying to get away from town. He says he has somewhere to go. I think we should consider going with him."

"Seriously?" she said.

"Seriously." Charlie said.

Bridger had told Kate that JW had gone to scout the neighborhood. He told her not told her not to worry. He told her a lot of things. It didn't matter. She had let him know in explicit detail what she thought of Bridger Preston allowing him to go out there. She had calmed down since but she still was worried. Raj and Tilly were sitting on the couch with Evelyn. Scott was sitting in JW's chair and Josh was sitting on the floor. Kate and Bridger came into the living room. Kate sat down on the floor.

"JW went out past the buses. He said he would be back soon. He was going to check out the rest of the neighborhood."

"By himself?" Raj asked.

"Yeah, he does that." Kate said.

"While we are waiting we need to figure out what we have and what we need. I have weapons for everyone. Anybody need a quick lesson just ask." Bridger said.

"We also need to get all of our food together. We need to make sure it is ready to go." He paused. "Just in case." He added.

They all gathered around Bridger's bag. He had two pump shotguns with pistol grips, two standard pump shotguns, three Colt AR Civilian models and one honest to goodness Special Ops issue M4 fully automatic rifle. That one was his. It had been with him a long time. He also had seven 9mm pistols of varying manufacturers. He had some ammo but not much beyond what was loaded in the weapons. He had several more shotgun rounds and pistol rounds but most of the other was what were in the magazines. Tilly and Raj chose the standard shotguns. Josh and Scott the pistol grips. They also had the rifles JW had given them. Along with Kate's pistol, she chose another pistol. Bridger took his M4 and the magazines from the other rifles.

"Ok, everybody keep your friends close and your guns closer." Bridger smirked.

They had brought some plastic totes in already and began emptying the pantry.

"From now on, everything we have at all times, has to be ready to go." Bridger added.

"I have food at my house too." Evelyn said.

"OK, we'll go get it. Raj, you wanna go with?" Bridger said.

"Ok." He looked at Tilly.

"I'm going too." Evelyn said. "It's my house, I need some things."

"Ok." Bridger said. He handed her one of the pistols. "Do you know how to use it?"

"Point and shoot?" She said. He showed her the safety.

"Red is Ready. Then point and shoot."

They went to the front door. Bridger looked out the peephole. He didn't see any movement. They moved the couch away and opened the front door. The street was empty. He stepped out into the sunlight. They crowded out behind him onto the front porch. Being outside seemed foreign to them already. They had been hidden behind those boarded windows for less than a day and already the sun seemed new. Bridger, Raj and Evelyn started across the cul-de-sac. The others went back inside and closed the door. The group reached Evelyn's front door and slipped inside. She went into the kitchen and started pulling things out of her pantry. Raj started loading it into garbage bags that she had given him. Bridger went into the garage and found some totes to put stuff in. He also found a garden cart he could use to get it back across the street. He pulled the cart into the kitchen and started loading things up. They had just about emptied the pantry.

"I need to get some things out of my bedroom. Some personal things." She said.

"Ok. Need any help?" Raj said.

"No, no. Just some small things." She said as she went out of the kitchen.

Bridger and Raj finished packing everything onto the cart. They rolled the cart out the front door and went back inside to grab the other few bags. Bridger noticed the pictures on the wall. It showed a happy couple on vacation and at holidays. It showed pets, but no children. Raj came from the kitchen with the last bag.

"Where's Mrs. Collins?" he asked.

"Where's Mr. Collins?" Bridger asked, smiling.

"Dead" Evelyn said, walking from around the corner.

Bridger's smile went away. She walked past them and out the front door.

"Well, that was fun, let's go." Evelyn said.

Standing in her front yard between her and the cart were two of the infected. Her voice had carried when she opened the door and both turned to the sound. The closest one was wearing work coveralls with the CXT railroad emblem. The coveralls were shredded around the legs, ripped by the thick underbrush it had passed through. The hands looked the same except instead of cotton and nylon it was flesh and muscle that was torn apart. The tips of the fingers were bone, the flesh completely ripped away. Blood oozed through the coveralls. The same thorns had lacerated the face, the slack skin easily giving way under their sharpness. The other infected appeared to be a teenage girl. She was wearing shorts and a t-shirt. Her leg had been bitten. She had the same slack skin and pale eyes as the man. Both turned in that same jerky way Bridger had witnessed earlier.

He raised the rifle. The first one jerked just as he fired and the round missed. It reached out and grabbed Evelyn. Raj fired over them as they fell and hit the other infected in the stomach. Bridger grabbed the one on Evelyn. Raj fired again. The girl (thing) in the yard fell. Bridger was holding on to the other with everything he had as it rapidly chomped for Evelyn's face. It was twisting and trying to turn and she was pushing it away as best she could. Raj tried to pull Evelyn from underneath it. They were all yelling. Boom. Everything exploded. Bridger fell backwards. The thing had quit struggling. Evelyn pulled herself from underneath with Raj's help. She had the pistol in her right her. She was covered in what had come out of the back of the things head. They just stood there for a second, each looking at the other confirming they were all ok. Evelyn was crying, but just a tear or two. Bridger was checking her over. Raj wiped her face off with a towel he grabbed from the kitchen.

"I'm fine. I'm fine. Just let me do that." She said, snatching the towel from him. "Sorry" she said.
"It's ok." He said.

They took a quick look around. They pulled the cart back across the cul-de-sac. The gunfire had alerted the others. They were standing in the front yard and rushed to the street to help when they saw them coming back. Tilly ran over to Raj and hugged him. Kate met Evelyn and helped her pull the cart. Bridger stopped and stood in the middle of the cul-de-sac. He looked up the road towards the buses. He looked at his watch. Not time to worry yet. He had another hour before he was even overdue. He looked at the sun, climbing higher in the sky. Nice weather, he thought. He turned and followed Raj and Tilly.

JW had reached the Home Depot. It was on the edge of the main part of town. Past the Home Depot was the college and just south of the college was downtown. He had encountered several infected but only randomly and he drove by them. As he approached the store, he could see more in the parking lot, wandering around. He stopped the car and opened the glove box. Binoculars.

He scanned the road ahead of the store and could see several more in the street. He walked to the back fence of the store and found a gate. He approached the back of the store and climbed the ladder mounted for the AC service. He got on the roof and walked to the front of the store. When he got to where he could see, he paused. The parking lot didn't just have some infected. It was full of them. He could see loudspeakers mounted on poles. There was some kind of aid station set up in the adjacent field the store had used for outbuilding displays.

There were dozens more infected shuffling in and out of the shelter. He had seen enough. He climbed back down. He convinced himself that what he wanted to do was the right move. He knew that it was a lie. It wasn't the right move. It was the only move. And it probably wasn't enough. He drove towards home.

Charlie Fair and his daughter walked back to their house. The group across the street were staying put. The couple that had taken shelter with Charlie, Amanda and Chris Bettis, were going to stay with Charlie. If he left they left. Counting them, his daughter and her friend Lori, Charlie's group totaled five. He told his daughter to start packing whatever food they have; he was going to make sure they were ready to go, if the time came.

"So do we need to pack clothes?" Amanda asked.

"Yep. I'll help." Charlie said. He and the couple headed next door.

"I don't want to leave. My parents, my brother. I don't know what happened to them. I can't leave." Lori said after they left.

"Lori, we have too." Jennifer said.

"Why?"

"Because we have too." They kept packing.

Charlie was in the neighbor's kitchen loading the food into plastic Magix bags. Chris brought in a few smiley face boxes to load the bags into. Amanda brought two suitcases from the bedroom and proclaimed that they were ready. Charlie put the bag into the box and they headed back next door. They could see someone walking down the road. They watched as it shuffled along. It turned towards the sound of a dog barking. They hurried inside. Charlie looked back as the police car pulled up.

"Be ready. Sometime this afternoon." JW said out the driver's window of the police car.

"How will we know it's time to go?" Charlie asked.

"It'll be just like being a kid again." JW drove off. Charlie walked inside shaking his head.

"Weird guy" he thought.

JW drove past the one infected walking the street. He parked the police car all the way past the buses. He crawled under and walked towards his house. He saw the two bodies lying in Evelyn's yard. He walked to his front door and knocked. He could hear them moving the couch and the dead bolt being opened. Scott opened the door. They hugged. He walked inside. Kate heard him come in and they all walked into the living room. Evelyn and Raj were sitting on the couch and Tilly came out of the bathroom and sat between them. Bridger was standing in the kitchen doorway. Josh was on the floor.

"I went to town. I got as far as the Home Depot. It all appears overrun," he continued, "The aid shelter was full of them. I don't think there is anything left. Anyone down there is either one of them or going to be if they don't get out. And that is what we are going to do."

"What?" Evelyn asked.

"We are going to get out. We are going to leave." He said.

"And go where." Raj asked.

"Nowhere, well actually the middle of nowhere."
Bridger said.

"What the hell are you talking about?" Tilly said.

"I have a piece of land and right now I think being as far away as possible from populated areas is the best way forward. We can load up everything we have in the buses."

"Oh great, the Partridge fucking family goes camping" Tilly said. JW cut her a glance.

"I'm Keith." Bridger said. Earning a glance of his own.

"We need to get everything packed up. All the food, anything we think we need." He said. "Anybody have anything questions?"

"For how long?" Evelyn asked.

"I don't know." He said. "We need to carry everything we can. We will take the two buses and Kate's SUV. My truck is already up there."

"Why?" Bridger asked.

"Why is my truck there? Long story." JW said, absentmindedly rubbing his head. "Why the buses? So we can carry more stuff but more importantly, when we get there, we can use them for shelter. We need to leave as soon as we can. I found another family in the neighborhood. We will stop to pick them up. After that we don't stop. I scouted all the way to the bridge. It is clear. Once we get across the bridge, I will stay ahead of the buses in the SUV. Kate you drive the first bus, Bridger you follow. Get everything ready. We move the buses in one hour. Let's get to work." He said. They started packing.

Caravan

JW and Kate were standing in their bedroom. It was really the first time they had been completely alone together since this all started. She sat on the bed. He was changing clothes.

"How you doing?" She asked.

"Huh?"

"How are you doing? Are you okay?" she asked again.

"I'm trying. Right now I am focused on getting us away from this."

"Ok. You don't have to do all the heavy lifting. We have a plan. We know what to do."

He finished getting dressed and they walked back into the living room. They had managed to fill it with boxes and totes of food, blankets, clothes and anything else they thought they needed. Everyone was sitting on a box or on the couch.

"Ok. Here's the plan. Bridger, Kate and I will go get the buses. The rest of you start moving everything into the garage. When we get back, we'll pull one bus against the garage and the other in the street. We'll load everything and everybody in one bus. The other bus will be just Bridger and Raj, it is Raj right?" JW said. Raj nodded. "I'll lead, Kate you next with everybody on board, then Bridger. Everybody be on alert. We don't know when these things are going to show up.

"Everybody ready?" They nodded

JW, Kate and Bridger walked out the front door and up the road to the buses. The sun had given way to clouds and it looked like the day was going to end in rain. They opened the door to the first bus as the drops began to fall. Bridger climbed on board followed by JW. They looked up the street. A few infected wandering at the far end of what they could see. Nothing else. They cranked up the bus and Bridger climbed off. Kate had the other bus running.

"Y'all pull down. Get everything loaded. I will watch the road. Now go." Bridger said.

JW and Kate pulled their buses down the cul-de-sac. Kate parked by the garage and JW parked in the street. He climbed down and went to where they were loading up. He grabbed his backpack out of Josh's car. He grabbed his toolbox, the first-aid kit from the deputy's car, an axe and a couple of other tools and threw them on the bus. He loaded the weapons still in his gun safe into the SUV. He walked back down the driveway and waved up the street to Bridger. He made sure everybody was loaded into the bus. He jumped in Kate's SUV and started to pull away, he looked back to make sure everyone was in line behind him. They set off.

Charlie was looking out his front door peephole. A bus pulled up to his driveway and opened the door. "Just like being a kid again." He smiled. "Let's go everybody. They're here."

JW parked and got out of his car. He was watching the street. Bridger stood in the stairwell of his bus. The first infected came from between the houses, by the time Bridger saw it there were at least a dozen more coming from behind the houses. Tilly and Raj were helping get the last few things from the house. Amanda was coming out of the door with them. The rest were halfway to the buses. JW ran towards the group trying to carry suitcases down the driveway. "Go, go get to the bus. NOW!!" he said in a muffled shout.

They paused, surprised. The first screams caused the infected to react. Bridger jumped down from his bus and covered one side of the driveway while JW was holding the other. Shots rang out of the bus windows from Josh, Kate and Scott. Most of the infected fell away. Charlie's group dropped everything and ran for the bus. Tilly and Amanda were coming out of the house when one of the infected came around the other side of the house. It was a girl, no more than 7 or 8 years old. It grabbed Amanda by the arm, Amanda jerked away from the small hands. She screamed. Tilly leveled the shotgun at its head and fired. It exploded. The child's body fell, headless to the ground. Amanda screamed again.

"Oh the humanity and all that shit, I get it. Now shut the fuck up before you get us killed." Tilly said.

One of the infected that JW shot fell at the feet of Charlie's daughter, she stopped and screamed. Everyone behind rushed against her and the whole group went down. Most of the infected were down too. "Ok folks, everybody up and on the bus." JW said reaching out to help them up.

The gunfire from the bus had stopped. Bridger was dispatching the few infected still coming from behind the house. Tilly, Raj and Amanda made their way down the driveway.

"Come on folks, don't have all fucking day." Tilly said. "It's just the fucking zombie apocalypse." Earning a few disapproving looks from the newcomers.

Tilly grabbed the suitcases, strolling around the bodies. She loaded them one at a time onto the back of the bus.

"Wouldn't want you to lose your panties." She said, climbing back on the bus. JW and Bridger gave each other an approving smile. JW didn't know where Bridger found this girl, but she had her moments.

They stood outside the bus. JW, Kate and Bridger. The rest were hanging their heads out listening. It was time.

"OK here we go. From this point on we do not plan on stopping." JW said. He hugged Kate. He looked up in the bus at his two sons.

"Saddle up." He and Bridger shook hands.

They slowly pulled to the end of the neighborhood. They turned left. As they passed a few houses they saw odd sights. Signs haphazardly painted on the doors. Save us, mainly. They occasionally saw a curtain move or a shadow pass by the window. No way to tell if it was living or dead. As they passed a church, its door flung open. The sound of the passing buses had awoken the congregation. They were streaming out in the same falling, stumble run they had seen before. Jennifer and Lori were looking out of the back of the bus. They could see the other bus behind them and the crowd of infected beyond that. They drove on. Kate was not prepared for the sight of her school. Cars abandoned, some burnt. Tents torn down and scattered. She could see the same windows JW had seen earlier. She knew which one was her classroom. She could see it as she passed the building. Tears came down her face as she saw the streaks of blood. They drove on. They approached the bridge.

JW stopped. What had been an empty bridge two hours ago now had a small gang of infected wandering around the car he had seen earlier. He stepped out of the SUV and walked back to Kate's bus. "Tell Josh to come up here and drive my car." He said.

Josh came out of the bus. JW saw Bridger walking up to him.

"Raj can drive my bus, I'll help." He said.

They walked around the SUV and started towards the bridge with the buses following behind. Bridger and JW methodically cleared the path. There were infected wearing military uniforms. Bridger took the opportunity to relieve them of any weapons as they passed by. From the variety of clothing among the others it appeared these were the poor souls who had encamped at the school. JW could see children and women among the infected. As they moved the caravan followed. They made their way around the car on the bridge. Once they made it across the bridge they stopped. JW climbed back in the SUV with Josh and Bridger back to his bus. They set out once again.

Tilly sat in the back of the bus. She rolled down the road looking at the smoke filled pine trees as the rain brought the smoke down to the ground. The fading light still provided enough for her to be able to make out the burnt out structure of the night before as they passed. She didn't know where they were, but she knew where she was.

"About twenty more miles." Scott said over the back of the seat in front of her.

"What?" she said.

"Twenty more miles until we get there. I come up here all the time. I think it is going to be a good place."

"A good place for what?" she asked.

"I don't know, a good place to get our heads together and figure out what to do next."

"And what is next?" she asked. He didn't answer.

Bridger was sitting in the first seat of the bus he and Raj were using. They both saw the dirt road and smoke. They didn't talk about it.

"What the hell?" Raj said, looking in his rearview mirror.

Bridger stood and walked down the aisle to the back of the bus. He looked out the window and saw two cars following them. He grabbed the walkie.

"JW, we have picked up a convoy. Two vehicles, unknown occupants."

"Ok, I am going to stop. If they stop behind you, wait for me to walk back."

"Aye aye cap'n" Bridger said.

As they slowed to a stop and pulled to the side of the road, the vehicles stopped too. Bridger watched them. Nobody got out. JW walked to the last bus and Bridger came out. They walked to the first car. JW approached the driver's window. It was down. A woman and two kids.

"Why are you following us?" he asked.

"We were at the school. We hid in our cars and didn't move. We haven't seen anyone come by in hours. You were the first ones we saw, we couldn't stay there any longer."

"The people behind you?" he asked.

"Neighbors. I'm Janice Walker. My son, Jeremiah and my nephew Clyde. Behind us are the Harrison's. An older couple who lived next door." She said.

"We are going to the woods. We have some provisions and we have weapons. If you would like to follow us, you are more than welcome. But, if you do, you follow our rules."

"OK. What are your rules?" she asked.

"Simple. Stay alive so you can keep others alive." He said.

She nodded her head. He walked to the other vehicle and had the same conversation. They would follow. He told them to get behind Kate's bus and let Bridger follow. They were growing their caravan.

Ahead JW could see the turn. They had seen a few vehicles abandoned on the way here, but not many. The road was fairly clear once they had crossed the bridge. A few houses and a few stores. They had seen no people. Living or dead. That was good. JW turned down the dirt road. Once he got everyone through the gate, he locked it. They made camp. JW got his truck started and they built a small fire. Tilly and Evelyn had taken upon themselves to coordinate sleeping arrangements. No one wanted to sleep. The darkness of the night was accentuated by the ghostly whispers of smoke lit by the moon. Charlie had brought a weather radio and was cranking it.

"Forecast for the weekend. Zombies. More at five." Tilly said, watching him crank.

He turned on the power. Static. He moved the dial. Static. He switched bands. Static. He switched to AM and all the way to the left of the dial, he got a signal.

PLEASE STAND BY FOR A MESSAGE FROM THE VICE PRESIDENT OF THE UNITED STATES.

PLEASE STAND BY FOR A MESSAGE FROM THE VICE PRESIDENT OF THE UNITED STATES.
■■
The message repeated several times. Charlie was just about to turn the dial and try another station.

■■

"This is Vice President Addison. Tonight we mourn the loss of so many, including President Wilson. I come to you tonight as a father and a friend. Washington has fallen. All information we have is that the city has been completely over run with Marionette. We have lost contact with all overseas military commands. We are at a secure location in Colorado and although we have contained it for now, it is inside the compound. People listening to my voice; please hold those you love tight tonight when you say your prayers. Stay strong. Be safe. God bless.

The group around the campfire looked at each other. All were searching the faces of strangers to find hope.

"We made it here. We are still here." Raj said.

Everyone slowly went to their bus. Nobody was sleeping. Everyone was sitting in a seat. Looking out the window into the darkness. Kate, Scott and Josh were sitting at the front of one bus. With them were people who joined the caravan past the bridge, and Evelyn Collins. The other bus held Tilly, Raj and Charlie's group, Jennifer, Lori, Amanda and Chris. Both buses passed the night watching the moon dance off the wet left by the rain and the smoke drifting through the trees.

"You were at the school?" Kate asked Janice.

"Yes."

"What happened?"

"It...it was bad. We were...just..."

"It's ok, we can talk tomorrow. Just rest." Kate said.

When the sun finally rose JW and Bridger walked down the road towards the gate. They cut through the woods. The came to the end of the stand of trees they were in and it opened into a field. They could see the road from this spot. Even though JW knew it wasn't on his land, he didn't think things like that were going to matter as much any more. The started across the field just to see what they could see.

"It looks like your plan might work." Bridger said.

"For now. But for how long, this thing has spread so fast. There wasn't even enough time to think. All we did was react."

"Lucky we had a chance to." Bridger said.

"From everything we have seen we were very lucky. But yeah, for right now, we are ok."

"We might have another problem."

"What's that?" JW asked

"We have maybe three weeks of food. Tops." He said "You remember laughing me off the phone about zombies in Madagascar?"

"Yeah." Bridger smiled and looked down.

"That was four days ago. Four days. Three weeks seems like a long time." He said, looking at the sunrise.

"Besides, we've got the rest of our lives to figure it out."

Walk with Me

By SB Poe
Marionette Zombie Series Book 2

This is a work of fiction. Names, characters, business, events and incidents are the products of the author's imagination. Any resemblance to actual persons, living or dead, or actual events is purely coincidental

Prologue

Janice, the Harrisons and the Boys

She had to find Dottie and Ray. They had been together since yesterday and she was not going to leave them. When the news reports began, she had turned to Dottie before anyone else. Dottie and Ray Harrison's back yard connected to the back of Janice's yard. They had been fence neighbors for over ten years. They were there when Jeremy was born. They were his godparents. They were there when Mac, her husband, had died of a heart attack a few years later. She wouldn't have made it through that time if Dottie and Ray hadn't been there to help her. They would sit with Jeremy while she struggled to work two jobs. It was hard, but she finally got things straightened out and she had settled into a job that didn't require her to be gone too many evenings. And then yesterday the world fell apart. They had gone to the church. Dottie and Ray had helped Janice get food and water loaded in her car. They also helped her keep Jeremy and his cousin Clyde calm.

The church had been open since yesterday. Most of the parishioners had gathered for an evening prayer and had decided to stay. Safety in numbers. Dottie was on the flower committee, and Agnes Weathers had called her to tell her to come to the church. They all went together. The church had stood with its doors open for over twelve hours welcoming people in. It became a home for the ill and infirmed that evening. Shortly after Janice and her group arrived, Agnes's husband had a massive stroke. Two hours after that all hell broke loose in the house of God. Janice saw Ray.

"Ray, where's Dottie?"

"She's coming. Go ahead. Get to your car. We're parked right next to you. Go. We'll meet at the school." Ray yelled.

Janice grabbed for Jeremy and Clyde and made her way out of the fellowship hall exit. They got to the car and drove to the school without looking back. She parked at the end of the lot facing the road so she could watch for Dottie and Ray. Janice watched as several military vehicles pulled around to the back of the school and watched them unload a few people on stretchers and take them into the back of the school. More military people arrived and went in front of the school. She saw Ray's car and flashed her lights. He pulled in next to her.

"Well. Did you check in yet?" Ray asked, rolling down his window.

"Not yet. I was waiting for you two." Janice said.

"Ok. Just wait here and let me go see what's what." Ray said.

"Ok."

Ray got out but left his window down so Dottie and Janice could speak to each other. He walked up to the side door but it wouldn't open. He waved back at them and disappeared around to the front of the school.

"What happened back there?" Janice finally asked.

"Tom Weathers had Marionette, I guess. He collapsed, and the preacher said he was dead, right before he rose up and attacked him."

"The preacher?"

"Yes. He killed him. Bit him. After that I just turned and left as quickly as I could. I could hear them screaming behind me. I swear Janice, I don't know what is happening, but it is evil. Pure evil."

"OPEN THE DOOR. OPEN THE DOOR" They heard Ray yelling as he came around the side of the school. Dottie opened the door.

Ray quickly jumped in and raised his window. As he did, several people came running from around the front of the school. A military person turned and raised his weapon and shot back towards the front of the school. Janice screamed inside the car. He kept firing and reloading until finally from around the front came a large crowd of other people. The people looked like the crowds she had seen in the videos on the TV. Shuffling, falling forward. The crowd came towards the growing line of military personnel gathered in front of them.

They watched the crowd approach the military line. The street on the opposite side began to fill with more of the dead. Janice looked back up the hill towards the church and saw Marionette infected coming from that way too. They were surrounded. She watched as the crowd finally overwhelmed the military. She watched it all. A few hours later, she watched as a sheriffs car rode by slowly and turned down the street towards the Home Depot. She thought about following it but couldn't. She just couldn't. Hours passed.

The crowd had moved away, mostly across the bridge. Ray rolled down his window just a little.

"Janice. Honey. Can you talk?" Ray asked.

"Yes. Yes. I" Janice started. Her voice was drowned out by the sound of a school bus.

"What the hell?" She heard Ray say.

"Let's go." Janice said.

"What?" Dottie asked.

"Let's go. Let's follow those buses. They may be headed somewhere safe."

Janice put the car in gear and pulled ahead. She watched as two men got out and cleared the infected from the bridge. It was two buses and a big SUV. If they made it across the bridge, she was going to follow. She watched the last bus pull across the bridge and she pulled out of the parking lot. Ray followed. They fell in behind the last bus. A short ways down the road the buses pulled over. She pulled over too. Ray and Dottie Harrison pulled in behind her. She watched as the two men she saw clearing the bridge approached her car. She rolled down the window.

In the Darkness

Lead me on my way

JW sat among the trees listening to the cicadas buzz. The mist brightened as the sun crept over the horizon. He could hear squirrels running around a pine trunk, their tiny claws rudely echoing through the morning quiet. He had been watching the road for almost two hours. The smell came again.

He was still processing the last two weeks. They had reacted so fast. Was it too fast? While everything he had seen told him that he'd made the right decision, sitting here now he began to wonder. Could they have held out at home? Maybe, maybe not. Now he had seventeen other people hoping this was the right plan. And the weather was going to get colder. Admittedly, Alabama in the winter isn't the Arctic Circle, but it still gets cold. And wet. Wet and cold is a bad combination. They had gone through the firewood in JW's truck and were spending their days gathering more. Groups of two or three would patrol around the camp watching the woods for infected but so far they had been completely unmolested. A few times they had heard cars on the road a few miles away, but only a few. The military aircraft that had filled the air for the first few nights were now mostly gone.

The wind shifted again and the smell of death came back. South. He waited a few more minutes so the sun could rise above the horizon. He pulled the walkie out of his pocket.

"Bridge?" he thumbed the button. A pause.

"Good morning sunshine." Bridger replied.

"I am going for a little walk south. I'll follow along the edge of the road and should be back by dark." He said.

"You think that's a good idea?"

"Don't know, but I have to see if I can tell where that smell is coming from. Whatever it is."

"You need me to come?" Bridger asked.

"Not this time. Just keep an eye on everyone. Make sure you keep everyone alert. And make sure everyone is armed."

"You get in trouble, you sing out. I'll come running."

"Will do."

JW put the walkie back in his pocket and stood. He waited for the wind to rise one more time. Death. It had been over a week since they came down this road to escape the Marionette virus and the infected.

At night, when the AM band could reach the heavens, they could hear Ohio, Missouri, Tennessee, Georgia, and on really clear nights, New York and Connecticut as they slowly scanned the radio dial. The radios in the cars weren't as effective as Charlie's weather radio but they could still pick up some things. They had run the battery down on Janice's car the first night. That next day Janice told them about the school. She told them how her and the boys went to the church for shelter and the National Guard had moved them to the school. Then the aid station in town got over run and the National Guard had evacuated those patients to the school too. That was how it got in. She also told them how it ended. The radio broadcasts were not much better.

Emergency broadcasts were interrupted by panicked local deejays. The military had closed Long Island, but the virus had already crossed over. Or maybe it was already there. They heard a broadcast from Atlanta directing people to a shelter. The military had closed off I-85 and it had reportedly created huge traffic jams coming out of the city. Folks were trapped on the interstates as the city fell. Two nights later brought the news that the military bombed the city to prevent the outbreak from spreading. The fate of the people stranded on the interstate was never mentioned again. The story was the same all over. The major cities fell quickly. Too many people, too few options. Most of the radio stations from the big cities died away by the third night. They listened as the world fell apart. Under the stars with the breeze blowing, they listened as Marionette marched across the radio dial into weaker and weaker bands until finally, nothing. Charlie continued to try to find something, anything, for another day. Cranking the handle for power and turning the dial. Nothing.

Then the smell came. It started as just a slight unpleasant odor on the morning breeze as they finished their first week in the woods. Throughout the day it would come and go. By nightfall it would linger in the air a little longer. It had the distinct smell of death, maybe a dead dog. JW decided to walk out to the road to see what he could see.

He stayed inside the wood line keeping the road on his left. He bought his land a few years ago and even though he came up here as often as he could, he didn't know anybody who lived in the few houses and the only landmarks he knew were the little country post office and the old fireworks stand down the road. He had noticed the stand when he came last time. It had a new coat of paint and hand painted sign in anticipation of the coming holidays. He knew the stand and the post office were about five miles away. He figured he could cover that distance and be back by nightfall. Any further would be a stretch unless he wanted to start walking the road. He wasn't ready for that. He wanted to use the cover of the trees and watch the road as he went. The smell was growing stronger the further south he went. He would watch the road for a bit and then move on. He wasn't hurrying, but he wasn't spending a lot of time waiting. He wanted to figure out what the smell was and get back. He didn't mind being alone, he actually enjoyed it but he wasn't enjoying it right now.

He could see a hand painted billboard. FIREWORKS 1000ft→. He looked up at the sky and then at his watch. Three hours. Not bad, he thought. He still had not seen anything that would explain the smell. But he was close. The wind didn't need to bring it to his nose any longer. It hung in the air now. He must be close. He paused in front of the little post office. The little white cinder block structure sat mockingly secure. The door was heavy steel and the small windows were covered with bars. He tried the latch. Locked. He walked around to the side and for the first time noticed the trail running into the woods from the back of the building. He followed the trail a few yards and saw a small house nestled back in the woods. The trail led right to the steps to the front porch. He stood there looking with his head cocked to the side, watching the little plume of smoke rise from the stone chimney.

Cameron Day had moved back to Berry over thirty years ago. He had left when he was eighteen to join the Navy. He spent a few years knocking around and finally moved back when his uncle asked him to come run the Post Office. Not a lot of pay but a free house and easy hours. After his uncle had passed away Cameron had renewed the contract and became the new Post Master for Berry. All 32 citizens. He mulled over the fact that he was probably going to be the last postmaster of Berry.
"No probably about it old boy. None at all." He said to himself after this started.

He had spent the last few years making the job even easier. He installed a CCTV system in the post office and had the feed sent to his cabin so he could sit in front of his shortwave radio listening to far away signals to record in his logbook. Shortwave had been part of his life since his Navy days, where he learned about the way radio signals bounce around the world. He didn't like to transmit and really had not even bought a decent microphone in twenty years. The one he owned was somewhere in the attic. He just listened. And he listened all the time. When the power bill got too high, he converted the whole system over to solar power with generator backup. The generator ran on liquid propane that he kept in a big tank behind the cabin. He put enough panels on the roof to run most of his electrical needs. He still had the power company hookup but his bill was in the single digits if he got a bill at all. When the grid dropped, he didn't even notice for a few hours until his generator kicked on to supplement the solar system. He began pulling everything off the system except for his radio, computer and CCTV system. His refrigerator was the first to come off, and he had spent the first full day of the official apocalypse stuffing his face with everything he pulled out. Anything he couldn't eat he put out in his compost pile. All these years of being mostly self-sufficient had unknowingly prepared him for the beginning of the end. He hadn't stockpiled food but he usually only made one trip a month to buy groceries. He had gone the same day Marionette jumped over to America. He had listened to the Surgeon General's speech on the trip back from the Wal-Mart in Collier. He had been glued to his short wave ever since. Nobody had bothered to check the mail since that day. Until now.

"Dammit Bridger, can't you talk some sense into him. We don't need him out wandering around the country. We need him here." Kate said as Bridger sheepishly put the walkie in his pocket. "You came down to help, now help."

"JW is out there doing what he thinks is the best thing to keep us all safe." He said.

"I came down here because I trust him. I don't like it but he is right. Until he is confident that Raj or Tilly or you or anyone else is able to go out and be an asset he'll just go alone. He wants me here at the camp, so that's what I do. It may not be a perfect scenario but it will have to work for now."

Kate knew Bridger was right, just like she knew JW was right when they had the same basic conversation last night when he was leaving. They had to know what was out there. If it hadn't been the smell that drew him out, it would have been something else. She knew he needed to go. Just to see.

As she walked away from Bridger, Evelyn fell in beside her.

"So, any word yet?" She asked.

"Nothing yet. He is heading further down the road to see if he can see anything."

"I know you're worried, I would be too."

"Thanks." Kate said.

"Anyway, me and Tilly will go with Charlie and his two daughters."

"Only Jennifer is his daughter, Lori is just a friend." Kate interrupted.

"Honestly, I can't keep it all straight. How do kids end up with not their parents during the apocalypse?" Evelyn mused. "Well Tilly, Charlie, Charlie's daughter and not Charlie's daughter and I are going to the creek and draw some water after lunch." She laughed.

"What's so funny?" Kate asked.

"Go to the creek and draw some water. Just another phrase I never imagined I would say."

"Well if we're saying things we never thought we would, here's one. Make sure the kids have guns." Kate smiled.

The group spent the rest of the morning taking turns gathering wood. They had an axe but they would mostly pick up what was on the forest floor. Once they had an armful, they would take it back to camp. Groups of three or four would go together with one person tasked to just be the lookout. They would carry a shotgun. The rest carried some kind of pistol.

Janice, her son and her nephew would go with Chris and Amanda. The boys would walk with Chris while he was on watch and he would help load their arms with tree limbs. Janice was happy to see the boys coping. Amanda would spend the time alone just within sight of the others. She had been having a hard time since the day they evacuated. That little girl had been right next to her. She saw her head explode. She felt it. And then stepping over those people to get on the bus. All that blood. She had woke more than a few times shaking, with Chris's hand over her mouth because she had been screaming. The rest of the camp was being polite, but she knew that a screaming woman in the middle of the night was probably not the best way to avoid these things. But she couldn't help it, she could see it all. It was all there, every night. She tried to use these moments alone in the woods to sort it out. She was getting a little better.

After they had gathered back together for a lunch of canned chicken and crackers some of them used JW's truck to haul the water from the creek. Tilly and Evelyn rode in the back with a Gatorade water cooler to carry the day's water back to camp. The water cooler was Charlie's contribution. He was driving with his daughter and Lori in the front of the truck. The girls were busy trying to tune the radio.

"Do you think we can go back and look for my parents?" Lori asked.

"I don't think so. Not yet." Charlie said.

"They don't know that I am ok. They should know." She said.

"Your parents aren't worried about you." Jennifer said.

"What?" Lori looked at her.

"They aren't worried about anything, except braaaaaaiiiiiiinnnnnnnssss." Jennifer said, leaning at Lori's neck as she said it.

As she did, Lori raised her shoulder and accidently hit Jennifer's chin, causing Jennifer to bite down on her tongue. Hard.

"Ow, you bitch." Jennifer said. Spitting a little blood.

"Bitch? Really. You deserved that. Sorry not sorry. Bitch."

"That's enough. Knock it off. Now." Charlie said. "Lori we will go as soon as we can. I don't know when that will be. Jennifer, you should be ashamed."

She looked at him wide-eyed and started to speak.

"Shut it. Shut it now." Charlie said as they pulled off to the trail to the creek. It was a short walk.

Evelyn and Tilly had heard the raised voices in the cab of the truck but not the substance; still they grabbed the cooler and started walking ahead of the others, best to avoid the drama. Both of them had been teenage girls before. Tilly had taken to Evelyn from the moment they met. Raj had told her about the uncomfortably funny remark she had made to Bridger about her late husband. She was quick witted and warmhearted, Tilly liked that. Evelyn had liked Tilly too. She was smart and confident, and her red hair and green eyes made her look fresh all the time. Evelyn could only imagine how unfresh she must look by now. She avoided all mirrors. They approached the creek bank.

"I think I am going to visit the bushes for a minute." Tilly said.

"Ok. I'll get started filling this" Evelyn said.

Tilly walked further down the creek. Charlie and the girls grabbed the duffle bag full of empty water bottles and headed down the trail. Each of the girls carried a shotgun and Charlie had a pistol on his hip.

"I miss them so much." Lori said to no one. "I just wish I knew. I mean, I just…"

"I don't know what to say Lori. I wish there was some way I could tell you I know what will happen, but I can't. Right now we just need to focus on staying safe and alive."

"Why? What's the point? If this is what we do now, why bother?" Lori asked.

"Because we just do." Jennifer said.

"But, oh never mind. Just never mind." Lori said as she started crying again. They could see Evelyn ahead.

Evelyn carried her late husbands .357 revolver on her hip. It was what she had retrieved from her bedroom, and she also had the pistol Bridger had given her, but she kept that in the bus. Kneeling, she used an empty can to dip water out of the creek and pour it into the cooler. She had draped part of a sheet over the cooler and secured it with a bungee cord. They still had to boil the water, but this helped keep bugs and stuff out.

"Everything ok?" Evelyn asked as she turned to them.

"I guess so." Charlie said, not sure.

"It's fine." Lori said.

"Well let's get this done. We still have to boil this when we get back. I hope Raj has the fire going." Evelyn said as she turned back to the creek. The others joined her and started filling the water bottles.

Tilly walked about fifty yards down the creek into a small honeysuckle stand. She put the stand between her and the others so she could have a little privacy to pee. The sun broke up into tiny shards as it passed through the canopy. The trees had turned the bright colors of fall and would rain down leaves when the wind blew. She felt the coolness of the day. The wind brought the smell again to corrupt another moment when she almost forgot about the world outside.

She and Raj had spent the last few days trying to wrap their heads around what was happening. Raj was coming to terms that he may not see his parents or brother again. She missed her mom, but she hadn't seen her since she and Raj got married almost two years ago. Her mom had chosen that day to announce to her she was divorcing Tilly's father. Tilly had taken it hard. She had said some awful things to her mother and made her mind up that she would start a new life with Raj. For two years she had done just that. She leaned her shotgun against a tree and stepped back. She wore her only pair of jeans. Expensive ones, the kind that hugged her backside, and that made them really uncomfortable when you had to live in them for a few days.

She had packed them for her and Raj's little honeymoon getaway. She had also packed a bunch of really sexy underwear, the kind that has dental floss up the back side and really delicate lace designs. The kind that suck in the apocalypse.

What she wouldn't give for a nice pair of granny panties right now.

She unbuttoned her pants and squeezed them down her hips. She bent forward and straightened her knees to slide them down to her ankles. She reached up and grabbed what passed for a waistband in the extremely small and uncomfortable panties she was wearing and pulled them down on top of her jeans. She reached up and grabbed the sapling in front of her and squatted down.

"Hey Ed, come see what I found." A voice came from behind her as she felt a hand wrap around her mouth.

This Dirty Road

He didn't know the man standing at the head of the trail to his house. The man was armed with at least one weapon that Cameron could see. The fact he was holding the rifle in his hand led Cameron to believe he probably wasn't infected. He grabbed the coffee cup off the table and stood. He walked to the front door and looked out the glass as the stranger walked up raising his right hand to wave and smiling.

"Good morning." JW said to the large man opening the door to the cabin. The man stood there with a disbelieving look on his face.

"Good morning to you. Can I help you with something?"

"Well, I don't know. I am trying to figure out what that smell is and accidently stumbled across your place. I didn't know this was back here." JW said slinging his rifle over his shoulder.

"So you're on a journey of discovery then?"

"What?"

"A journey of discovery. You are trying to discover things and in that search you found something, although it wasn't what you thought you were looking for." Cameron said.

"Ok." JW said, mouth slightly agape.

"Just messing with you. Come on in. I got coffee."

"No shit?"

"No shit, just coffee." He smiled as he turned back into the cabin.

JW walked up the few steps onto the porch. The man was standing at the screen door, holding it open. JW stepped through. The room was warm. There was a fireplace with a small kettle warming over it. The walls were unfinished logs, matching the outside. There were a few pictures but not many. There was an old oval area rug on the floor that reminded JW of when he was a little boy. He had set his train track up on a rug like it at his grandparent's house at Christmas and watched it go round and round. He always thought of toy trains when he saw a rug like that. The man walked by him and turned around.

"Cameron. Cameron Day." He stuck his hand out.

"JW Toles." He shook it.

"Toles, you say? You're not the Toles that bought the old Watson place?" He asked, raising one eyebrow.

"That's what the realtor called it too." JW said.

"Well, I grew up here, and that's what it was called when I was a kid and I guess it stuck. There hasn't been an actual Watson up here since before I was born, as far as I know. And I would know."

"Yeah, why is that?" JW asked.

"Well, ain't no Watson ever picked up no mail from me and if they didn't pick it up from me they didn't get it. Don't know too many folks who don't get some kind of mail."

"Makes sense."

"Glad something does, the last couple of weeks nothing else has. Haven't had many visitors since this all started." Cameron broached the small talk.

"Yeah, I know. We came up to my place almost immediately. You're the first person outside our group I have seen since this all began. We have been listening to the radio but most of that is either gone or just repeating old government broadcasts." JW admitted.

"It's mostly the same everywhere. I do get to listen to a few guys like me giving updates and passing on information." Cameron said, nodding towards the glowing radio in the corner.

"Does that have power?" JW asked.

"Shit yeah. Solar. And generator. But mostly solar. I can shut everything down and run that thing forever on just my solar panels. As long as they don't go tits up, I got power." Cameron said proudly.

"So who do you talk too?"

"Oh I don't talk. I just listen."

"Why?"

"Well I got into radio in the Navy. I worked at a listening station. We just listened. We didn't talk. I guess once you get trained to do it one way, it just gets comfortable. Besides, I ain't got nothing to say."

"Fair enough. So what have you heard?"

"Probably would be better to ask what you have heard, so I don't repeat things."

"Fair enough. We know about DC of course. We heard the VP statement. We know about Atlanta. We assume Birmingham and Mobile are the same. We haven't heard anything for two nights."

"Ok. Well your assumptions are right. Birmingham and Mobile along with New Orleans, Biloxi and just about any place that warrants a dot on the map. It is amazing how quickly things fell apart. I hear folks all over the world. Or did. Some places are gone completely. Whole countries. Nothing. The US and China are holding on by a thread. The only place that is been spared so far is Greenland. There are a few places there that I can pick up and some are trying to figure out how to rescue folks and others are trying to figure out how to keep everyone out. The UK and Europe are iffy. All that is left is just like here. Pockets. Just pockets."

JW had leaned against a small table and crossed his arms. He was looking down at the rug, absorbing the devastation this stranger was laying out.

"You said you hadn't seen too many folks since this began. Does that mean you have seen someone?" JW asked.

"Oh yeah. Russell Davis. His family owns some land just a few miles past your place. Old Russell is one of them survivalists. His daddy made a fortune in timber but drank most of it away. Russell got the land and half million dollars when his daddy died. He would brag that he built himself a compound and was getting ready for the fall of the country. He would talk about all kinds of conspiracies and biblical prophecies. He would come in here from time to time to pick up parcels. Mostly ammunition, I know because it had to be signed for. He said he would have it sent here to confuse the government. Like the government gave a shit about Russell Davis. Anyway, he came in here the day of the Surgeon General announcement, you know the one?" nodding at JW.

JW nodded back.

"Well he came in here all smiling and giddy, like a girl getting a pony, and said he'd see me in the new world. He's squirrelly as a pecan tree. You might want to avoid him."

"Ok. Good to know." He looked at Cameron and kind of winced. Cameron was looking at JW with the same quizzical expression. They both scrunched their noses and eyebrows. The smell. They could see the shadows passing by the windows.

Tilly tried to scream but as she did the man behind her managed to cover her mouth and all that came out was a short squeak. He wrapped his other arm around her shoulders and pushed her forward into the dirt. Her pants were still down and the dirt and twigs scratched her legs as he shoved her down. She tried to break his grip, but he managed to grab her wrist and pin it to the ground. Her other arm was trapped under her body as he put his weight on top of her.

"No, no, no, missy. You just keep quiet. I got plans for you. Big plans." he said as he leaned his face to hers, this last part delivered in an excited whisper.

Tilly could feel his beard stubble against her face. She could smell his breath, a mixture of scrambled eggs and last night's whiskey. He forced her flat on her stomach and relaxed his grip on her wrist. Tilly took the chance to deliver an elbow to whatever she could. She hit his stomach, and he huffed. The next thing Tilly saw was stars exploding as he punched her in the back of the head.

"Nope, bitch. You don't get to do that. That is a big no no. You'll learn. I'll fucking teach you. Now sit still. You'll thank old Russell after. I promise."

Ed wasn't sure about this guy. He had met him while he was working the sporting goods department at the Collier Wal-Mart. Collier was a small town about twenty miles north and the Wal-Mart had been the second largest employer. This guy had been a customer. He would order guns online and have them delivered to the Wal-Mart. The store would do the background check on him when he came to pick them up. Ed had helped him a few times, and they had struck up a conversation. He was one of those folks who liked to prepare for the worst. Ed thought he was mostly talk, until the guy came in the day before the rest of the world would realize how bad Marionette was going to be. He had been on the Internet and watched some videos and had come to a pretty quick decision. He was there to buy every round left in the store. He had brought all the cash he could get his hands on, which was considerably more than Ed could have ever imagined and spent $6,450.00 on ammunition and two more rifles from stock. Ed became convinced that this guy was on to something while listening to his take on the videos they had all seen. Ed wasn't really tied to anyone or anything and asked him if he could join him. The guy just smiled and said, "Sure, it all starts over now, anyway." Ed wasn't sure what that meant; he had begun to find out.

Ed stepped around the big oak tree and saw Russell on the ground on top of some red-haired girl. Her pants were down around her ankles, her face contorted in a look of shock, anger and fear. Russell was whispering into her ear and had pulled one knee up and raised his hips off of her. He reached with his free hand and started unbuckling his belt.

"What the hell man? What do you think you're doing?" Ed said. Looking shocked.

"Shut up. I am doing what I said I was going to do. New rules. New world."

He looked at Ed to make sure he wasn't going to interfere. He was pretty confident that wuss wouldn't do a thing. He had been a little bitch this whole time. He'll take care of that shit next. Now down to business. He managed to get his belt unbuckled and started on the zipper. Tilly tried to elbow him again.

"Oh no no. Just wait. This is gonna be good." Russell said, leaning down to kiss her cheek.

Tilly could not do anything. He was too heavy and too strong. She tried to roll, and he just let his weight down on top of her. She tried to move his hand off her mouth and couldn't. She tried screaming but no sound that would carry could come out. She smelled him. Not his breath, or his clothes. She smelled *him*. That musky, sweaty smell that everyone has when you get right against the skin. Past everything else. The pheromones or something. She began to realize that no matter how much she wanted this not to happen, all the want to in world wasn't going to stop it. She felt weak. She felt ashamed. She felt pissed. She wanted to fight but couldn't. She hated him. She hated every fucking thing about him. She closed her eyes preparing for the next part. She fucking hated this. She squeezed her eyes so tight the tears streamed like water. He felt her relax as she began to cry.

"Oh yeah, just you wait. You gonna be crying that you waited so long to get you some Russell. Yes you will." He breathed into her ear, still trying to fish it out of his underwear.

He heard the click and felt a cold steel barrel pressed against the back of his neck.

"I know you ain't pulled a god damn gun on me Ed." Russell said.

"Nope. I did. Get your ass up right now." Evelyn said.

JW and Cameron stood by the kitchen table, completely motionless except for their eyes. They both were looking past the other out the windows. It was a mass of heads and shoulders moving by. JW supposed that if you get a few dozen dead folks together they tend to stink up the joint. Mystery solved. He smiled slightly. Cameron saw it and raised one eyebrow. JW just smiled wider and brought his index finger up to his lip. Cameron didn't see anything to smile about and he damn sure didn't need to be told to keep quiet. He was afraid he would piss his pants. The end of the world had been on his radio so far. He hadn't seen anything to disprove that it was just a "War of the Worlds" media event. He had now. He swallowed hard. They stood and watched. It took about twenty minutes for the crowd to move by. They waited another twenty minutes before they decided to go outside. The infected hadn't been able to climb the steps to the porch. A few had stood in front of it bumping their shins against the first step but couldn't quite figure out how to step up. One had fallen over and was stuck trying to drag itself up the steps. The wooden steps had no faces. Its foot had slipped through the hole between the first and second step. It couldn't get it out. When JW and Cameron stepped out onto the porch, they could see the path the crowd had taken. All the small trees and bushes were trampled down. It cut a swath through the underbrush leaving torn clothing and some flesh caught in the briars. The path led towards the post office, they couldn't see beyond that. There was only one left, it was still hung between the first and second step.

Cameron stepped in front of JW and looked at the man trapped in the step. It was still trying to pull free. His legs had been torn up on whatever hellish journey he had endured and trying to pry the leg loose was ripping more flesh away. He was wearing a coat and tie and the front of his shirt was covered in dried vomit and bloodstains. The arms of the jacket were frayed and bloody. Part of the right arm and shoulder was exposed. Cameron could see the vicious open wounds. Bites. Cameron leaned over the railing and puked. He looked back at the thing on his step. The muscle and skin of the wounds were scabbed over and covered with dirt. Puss and blood oozed out of the cracks. JW raised his rifle.

"Wait." Cameron said.

"Why?"

"You think that crowd has moved on enough not to turn back?" Cameron said.

"What makes you ask that?" JW asked.

"I have been listening to folks talk about their encounters with these things and I know they tend to follow loud sounds." Cameron said.

"I've seen that." JW admitted. "What else have you heard?"

"I have heard a lot of things. I don't know how much is true. I heard they could smell better than we can but can't see for shit. I have heard they are attracted to noise and light. I guess that kind of makes sense if they can't see well. I hadn't seen any yet, but I have heard them called deadheads, z people, walkers, lamebrains, the dead and poppers." Cameron added.

"Poppers?" JW asked.

"Apparently they make a popping sound when their skull is cracked open or stabbed. Something about the pressure in their head or something"

"Interesting." JW said. "What do you call them?"

"I don't have a name but if you say zombie I wouldn't disagree. They seem to follow all the zombie rules"

"Zombie rules?"

"Yeah. I learned those from some kid in Ohio last night. They come back from the dead, attack people, eat people, get bit turn into one, die turn into one and the only way to stop them is to get the head. Zombie rules."

"What about eating brains?" JW asked.

"I don't really think that it matters what part they eat, they just eat. I think it has more to do with the blood, but that's just me."

He looked down at the thing trying to climb the steps. It was looking between them and back at its leg. JW and Cameron were standing about ten feet away from it and it was just jerking its trapped foot trying to move forward. He grabbed a big rock out of the planter sitting on the porch.

"You mind?" JW asked.

"Go right ahead."

JW moved closer. He studied it a little more but when it its opaque eyes turned up to him he brought the rock down on his forehead. Nothing.

"Harder. And more to the side." Cameron said.

"You wanna do this?" JW asked.

"Nope. Sorry. Just trying to help."

JW had not struck it very hard intentionally. He wanted to see what the minimum effort was, and he didn't think he was going to have more test subjects so willing. He swung again, a little harder. Nothing. Again. Nothing. The infected was becoming more and more angry. It was wildly reaching for JW with each swing. JW brought the rock down almost full strength into the top of its head. He felt the skull crack.

POP. It collapsed.

JW stepped back. He turned to Cameron. They both looked at each other and smiled.

"Did you hear that?" JW asked.

"Yeah. Sounded like those things we made when we were kids. With balloons and wet newspaper."

"Paper Mache" JW said.

"That's it. Blow up the balloon. Cover it with wet newspaper. Let it dry then...."

"Pop" JW finished.

"That same kind of muffled pop. Exactly." Cameron said.

"Exactly" JW agreed.

"Ok. So, what now?" Cameron asked

"That crowd may be headed towards my camp, I need to keep an eye on it." JW said.

"Fair enough. Hope you'll make it back this way." Cameron replied.

"Oh I'll make it back. I still want to hear some more about that radio." JW said.

After seeing the crowd of infected that just passed by Cameron doubted he would be seeing JW again. He gave JW about a twenty percent chance. Cameron had had his first encounter with the infected and survived. He was going to make sure he kept those encounters to a minimum.

He stuck his hand out and JW shook it. JW made his way down the steps and started back on the path towards the road. He walked by the little post office and stopped long enough to kick in the backdoor to the fireworks stand. He stepped inside briefly and came back out. He started out again beside the road. JW picked up the pace a little.

That I should Rise

And You should not

Russell looked back and saw Ed standing next to some man and two teenage girls. The man was holding Ed's gun on Ed. He looked further back over his shoulder and saw a middle-aged woman with streaks of gray in her hair standing over him holding a big ass revolver.

"Hold on honey. You sure you know how to use that thing."

Evelyn answered by firing a round into the air above his head. He ducked.

She brought the gun back down and this time the barrel was hot against his neck. Russell quickly decided to give up. He'd figure this out when he buttoned his pants up and he'd make sure this bitch got hers too. He stood buckling his belt and raising his hands. Evelyn took the gun he had in his holster.

"Hey, I need that. You know, for protection." Russell said, smiling at Evelyn.

Tilly rolled over and pulled her pants up. She scrambled backwards away from Russell, never taking her eyes off him. She dropped down against the honeysuckle and started crying. She looked through her tear-stained eyes at him. Lori walked past the man holding his hands up and knelt down beside her trying to comfort her. Tilly ignored her.

"Alright. So what now?" Russell asked. "What you gonna do? Call the cops. File charges. Give me my gun back and we'll just be on our way. That's what gonna happen now. Understand?"

"I don't think so." Ed said.

"What?" Russell looked surprised at Ed.

"That was fucked up. I thought you were pretty much full of shit with your compound and all but I didn't think you would try some shit like that."

"Shut up about that shit. Shut the fuck up." Russell was visibly angry now.

"About what, your little fucking apocalypse bunker? That shit?" Ed said.

"Both of you shut up. Right now." Evelyn said.

"Look honey, just let us go. We'll leave and the world will go on." Russell said, smiling his best "yes mam, we were just leaving" smile.

Evelyn watched Tilly stand up from the honeysuckle behind the smiling jackass in front of her. She saw her walk towards him. She saw the shotgun come up to the back of his head.

"New rules. New world. And assholes like you don't get to fucking participate." Tilly said as Russell wheeled on his heels to face her.

The realization of the shotgun in his face was the last thing to go through his mind, that and a dozen buckshot pellets.

Ed started shaking. He had watched the back of Russell's head come apart when the red-haired girl pulled the trigger. Evelyn reached up and wiped away the little droplet of blood that had landed on her cheek. She paused and put her revolver back into her holster. She stepped over the man on the ground and put her arms around Tilly. She felt her start to shake and then she felt her push away. Tilly stepped back and took a defiant breath. She wiped her eyes.

"Fuck him."

She turned and walked back up the trail towards the truck. Lori and Jennifer followed her. Charlie wiped his forehead. Evelyn watched the girls walk away.

"So, what do we do with you?" She said turning to Ed.

He was still looking at the man on the ground. He had not taken his eyes off of him. He did now. He raised his hands again.

"Hey listen, I didn't know he was like that. Not really. I mean he was crazy, but he seemed to have a plan. I didn't know it involved shit like this. I swear. Please don't kill me." Ed was almost crying.

"Look dude calm down. We're not gonna kill ya."

"So I'm free to go?" Ed perked up.

"Nope. I don't know what to do with you. Evelyn, what do you think?" Charlie said turning to Evelyn.

"I think he goes with us for now. We'll get back and tell Kate what happened. We'll let her decide."

"Decide what?" Ed said.

"Whether to kill you or not. Start walking." Evelyn said.

They walked back towards the truck with Charlie next to Ed. Evelyn was pulling the rear and watched Ed as he animatedly told Charlie whatever he was telling him. She was far enough behind that she couldn't really hear. She heard the name Russell a few times. She assumed that was the dead jackass they had left by the creek. She stopped.

"Charlie." She said.

Charlie stopped and turned around. Ed did too. "We can't just leave him there. We have to bury him. Or burn him."

Evelyn came out of the woods and walked to the truck. Lori and Jennifer were sitting on the ground leaned against the door. Tilly was in the passengers seat. She didn't look when Evelyn spoke.

"We have to burn the body. I just came to get some gas. Your Dad is gathering up some wood."

"What about that other asshole?" Jennifer asked.

"That other asshole is helping. And I am not sure he's an asshole. Maybe he just has asshole friends. Anyway, he's helping right now, and he seems like he didn't really know the other asshole. The dead asshole." She said the last part looking into the window at Tilly. Tilly ignored her.

Evelyn grabbed the gas can and tapped the side of the door. Tilly looked at her. Evelyn looked at her with her best, "I am here for you" expression. Tilly nodded and turned back to starring straight ahead.

Charlie and Ed had managed to gather a small matt of limbs and leaves onto a wide sandy spot and laid the body on it. Evelyn came down the path with the gas can. She started dousing the pyre. Once she was satisfied with her effort, she stepped back and brushed her hands against her pockets.

"I don't smoke. I don't have any matches." Evelyn said.

"Neither do I," said Charlie.

Ed reached into his pocket on his shirt and produced a magnesium stick. He pulled his pocketknife out. He reached down and tore a piece off of Russell's t-shirt and wrapped it around the end of one of the sticks making a torch. He rolled the torch into some puddled gas and laid it on the ground. He held the magnesium stick over the torch and scraped it with his knife, letting the shavings drop onto it. He hit the striker on the other side of the magnesium stick with the blade his knife and a spark jumped onto the shavings. The shavings sparked too. Enough for the gas vapors to ignite. He stood. He tossed the torch onto the pile. They stood and watched as the flames caught. They turned and walk away.

JW had covered about half the distance when he stopped to drink some water. He looked at his watch. He had been traveling for an hour. He had followed the crowd's trail. They had stayed close to the road too. He didn't know where they came from or where they were going but he was catching them. He topped a small rise and the valley floor opened up below him. Laying just over the rise was one of them. Below him, a few hundred yards further in the valley he could see the infected. He watched them through the small binoculars he kept in his pocket. Most were just shuffling along with a few falling over and being trampled. Once the crowd passed over them, they would stand back up and start shuffling again.

A shot rang out. It sounded like a pistol and it came from the direction of camp. He looked in that way and then back at the crowd. They had stopped. Some were turning their heads toward the sound; the rest just stood starring at the ground. The straggler near him began to try to stand again. He made his way closer. It was a child. He crept up beside it. It kept trying to stand but one leg would just buckle when it stepped and it would fall down again. The Achilles tendon had been bitten through. One of its arms no longer worked for some reason. JW couldn't see any obvious injury but it hung by its side and never tried to bend. There were spots of skull exposed where it had either fallen hard or had been hit by something. He pulled his knife out. It was a useful tool. It had a butt plate of hardened steel that worked just fine as a hammer.

He noticed the shoes as the thing toppled over again. He stopped. They were gray Nike's with a blue swoosh. The same type shoe that Scott had worn his whole life. His mother had bought him a pair when he was about three and he loved them. He said they made him fast. It was cute. But since then, every time he bought new shoes, he got a new pair of that same shoe. He had been wearing them his whole life. JW suddenly thought about the terrible end to this child. What horror had it witnessed in its final moments? Did it leave this world screaming in pain wondering why his mother and father had let this happen? Did it die afraid and alone? Or did his parents feed him rat poison trying to spare him this?

Every time it made an attempt to walk JW almost found himself rooting for it. A second shot rang out. More muffled but from the same direction, snapping him out of his thoughts. He caught himself. Whatever this thing had been is gone. What this is now is not a child. It is dangerous. He got closer and flipped his knife in his hand so the blade pointed up. He kicked the good leg out from under it as it made another attempt to stand. He fell on its back and shoved the knife behind the ear. He drove it up and in.
Pop. The thing went limp.

JW stood up and looked around. The crowd had started walking towards the sound of the gunshots. He pulled the walkie out of his pocket.
"Bridger, you there?"
"Bridger, are you there?" He released the button.

The group gathered around the campfire to get the evening meal together. They still had several cans of Spam and plenty of canned vegetables. They could still choose from Vienna Sausages and canned chicken. Most were glad the canned chili was gone. Tonight they were having Spam and beans. They also had some canned peaches for desert. The Toles had brought a good stash but Evelyn and Charlie had brought plenty too. Janice had a few things but most of what she had packed was lost at the church. They still had enough food to last another week or so. Bridger had been telling Raj he could construct some squirrel poles to start catching them for food if they needed to. Raj had no idea what a squirrel pole was but Bridger had convinced him that it worked like a charm. He would show him tomorrow. Raj had the fire going. They were just waiting for the water.

"So who wants Spam?" Janice asked nudging Clyde who was smiling and nodding yes.

"I do." Clyde said.

"I do too." Jeremy chimed in.

"Well good." Janice laughed.

A pistol shot rang out.

"What was that?" Jennifer asked.

"Sounded like a gun." Ray Harrison said.

Ray and his wife Dottie had been with Janice at the church and then at the school. They had been neighbors of a sort. Janice's family rented the house behind them and the chain-link fence separating the yard didn't keep them from getting to know each other. The Harrison's had helped Janice by babysitting Jeremy so she could go back to work after her husband died. They knew her nephew, Clyde, from church too. They had all attended Forest Grove Methodist in South Springs. They had all gathered there seeking shelter from this storm. They found none.

"So what do we do?" Amanda asked.

"*We* don't do anything." Bridger said. "I will go see what is going on."

"We can't just sit here. They might need help." Chris added.

"They might. But since we haven't heard any additional shots, they might have just come across a snake trying to find a good spot for the winter." Bridger said. He walked over to the side of the bus and grabbed his rifle. He turned to say something.

The second shot rang out. This one sounded different. More muffled.

"You were saying?" Raj looked at Bridger.

They all stood. Kate and Dottie came from the back of the bus over to the fire. They were all looking in the same direction. Josh and Scott came out of the woods on the other side of the camp into the corral. They had been on patrol and heard the first shot.

"Ok. Everybody just relax. I will walk down and see what I can see." Bridger said.

"I am coming with you." Raj said.

"Get everybody on the buses and close the doors. Just in case." Bridger told Kate as he checked to make sure he had a round in the chamber.

Bridger watched as Kate got everyone on the bus. Raj walked up to him shouldering a shotgun.

"You ready?" Raj asked.

"Are you?" Bridger replied, raising one eyebrow.

The buses were parked on either side of the dirt road with their side doors facing the center. They had parked the Harrison's and Janice's cars across the road on one end and Kate's SUV across the road on the other. They had started referring to the area in the middle as the corral. They had their fire in the middle with all their various chairs gathered around it. They hung the few things they had washed on a line made from the bailing wire they had found in the trunk of Ray's car. He had picked it up at a garage sale for a quarter, or so the handwritten sticker said. He may have dickered on the price.

Bridger and Raj walked between the bus and Kate's SUV and got down the road about a hundred yards. Raj started walking a little faster.

"Whoa, slow down." Bridger said.

"Why?"

"We don't know…" the walkie crackled.

"Bridger, you there?"

"Bridger, are you there?" JW's voice came from the speaker.

"Yeah, right here. Any news on the smell?" Bridger asked.

"None of it good. There is a crowd of them. I had to hunker to let it pass. There are dozens of them. They may have turned your way. I think they heard those gun shots."

"Checking on those now." Bridger said.

"I am heading your way. Let me know what you find out but be alert."

Bridger put the walkie back in his pocket and looked at Raj.

"Shit. Did he say dozens?" Raj asked.

"That's what it sounded like. Listen, we don't know what's out there. We need to be cautious. Shit."

"What?" Raj asked.

"I have the walkie, they don't know back there." Bridger said pointing back down the dirt road. "We need to make sure they know."

"Ok. I'll go on to the creek and check on Tilly and the others and you go back." Raj said.

Bridger smiled. He had great teeth. Being on TV, the dentist was on the expense account. He had always been particular about his teeth but the guy they had on retainer at the network was great.

"Ok. I get it, I do. But it would be best for you to go back and tell them what we know." Bridger said.

"You think that since you were once some kind of soldier that you can do things we mere mortal civilians can't?" Raj asked.

"Yes." Bridger's smile faded. Raj had known Bridger for about two weeks under extremely difficult circumstance, to say the least. Bridger had always smiled. For the first time Raj took the full measure of the man standing in front of him He was at least six foot two and built a lot better than most men half his age. His head was as close to bald as Bridger could keep it with a dull razor and cold water. His forearms muscles were clearly defined underneath his chestnut skin. He looked at Bridger's eyes. Raj stepped back a bit.

"Just screwing with you." The smile returned and Raj exhaled. "But seriously, I'll go to the creek. You head back and tell them what we know. Just make sure everyone stays on the bus. Until..."

"Until what?" Raj asked.

"Just until."

Raj looked at him one more time. He turned and started back to the buses. Bridger watched him for a minute and turned down the dirt road and headed for the creek. He kept listening for screams or shots or anything. He heard nothing. He kept scanning the woods for any movement. Everything seemed to be as it should be. That made him a little nervous. He could finally see the truck up ahead parked by the side of the road. He could see a line of black smoke rising from over the trees against the purple sky of the setting sun. He shouldered his rifle to look through the ACOG scope. He could see red hair sitting in the passenger seat. Tilly. He couldn't see anyone else. He started to lower his rifle to walk over when he saw Charlie come out of the woods with some man Bridger didn't know.

Lori and Jennifer, who had been sitting on the ground on the other side of the truck, stood up. He saw Evelyn, carrying a gas can walk out of the woods behind Charlie and the new guy. He watched Charlie, the new guy and the two girls climb in the bed of the truck. Evelyn leaned in the passenger window and said something to Tilly but she didn't respond. He saw Evelyn get in the driver seat and start driving back down the road. He slung his rifle over his shoulder and stepped out. The truck made its way towards him, headlights burning in the evening dusk.

Easier than just

Waiting around to die

Evelyn stopped the truck when she saw Bridger standing in the middle of the road. He hung his head in.

"Everything ok? We heard some shots," he asked, smiling.

"Long story, you can hear it when we get back. And everything will be ok." Turning her head towards Tilly.

She put the truck in park, opened the driver's door and slid over in the middle.

"You drive."

He got in the truck and put it in gear. It was slightly less than a mile to where they had made their home. Just a few minutes drive.

"I talked to JW, we have a problem." Bridger said as they pulled off.

"There may be a crowd of them headed this way. He said he had hunkered down to let them pass. I think we should do the same thing."

"Hunker down. Just wait for them?" Evelyn asked.

"Well, not wait for them, wait them out. Just let them walk by. Hopefully they will." Bridger said.

"Hopefully." Evelyn replied. Tilly had said nothing. She just stared straight ahead watching the bugs dance in the headlight glare.

They pulled up to Janice's car and parked. Tilly opened the door and walked towards the corral. Raj saw her and came off the bus to meet her. She looked at him. He knew something was wrong. He wrapped his arm around her and led her around the front of the bus; it was the closest thing to privacy he could muster.

"Tilly, what happened?" Raj asked.

"Nothing happened. Well mostly nothing. This stranger tried to attack me."

"This guy?" Raj interrupted. He pointed at the stranger climbing out of the back of the truck. Raj took a step away and Tilly reached out and grabbed his arm.

"No. Not that guy. I don't know who that guy is. The guy that attacked me isn't here."

"Where is he?" Raj asked.

"I killed him." Tilly said.

Raj just looked at her. He could see the resolve in her eyes but he could see her losing the battle against her tears. She would cry now, and he would comfort her but he knew she would hold most of it inside.

"I know this is hard but we all need to talk." Evelyn stuck her head around the front of the bus. "I don't want to interrupt but this can't wait."

"It's ok. We'll be right there." Tilly said, mustering half a smile and wiping her eyes.

"On our way." Raj said. Turning back to Tilly. "You ok?"

"I will be." Tilly said.

Kate met Bridger as he came into the corral.

"Is he ok?" she asked.

"He sounded fine last I talked to him." Bridger said.

"Give it to me." Kate said, holding out her hand. He handed her the walkie.

"JW, JW, you there?" she thumbed the button.

"JW, this is Kate, are you there?" she was met with static.

She looked at Bridger.

"It don't mean anything. He is probably just a little close to them and turned it off so it didn't make a noise at the wrong time. Just being smart."

"You'd better be right." Kate said, thrusting the walkie back at him.

They joined the others in the corral. Bridger looked around. Janice, Jeremy, Clyde, Ray, Dottie, Josh, Scott, Kate, Charlie, Jennifer, Lori, Chris, Amanda and the new guy all sat around the campfire. Evelyn came from around the front of the bus followed shortly by Raj and Tilly. Charlie and the new guy were whispering to each other as Bridger cleared his throat, they all looked at him.

"Ok folks, here is the deal. We don't have a lot of time to discuss this, as a matter of fact, I have no idea how much time we have. We have a crowd of infected that may be headed our way. We are going to assume they are but we are not going to panic. I want everybody to get on the buses. We will wait them out. We will let them walk right by. And we will be very quiet." He glanced at Amanda. "Any questions?"

"How long?" Dottie asked. "How long do we wait?"

"Until they pass by or JW gets here and gives us the all clear."

"Why don't we just load up the buses and leave?" Josh said.

"We could, but we don't have anywhere to go. We can't just drive off and hope. That is something we need to discuss later, but right now we are going to stay and ride this out. Everybody ready?" Bridger concluded by kicking dirt on the fire until it had mostly died out. As the others made their way into their buses, he could hear the unmistakable sound of weapons being checked and loaded. Once everyone was on the bus he was left standing alone in the corral. The sun was gone, and the sky was dark purple. He could see Venus and the crescent moon.

"Ok, folks. Here we go. Remember. Quiet." He climbed onto his bus.

JW started jogging after the crowd again. He knew that Bridger would have everyone ready, although he didn't know what ready meant. He should have told him to get everyone on the bus and drive away but he knew Bridger wouldn't leave without him. JW wouldn't leave Bridger out here either. Maybe they could get on the bus and just let them pass by. That had worked for him. He reached up and knocked on his head with his knuckles for not coming up with that already. He was a hundred yards or so behind the crowd. He stopped. He leaned his back against a tree and reached into his pocket for the walkie. He felt pressure on his foot. He looked down and saw one of the infected on the ground bending around from the other side of the tree. He grabbed the knife. As he did, the thing grabbed his leg and knocked him off balance. He dropped the knife. He tried to grab it but it was out of reach. He tried to shake loose but the thing would not let go. JW was surprised at how strong it was. He kicked at it and managed to momentarily break its grip. He pulled the walkie out of his pocket.

"No you don't you shithead. No the hell you don't." He hit the top of its head as hard as he could.

The skull popped, and the walkie shattered. Both died. He dropped down on his bottom and pulled himself away a few feet. Shit.

He gathered himself and picked up his knife. He needed to keep moving. The loss of the walkie increased the urgency in his mind. He had to make sure he was there to help. He looked down at the thing on the ground. He spit on it.

"Fuck you." He started after the crowd again.

Bridger looked out the window of the bus. The moon was just a crescent, but the skies were clear. The light reflecting from the moon cast off the atmosphere and brightened the sky. Since the world had gone dark, those surviving had been treated to the most spectacular views of the night sky, even though most had spent the time huddled in the dark trying to stay alive. When he was in the desert just outside Mosul all those years ago, he would stare at the sky. The stars in the sky stared back. Unchanging. Things down here had certainly changed.

He could see through the trees as the cool air settled into a shimmering mist on the ground. The trees were just shadows divided by shards of moonlight slicing through the mostly bare limbs. As he watched, black shapes moved. One, then another. The crowd began to appear, first as shadows and then into the light filtering between the trees. He looked back to the interior of the bus. Everyone was up against a window looking out. He quietly backed out of the seat he was leaning in and walked down the center aisle tapping each person. They all pulled away from the windows a little and watched from the darkness.

The angle didn't let them see right next to the bus without leaning against the window. They didn't need to see. They could hear them bumping up against the side of the bus. Occasionally a hand would shoot up against a window. When that would happen, Bridger expected for someone to cry out. Hell, the first time it happened it was almost him that did it. He was impressed by how well the group in his bus was holding on. He wondered about the other bus.

The windows facing the corral changed from the silvery white of the moon to a dull orange. Bridger rose up in the seat to look. They had dug a shallow pit and surrounded it with larger stones they had found by the creek to build their fire in. One of the infected had fallen into it and apparently the fire had not been completely out. It had rolled around and struggled enough that the coals had reignited and the tattered clothing had caught. It managed to stand up as the flames climbed its back. The dress burned around its legs and its long hair started to catch. It was oblivious to it. The fire engulfed its hair and burned quickly. Others had been drawn to the dancing embers floating from the burning living corpse. There were now maybe half a dozen inside the corral and the fire had spread to each one as they came too close to the first. As each one caught fire they would continue their aimless shuffling. They seemed completely unfazed by the flames. He could see their faces start to blacken and crack from the fire engulfing them.

Bridger looked down the aisle of the bus again. He could see disbelief reflected by the firelight outside the windows. He could hear mumbled words of shock but nothing that would carry. He raised his head again, happy that everyone had held it together. He could see a face reflected in the bus across the corral. The face slowly grew out of the darkness and Bridger was thinking to himself, "Please get back". He realized a moment later that the face was growing because the light was coming closer to it. One of the infected was walking towards it. The face withdrew a little further into the darkness. Raj. The thing outside stopped right against the side of the bus. Bridger watched, as it turned around and just stood there burning. The flames were licking the side of the bus. A few other infected had walked over to it and now they were all against the side of the bus across the corral. All of them were on fire.

Raj had watched as the burning things slammed against the side of the bus. He turned, wide-eyed, down the aisle looking at the other people on the bus. Tilly was right next to him. She was still looking out of the window at the growing crowd of burning dead. Janice and her boys huddled in the back next to the emergency exit door. Ray and Dottie were just in front of them. Chris and Amanda were sitting in the front of the bus.

"We have to do something." Chris said.

"What?" Tilly said.

"I don't know but we can't stay in here. This bus is about to catch on fire." Chris said.

Raj got up and walked to the back of the bus. He leaned over Janice and looked out of the back door. He could only see as far as the glow cast from the walking torches. He didn't see any other dead. He glanced over his shoulder at the flames as they licked up the side of the bus. The rest of the people on the bus had lined up behind him, anticipating his next words.

"We have to go, now." Raj reached for the door handle. Janice jumped out first, followed by Jeremy and Clyde. As Ray jumped down, he landed awkwardly. They all heard the snap when his leg broke. He yelled. His voice carried, and they all looked into the darkness beyond the bus. One by one, as the crowd turned to face the sound, their eyes reflected the firelight. The dark woods filled up with dozens of glowing red eyes. Janice screamed.

The rest of them were still on the bus. Raj, Tilly, Chris and Amanda watched as Janice snatched Jeremy and Clyde's hands and took off running into the woods away from the glowing eyes. Dottie climbed down and was on the ground trying to help Ray. Chris jumped down and tried to help Ray stand. He couldn't. Raj and Tilly helped Amanda off the bus after them. Raj knelt down and slid one hand under Ray's leg and the other around his back.

"Chris, grab my hands. Form a seat and let's carry him." Raj said. Chris caught on and grabbed Raj's hands. They lifted Ray and started to go. Out of the darkness came one of the infected. It was one of the burnt ones. The fire had run out of things to burn on it. The thing standing in front of them had no clothes, no hair, no lips and no eyelids. It was blackened, and the skin had cracked. Blood and rot was oozing through the cracks. Amanda screamed.

"Damn, can you not do that all the time?" Tilly looked at her. She shouldered the shotgun she was carrying and fired at the infected. "Let's go."

She grabbed Amanda's hand and headed around to the front of the bus. Janice and the boys were nowhere to be seen. As they reached the back of Kate's SUV, Chris tripped. He, Raj and Ray all went to the ground. One of the infected came around the other side of the SUV between Ray and the other two. It wasn't a burnt one. It had once been a man wearing a sweater with khaki pants. The pants were ripped at the bottom and the sweater was now just ribbon. The arms of the infected were covered in bruises and open wounds. There was a large bite mark on its face and the surrounding skin had puckered and swollen into an angry gaping wound. Parts of its teeth were visible in the hole. Ray was trying to drag himself away. He looked up into its face. The things hair was matted and bloody. The opaque eyes turned downward to Ray. He rolled over and tried to raise himself up on his leg but it gave way. As he fell back down to the ground the infected fell on top of him, biting into his back. Ray yelled in pain. Raj tried to grab Ray but as he did another infected came out of the darkness. He and Chris scrambled back and ducked into the woods. Raj looked back at Ray, he couldn't help him. He and Chris ran a few yards and stopped as another one of the dead stepped in front of them.

Dottie, who had gone around the other side of the SUV with Tilly and Amanda, stopped and turned towards the voice of the man she had shared the last 42 years with. Tilly tried to grab her arm, but she shook it off and went towards him. Tilly and Amanda followed her around the other side of the SUV. They saw Ray lying on his belly with an infected taking a bite out of his lower back. Tilly raised the shotgun and hit the thing in the back of the head with the butt. It made an audible pop. The thing went limp. Dottie dropped to the ground and put her hand on Ray's back.

"Ray, Ray. Please, please you have to get up. You have too." Dottie said. Tilly was standing over the couple holding the shotgun and looking for any nearby infected. Amanda pulled out the revolver Bridger had given her. Ray was on his knees looking over his shoulder at Dottie.

"I can't. Besides what's the point?" reaching his hand back and touching the bite over his kidney. Dottie put her hand on top of his and looked into his eyes.

"What do I do, what do I do?" She frantically asked.

"Run" Ray said. "I love ya darling but you gotta go." Ray said. He looked at her, half smiling with tears in his eyes. She cradled his face and kissed him. He ran his hand through her hair one more time.

"Go, you have too." Ray said as another infected came out of the woods. Dottie kept her hand on his face. She heard Amanda scream and fire at the infected coming out of the tree line.

Dottie looked at her husband. He had jerked under her grip. He was looking down at his chest as the blood bloomed on his shirt. He looked back at Dottie with shock. She understood quickly what had happened. He teetered and fell over. Amanda looked over the gun at Dottie, tendrils of smoke still coming from the barrel. She dropped the gun. Tilly had seen enough. She grabbed Dottie and pulled her to the back of the SUV. She popped open the rear hatch and roughly shoved Dottie into the back. She looked back over her shoulder at Amanda who was still standing in shock looking down at Ray. He had quit moving.

"Get in here NOW!" Tilly yelled, snapping Amanda out of her trance. She looked at Tilly and dove into the back. Tilly jumped in behind her and pulled the door down. Dottie looked out the window, never taking her eyes off of her husband, her face wet with tears.

Now I Lay Me Down to Sleep

Bridger watched as the fiery infected gathered around the other bus. The flames reflected off the windows and he knew that it was only a matter of time before the bus would become an oven, or worse. He saw the back door swing open and someone jumped out. He couldn't tell who it was, but they were quickly followed by two smaller figures, Jeremy and Clyde, he thought. He saw Ray jump out and fall to the ground. The next one out knelt down by him. They were in trouble. He had to help.

"I am going. Stay here." Bridger said facing the group in his bus.

"Like hell." Kate said. Bridger looked at her, trying to convince her with his eyes. It didn't work.

"I'll stay here with Jennifer and Lori and I'll keep an eye on this guy" Evelyn said, tapping her sidearm and nodding towards Ed.

"Thank you." Charlie said.

Jennifer and Lori were still looking out the window. Ed rose up in his seat to look too. They saw Janice and the boys run off into the woods towards the creek, away from the crowd that had just passed. The bright flash and boom from a shotgun blast got everyone's attention again.

Scott, Josh and Charlie all went out the back. Another shot rang out from across the corral. Bridger and Kate went out the side. They all started across the corral to the other bus. As they did, the infected began to stream around the parked cars. They all turned to meet the threat. The night rang with the sound of gunfire.

Tilly, Dottie and Amanda were all startled when the shots started. Tilly crawled over the rear seat and climbed into the driver's side. She turned back to the others.

"Stay here. Don't get out." Tilly said. "I have to find Raj."

She opened the door and stepped out. Just as she did Raj came from the other direction.

"Are you okay?" He said as he came up to her.

"Fine. Where are the others?" She said. "Where is Chris and Janice?"

"Chris and I got separated. Janice and the boys ran into the woods and I haven't seen them." As they spoke another one of the dead wandered out of the woods. Tilly fired, and the buckshot ripped its chest open. It kept coming. She fired again and half of its face came apart. It fell. They scrambled into the SUV and shut the door again.

"Chris, what about Chris?" Amanda demanded.

"I'm sorry, I don't know. They came at us and we got split up. I don't know where he is." Raj said.

The infected surrounded the vehicle. Every window was full of disfigured dead. They huddled as far away from the windows as they could. The raspy exhalations of the infected gathered around the SUV quickly drowned the subtle sobs and nervous breaths of Dottie and Amanda. Dottie looked out the window at the ground. Ray was gone.

JW heard the sound of gunfire ahead. He began to run. He could see a glow through the trees. He stepped out of the woods onto the dirt road. He could see the outline of the SUV back-lit by fire. The dead surrounded it. The gunfire that had erupted a few minutes ago was moving away from the camp, into the woods. He didn't know who was firing, but he knew someone was trapped in the SUV. He raised his rifle to fire, but he quickly lowered it. He wasn't going to risk accidently shooting into the vehicle. He reached into his back pocket and retrieved what he had taken when he paused at the fireworks stand. He pulled the lighter out of his pocket and lit the fuse. He tossed the strand of firecrackers into the woods to his left as far as he could throw it. As the first ones began to go off, he tossed the next strand in the same direction. The repeated banging of the firecrackers had the intended effect. The dead began to turn towards the sound and move away from the vehicle. As they cleared it JW raised his rifle again and began firing. He dropped six or seven when he realized someone had exited the SUV and was firing at them from that direction too. The crowd that had gathered around the vehicle was mostly down and JW approached the SUV. Tilly was standing on the hood, shotgun raised, looking into the woods waiting for more infected to arrive. Raj was standing on the corral side of the vehicle.

"Where is Kate and Bridger? Where is Scott and Josh?" JW yelled up.

"I don't know. They were in the other bus. I guess they are the ones shooting." Tilly said.

"Stay put. I'll be back." JW said as he disappeared back into the darkness on the other side of the bus.

Dottie managed to slide out of the back and went to the side of the SUV. She looked on the ground. "Ray, Raaay. Where are you?" She yelled.

"Be quiet." Tilly snapped.

"But he's not here. He's gone. He was bitten." As she said the last part out loud the truth finally snapped into her mind. Ray was walking with the dead. She quit yelling and climbed back into the vehicle, she didn't want to see him like that.

Tilly stood on the hood and continued to look alternatively into the darkness and back across the corral. Everything inside the corral was on fire. The bus they had been on was smoking and she could see flames coming from underneath. Some infected had somehow gotten under it and were now just lumps of smoldering flesh. She was surprised that the gas tank hadn't erupted. As the thought crossed her mind, the bus exploded in a huge fireball, knocking her off the hood and to the ground. Raj was thrown against the side of the SUV and it knocked the breath out of him. The bus had become an inferno. Raj crawled around to the front and saw Tilly picking her self up. They both climbed back into the SUV. She turned the key and quickly pulled down the dirt road until they were clear of the fire. She stopped. They got out and looked back down the road.

"Should we go back?" Raj asked. They heard more gunfire.

"We should but I don't want someone randomly shooting me." Tilly said. Raj hadn't seen what happened with Ray. Amanda heard Tilly's words. She didn't respond.

Chris was crouched behind a tree looking back towards the glow through the woods. He could see shapes moving between the trees. He had lost sight of Raj. He had lost sight of everyone. He sat there for another minute trying to figure out what to do next. He had dropped the shotgun he was carrying when he and Raj picked Ray up. He decided to work his way back towards the other bus. He moved past a clump of bushes and felt something rip at his leg. One of the infected had fell into it and Chris hadn't seen it. All he could see was the top of the things head as it reached out and grabbed him again. He tried to pull away, but the thing was stronger than he was prepared for. He couldn't break free. He felt the searing pain as the thing bit down into his calf. He twisted and cried out but it was useless. The thing grabbed his other leg while still biting and took Chris to the ground. He beat against its head. He beat against its shoulders and arms. He continued to beat against the thing as it tore through the muscle on his stomach and ripped his guts out. Chris watched as the thing began eating the intestines being pulled from his stomach. He could feel it as it used its hands to tear the rest of his belly open. As the blood left his body, he lay back. He had no fight left. His eyes fixed on the sky and he drew his last breath to the slurps and gurgles of his own devouring.

Janice had taken the boys several yards into the woods when she realized she had no idea where she was going. They had no flashlights, and they had run far enough away from the fire that the woods had grown dark again. They stopped.
"Momma, where are we?" Jeremy asked.
"I don't know, I think we are close to the creek now but I can't see anything" Janice said. She knelt down. "But we are ok. Just stay close."

She reached out and took their hands again. They slowly started walking into the dark woods. They could hear gunshots. Lots of gunshots. Then the bus detonated. The woods lit up as the fireball from the exploding gas tank expanded skyward. Janice could see. It wasn't good. The woods ahead of her were full of moving shadows. She tightened her grip on their hands and turned to run in the other direction.

"Yaaaaaaaaaaa" Jeremy screamed. One of the dead had been slowly following them and when they turned it reached out and grabbed Jeremy in a bear hug. It lifted him off the ground, ripping him from his mother's hands. It bit hard into his shoulder.

"Stop, stop, no, no." Janice yelled, trying to hit the thing as hard as she could. It didn't help. The thing bit down one more time and dropped to the ground, still holding Jeremy in its arms. As it lifted its head to take another bite of the boy, Janice kicked it in the side. The thing in front of her was at least a foot taller than her and probably doubled her weight. When it turned she saw its face. The thing had long hair and a full beard. Except it didn't. Half of its scalp was peeled from the top center to just over its left ear. The skin was bunched up in a semicircle around the side its head with much of the left side of its skull clearly exposed. The skin was also split along its jawline on the same side and it was pushed down into the same semicircle pattern around the left side of its neck, exposing the bottom of its jaw and all the muscle and tissue. She screamed and kicked again.

The thing let Jeremy go and began to stand up. Janice reached down to pull Jeremy away. As she did, she heard a pop and saw the infected fall to the ground. As it fell, she could see Clyde standing behind it hold a big rock in his hand. He had struck the thing as it had struggled to stand and he had struck it in the right place. Clyde had a look of disbelief on his face. That was not what he had expected. He dropped the rock. He and Janice tried to get Jeremy to stand. He wasn't moving. Janice couldn't get him respond to her. There was so much blood. She knew. She looked up and saw another shape limping towards them. In the light she recognized Ray. He came closer.

"Ray, over here. Please help me. Please, please help me. They got Jeremy, he's hurt bad." She looked back down at Jeremy. Clyde had turned to look at Ray when she first called to him. He turned back to Janice as Ray was coming up behind him.

She was looking down when the thing that had once been Ray Harrison fell on top of Clyde, pushing him down onto her and her onto Jeremy. As they all went to the ground, the thing took a deep bite into Clyde's leg. Clyde screamed. Janice was trapped between Clyde, Jeremy and this thing. She couldn't move. Her cheek pressed against the side of Jeremy's face and she pulled her head back a little to see him. His eyes were closed. He looked like he was sleeping. She whispered to him.

"Oh baby boy, please come back to me. Please."

As if hearing her plea, his eyes opened, and he turned his face towards the sound of her voice. She looked at the opaque lenses fogging his vision. She started to scream again but stopped. Her husband was dead. Her neighbor was dead. And now her child was dead too.

"It's ok baby boy. I love you." Janice said as she placed her mouth on the side of his face to kiss him.

As she did, he turned his mouth towards hers, closed down on her lower lip and bit it off. She didn't make a sound. The tears streaming down her face reached her mouth. She tasted the mixture of blood and tears. The thing on top of them finally rolled to one side, and she was able to move. She didn't. Instead she reached out, knocking the hands of the child she had brought into the world away as it tried to grab her. She grabbed the things head and brought it in close to her chest. It was biting and thrashing. It bit into her breast, the same breast she had used to feed it just a few years ago. It bit several more times. The whole time Janice was just pulling it tighter and tighter her, singing a lullaby.

"Hush little baby, don't say a word. Momma's gonna buy you a..." the thing bit into her neck. They both fell over. She lay back on the ground and looked to the side as her child began feeding on her. She could see the thing that had once been Ray bent over Clyde. Clyde wasn't moving any more either.

As JW moved around the SUV and towards the other bus, he could see the back door standing open. He jumped in the back and looked around.

"Kate, Josh, Scott. Where are you?" He said.

"They left. They went to help the others." Evelyn said, rising from the seat.

He could see Evelyn's face in the glow of the fire. Jennifer and Lori stood. Just behind them a man JW didn't know stood too.

"Who the hell are you?" he said.

"It's a long story JW. We can tell it later." Evelyn said.

JW started to say something, but the world exploded outside the windows and bus filled with light. The shock wave from the explosion of the other bus' gas tank lifted their bus off the ground and it hovered briefly tilted to one side, completely off the ground. It threw everyone on the bus against the wall on the opposite side. It violently came back down to the ground and slammed them all to the floor. JW tried to raise his head but the ringing in his ears made his vision blur. Evelyn was draped over the back of one of the seats trying to rise up. Ed crawled out from under the seat next to her and saw her gun lying on the floor. He reached over and helped her sit up and looked at the gash over her eyebrow. It was bleeding pretty good. The bus had been a makeshift home for the last few weeks. All the clothing and personal items they had kept in it were now scattered and tossed all over the interior. Ed grabbed the first thing he found, one of Scott's shirts, and put it up against Evelyn's forehead. "Thank you." Evelyn said. She looked up at her benefactor and for the first time realized it was Ed. Her eyes widened.

He reached down and picked up her pistol. He held it in his hand and turned it this way and that, looking over it into her eyes. JW slowly managed to raise his rifle. Ed shrugged his shoulders and handed the gun back to Evelyn. She smiled. She glanced over Ed's shoulder and made eye contact with JW. He lowered the rifle.

Kate turned to see the infected coming around the other cars. Bridger stopped when she did. Josh and Scott took another step but when Bridger opened fire to their right, they wheeled around. They could see the dead coming into the corral and they began firing into them. Bridger glanced down to reload and caught movement out of the corner of his eye. He saw Janice and the boys run into the woods towards the creek. He started walking towards the few infected still in front of him and tried to clear a path to the back of the bus. It wouldn't work. There was too much fire growing around it. He turned back towards the cars parked across the road.

"Come on, we can get to them this way." He said looking back at Kate.

They worked their way around the back of the car and went down the road just a few yards. Bridger and Kate turned into the woods. Josh took a few more steps and turned into the trees. Scott stepped into the woods with Josh just in front of him. Josh turned to look back at him when one of the infected came around a tree and reached out for him. Josh felt the pressure on his back as Scott's eyes widened. As he ducked the thing fell over him and landed on the ground. Josh didn't even think. He pointed the muzzle of his shotgun and pulled the trigger. The splatter of rotted brains and blood covered Scott. Josh looked up at him.

"Shit." He said.

"Shit? Man I would welcome shit compared to how this smells." Scott said wiping his face.

"Hey, you okay?" Kate said as she reached out and grabbed Josh's shoulder from behind.

He wheeled, startled. Bridger reached out and lowered the barrel of Josh's gun, which Josh had brought up almost to his head.

"Whoa." Bridger said, as he ducked his head to the side.

"Sorry. Yes, we're ok." Josh said.

"Ok. Let's go." Bridger said.

They slipped further into the woods, trying to flank around to the other side of the bus. Bridger didn't know how many of the others had gone into the woods but he knew for sure he had seen Janice and the boys. He figured the rest of them went that way too. As they moved a little further away from the glow of the fire they slowed. Bridger reached up and turned the flashlight rail attachment on. It cast a narrow beam of white light into the trees. They could see several of the dead moving away from them. They followed them. When his light would land on one of the infected, he would pull the trigger. They were leaving a trail of dead as they went.

"Where are we going?" Charlie asked.

"I saw some of our people run into the woods this way. I am not sure where they went after that." Bridger said, pointing the light into the woods.

They had covered another few yards when Bridger stopped.

"I don't know. I don't see anybody. Maybe we should..." The explosion interrupted him. They all ducked their heads and snapped back around to face the buses. The woods lit up.

"My god." Kate said.

They looked around in the glow of the fireball in the sky. All the infected they could see turned towards the fireball and started walking.

"They are all going towards the fire. All of them." Charlie said.

JW stood and looked out the window. A dozen or so dead were coming out of the shadows into the light of the fire. For an instant it looked like a crowd gathered around cheering a Friday night bonfire, but the dead didn't cheer. Or stop. They walked into the fire. He watched as they began to burn. Some started to cross the corral towards the bus he was on. He wasn't going to let them get to it. He stuck the barrel of his rifle out of the window. When he finished, all that was left were piles of burning corpses. He looked over at Evelyn and Ed. Jennifer and Lori had crawled out from under the other seats. None of them looked like they were injured too badly. He stepped out of the back. He winced when he hit the ground. He looked into the woods and could see the outline of the trees to the east, back-lit by the rising sun.

Through the Darkness
See the Light

Tilly, Amanda, Dottie and Raj emerged from the SUV. The smoldering remains of the bus blanketed the woods with smoke. The rising sun cast its light into the haze. Their eyes were adjusting to the light. No shapes moved. The air was still. And quiet. The morning crept into the world bringing the truth of the night before. A shadow moved across the corral. Tilly raised her shotgun. JW, Evelyn, Ed, Jennifer and Lori stepped through the smoke towards them.

As the sun rose a little further, the breeze began to carry the smoke away. The veil lifted off the bodies that littered the ground. Some burnt, some not. Some small, some not. But all of them dead. Really dead. They made their way around the piles on the ground towards each other. JW looked as hard as he could at the group coming to them but didn't see his family. "Which way did they go?" JW asked Tilly.

It took her a second to remember where their last conversation had left off.

"That way." Tilly said. Pointing past the cars at the other end of the corral. He turned to go.

"Wait." Raj said. "I will go with you."

"Me too. We all will. We all stay together." Tilly said. She didn't appear to be open to negotiation.

"Fine. Let's go." JW said.

JW didn't care. If they wanted to go, fine. If they didn't, fine. He was going. He turned and started across the corral.

"Where you going?" Bridger called as he stepped around the burnt out husk of the other bus. They all turned to his voice.

Bridger stepped out of the haze. Followed by Kate, Josh, Scott and Charlie. Kate's eyes met JW's. "John." She said as she ran towards him.

"Dad." Josh and Scott said in unison. They all met over the burnt remains of lawn chairs and dead scattered around the corral. He hugged all of them at once.

"Are you ok?" JW asked while cupping Kate's face in his hands.

"Yes, yes. We're fine." Kate said. She smiled through her tears. She kissed him.

"Boys. Y'all ok?" He said. Looking each of them in the face.

"Good." Josh said. Scott just gave him thumbs up. JW hugged them all together again.

"Where are the others?" Bridger asked. "Where is Janice? Where is Jeremy and Clyde?"

"They ran." Raj said.

"Into the woods." Tilly added, pointing in the direction they went.

"Chris?" Bridger asked.

"I don't know. We were together for a minute but there were too many. We got split up." Raj said. Then turning to Amanda. "I'm sorry."

Amanda just looked at him and nodded. She was biting her lower lip as she let the tears flow down her cheeks. Dottie reached around her shoulder to comfort her. Dottie didn't blame her. Now Amanda knew it. She felt a little better.

"Ray?" Kate asked.

Dottie just looked up into her eyes and shook her head no. Kate looked down. "Oh" was all she said.

"Well let's get started." Bridger said.

"Started what?" Lori asked.

"Looking." He said.

"We don't know what's out there." Jennifer said.

"Yes we do. For the first time since this all started, we know exactly what's out there." Dottie said. "Hell"

"And if you're going through hell, just keep going." Bridger said, recalling the words to one of the few country songs he could remember. He smiled. Dottie didn't.

"Listen. We can't just sit here. We have to look. We have to." Charlie said. Most of them nodded.

"Ok. But let's be smart. Let's give it another minute and let the sun come up a little more and maybe some smoke will clear out." Bridger said.

Kate walked over to Evelyn and pulled the makeshift bandage off her forehead. They both winced. "Ooh. That's deep." Kate said. "Raj, take a look at this."

Raj stepped in front of JW and over to Evelyn. JW turned and grabbed the back of Scott's head and pulled his forehead to his. He did the same to Josh. He took a long look at each of them. He turned and squeezed Kate's shoulder as she tended to Evelyn. He walked over to the other side of the SUV and sat down in the open rear compartment. Charlie walked over to Jennifer and Lori.

"Stay here. We will go and look." He said to Jennifer.

Scott walked over to the burned out bus and looked over into it. Lori and Jennifer walked over to him.

"What are you looking for?" Lori asked.

"Well, since that bus had almost all the food on it, I was hoping some cans might have survived." He said.

Bridger released the magazine from his rifle and inserted a full one.

"Ok. Charlie and I will head this way." Bridger said, pointing. "Everyone else just wait here. We will be back in twenty minutes. Until then everyone stay put."

There was no objection. They had all had enough for one night. Bridger and Charlie walked out of the corral.

"You think we'll find them?" Charlie asked as they turned.

"We'll find them, one way or the other." Bridger said.

They walked a few yards beyond the bus. They came upon one of the infected. It had been close to the bus when it exploded and one of its legs was missing. The other leg was ripped apart just above the knee. The femur bone stuck out of the charred stump and it was dragging itself towards some unknown place. Bridger handed his rifle to Charlie and pulled out his knife.

"What are you doing?" Charlie asked.

"Well, I don't want the rest of them to get all worked up again because they hear a gunshot."

Bridger walked over and put his boot in the middle of the things back and pushed it against the ground. He dropped his knee down and drove the knife into the base of its skull. There was an audible pop. Both Bridger and Charlie jumped back just a bit.

"What the hell was that?" Charlie asked.

"I think that was its damn head."

"Damn" Charlie said, handing the rifle back to Bridger.

"So, now that we have a moment, who the hell is the new guy?" Bridger asked.

Charlie realized that since they had picked up Bridger walking out of the woods yesterday, they still hadn't had a chance to tell him what had happened to Tilly. He began to recount the entire ordeal, including parts of the conversation between him and Ed.

"And you think this other guy, the guy back at camp, Ed, you think he isn't a bad guy? He damn sure hung out with a piece of shit." Bridger said after hearing the story.

"Hell, I thought JW was some psycho crazy loner dude until he pulled up to my house with two buses and a way out of town. Sometimes you get lucky, sometimes you get assholes." Charlie said.

"Well JW is some psycho crazy loner dude, but you still got lucky. I did too. We are in the middle of nowhere and that just happened. Can you imagine what it's like where people actually are?" Bridger said.

Charlie hadn't thought about it that far. He did now. They had all been living in a kind of state of suspended belief. Sure they could hear some things on the radio and they had even seen a thing or two when they were trying to get out but it had been tempered by a week of isolation. They had been able to keep it at a distance. It hadn't touched them. Until now. He realized that whatever they had been doing for the last few days, trying to adjust or whatever, they were fooling themselves. What Bridger had just said made him realize that this was not going to get better. At least not for a long time.

"Where was this place this guy was telling you about? This *compound*?" Bridger said.

"He said..." Bridger stuck his hand in front of Charlie and brought his index finger to his lip. He pointed to Charlie's left.

About ten yards away they could see one of the infected. Charlie recognized the shirt. Ray had managed to pack three shirts when he was evacuated. All of them were some kind of bright Hawaiian print. This was the blue one. It was kneeling on the ground with its back to them. It's head down near the ground. They slowly walked up behind it. Bridger looked down at his belt to pull his knife out again.

"Holy shit." Charlie said. Bridger's eyes snapped to Charlie, then to the thing on the ground.

It started to turn around. Bridger saw the face of its meal. It was Janice. As the thing turned its body, he could see another infected eating the other side of Janice's body. This one was smaller, a child. He raised his rifle and fired twice. He turned his head and emptied his stomach.

Kate walked to the bus and grabbed the first-aid bag. JW had snagged it from the deputy's car what seemed like a lifetime ago now. Good thing. It had a suture kit in it. She brought it over to Raj, and he started cleaning Evelyn's wound.
"I don't think you have a concussion." Raj said. "I think a couple of stitches should just about take care of it."
"Thanks" Evelyn said.
Kate squeezed her hand and walked around to back of the SUV. JW was facing away from her. He had one of his boots in his hand.
"Hey what are..." she froze.
She could see the tear on the top of the boot. Her eyes went from the boot to JW, who had swung his head around as she spoke. His face was wet.
"Is that? It's not..?" her hand coming up to her mouth.
He pulled the sock off his foot to expose the small marks. They were each less than an inch long and less than a half inch deep. Individually they were unremarkable; together they formed a perfect bite mark. They stared at each other for another minute. Then she just walked over and stood next to him, pulling his head against her chest. He looked at the ground. She looked at the sky. Two shots rang out in the distance. They ignored it.

Bridger held it to two retches before straightening back up. He wiped his mouth and turned back around. Charlie was looking at the scene in front of him trying to understand. He couldn't.

"What now?" Charlie asked.

"I don't know. I think we keep looking. We still need to find Clyde and Chris." Bridger said.

"I think we found Clyde." Charlie said, pointing to another small body a few feet away.

Bridger turned and looked. He looked down at the ground again.

"Let's go back. I don't think finding Chris is going to change anything. I think we know how it ended." They turned and started back to the camp.

Josh grabbed his rifle when he heard Bridger fire. He was standing next to Janice's car looking out in the direction the shots came from. Lori sat down on the ground next to the car.

"Do you think they found them?" Lori asked.

"Maybe but I wouldn't count on it." He said.

"Why not?"

"Didn't you see what just happened here?"

"Yes but that doesn't mean it's hopeless."

"It's pretty close." He said, turning to look at her.

"But it's not hopeless everywhere." She said, almost asking.

"I wouldn't know." He said.

"Well, I mean, my parents may still be out there. We don't know for sure."

"No we don't, but I don't know how we could ever be sure anymore."

"We could look." She said, looking up without raising her head.

He looked at her. He looked back out into the woods.

"We could." He said. She smiled.

"When?" Kate finally managed to ask. "When did it happen?"

"On my way back. I stopped for a second to use the walkie. I didn't see it until it had done it. It was on the other side of a tree and I just put my foot in the wrong place." He said.

She sat down next to him.

"What now? I mean, what is going to happen? To you?"

"I think we both know how this ends up. I think we need to bring Bridger in on this pretty quick." He said.

"What about the boys?" She asked.

"Bridger first. I want to make sure that if, you know, something happens, he is ready." He said. "Pretty sure he's wanted to crack my skull a time or two, anyway." He smiled.

"Don't joke about this John." She said.

"It's really all I can do, honey."

Josh saw Bridger and Charlie walking out of the woods. He turned to Lori.

"Wait here."

He went to meet them.

"Well?" he said as he fell beside them.

"We found them. Most of them. Their gone." Bridger said.

"Gone?" Josh said, stopping.

"Yes, gone. We found Ray, Janice, Jeremy and Clyde. They were all gone." Charlie said, still walking.

"Chris?"

"Listen Josh, they are all gone. Just leave it alone." Bridger said, stopping and looking Josh in the eye.

"Ok" Josh said. They all walked around the back of Janice's car and into the corral.

Most of them gathered around the center of what had been their home. The pit they had prepared for their fire was still there. It now had two dead infected in it. Scattered around the ground was a mixture of scorched signs of life and roasting corpses. Evelyn, Ed and Raj joined Jennifer and Lori along with Scott and Josh. Dottie and Amanda were leaning against the tires of the remaining bus. Bridger and Charlie stepped into the middle of the group.

"I'm sorry." Bridger said, looking at Dottie and Amanda.

"The others?" Evelyn asked.

"No." Charlie said, shaking his head.

They all briefly looked at the ground.

"We need to figure out what comes next." Bridger said. "For now, let's start trying to clean some of this shit out of here." He said, delivering a swift kick the dead thing in the pit.

He looked at Evelyn.

"Where's JW and Kate?" Bridger asked. Evelyn just nodded towards the SUV. He started walking.

Kate had overheard Bridger and knew he was headed towards them. She turned and met him as he came around to the back of the SUV. She couldn't disguise her eyes.

"What's wrong?" Bridger asked, suddenly aware that Kate had been crying.

"It's John." She said, stepping to the side so he could pass.

She followed him back around. Bridger stopped and looked down at JW. He was sitting in the back of the SUV with one sock off. His eyes went to his foot. He saw the bite mark. He looked back and forth between JW's eyes and his foot two more times.

"Well shit." Bridger said.

"Yeah, that's what I said." JW smiled.

"So now what? I mean what comes next for you?"
Bridger asked.
"I don't know. I'm not quite sure how this works but I
am pretty sure we all know how it is going to end." He
glanced down at one of the burnt corpses scattered
around the SUV.
"We have to tell the boys?" Kate said.
"We will, honey, but we need to make sure I am not a
threat first."
"You're not a threat, you're just…" Kate said
"Bitten. And that means we don't know what I am
now." JW said.

Another Hard Life

Long forgotten

JW sat up against the back of the seat. He had been stretched out in the SUV for long enough. He had made them isolate him in here after they told the boys and the rest of the group. He knew that last night had taken most of the fight out of everyone and he didn't want them to sit around and watch him die. He knew time was shutting down for him. He could feel his body dying. It was a strange sensation. He was beginning to notice parts of himself going numb. Not a foot or arm but just spots. Under his arms, the backs of his hands or the side of his face. Like having random shots of Novocain. The feeling would return but it was happening more often and over more of his body. He felt cold, which meant he was probably running a fever. He looked over his shoulder into the rearview mirror. His eyes were set back, and he had dark circles under them. He looked tired. But more than that the skin that covered his cheekbones was starting to relax. His lips were still pink but there was a tell tale bluing around the corners. He leaned forward and lifted the towel he had draped over his foot. The bite was just two small tears in the skin when he first pulled his sock off to show Bridger and Kate. Both spots were now at least three inches wide and the hole in the middle smelled, the same smell he had been searching for, like a dead dog but different. More ammonia. It was acrid and in an enclosed space like this it made his eyes water. He reached down and opened the door next to him. The sunlight streamed in and the fresh air made him feel a little better. Bridger walked over to the open door.

"How you doing?" Bridger asked.

"Still able to open the door." JW smiled. "Guess I am still here. For now."

"Come on man, you look good." Bridger lied.

"I think you need to bring my family over." JW said. He and Bridger had talked about this when he first locked himself into the SUV this morning.

"Are you sure?" Bridger reached out and touched JW on the shoulder. JW smiled up at him, squinting in the bright light.

"Yeah, I think I am getting close. I need to say goodbye and when I am done you and I can go for a drive." JW smiled again. Bridger looked down out the ground and shrugged his shoulders. They had talked about this part too; he knew he would be the only one coming back.

Bridger walked over to the corral. Kate, Josh and Scott were sitting on the ground, the chairs lost in the fire. They all looked up. They all looked back down again after they saw the expression on his face.

"Is he..?" Scott mumbled.

"No. But it won't be long. He wants to see y'all." Bridger said.

They all stood. Josh linked his arm with Kate's. She moved her hand down to hold his hand. She looked over at Scott and stuck her hand out. He took it. They walked past the surviving bus and around to the side of the SUV. The door was open. Bridger walked slightly ahead of them, pistol in hand.

"Here we come." He called to the SUV.

"Come on, I won't bite." JW said with a laugh, a laugh that quickly devolved into coughing.

Bridger looked into the SUV and then backed off to the side so the others could gather around the door. Kate sat down on the door kick plate and reached for JW's hand. He took it and looked down at her, smiling. Josh and Scott stood awkwardly silent.

"Hey guys, it's still me. I haven't gone anywhere yet. I want y'all to know how much I love you." JW said.

"We love you too, Dad." Scott said.

"We love you." Josh added.

Kate couldn't speak. She couldn't. She was choking back tears watching the man she loves say goodbye to their children. She couldn't take her eyes off him. His cheeks were sunken but not as deeply as his eyes. She could tell he was in pain. She could always tell.

"Boys, I want you to know, no matter what you do, I have always been and always will be proud to call you my sons. I don't know what comes next. This world is something I wasn't prepared for. I wanted to give you each a talk like this when you went off to college. I wanted to tell you to figure out what you want to be and go be it. I wanted to fill you with courage and confidence and send you out into the world to make your way. I don't know if I have prepared you for this world. I hope I have but you'll have to figure it out on your own. I love you both. I love you so much." He reached out to each of them and pulled them close. He breathed deeply the smell of their hair. He pulled back and took each ones hand. He looked at their hands, remembering when they were so tiny, so little. He brought their hands up to his face and kissed them, smelling their skin. He looked up at each of them.

"Goodbye, boys. I love you."

"I love you Dad." Josh said.

"I love you Dad." Scott said. They both turned and walked back towards the corral. Kate was still sitting on the kick plate looking up at him. She had let the tears flow while he was talking. She had gathered herself together just slightly. He looked down at her.

"Well, I guess we managed to get a little alone time." He smiled.

"So that was the plan?" she said, smiling through her tears.

"Sort of." JW said. "I am so sorry. I screwed up."

"John, just stop. You didn't screw up. You saved people. A lot of people."

"I love you. I have always loved you."

"I know, I love you too." Kate said.

"You remember when you pulled me together after the deputy thing with Josh?" He said. She nodded that she did.

"You said you needed me to be the man I needed to be for you. I tried." He said.

"You did." She said.

"Well I need you to be the woman who wouldn't take any shit off me or anyone else. I need you to be strong. I need to know you are going to make it." He said.

"John." She started to interrupt.

"No, tell me. Tell me you will make it. Tell me I didn't bring us all out here to die."

"You brought us here to live, and that is what we will do." Kate said. "I promise."

He looked at her face. He believed her. He leaned his head back and drew a breath. His chest felt heavy, and it felt like he was breathing through a straw. He looked back at her.

"It's time." He said.

"I love you. I will always love you." He said.

"I love you too, John. I love you." She stood and leaned against him. He held her head against his chest and stroked her hair. She had always loved it when he stroked her hair. She used to make him stroke her hair to help her sleep, so much so that it had been a running joke between them. A smile crossed his lips as he looked down at the top of her head. He kissed her head. She looked up at him. She could see his eyes were starting to get swimmy and his skin had begun to turn ashen. She leaned up and pressed her lips to his. Cold. He kissed her back. They held each other for a few more minutes.

"You have to go." JW said.

"I know." Kate said. She stood.

"Goodbye. God gave me the greatest gift in the world when he brought you into my life. I love you. I love you." JW said.

"I love you. I will always love you." Kate said. She kissed him one more time. She turned and walked away. He watched her walk around the bus.

"Let's go, I don't think I have much time." JW said, knowing Bridger was listening even though he was trying hard not too.

"Alright." Bridger said. He climbed into the SUV and cranked it up.

They pulled away from the bus. JW looked out the back window and saw Kate, Josh and Scott reemerge from the other side. They were standing there watching the SUV pull away, and he thought about that day, not so long ago, when he was pulling away from the house and saw them in the bay window. He held that image in his mind now.

"How you doing back there?" Bridger asked.

"Dying." JW said.

"Well, whatcha waiting on." Bridger said attempting a joke.

"I'm scared."

"I know brother."

"Bridge?" JW said. "After, you know?.."

"Don't talk about it."

"Listen, after I am gone, make sure you burn me. Don't bury me. And then move on."

"But why man, why is that so important to you? I know they all bought that crap about keeping the virus from spreading but you and I know that's mostly bullshit. It doesn't spread that way. So why is it a big deal?" Bridger said.

"Because if there is a grave, she won't leave. And I think you are going to have to leave."

JW said, his voice almost a whisper now.

They drove down the road past the creek. They stopped. Bridger got out and opened the door for JW. JW slid his feet out and touched them on the ground. He couldn't put any weight on the bit foot without it sending shock waves of pain through him. Bridger stood beside him and reached around his waist to support him. JW wrapped his arm around Bridger's shoulders.

"Over there, by that big tree."

"The pine tree?" Bridger asked.

"Hell no, I hate pine trees. Damn tick factories. Over there, by that oak." JW pointed.

They made their three-legged walk over to the tree. Bridger gently helped him down. JW straightened himself against the tree and looked up and Bridger. Bridger knelt down beside him.

"Brother, we have been through a lot of shit together, but this. Man I wasn't ready for this." JW said.

"Yes you were. You did everything right. You have to know that. I came here because I trusted you. I was not wrong. You saved us. You did."

They sat there for a few minutes without saying another word. Bridger listened to JW breath. It was coarse and shallow. He looked at his eyes. The whites were turning yellow, and the corners were starting to fill up with blood. His fingernails had turned blue. JW broke the silence.

"I'm scared. I never had to do this before."

"What's that?" Bridger asked.

"Die. I never did it before. I don't want to go." JW said.

"Brother, I am here. I am going to let you live every last second." Bridger said.

"You should just let me do it." JW said.

"Too bad you don't get to decide." Bridger said.

"You're my brother, you know that." JW said.

"I know. I love you man." Bridger said.

"I love you to brother." JW reached up and took Bridger's hand.

"After this, you have to move on. You have to make Kate move on. You have too. Promise me."

"I promise."

JW leaned back against the tree. He could hear the cicadas buzzing and a robin singing. He could see the bright morning sun..shit. He opened his mouth. He tried to tell him to go to the post office and to find Cameron Day. He has a radio. He can help. But Bridger heard

"Go post, day radio with the help."

Bridger leaned in and nodded at JW just to keep him at peace. He looked into his eyes. They were fixed on the horizon. His breathing was very shallow. A few moments later, underneath an oak tree with the sun beaming down on his face and the birds singing in his ear, the image of Kate, Josh and Scott firmly locked in his mind, JW died.

Bridger looked at him hard. He stepped around the tree and knelt down behind JW. He pulled JW's knife out and held it in his hands. He watched for any movement. JW just sat there. After another minute or so Bridger saw his chest rise and fall one time. Another. A third.

"JW?" Bridger whispered in his ear.

Its arm jerked forward and a raspy exhale came from the dead lungs. Bridger reached up and grabbed the things collar and pulled it back against the tree. The thing tried to pull away but Bridger pulled it back. Now both arms were grabbing the air trying to get a hold of something. Bridger brought the knife up the back of its neck and drove it in. Upward. Pop. JW went limp. Bridger sat there with his friend for another half hour, crying. He finally stood and gathered some wood for a pyre. He took the gas can from the front seat floorboard and poured it on the wood. He laid his friend on top of it and poured more gasoline over him.

"Godspeed, brother. You deserved better." He tossed the match.

He walked back to the SUV and pulled away. He looked back through the rearview mirror and saw the black smoke rising. Kate could see it too, over the trees. She knew what it meant. She started crying and went to the ground. Evelyn walked over and knelt down next to her, gently rubbing her hand across her back.

"I know this doesn't help but this, this right now, this moment. This is the hardest moment. It will get better. I am so sorry." Evelyn said.

Run to You

Walk with Me

Charlie and Raj walked around the other side of the bus and grabbed the ankles of one of the dead. They had decided to drag them away from the camp and begin burning them all. What JW had said about the infection spreading made sense. Kind of. Raj knew that the spread of the Marionette virus had already happened and was pretty sure everyone was infected. He had seen the old man come back, and he didn't have any bites. But having rotting corpses around presents its own set of problems. Burning them made sense. He glanced towards the bus and saw Kate on the ground with Evelyn next to her.

"What now?" Raj asked.

"What?" Charlie said.

"What now? With JW gone. I mean he was the one who kind of got us all out here. What is the plan now?" Raj asked.

"Not sure. Maybe we should all start talking about it. I been talking to..." Charlie paused. He wasn't sure if Raj had formed an opinion on Ed but he was pretty sure Tilly had.

"The asshole's friend?" Raj interjected.

"Listen, I..." Charlie stopped. They heard the SUV coming back down the road.

"We can talk about it later." Raj said.

They dropped the thing they were carrying on the pile and walked back to the corral. Josh and Scott had joined their mother, and they were all huddled together away from the others. Evelyn stood watch over the family, offering a comforting hug or gentle hand when needed. Some of the group wandered by and Dottie and Amanda stayed. The rest gathered in the freshly cleaned out corral. Bridger got out of the SUV and walked over to Kate.

"He's gone?" Kate asked, already knowing the answer.

"Yes."

"Thank you. Really. Thank you." Kate said. She hugged Bridger. He stood and walked over to the corral.

"OK folks. We have to get organized. We need to..." Bridger was interrupted.

"Can't we just stop?" Evelyn said, walking over.

"What?" Bridger said, shocked.

"Just stop. For one minute. We need that. We need to mourn. We need to breathe."

"Ok. I get that but that means we have a minute. Right now, I don't know if we have a minute. Last night we had warning. JW died making sure we knew what was out there. And this still happened. We need to get organized." Bridger said, ending the dissention.

"Organized how?" Charlie asked.

"We need to figure out what we lost in the fire. We need to gather our resources together."

"We need to figure out where to go." Josh said. Everyone turned to his voice.

"Where to go? Did you say where to go? Who is going anywhere?" Raj said.

"We can't stay here. At least I can't. I am not going to just sit around and wait for death to walk out of the trees." He said.

"He's right." Lori said. "We can't just sit in the woods. We need walls and roofs."

"The kid's on to something." Dottie said. "We can't stay here."

"Maybe go back to South Springs." Josh said, glancing at Lori.

"You want to go back into that?" Raj said.

"We don't know what happened. We left. We don't know." Lori said.

"We can take a damn good guess." Tilly said.

"Yeah, but we don't *know*." Josh said.

Bridger watched the conversation circle around the group. No one knew where to go but one thing was clear, no one wanted to stay here. He wasn't sure how long it was going to take to decide but he knew some things had to be taken care of now.

"Ok. Stop. It is pretty clear we have a decision to make. Everyone let's spend a little time thinking about it as we get this place organized. We need to know what we have before we can decide, anyway. Ok?" He looked around the group.

"One thing, before we start to think about it, I think we need consider something." Charlie said. "Ed?" He pointed to the stranger standing next to him. Everyone turned.

"Uh, ok. Listen, that guy I was with..."

"Your asshole friend?" Tilly asked.

"Yeah, but he really wasn't my friend."

"Right." Tilly.

"Listen. He wasn't my friend. I knew him. He shopped where I worked. When the shit hit the fan, he seemed to have a plan. It seemed to me that any kind of plan was better than mine because I didn't fucking have one. Ok?"

"Kinda like us. I guess you too?" Charlie said, looking at Tilly.

"Fine." Tilly said.

"I am sorry. I really didn't know."

"Do you want a trophy?" Tilly said.

"Ok. Listen, the guy I was with, I hooked up with him when the world went to shit. He said he needed help and that he had a secure place."

"Just hooked up with him. You didn't know him but you just decided to, go?" Raj asked.

"Well I had just watched all them damn videos in the break room and well, I had just smoked a fat one too, and everyone else was starting to just say fuck it and leave. He came in and bought a bunch of ammo and few rifles and hell, I went with him. He had bought stuff from me before but never this much at once."

"So where did you go?" Raj asked again.

"We ended up down here at his place. But it was more like a dang ghost town than anything. He had been hauling in old shacks and buildings over the years and set it up like a little town. It looks like shit but there are at least ten buildings and he put a big old game fence around everything. He built one building out of cinder block that he lived in. I never went in there but I am pretty sure it's full of guns and food. He bought a lot of that shit from me over the years at Wal-Mart."

"And it was just you and him?" Josh asked.

"Yep. We had been pretty much locked inside the fence until yesterday. He decided that it was time to do a little scouting since the radio quit broadcasting."

"Yesterday?" Josh said.

"Yep. Been in there almost two weeks. Went out yesterday, that's how we found you." Ed said, looking at Tilly. She wasn't smiling.

"And he didn't talk about anyone else coming or anything." Bridger said.

"Nope. To be honest, I think he was starting to wish he hadn't included me either." Ed said.

"And where is this place?" Bridger said.

"Just a few miles..." Ed started.

"You're not serious?" Josh said. "I mean, you can't be seriously thinking about that?"

"Why not?" Raj asked.

"We don't know this guy. This may be some drug-induced fantasy. You heard him." Josh said.

"A two-week fantasy?" Jennifer said.

"I don't know. Shit. But we ain't trusting him, are we?" Josh said, turning to Bridger.

"We'll see. Right now let's just get this place together. Raj, you and Tilly rest up. I want y'all to plan on being on watch tonight." Bridger said.

Josh walked over and sat down next to Kate.

"What do you think Mom?" Josh asked.

"I don't know son. I'm not sure I could make a good decision right now."

Evelyn walked over with a granola bar she had been saving.

"Here, you need to eat something." She said, handing it to Kate.

"Not hungry."

"Yes you are, you just can't feel it. Take a bite. You need it." Evelyn insisted.

She took the bar and gave Evelyn a half smile. When Evelyn's husband had died, Kate had been one of the many who brought food to Evelyn's house that week. It was a tradition, but it is also a well-known fact that food helps ease the pain. At least it does in the south. She smiled a little more and took a bite. She was hungry. Josh stood and walked around to the bus. Scott was sitting on the ground. Josh sat down next to him.

"How you doing?" Josh asked.

"I don't know. It's weird, you know. Him being gone."

"I know. I keep waiting to hear him deep breathe when someone says something he doesn't approve of. Or roll his eyes."

"Yeah, he would roll his eyes and rub his chin. Like he had a beard." Scott said, smiling.

"Yeah." Josh smiled.

"I'm gonna miss him." Scott said.

"Me too."

They sat there for a minute looking at the sun climbing in the sky. They were both trying to figure out what came next.

"Can I talk to you?" Lori stepped in front of Josh, blocking the sun. Scott squinted and shielded his eyes to see who it was.

"Sure." Josh said, standing. They walked off.

Scott stood and walked around the other side of the bus and sat down next to Kate. She looked into his eyes as she took his hand.

"It will be ok. Ok?" she said.

"I know. I will make sure of that." Scott said smiling.

"What do you mean?" Kate said.

"I am just going to do everything I can to keep us safe. All of us." He said. "That's what Dad would have wanted."

"Yes he would. He did."

Bridger and Charlie had brought the last of the dead from around the campsite to the burn pile. They had gathered thirty-one plus the four of their own they found. Chris was still missing but nobody was looking any more. There had been some objection to burning the bodies but JW put that to rest before he died.

"The way this new world works seems if you bury folks you end up spending all the time you have left either dying or digging." JW said. And that was that.

Before they had brought the last one from around the campsite Charlie had approached Dottie.

"Do you want to see him?" he asked as gently as he could.

"No. I don't. I don't need to." She said, gathering her hand across her shirt. "I can't"

Charlie just nodded and patted her on the shoulder. What else could he do?

He and Bridger brought the last one to the pile. They had put their own people in the middle so they wouldn't have to see the faces. Moving the two boys was hard. Janice had been just about eaten from the waist up. Her face was unrecognizable but the two boys looked normal. Well normal for having large bite marks and a bullet hole in Jeremy's forehead. They put them on top of Janice and then Ray on top of that, the whole time pouring gasoline over the pile.

"You think we're using too much gas? I mean, not to burn, but do you think we might need the gas?" Charlie asked.

"Probably, but that bus back there holds about two hundred gallons and the gauge says over half full. We can spare a few." Bridger said. "We just don't need to make this a habit, so how about let's start trying to figure out how to survive a little while longer?"

"Sounds good to me."

Josh and Lori walked towards the creek. The sun was approaching its highest point and the cold morning had turned a little warmer. They still wore the same sweatshirts and jeans they had on yesterday. Lori pulled her sweatshirt over her head and tied it around her waist.

"So, what do you think they will decide?" she asked.

"I don't know. I think they may actually try to see if that guy is telling the truth. But even if he is, I don't want to go." He said.

"Why not?"

"I just think that if it is there, it's just the same as here. Hiding in the woods, waiting. I don't want to do that. I want to be out there, like my father was."

"Your father died because of that." She said.

"I know. I know." He looked down. She touched his shoulder. "But I still can't stay."

"I'll go with you." She said, looking up at him.

He kissed her. He didn't know why, but he did. She kissed him back. They stepped back from each other. She turned and stepped past a bush. Her foot felt something squish under it. She looked down and screamed. They had found Chris.

Raj and Tilly were trying to sort through the rubble of the burnt bus. They were hoping to find some food stores safe. So far they had not been lucky. Finally Tilly pushed one of the seats over and found a scorched cooler. She opened the lid and even though the outside was singed, the inside was still safe. They had stored canned goods in the coolers to save space. She reached in and pulled out a can of green beans and thrust it towards the sky in victory.
"Look what I found." She said, a screamed pierced the air. "Come on green beans aren't that bad."
"I think that was Lori." Raj said. "That way."
They hustled towards the sound of the scream and Lori came running past them.
"Wait, what is happening?" Tilly said, grabbing her as she went by.
"Back there, it's back there." Lori said, pulling away from her.
Raj walked a little further and saw Josh looking down on the ground. He followed his eyes down. Lying next to the bush was Chris. His arms were reached back over his head and below his chest was, nothing. His rib cage was open from the bottom and they could see his spine. His arms were not moving. The only movement was a methodical chomping of his teeth. Bridger and Charlie came through the trees to see the crowd gathered round.
"Was that Lori? The scream? Where is she?" Charlie asked Tilly. Tilly pointed back to camp.
"She's fine. Just a little shook, from this." She said, looking down at the thing on the ground.

She turned to look towards camp and saw Dottie and Amanda coming. She headed them off.

"You don't need to see." She said, taking Amanda's hand.

"Is it, is it Chris?" Amanda said, wide eyed. "Let me go. Let me go now." She said, pulling free. She turned a walked forward. She looked down.

"Oh my God. Ohhh" she got weak in the knees and Raj helped catch her as she started down. He put his arm around her and turned her back around. He and Dottie walked her back to camp.

The rest had gathered around the thing on the ground. Bridger pulled out his knife. He knelt down on the ground and put his hand on the things forehead. He brought the knife next to the temple and gently slid it in. Pop. It made him stand up quickly while the rest of them jumped back a little.

"It did it again." Bridger said, looking at Charlie.

"Did what?" Josh said. "That sound?"

"Yeah, we had another one do that." Charlie said.

"I had one do that too." Tilly added.

"Do they all do that?" Josh asked. "Why?"

"I don't know." Bridger said.

Bridger and Charlie took what was left of Chris back through the woods to the burn pile as the rest of them returned to camp. Charlie poured one more pour of gasoline on the pile and grabbed the stick they had wrapped to use as a torch. He tossed it onto the pile and they stood back as it caught fire. The breeze carried most of the smell away from camp but now and then a little wisp of wind would bring the sickening sweet smell of burning flesh drifting into camp. They all spent the rest of the evening trying to ignore it.

Empty Spaces

Abandoned Places

Kate and Evelyn joined Dottie and Amanda in the bus for the night. Charlie and Jennifer were settling into the front of the bus and Lori was helping Josh move his stuff from the bus to the truck. After the fire Dottie and Amanda along with Tilly and Raj were left homeless. Raj and Tilly decided they would use the SUV so Josh and Scott moved to the truck to give more room to Dottie and Amanda. Bridger moved Ed to the Harrison's car so he could keep an eye on him.

They had cleaned up the camp enough that they could sit and eat. They had scrounged through all the remains of the bus and had brought together everything they could find. Even with their reduced numbers they all knew they only had a couple of days left. They could stretch it but not much. Evelyn had spoke up at dinner.

"Guys, as far as shitty days go, this one is on top. I know we have things to think about." She looked at Bridger. "But we have lost a lot today. We can start again tomorrow."

After that they all found their own place to think about what they lost and what came next. Raj and Tilly knew that Bridger would be coming by to get them for watch soon so they found their way to the SUV for a few minutes alone. They opened the rear gate, and she sat down. He stood.

"I have not had a chance to really talk to you since yesterday." Raj started. "Are you sure you're ok? Is there something you're not telling me?"

"No. I'm fine. It shook me, I admit it. But after what happened last night, it seems like a long time ago. Besides, I dealt with it." Tilly said.

"You killed him. That's what you said. Is that dealing with it?"

"New rules, new world." Tilly said.

"What?"

"Just something that asshole said. I just decided he wasn't going to be the one making the rules." She said.

"And who gets to make the rules? You?" He asked.

"Maybe"

"Are you going to include me in that?" He asked.

"Only if you're very good to me." She said, smiling and wrapping her arms around him. It felt good to hold him. He had always understood her. Even when she didn't understand herself, Raj always knew what she needed. He knew how to make her feel strong and safe at the same time.

"I'll always be good to you." He said.

"I know" She kissed him.

Bridger knocked on the hood of the SUV. Raj walked around from the back. Tilly joined them.

"OK guys. I need you two to watch this place tonight. It's not going to be business as usual. You need to be good with this." Bridger said.

"What do you mean? Good with what?" Tilly asked.

"I need you two to step up because the others are wiped out. Plus I have to leave for a bit."

"What? Where are you going?" Raj asked.

"I plan to take that Ed guy and make him take me to this compound or bunker or whatever the hell it is. If he is telling the truth, it could be a huge stroke of luck."

"You're calling what his friend tried to do to me lucky?" Tilly said.

"That's not what I mean. I'm sorry about that but if this guy does have a stash of food and weapons, it could be a big deal. I particularly like the whole not starving to death part." Bridger said. "And he seems like he just wants to help."

"And you trust him." Raj asked.

"Nope. That's why I am going to take a little trip with him. Find out if it's bullshit or not."

"And if it is?"

"Well, I'll deal with it." Bridger said, matter of fact. "Listen, this was always JW's gig. He was the guy who knew what to pick up on. He could spot problems in the corners. But he's gone. The only way I know to do things is to ferret out the bad choices. This one is fifty fifty. And after last night, that's pretty damn good odds."

"So what do you need us to do?" Tilly asked.

"Stay awake and alert. Charlie said this guy told him it was just a mile or two up the creek from here. I should be back by midmorning. Just keep everyone busy until I get back. Make sure folks stay alert." Bridger said.

"Ok. We can do that." Raj said. He and Tilly grabbed their shotguns out of the back of the SUV and made sure they were loaded. They both carried 9MM pistols in holsters on their hips. They checked them too. Bridger had spent some time with them over the past week showing them how everything worked and how to keep it working. After doing the weapons check they both looked at each other. They giggled a little.

"Look at us. Regular Mr. and Mrs. Smith." Tilly said.

"Love you." Raj said.

"Love you too" Tilly smiled as she turned to walk into the woods.

Raj watched her fade into the darkness. They would cross paths on the other side of the camp. The rest of the night would be spent making these circles around the camp. They would stop and talk, occasionally sitting back-to-back watching the woods. Bridger waited an hour or so before getting Ed.

"Get up." Bridger said as he opened the door of the Harrison's car.

"What?" Ed said, leaning forward in the reclined seat.

"Get up. We're going for a walk."

"Damn man, please, no don't kill me..." Ed said, eyes wide.

"I ain't gonna kill you. I want you to take me to that place. Your place. Can you do that?"

"I think so. I don't know for sure but I know we followed that creek here. The creek backed up to his place just inside the woods. I think I can find the spot. Yeah. I can find it." Ed said.

"You sure?" Bridger said.

"Pretty damn sure. Besides, what choice do I have?" Ed said.

"None." Bridger reached down his hand. "Let's go."

Josh was lying in the bed of the truck looking up at the stars. Lori was lying next to him. Scott was sitting in the front seat trying to see if he could get anything on the radio. As he turned the dial he picked up a voice.
■■

■■■
This is the Emergency Broadcast System Zone 3 Refugee Camp Update #1.

Refugee Camp 12 Mile Marker 112 I-20 East Madison County - Closed
Refugee Camp 9 Mile Marker 93 I-20 West Jefferson County -Open
Refugee Camp 3 Mile Marker 64 I-10 Mobile County - Open
No other active refugee camps to report on at this time.
This is the Emergency Broadcast System Zone 3
▪▪

It repeated the same message twice more. Lori jumped out of the bed of the truck to listen.

"What does that mean?" Lori asked.

"I think it means that there is still some people out there, somewhere." Scott said.

"Not just somewhere. Jefferson County is near here. Zone 3. I wonder what that means." Josh said.

"Well the rest of the places were in Alabama. Maybe we're Zone 3 now. Doesn't have the same ring to it. Not saying I hate it, but..." Scott said.

"Will you shut up?" Josh said.

"Um. Ok." Scott said.

"I wonder how old that message is. I mean it could be just repeating something." Scott added.

"I said shut... ok. That may be a valid point." Josh conceded. "But it can't be more than a day or two old or we would have heard it. Someone would have heard it."

"Makes sense." Scott said.

"We can check it again in the morning." Lori said, climbing back into the bed of the truck. She didn't want to walk back to the bus. Not tonight. The shock of seeing Chris's head like she had was horrifying, but it was more than that. For the first time since this had all started she felt safe for just a second. When she kissed him.

Josh looked back at Lori as she climbed into the truck. He smiled at her and reached in and patted Scott on the shoulder.

"Get some sleep little brother." He said.
"You too."

       Bridger and Ed followed the creek for almost two miles when Ed stopped.
"Here. I think it was right here." Ed said.
"You said that once already." Bridger said. "Is this just bullshit?"
"No. No it's not bullshit. It was just, it's night, and I wasn't sure. This time I am sure. I remember that gnarled up old tree stump. That was just opposite where we came down the bank. So it's right up there." Ed said, pointing up the small bank towards the trees.
"Let's go." Bridger said.
       They climbed the small bank and walked a few yards into the trees. Bridger could see the camouflage netting hanging on the fence. It was one of those shapes that if you spend a good portion of your youth living under, you recognize right away. They both walked up to the fence.
"Ok. So how do we get in?" Bridger turned to Ed.
"This way." Ed started down the fence. "Shit"
       Ed stopped. One of the dead was standing just ahead. It was leaned against the fence with its head down. There was a small trench under its feet because it was still trying to walk. The fence was slightly bowed from the constant pressure against it but was holding strong. Bridger walked up behind it with his knife out. Pop. He let it slide down to the ground.
"Do they all make that sound?" Ed asked.
"I don't know. I think they might. Let's go."
       They followed the fence around to where it crossed what looked like a logging road. The fence had a gate in it. They approached the lock.
"You got the key." Bridger asked.

"No key. Kinda neat actually. They gate is a sham. If you break the lock it still won't open, look at the top." Ed said pointing up.

Bridger looked up and saw the top rail of the gate was actually a solid piece all the way across. The gate doors wouldn't open. He looked back at Ed. He was pulling a hidden pin through the post the gate was hooked too. He slid the pin out and lifted the whole post out of the ground. The fence swung open.

"Neat, huh?"

"Why do some shit like that?"

"Russell said it was so he could keep it locked up without having to keep up with the key."

"Russell? I guess that is asshole guy."

"Yeah, that was asshole guy." Ed said.

"Probably want to stick with calling him asshole guy." Bridger said.

"Point taken." Ed said. They walked through the gate and Ed set the post back in its hole.

Bridger looked around. He was standing in the middle of the logging trail and on either side of him was a row of old wooden buildings. Most of them were old shotgun shacks or dogtrot houses that had been brought from the surrounding area. There were two old barns and at the far end of the trail he could see a squat block building with a door. He started walking towards it looking in each building as he went.

"So you had never been here before you evacuated?" Bridger asked.

"No. He had told me about it a time or two but he never invited me to come see it. Until that day." Ed said.

"And what did he tell you when you got here?"

"Just that he might need some help to get the new world started and shit like that. I never took him too serious. I mean he had that, spent too many days in the sun, look about him, but he didn't seem all that dangerous. He seemed kind of excited about it. Like he was hoping something like this would happen. Crazy, huh?"

"Folks have been hoping for the end of days since days began. For some folks crazy is their religion." Bridger said.

"What's in there?" Bridger asked, pointing towards the two-story building with saloon painted on the front.

"Just what it says. Got a bunch of canned beer and a few cases of Jim Beam. Maybe a bottle or two of rum somewhere."

"Tequila?" Bridger asked.

"Probably." Ed said. "In Russ-er I mean, the assholes house." He pointed at the block building.

"Where did you stay?" Bridger asked.

"Right over there. That little place right there." He pointed across the street to a small shack.

"Where do you keep your food?"

"Most of the canned goods are in the barn, but there is food kind of stashed all over the place. Ammo too. Assholes plan."

"How big an area is fenced in?" Bridger asked.

"It's about two acres. Just a game fence but it is ten feet tall. Keeps the deer out. Kept the Draugers out so far too."

"Draugers?

"Yeah, Russ-asshole called em that. Said it was some Viking word for walking dead or some shit."

"This guy was a piece of work wasn't he?" Bridger said.

"Well, he did have a plan. I didn't" Ed said.

"Fair enough. Let's check out his room."

They approached the block building. The door was set in a frame. It had a pad lock on it but no door handle.

"Got a key for this?" Bridger asked.

"Well, he didn't know I did, but I saw him hide it. It's right here." Ed lifted the old metal chair leaning against the wall of the building. The key was under one of the legs. He put it in the lock.

They swung the door open and stepped inside. Bridger reached up and toggled on his flashlight. He swung it around the room. It was impressive. He had not seen this many centerfolds plastered on a wall since that awkward freshman year at Georgia and his roommates obsession with some girl in one of these magazines. He thought that one looked familiar, shining his light on the far wall. He could see a bed and a bunch of boxes on one wall. Another wall had an armory type gun rack with at least half a dozen rifles. He could see several pistols hanging on another rack and several dozen boxes of ammunition. He looked around the room one more time and something caught his eye. One of the walls wasn't block. It looked like paneling. He walked over to it. He knocked on it and it sounded hollow. He walked the length of the wall knocking on it and found a seam. He pressed against the paneling and it clicked. A door swung open. He swung his flashlight inside.

He saw a small room. Just really a walled off section about three feet wide the length of the wall. The end he was in had a chair with a small table. It faced the other end. At that end, attached to the block wall was a chain with a collar. Bridger walked up to it and looked at the collar. He followed the chain up to the wall.

"Find something to break this shit off this wall. Right fucking now." Bridger flashed at Ed.

Ed turned and swept his flashlight around the room and saw a crowbar leaning against one of the gun racks. He grabbed it and handed it to Bridger. He ripped the shackle from the wall and threw it down. He walked back out and closed the door.

"Yeah, he was definitely an asshole. And after seeing what he thought he was going to get away with, well, he got what he deserved." Bridger said. He handed the crow bar back to Ed.

Ed just nodded.

"So now what?" Ed asked.

"I needed to see. To see if you were telling the truth."

"I know. It's cool."

"Yeah, but are you cool? Can I trust you?" Bridger asked.

"Look man. I wasn't loyal to this guy, just like I ain't really loyal to you. I am loyal to staying alive. That's it. Right now you seem like a decent bet to help me in that so I am loyal to that."

"An honest man, huh?" Bridger said, raising his eyebrow.

"Nope. Just honest about that."

Bridger chuckled. He still wasn't sure, but he felt a little better. They went around the room taking a quick look at what they could. Stacks of conspiracy books in one corner and VHS porn tapes in the other.

"Did he have power for a TV?"

"Yeah there's a generator. He burnt through the gas. That was why we went out looking that day. For gas." Ed said.

"Where's the generator?"

"In the next building. He put it in there to keep the noise down. It's pretty quiet but in that building, you can't hear it unless you're standing right next to it. Dead never seemed to hear it."

"Let's take a look." Bridger said. He motioned for Ed to go ahead of him. Ed stepped out of the building and Bridger turned to look one more time.

"Yep. Gotta have a housecleaning before Tilly sees this." Bridger said under his breath as he walked out the door. He locked the padlock and put the key in his pocket. Ed didn't object. They found the generator and Bridger was satisfied. They started back to camp.

For just a While

Feel at Home again

Josh awoke with Lori lying next to him with her head against his chest. He looked down at her hair and ran his hands through it. It was dirty but soft. She rolled away and sat up yawning.

"Good morning." He said.

"Good morning to you." She said.

"Good morning to the both of you." Scott said.

They got out of the truck. The sun was just coming through the trees and they walked to the corral. The others were slowly making their way around camp. Josh grabbed the bundle of firewood they had gathered yesterday and began to rekindle the fire. By the time the rest of them gathered around he had boiled some water and dug out the last tin of instant coffee. Every one sat down as he poured out water for the ones who wanted it. Every one except Jennifer took some. Raj and Tilly walked up just in time.

"So last night, we heard something on the radio." Josh started.

"Yeah. It was some kind of emergency broadcast." Scott said.

"What, were they warning about the possibility of dead people coming back or something?" Tilly said.

"No. We're serious. It was new." Lori said.

"It said there was a Refugee center nearby." Josh said.

"Nearby where?" Charlie said.

"Jefferson County. Interstate 20 Mile marker 93." Scott said.

"Jefferson County? Really?" Charlie said.

"Not from here, hello" Tilly said waving her hand.

"Where is Jefferson County?"

"Well as the crow flies, that spot on I20 is about ten miles that way." Charlie said, pointing east.

"How far is it as the bus drives around dead and undead?" Tilly asked.

"A bit further." Charlie replied. "I would think."

"Where's Bridger?" Kate said over her cup.

"Um. He uh, he left." Raj said.

"Uh huh." Kate said. "Where did he go?"

"He took Ed and went to find or to see if that place is real." Raj stuttered.

"So he just decided to go and find out by himself. Without telling anyone?" Kate asked.

"He told us. He thought you could use the rest, and he knew we could keep watch." Tilly said. "So he did tell someone."

"Did he say when he should be back?" Evelyn asked.

"He said by mid morning. He said to just sit tight until then." Raj answered.

"Did y'all not hear what we just said?" Lori asked. "They said a refugee center. Nearby."

"Really. We should just go to there. Forget this other place." Josh said.

"But we don't know enough. When did you hear this broadcast?" Amanda asked.

"Last night." Scott answered.

"And nothing since then?" Charlie added.

"No. But we haven't been listening since we came over hear." Josh said.

"Ok. Scott you and I can go back over and listen on the truck and I'll see if I can find it on my weather radio too." Charlie said. "We can do that until Bridger gets back, anyway."

Scott and Charlie stood and walked back over to the front of the truck. They started listening. Josh stood and walked over to Kate.

"How are you doing this morning?" Josh asked, kneeling down next to her.

"I'm ok. I'm doing ok. How are you doing?" she asked.

"I guess I'm doing ok too." He said. "You need anything?"

"Nope. Just going to sit here with Evelyn and drink a little coffee flavored water."

"Ok. Raj asked me to take the next watch, so Lori and I are going to start walking."

"Be careful."

"I will"

Kate watched as Lori met Josh as he crossed across the corral. She turned to Evelyn.

"What do you make of that?" she asked.

"Well when boys and girls reach a certain age..." Evelyn started.

"Not that." She said, smiling.

"I know, I just wanted you to smile today. I think they are doing what we are all doing."

"What's that?"

"Figuring it out as they go." Evelyn said.

Bridger and Ed walked the logging road all the way back to the main road. It was a further this way but Bridger needed to be able to get the bus and the other cars over here so he needed to know where this logging road came out. He had already decided that he was going to try to get everyone to come over here. It wasn't perfect, but it was a hell of a lot better than what they had now. The fence could at least slow the infected down and the buildings would help keep off the cold. And winter is coming. After getting back to the main road he figured it was less than a mile to the turn off to the dirt road on JW's place. Pretty close. They started walking along the edge of the road.

"So you live around here somewhere?" Bridger asked.

"Not really. Up the road about twenty miles. Collier? Little town. Lived in my grandma's house. She been dead a few years. My momma run off with some guy before that. Never knew my pops." Ed blurted out, still carrying the crow bar over his shoulder.

"Well, at least you're getting to meet some new people." Bridger said.

"At least there's that." Ed said.

They rounded the next corner in silence. They could see several of the infected in the road in front of them. They were gathered around something in the middle of the road. All of them were on the ground. Bridger and Ed ducked down and watched for a minute to make sure there were not any more around. Most of the infected were knelt down over the main carcass, it looked like a deer, but a few had managed to pull off a leg and were off to the side of the main group. Bridger didn't want to shoot them. He was afraid of what the sound might attract.

"Let's go around." Ed said.

"Nope. Can't just hope they wander off the right way. We don't leave them for someone else to have to deal with."

"So what do you suggest?" Ed said. Bridger motioned for him to back up back around the bend in the road.

"Well, I suggest you giving me that crowbar for a minute." Bridger said.

"I won't have anything." Ed said.

Bridger looked at his rifle. He handed it to Ed.

"Don't shoot it. Unless I tell you too. Ok?"

"You trust me now?"

"Not really. But after this I might." Bridger said.

Ed handed over the crowbar and took the rifle. He looked it over. It was not like anything he sold at Wal-Mart, that was for sure. This one was heavier with a much heavier barrel. It was marked and scratched like an old tool. This wasn't some weekend plinker's gun, this gun had a history. He looked up at Bridger again. Bridger smiled at him. He took the crowbar and walked back around the bend in the road. He approached the first infected and didn't hesitate. He brought the crowbar down into the back of its head with such force that it exploded like a watermelon. The pop sounded like a firecracker. The rest turned from their feast.

"Well shit, that didn't go as planned." Bridger said to himself. He brought the crowbar back up and swung it like a bat into the closest one to him.

The crowbar struck the dead in the side of the head and ruptured its skull. It also broke the vertebra holding the head attached and the whole thing came off except for one ligament on the opposite side. The head flopped over to one side as the thing collapsed.

"Shit." Ed said, watching from a few yards behind.

Bridger swung the crowbar back around and connected with the forehead of the next infected. It split open. He flipped the crowbar in his hand so he was holding it like a cane. He shoved the end up under the chin of the next infected and drove it out the top of its skull. It twisted in his hand and he wasn't able to pull it straight back out. Another infected stumbled towards him and he dropped the crowbar and the dead still attached to it. He pulled his knife and drove it straight into the eye of the dead woman in front of him. He pulled it out and wheeled around and drove it into the eye of the dead man behind him. He reached down and grabbed the crowbar again, placing his foot on the face of the thing and pulling the crowbar back out of its chin. He flipped it again in his hand and swung one more time at the last of the infected, a small child, no more than a toddler. He never hesitated. Pop. Bridger stood breathing deeply. He was covered in blood and rot. He turned and walked back over to Ed.

"Damn dude." Ed said.

"I just needed to work some things out. Been a rough week at the office." Bridger said.

He took the rifle back and slung it over his shoulder. He stuck the end of the crowbar under his arm and drew it back out, wiping the big bits off. He handed it back to Ed.

Josh and Lori made their second circuit around the camp. They weren't straying too far from the center but they were still far enough away they couldn't be heard.

"I am not going to stay in these woods. I am just not doing it." Josh said.

"You know I feel that way too but how?" Lori asked. "How are we supposed to convince them to go to the refugee center?"

"I don't know. I am not sure that the refugee center is still there either." Josh said.

"But you said."

"I know. But it has been a while now and we really don't know how long it has been playing. It could be a few hours old or a few days. A few hours means it might be there, a few days might as well be a few years."

"So what are you saying?" Lori asked.

"I'm saying I might want to try going somewhere else."

"Where?"

"Home" Josh said.

"That's a lot further away."

"Yeah, but at least we know the area and we're not just wandering around the woods like cavemen."

"But won't there be more of those things?"

"I don't know. Maybe, maybe not. We could go look"

"We could." She said, smiling.

Josh and Lori walked back into camp since their shift was just about over. Scott and Charlie were due to go out next but they would wait until after lunch. The woods had been quiet for the day so far. Dottie and Amanda had spent most of the morning together in the bus trying to straighten things out. Raj and Tilly had rested as soon as Josh had taken over the watch. Kate and Evelyn were with Charlie, Scott and Jennifer in the corral when Bridger and Ed returned.

"What the hell happened to you?" Evelyn asked.

"Doing what I have too to get back to you." Bridger smiled, wiping his pants off.

"Save it."

"Did you find the place?" Charlie asked.

"Yep. Just what he said it was. Maybe a little better."

"Better?" Kate said.

"There's a rumor there is tequila." Bridger said.

"Of course." Kate smiled, remembering when JW had first introduced her to Bridger.

"So what now?" Josh asked.

"I guess we go." Evelyn said.

"You guess?" Josh said.

"Well, what else is there?" Evelyn asked.

"The refugee center." Lori said.

"We haven't heard anything else about a refugee center." Evelyn said.

"She's right Lori. Scott and I have been listening all morning. Nothing." Charlie said.

"Well how about going back to South Springs?" Josh asked.

"No. Absolutely not." Kate said. "We are not going back there. It is too far, and it is too dangerous."

"But we don't know that." Josh said.

"I said no, Josh. That's the end of it." Kate said. Josh didn't respond.

"Ok. Well now that is settled. We can leave as soon as we're ready." Bridger said.

"Today?" Jennifer asked.

"It's a mile or so down the road to where we will have to turn back into the woods and follow an old logging road. I am pretty sure the bus and the vehicles can all make it in. There was one really slick spot but I don't think it will be a problem. So yeah, today. We just need to get everything loaded and go."

Everyone began to leave the corral as though a spell had been broken. They each went about trying to make sure they could get everything loaded as quickly as possible.

Josh pulled Lori aside.

"Listen. We don't have a lot of time to decide. I think we should just go. On our own." Josh said.

"What?" Lori asked.

"Really. We can do this. I can stash a couple of guns in Janice's car already and I can get a couple more. If you can grab some food, it doesn't have to be much. I can hunt and fish if we need too."

"Ok."

"Really?"

"Sure. Ok." She said.

"Put everything in Janice's car. It has plenty of gas and she doesn't need it anymore. Sorry that was..." Josh paused.

"I know what you mean, it's ok." Lori said, reaching out and touching his arm.

"Ok meet me at Janice's car in twenty minutes" Josh said.

"Ok."

Evelyn and Kate were standing at the rear of the bus helping load the few things remaining onto it. Raj and Tilly had finished loading the SUV and most everyone was gathered back in the corral. Kate watched as Josh walked to Janice's car for the third time in the last ten minutes.

"Do you think maybe he is making a rational decision?" Evelyn asked.

"Evelyn, his father just died. I am pretty sure he is not making anything close to a rational decision." Kate said.

"Well, at least hear him out. He deserves that. His father just died." Evelyn said. Kate nodded.

Josh glanced at his mother as she started walking towards him. He stopped. He knew he was caught. He didn't know how she did it, but she always did.

"So, were you going to sneak off without saying anything?" Kate asked.

"I didn't want to." Josh said.

"Did you feel like you had too?"

"Maybe. I guess so, yes." Josh said.

"Maybe you did. But I know I can't stop you. Your father reminded me of that not too long ago. But I need to know why? Why are you leaving? Is it because of what happened? To your father?"

"No. Not because of it. Not really. I need to not be hiding. I don't know how to explain it." Josh said.

"Josh, you don't need to. It is the same way your father felt. Inside."

"But he brought us out here to hide." Josh said.

"Yes. He brought you and me and Scott and everyone else out here to hide. But he couldn't hide. He brought us here so he could feel we were safe. He knew he had to take us somewhere that he thought we would be safe, without him. Because he knew he would go out there again. He knew he had too. You are more like him than you will ever know." Kate said. She was crying.

"Why are you crying mom?" Scott asked. Josh hadn't seen him walking up behind him.

"Because Josh is leaving. He and Lori are leaving." She said this last part loud enough for most of the rest to hear. They all gathered around.

"Leaving?" Charlie said. "No one's leaving."

"Yes I am. We are." Lori said.

"Are you crazy?" Charlie asked.

"No Charlie. They're not crazy. Not any crazier than the rest of us. They have as much a chance to make it as we do. I wish they wouldn't go but it's not up to me. Or you. It's up to them." Kate said. "I hate it. I really do, but I get it."

"I don't." Scott said. "Why do you want to go? You shouldn't want to go?"

"I have too." Josh said.

"That's bullshit. You don't have to do anything."

"You'll understand one day." Josh said.

"That's bullshit too." Scott said.

"I love you little brother." Josh said. He hugged him.

"Don't go" Scott said.

"I love you" Josh said.

"I love you too." Scott said. They hugged again.

Josh and Lori said their goodbyes to everyone. Evelyn had given them some food supplies. Enough to last a few days at least. Bridger had told Josh how to find the logging road in case they changed their mind when they got there. Or whenever.

Kate leaned in the window with tears in her eyes. Josh was fighting back his own. Lori hugged Jennifer out of the other window.

"Be careful. I love you." Kate said.

"We will. I love you too. We'll see each other again. I know that for sure." Josh said.

"I know. Me too." Kate said. He touched her hand as he pulled away.

216

They watched until they couldn't see them through the trees any more. They all looked around. This wide spot in the road, where their friends and family lived and died, had become home. They all loaded into their vehicles. Dottie and Amanda on the bus with Kate, Evelyn and Scott. Raj and Tilly in the SUV. Scott and Charlie driving the Harrison's car and Bridger and Ed leading the way in JW's truck. They pulled back down the dirt road they had driven two weeks ago to escape one version of hell. They pulled back out onto the asphalt past the mass of dead that had been left by Bridger.

They pulled back off the asphalt just down the road and made their way deep into the woods. The one spot Bridger had seen turned out to be nothing. It was the three he didn't notice that slowed them down but not so much so that they weren't pulling through the gate of the compound just as the sun began setting in the sky. They pulled the gate back shut, and they all walked up to the fence. They couldn't see anything in the woods. They couldn't hear anything in the woods. But they could all feel the fence under their fingers. They all felt just a little safer than they did this morning. It might not be perfect, but things seemed better.

Josh and Lori passed the old post office without noticing it at all. The sun was setting and the glare on the dirty windshield made seeing anything beyond the road difficult. He used the windshield washer until the fluid was gone and it was a little better. The problem was the wiper blades were worn out. Things you never think about until it's raining, or it's the apocalypse. Josh smiled.

"What?" Lori said, catching his smile.

"Something my mom said, about me being more like my dad than I think. Well I just heard his voice tell a joke in my head."
"Was it funny?"
"A little"

The Hard Day

Book 3

The Marionette Zombie Series

SB Poe

They can take our Bones

Lori stood looking at the door as her father walked into the living room. She thought she heard someone knocking but her father didn't seem to hear it so she ignored it.

"Honey, can you come in here and help me with this?" Elaine Jenkins called from the kitchen.

"Of course. Heaven knows you need it." Gary Jenkins said.

"Oh, stop it you big goof." Elaine sang out.

"Did I miss something?" Lori asked.

"What do you mean, honey?" Gary asked his daughter.

"I don't know. It just feels like I missed something. Like something happened and it... I don't know. It's hard to explain."

"Maybe you stayed up too late last night studying." Elaine said as she walked into the living room wearing an apron and carrying a big plate of waffles and bacon.

"I am pretty sure that wasn't it. But I don't..." Lori heard the knocking again, very softly.

"You don't what honey?" Gary asked.

"Do you hear that?" Lori asked.

"Hear what?" Elaine said.

"Nothing, never mind." Lori said.

"Great. Are you ready to eat?" Gary asked, clapping his hands together.

"I present breakfast." Elaine said, standing back from the table, waving over it like a game show hostesses presenting a new car.

The knock came again. This time it was louder. She was sure they had heard it. She looked at them but they were both standing there with silly grins on their faces. Knock, knock. She looked back at the door. "Do you not hear that?" Lori asked, looking at her parents again. They just smiled.

She turned and reached for the knob but missed. She looked down again and grabbed for the knob (handle). She felt something grab her arm.

"What are you doing?" Josh asked, holding her wrist.

It took her another second to wake up. She looked around. It was still dark outside, but the first signs of gray were starting to show. She was still reclined in the passenger's seat of Janice's car and they were still on this side of the bridge. Knock, knock. The number of infected that had been gathered outside the car since late last night had dropped to just one. And it was still knocking on the window.

"What time is it?" Lori asked.

"Almost five." Josh said. "You were reaching for the door."

"Yeah, weird dream. So what do you want to do today?" She said smiling and sitting up. Her movement excited the infected outside, and it put its face against the window and chomped its teeth. She instinctively jerked away from it and her head hit Josh in the chin.

"Ok. That hurt." Josh said rubbing his jaw.

"Sorry." She giggled.

"Not that funny." Josh said.

"I know. I'm sorry. I did the same thing to Jennifer when she said something about my parents" she said, the smile fading from her face as she thought about the dream.

"Cross that bridge." Josh said.

"Huh?" Lori asked.

"You asked me what I wanted to do today. I want to cross that bridge." He pointed at the two-lane bridge that would take them back into South Springs.

"Are we really going to try?" Lori asked.

Last night they had approached the bridge just before the sun went down. A few infected were wandering on it. More infected had been sitting or lying on the bridge, and when they started across it quickly became a small crowd. They had to back up. The crowd followed. Josh turned around and drove back up the hill away from the bridge and stopped. Some of the crowd kept coming but most lost interest when he turned off the car.

"I have been watching the crowd for a few hours now. Most of them wandered off towards the interstate. Just a few went back onto the bridge. I think we can make it now." Josh said.

"And if not." She asked.

"If we can't get across, we'll come back here and try something else. But I think we can make it."

"If we do make it, then what."

"I figured we would just stay on this road for a little while. We can make our way to your house but I don't think we should go straight through town." Josh said.

"I know a shortcut. If you turn left at the church, you can cut through the college. That might not be so bad." Lori said.

"We'll see. First let's get across this bridge." Josh said.

He started the car. The infected standing outside started knocking its head against the glass again. Lori turned her face towards it and looked up, smiling. She raised her middle finger.

"See ya, dickhead." She said. They pulled towards the bridge.

Leave somehow

Bridger was making his way around the perimeter of the fence for the fourth time. He thought to himself that Ed probably needed to refigure his two-acre estimate. He counted his steps the second time around and by his quick calculation, the fence enclosed closer to five acres and he had not found anything wrong with it at all. It was ten feet tall with vertical posts every six feet. It had two horizontal cross members with a top rail. It was pretty damn sturdy. It could probably hold up well unless a bunch of them came at the same spot.

He made his way back to the main barn. It was closest to the gate. Everyone had settled on staying in one building for the night. Bridger had spent the night on watch. He let everyone sleep. He knew he would not be sleeping for a day or two, anyway. He remembered the days that he and JW had spent together in far away places. They knew when sleep wasn't going to be coming soon. They had learned, like so many others, how to turn off the need for it for a while. Eventually it will catch up to you but you can fight it if you have to and he thought for the next few days he would have to. He needed to do that for JW. He owed him that. "Knock knock." Bridger said, tapping on the side of the barn as he walked through the door.

The floor of the barn was a scatter of sleeping bags and blankets. They had unloaded most of the things from the bus and set it all in one corner. After that they had grabbed whatever piece of dirt they could and slept. Some slept. Some spent the night starring at the darkness. Some spent it letting tears rolls down their cheeks. But some slept.

"I said knock knock." Bridger said again.

"Yeah, we were ignoring you." Tilly said.

"I appreciate that, I really do." Bridger said.

"I would not worry too much, she does it to me quite regularly." Raj said, earning an elbow from Tilly.

"Is it morning already?" Ed said, crawling from under a blanket piled against the wall.

"Pretty close." Bridger said. "Why didn't you sleep in your shack?"

"Well no one gave me the ok, and I didn't want this one to shoot me for trying to escape." Ed said, nodding towards Tilly.

"I would have." She said.

"So here I am." Ed said.

"Ok. I mean you have the ok. You can go back to your building." Bridger said.

"Hold on. Really?" Tilly said.

"Why not?" Bridger asked.

"Because we don't know him. How can we trust him?" Tilly said.

"You didn't know me, and yet here you are." Bridger raised an eyebrow.

"It's on you." Tilly said.

"Thanks." Ed said, looking at Bridger.

"Don't thank me, thank her. If she had said no, you would have been hogtied." Bridger said.

"Wait, what?" Tilly said.

"Nope, too late. No take backs." Bridger said smiling.

"What he said." Ed smiled.

Ed stood and made his way out of the barn and to his shack. Tilly and Raj walked out shortly after with Bridger in tow. The rest were still waiting for actual light to break the morning darkness instead of this predawn gray.

"The saloon seems to be the main storage area for food. There is a barbecue pit out the back door and there is a wood-burning stove." Bridger said. "We should start by doing a basic search. Each building. Ed said there might be food and ammo stashed around. We need to find it and put it together."

"Why?" Raj asked.

"Well for one, we just need to see how much we have."

"Of food or ammo?" Tilly asked.

"Both."

"You want us to bring it all to the saloon?" Raj asked.

"For now." Bridger said. "We'll divide it between the saloon and the Alamo."

"The what?" Tilly asked.

"The Alamo. I am officially calling the block building the Alamo. I am going to clean it out and put food in it." Bridger said.

"What's in it now?" Tilly asked.

"Just trash. Mostly." He said.

"Do you need us to help?" Raj asked.

"Nope. I'll grab Ed."

"So just bring everything to the saloon for now?" Raj asked again.

"Yep." Bridger said.

"Bring what where?" Evelyn said, walking out of the barn.

"Oh, we were just going to start checking each of these buildings for beans and bullets. Ed says the asshole stashed shit around like crazy asshole's do and for some reason Bridger here doesn't want us to see what's in that brick building." Tilly said pointing her thumb back over her shoulder.

"Why not?" Evelyn asked.

"Ask him." Tilly said.

"Bridger?" Evelyn said.

"Look, it's nothing. Just some pinups and shit. I just wanted to have a chance to get it out of there. We need that place, this place. It would just be easier."

"You think keeping me from seeing some porn this prick had is going to make things easier. Oh you mean easier for you." Tilly said.

"No really, don't hold it back. Tell me how you really feel." Bridger said, smiling.

"I just did." Tilly said, not smiling.

"Well ok. I would extract myself from this conversation but I don't have anywhere to go." Evelyn said.

"You can go with me." Bridger said. "We'll head over to the saloon and see if we can get something for breakfast for everyone. After that we'll get to work. Right Tilly?"

"Right. I just don't want you thinking you need to do whatever it was you thought you were doing." Tilly said.

"Fair enough." Bridger said.

Bridger and Evelyn made their way to the saloon. The building was an old general store that had been gutted. A wooden bar with a cracked mirror stood against one wall. The tables and chairs were standard southern convenience store/burger joint. All mismatched metal and wood gathered together in a menagerie of furniture. There were even a few old metal-framed plastic folding chairs thrown in for good measure. The floor was covered in cheap linoleum that gave the whole place a musty plastic smell. There were two windows on either side of the screen door they came through. The wooden door was permanently propped open against the wall. They walked inside.

"So all the food is supposed to be in here?" Evelyn asked.

"Half maybe. Ed says the other barn, the one at the other end of the row, has food in it too." Bridger said.

"So where is it?" Evelyn asked, scanning the room.

They both walked around the bar and saw all the liquor lined up below eye level. Evelyn reached down and grabbed a bottle.

"Jack, so glad to see you survived the end of the world. We're gonna need you." Evelyn said.

"I hope his cousin Jose' made it. Ed said there was beer too. But I don't see any beer."

"Do we need to get Ed?" Evelyn asked.

"Not yet. We can look around. How is Kate doing?" Bridger asked.

"As well as can be expected."

"Yeah, ok. But I don't know what that means."

"She's holding up, I think."

"What do you mean?"

"Well, it just struck me as odd how she handled Josh leaving. I thought she would be a little more hysterical. I would have been, I guess. But anyway, I asked her about it last night, just said something like she handled it well. And she just shut down. Said she didn't want to talk about it any more."

"You found that odd?" Bridger said.

"Well, I don't know. I don't know her that well and she had been talking up until I said something about Josh."

"You were neighbors, what do you mean you don't know her too well?

"We were street neighbors, you know, the kind that live next door but the only conversation is just saying 'hey' in the street."

"Gotcha. So you didn't know JW either."

"Less."

"So you never heard the story of how they met?" Bridger asked.

"Nope."

"Fairy tale stuff." Bridger said.

"Really?"

"I shit you not. Right out of some Meg Ryan movie."

Evelyn smiled at that. Her and Bridger were close enough in age they got some of the same references. This one didn't miss the mark. They opened the door beside the bar and went into the kitchen. They found the beer. And the food.

"Shit" Bridger said.

"What?" Evelyn asked.

"MRE's. The only thing in the world that would make me rethink the downside of starving to death. And this shithead bought them by the pallet." Bridger said, looking at the MRE boxes stacked against the wall.

"That bad?"

"The really bad part is that I have eaten enough of these to know how to make them actually taste good."

"That's good. You can be the chef. You just need to see the silver lining." Evelyn said.

Bridger smiled.

They counted 56 cases of MRE's. They also found boxes of canned meats along with canned fruits and vegetables. One corner was stacked floor to ceiling with beer cases and the other corner was stacked with dried beans and rice.

"This asshole was thorough, I'll say that."

"This asshole got what he deserved." Evelyn said coldly. "You were there. Charlie told me some of it but I think he might have been glossing over some of it to keep the heat off Ed. What happened out there?"

"It was pretty bad. Charlie, Lori, Jennifer and I were getting water, and I thought I heard a man's voice. It said something like 'Look what I found'. We went towards where Tilly had gone to use the bathroom and when we stepped around a big honeysuckle vine, there they were. He was on top of her. Her pants were down and he was trying to get his down. Charlie walked up to the other guy, Ed, and just put his gun against his back and took the gun from him. As he did that I walked up behind the asshole, Russell is the name Ed kept using, and I made him get up."

"You made him get up?"

"Well I fired a shot over his head and he got the message."

"Effective. What did he do?" Bridger asked.

"Well he got up and tried to talk his way out of it. He wanted us to let him and Ed go and just forget the whole thing. He said there wasn't anything we could do about it anyway."

"Then what happened?" Bridger asked.

"Then I took a shotgun and blew the son of a bitch's head off." Tilly said, walking through the kitchen door with a box in her hands. She looked over at the stove and saw the frying pan with leftover scrambled eggs. "And this was his last meal." She said, tossing the frying pan against the wall. "I know, because I smelled the eggs on his breath. I could also smell the whiskey from that bottle out there on the bar. Go ahead. Ask me what else. Did I feel his beard against my face? Yes. Did it hurt when he punched me in the back of the head? Yes. Was I angry when I pulled that trigger? Yes." Tilly stood defiant. "Was I glad I did it? You bet your fucking ass."

"Listen, I" Bridger started.

229

"No, you listen. You have been dancing around this whole thing. Trying in some fucked up way to protect my feelings or some shit. Stop. I don't need you to look out for my feelings." She said.

"I just wanted to know what happened. Sorry." Bridger conceded.

"Well now you know." Tilly said, as she turned and walked back out of the kitchen.

"Ok. That was fun." Evelyn said.

"Yeah, except it wasn't. No matter how bad the other guy deserved it, it still leaves a mark. We need to keep an eye on this."

"How?" Evelyn asked.

"Just let her vent for now. Sometimes that's all it takes. We'll see." Bridger said.

They walked out of the kitchen bringing a case of MRE's with them. They headed back to the barn.

"So, what now?" Evelyn said.

"Not sure. We all need to talk this over. Together. I don't want people to think I have a plan. Because I don't." Bridger said.

"Well, you convinced everyone to come to this place."

"Let's see, fence or no fence. After the last two days not really a tough sell job." Bridger said.

"Yeah." Evelyn said, smiling.

Nothing has changed

Except the wind and the rain

Josh maneuvered across the bridge. A few cars stood sentry marking the last flailing efforts of their occupants to reach safety. Some of those occupants were now rotting away and becoming part of the bridge itself. He tried to avoid them. He was mostly successful. The one infected they encountered had failed to hear their approach and rose as they passed by. It shuffled a few steps and collapsed again. They drove on.

As the car passed the school Lori could see the front entrance. The fallen leaves mixed with bits of paper and the wind gathered it all against the doors. More paper and leaves blew across the parking lot and collected on the windshields of the abandoned cars. The cars were streaked with dirt and rain and Lori wondered if they would ever move again. The street in front of them was peppered with more leaves and trash. Occasionally they would see overturned garbage carts with the contents adding to the collage of finality. Everywhere they looked they saw disarray. Cars driven into yards, doors of homes standing open, broken windows with curtains billowing in the breeze. And paper. Everywhere paper. All carried on the wind and deposited where it fell, waiting for the next gust to carry it along on its journey to nowhere.

They also noticed the smell. It wasn't the same smell they had encountered in the woods. This wasn't infected. This was decay. The smell hung in the air. Even with a breeze it just became recycled from stale stench to fresh stench. They approached the intersection where the church stood.

"Do you want to try the shortcut?" Lori asked.

"We will. But I have to see." Josh said.

"See what?"

"My house. It's just another mile or so from here. I need to."

"Ok." Lori said. Josh was expecting some resistance. She just smiled.

"Ok." Josh said.

They came to the corner where the church stood. The doors were still standing open. Ahead they saw a stroller resting overturned against the curb. A car was halfway up the steps to the church and a decomposing body pierced the windshield. Lori could see the dirt covered pink bundle in the street as they passed by. It wasn't moving. She looked back at the impaled body sticking out of the car windshield and saw the arms start to move. She looked away. A few infected wandered out of the church as they drove past. They could still see the signs painted on the houses they had driven by weeks ago. Save us. Help us. Living inside. Each one a desperate call for help that never came.

He approached the four-way stop. It had been almost a month since they had left this spot behind. He turned to the right, and they started the mile long journey through his old neighborhood to his house. "There's Jennifer's house." Lori said pointing to the brick house on the left. The bodies they had stepped over to get on the buses lay rotting in the yard.

Josh noticed that most of the houses they passed had their front doors standing open. The others had windows smashed out and all of them had shit scattered across the front yard. His first thought was looters but realized at the end of the world, we all become looters. He drove on.

He knew what the dark shape in the road was before he saw it. He knew it would still be there. The deputy. Rotting away. This was where it had become real. For him and his father. His father may have saved him but what if he hadn't? What if this body on the ground wasn't infected? If his father hadn't fired that shot maybe he would be here now? Butterfly wings. He could see the deputy's vehicle that JW had first commandeered and then abandoned. He came to the end of the street and took the angled turn down the hill. The lower lying cul-de-sac had been a depository for all the leaves and paper blowing down the street. They navigated the car through the sea of leaves.

"Which one is yours?" Lori asked.

"That one, on the right." Josh said pointing to his home.

He could see the bay window and the garage. The door was still up. The driveway was covered in leaves and paper, as was most of the front porch. A fresh gust of wind scattered more along the yard. They parked the car in the middle of the street.

"We'll just go in for a quick look around. See if there is anything we need. Then we go to your house." Josh said, reaching in and grabbing one of the shotguns.

"Ok." Lori said, putting on an empty backpack and grabbing the other shotgun.

He quietly closed the door, and she mimicked him. They walked into the garage. The door to his father's small storage room was open. The gun safe was unlocked, so he looked inside. It was empty except for two small pieces of metal hanging from a small beaded metal chain suspended from a storage hook. It was his father's dog tags.

Toles John Walker

01March1969

B NEG

XXX-XXX-4356

Baptist

He read the punched metal letters through misty eyes. He hung them around his neck.

"I need these." He said, mainly to himself.

He turned and went to the kitchen door. Lori followed. He turned the knob and swung the door open. He stuck his head in and tapped on the wall. He waited. He couldn't hear anything. He cautiously stepped inside.

"Well close the door behind you." A female voice called from the living room. He heard someone walking around the corner.

"Who the hell are you?" A guy a little older than Josh said as he came around the doorframe.

Josh turned, inadvertently turning the shotgun with him.

"Hey, hey it's cool." The guy said, putting his hands up.

"What the hell?" the girl said as she ran into the back of the guy with his hands up.

"Who are you?" Josh asked. Making a demonstration of lowering the gun.

"I asked first."

"This is my house." Josh said.

"No it isn't." the guy said. "We been here like all night and ain't seen you once."

"I been busy." Josh said.

"Hey, he does kind of look like the guy in that picture." The girl said.

"What picture?" the guy asked.

"You know. The one on the mantle you turned down because you said it gave you the creeps." She said.

"Yeah, he kinda does." He said, squinting his eyes at Josh.

"What the hell? Is this a joke?" Josh asked.

"Yeah, we planned this whole Marionette thing with dead bodies and walking corpses just to punk you. Gotcha." The girl said winking with a tilt of her hip and pointing both index fingers at Josh.

Lori laughed in spite of herself. So suddenly it surprised even her. It surprised the others more. The girl leaned around the guy and raised her eyebrows at Lori.

"You ok there honey?" the girl asked.

"Yes. Sorry." Lori said, covering her smile.

"Listen. What the hell? Who are you people?" Josh asked again, a bit more agitated.

"I'm Devin and this is Jahda," the guy said first pointing to himself then to the girl.

"We are just trying to make it man, nothing more. We didn't know that this home still had folks in it."

"Well now you do." Josh said.

"Yeah, but the thing is, we can't leave. Not yet." Devin said.

"Why?" Josh asked.

"We're waiting on someone." Jahda said.

"Who?" Lori said.

"Us"

Josh looked back through the open door and saw a man in a baseball cap with a gray beard and a girl about ten or twelve years old. The girl had a rifle slung over her back and the man had a quiver on his back holding a baseball bat. Josh had to do a double take, but it was definitely a baseball bat. They were carrying a large cooler, one on each end.

"I'm Martin. This is Ham. My granddaughter."

"Ham?" Lori asked.

"Oh. Katie. But we call her Ham." Martin said.

"Katie? That's my mother's name." Josh said, nodding at the girl.

"Who are you?" Ham asked.

"Apparently the homeowner." Jahda said.

"Um. Ok." Martin said nervously eyeing Josh's shotgun.

Josh saw his eyes and calmly set the shotgun against the wall.

"Look, it's cool. We all have to..." Josh started.

His eyes widened as the first of the infected came past the trees blocking the view up the road and started walking down the driveway. He reached back down for the shotgun as Martin turned to look behind him. He quickly looked back at Josh.

"No. There are just a few. They have been following us for a while. I thought they would stop when we came down the hill but I guess not." He set down the end of the cooler he was carrying and drew the baseball bat from the homemade quiver on his back.

Devin stepped past Lori drawing out his machete. They both met the infected halfway down the driveway. Martin came to the first one. A woman. Her clothing was torn and dirty but her face was almost normal. One of her legs had a large wound that was seeping blood and puss. She would stumble when she put weight on it, not quite falling but slowing down her advance dramatically. She lunged as Martin approached and her leg gave way. When she paused Martin brought the bat down on her head. Pop.

Devin went past them and took the machete and drove it, tip first, through the eye of the next infected. Pop. He pulled it out and side stepped the next infected, bypassing it. It turned. As it did Martin brought the bat down on the back of its head. Pop. Devin meanwhile was doing the eye poke thing to the next infected. Pop.

The last one came down the driveway. Its skin was blackened but not by fire. It was almost putrefied. The pieces of flesh hung loose against the muscle below. The stomach was bloated and black beneath ribs so taut against the chest some were peaking through, bright against the black rotted flesh trying to stay together. It would take a labored step or two and then stop, trying to maintain its fight against gravity. Then it would take another few steps. Its face appeared to be looking down but as it got closer Lori realized that its face was ripping apart and sliding towards the ground. Its opaque eyes were partially obscured by the brow that was being pulled down. It turned towards Devin. Martin walked up and delivered two quick blows to the back of its head. Pop.

Devin walked to the end of the driveway and looked back up the hill. He didn't see any more infected. He joined Martin who paused to examine the first infected he had popped. The woman. Martin was looking down at her as Josh and Lori walked up.

"This is the freshest one." Martin said to Devin.

"And she's pretty rotten." Devin agreed.

"Freshest?" Josh asked.

"Well, some of these are..." Martin started.

"You think we can do this behind some walls?" Jahda said.

"Sure. If our friend here doesn't mind." Martin said, motioning to Josh.

"Why me?" Josh asked.

"Well, it's your house." Martin said. They walked in through the garage and closed the kitchen door.

Martin and Ham sat the cooler down on the kitchen floor and opened it up. Inside were a few bottles of water and a couple of large cans. There was a small satchel in there too and Ham pulled it out. She reached inside and produced a can opener and grabbed one of the cans. Devin grabbed a couple of water bottles and they all walked into the living room.

Josh sat down in his father's recliner and Lori sat down on the floor next to him. Ham sat the can down on the coffee table. She knelt down beside it and started opening it. Devin handed one of the bottles to Martin who passed it, unopened to Jahda. Devin and Jahda sat on the couch. Martin stood.

"So, where are y'all from?" Josh finally asked.

"We're from Willow Haven." Martin said.

"Where's Willow Haven?" Lori said.

"South of Talladega, over by the Georgia line." Devin said.

"How did you end up here?" Lori asked.

"We started out heading towards the big shelter in Atlanta. We were just about there too." Jahda said

"You could see the sky get bright and then this rumbling sound came. Like thunder but close to the ground. It was bad." Ham said.

"The military bombed the city. We were on the interstate about twenty miles away." Martin said.

"We heard that on the radio. Didn't know it was true, for sure."

"It's true." Jahda said.

"As soon as the bombs finished dropping everyone fled like roaches when the light comes on. Tires squealing, engines revving and smoke flying." Devin said.

"Cars wrecking, lanes blocking." Jahda added.

"Yeah, we couldn't go anywhere fast." Devin said.

"It was scary." Ham said as she gently removed the lid from the can. Josh stood and walked to the kitchen and grabbed four bowls and four spoons.

He looked in the drawer and thought about the last meal they had eaten here as a family. His father had eaten eight pieces of bacon. They had been cleaning out the fridge after the power went out. He brought the dishes into the living room.

"None for you?" Jahda asked as he sat the bowls in front of each of them.

"No. We have our own food."

"Ridiculous. Have some peaches." Martin said.

Josh stood and retrieved two more bowls. Ham spooned peaches into each bowl.

"So then what?" Lori said.

"Well. After folks finally calmed down some people moved some wrecked cars, and we were able to exit off."

"Where did you go?" Josh asked.

"Well we wanted to go to some military place like Ft. Benning or maybe Ft. Stewart over by the coast but didn't go." Devin said.

"Why not?"

"Couldn't. Every time we got going on any road there'd be a wreck we couldn't get around or a big bunch of stringers." Ham said.

"Stringers?" Josh asked.

"She calls them stringers. Like a Marionette." Martin said mimicking a puppeteer.

"Oh, ok." Josh said.

"So we just kind of followed the path of least resistance and it took us west." Martin said.

"You've been on the road this whole time?" Josh asked.

"It's been almost a month since we heard about Atlanta being bombed. You've survived this whole time traveling from place to place?"

"We left Willow Haven with twelve people. Some didn't make it." Jahda said.

"What about you guys?" Martin asked. "You said this is your house, and I ain't doubting you, but you were gone. Where?"

"The woods. We were in the woods." Josh said.

"Just the two of ya?" Ham asked.

"Not just us. We had eighteen folks. My dad got us out of town and to our land near Berry." Josh said.

"Eighteen. What did you use, a bus?" Jahda said, laughing.

"Two actually. They took them from the school and got everyone to safety." Lori said, looking up and squeezing Josh's hand.

"Really?" Devin said, sitting up on the couch.

"Yep. My dad, my mom, my brother and I took the buses. First, we used them to block the street out there and when it started getting bad, we used them to evacuate." Josh said.

"You do this too?" Martin asked, placing his hand on the doors Josh and his family had had used to board up the windows that first night. Josh nodded.

"You had eighteen people in this house?" Devin asked.

"No. We picked some up on the way out of the neighborhood. Lori was one of them. Mrs. Collins from across the street was here and my dad's old army buddy showed up right before we left and he was carrying a couple of people he had, I guess rescued." Josh said.

"The rest followed us on the way out of town."

"And when was this?" Martin asked.

"Weeks ago. We left pretty quick." Josh said.

"Why did you come back?" Martin asked.

Josh looked down at Lori. She squeezed his hand and spoke.

"Things happened. Some of us didn't make it either."

They all just sat there for a minute and ate their peaches.

"Anyway. How did you end up coming here? To South Springs." Josh finally asked.

"Well, we've been kind of working our way generally west. Hoping to find somewhere safe. Devin had been a student at the college here a few years ago so we just headed this way. We were looking to get across the river when we found this place."

"Why cross the river?" Lori asked.

"No reason. Just next thing on the map." Martin said.

"That's it? Just the next thing?" Lori asked.

"For the last few days it has been." Jahda said.

"We've kind of been just trying to get our bearings since..." Martin paused.

"Since what?" Josh asked.

We come a long road

Still got miles to go

Martin had finished siphoning the gas out of the tractor. He knew the diesel wouldn't work for the cars but it worked great to help get a fire going. He started walking back across the field again. Ham climbed down from the tractor seat and fell in beside him. He would never regret teaching her to hunt and fish just like she was a boy even if the world hadn't fallen apart. He was thankful for it now. It taught her to be quiet and being quiet was sometimes the difference between making it or not.

His oldest daughter had shown up with her when she was just a few months old. The next morning his daughter was gone, but Katie stayed. His wife, Abbie had nicknamed her Ham. Abbie died a few years ago when Ham was just about nine. Since then it had just been them. She was very outgoing growing up and he took her everywhere with him even before his wife died. The last few weeks had been one long nightmare but Ham had handled it. She was used to the woods, and she wasn't afraid of the dark. She knew how to shoot and knew it was ok to shoot the stringers if you had too. They were dangerous. And not people.

"So you think we can find somewhere to fish?" Ham asked.

"I don't know. We'll check the map and see if there is anything nearby." Martin said.

"Ok, Opa." Ham said.

"Opa?" Martin said. "Is that the Italian one or Swahili?"

"German." Ham had learned ten different ways to say grandfather and used all of them. But when it mattered she had always called him Martin. He didn't know why but whenever she got hurt or scared, she always called him by his name.

They walked up to the campsite. Devin and Hector had the hood up of Hector's car. Hector poured water into the radiator to make sure it was topped off. They had been driving a few miles, stopping and letting it cool off for a while then adding water to it. They were winding their way west with no real destination in mind. Right now moving just felt safer.

"So what's the verdict?" Martin asked patting Devin on the back.

"Well, it runs. And I don't think we have much option, but we have to find another car." Hector said.

"We need to get off these back roads. No houses, no cars, no nothing." Jahda said.

"No stringers." Ham said.

"Well fewer stringers but Hector's right." Martin said. "We need to find another car. Everyone can't ride in the back of my truck."

Since they escaped the panic outside of Atlanta, the group had abandoned Rick Dabner's van when the axle broke. That meant ten people in two vehicles and one of those was Martin's single cab truck. Devin and Jahda rode with Hector and his wife in Hector's car. The four Dabner brothers rode in the bed of Martin's truck. Martin and Ham rode in the front.

"Let's eat something and get some sleep. We'll find another car tomorrow." Maria, Hector's wife, said.

"Sounds good." Rick Dabner said.

The Dabner brothers ranged in age from about twenty to forty, Rick was the oldest. They owned a furniture store together. Their father founded it in the fifties. He retired two years ago but he and his new wife had been killed in a plane crash. His first wife, the boys' mother, had died of cancer several years ago. Henry, the youngest, was still in college but managed the entire inventory. George and James, the twins, took care of sales and Rick did the rest. None of that mattered now.

The group sat around the small campfire warming their cans of food. The night was brisk and threatened rain. As soon as they finished eating, they doused the fire with dirt and sat in the dark talking softly. The first stringer wandered by the front of Hector's car. They heard the wheeze of the rotten lungs. Rick tapped George on the shoulder and they rose in unison. The rest of the group stood and looked around. They each had either unsheathed a knife or gripped another weapon. They all had guns but none were drawn. It had been hard lessons to learn about how sound draws more of them.

Martin counted five stringers in the starlight. The group spread out. Ham stood behind Martin facing away from him. Devin and Jahda went around the back of the truck and stepped into the road. The movement drew the attention of the stringers and they all started shuffling towards them. The Dabner brothers all went around the other side of the car and got behind the crowd. Rick opened the back of the first ones head with one swing of his axe.

George took an arrow and drove it into the eye of the one who turned when Rick swung. Pop. Pop. The other three stringers turned. Devin brought his pipe down onto the head of the first one. Jahda kicked the feet out from under the next one and drove her machete through its eye when it hit the ground. Pop. Pop. The last one paused, trying to decide between Devin and Jahda. Hector stepped from behind the truck and swung his bat, striking the temple of the stringer. Pop.

"Nice follow through." Devin said, stepping over the corpse.

"Been working on it during the off season." Hector said.

"Is that all of them?" Martin asked looking around.

"I think so. We'll take a quick look around to make sure." James said.

The brothers split into two groups and walked in opposite directions down the country road they had camped beside. Hector and Devin grabbed the stringers on the ground and piled them up away from the camp. The brothers returned without seeing any more of the dead.

"Makes you wonder why we keep seeing these little groups way out here." Jahda observed.

"My guess is that most of them are folks headed to somewhere they thought was safe." Martin said.

"Maybe we should head to their house. Nobody's home." Devin said nodding at the pile of dead.

"You know something Devin, you can be pretty thick at times." Jahda said.

"Not disagreeing with you Jahda" Martin said smiling at Devin, "but I think Devin actually might be on to something."

"You fricking kidding right?" Rick said.

"Well, I don't mean we should find these poor bastards' house and go there but think about it. We have been mostly off the beaten path for almost a month now and yet we keep running into these little packs of stringers. Why?" Martin asked. Everybody just shrugged.

"These folks evacuated. They didn't make it." Martin said. "I would bet almost all of these little packs are folks who got caught on the interstate or trying to get to it and since the interstate basically splits the state north to south, these stringers just wandered into the countryside."

"So?" Jahda said

"Well they left from somewhere. And that somewhere is where we should go. Find a town and see how much has been evacuated. Maybe the safest place now is where everyone ran from in the beginning. It just needs to be not so big folks wouldn't have been able to leave." Martin said the last part out loud but it was a thought that just crossed his mind. "Get the map."

George pulled out the map from the glove box of Martin's truck. Martin had been in charge of most of the navigation mainly because he was old and had a map. George handed the map to Martin who spread it out on the ground. Hector stood over it with his flashlight.

"We're roughly here." Martin said putting his index finger on the map.

He studied the map for a minute and made a few culls but there were still a few possibilities. He would let the group decide.

"Ok. So the closest places are Haleyville and South Springs. If we keep going for another few miles on this road, we'll cross 44. If we turn left, we get to Haleyville in about twenty-five miles. South Springs is about twenty miles to the right. What do y'all think?" Martin asked.

"I went to college in South Springs for two years. It was a few years ago but I still remember where things are in the town." Devin said.

"We went to Haleyville to set up a store one time, but the lease fell through and that was ten years ago. South Springs is closer anyway." George said. The others nodded.

"Ok. South Springs." Martin said.

"What if you're wrong?" Maria asked. "What if there are just more stringers there than out here?"

"It wouldn't be the first time I was wrong Maria, but at least we might be able to find another car." Martin said. She nodded.

Martin walked with Ham and she climbed up in the front of the truck to get ready to go to sleep.

"I think we need to plan on tomorrow being a hard day." Martin said.

"I wish we could get an easy day."

"I do too honey. But some will be harder than others. And I think tomorrow might be one of those days." Martin said.

She sat up as he walked to the back of the truck and opened the camper shell. He reached in and grabbed a bottle of water. He also grabbed her toothbrush.

"Here brush."

"Yes Babu."

"That's the Swahili one." He said, pointing his toothbrush at her. She winked.

They decided to call it a night. The Dabner brothers had set up their tent a few yards away from the back of Martin's truck. Martin slept in the bed of his truck. Hector and Maria slept in their car. Devin and Jahda had the watch for the rest of the night. It would only be a few more hours until dawn. After a while they walked across the road and sat down on the guardrail of the bridge that passed over a small creek.

"So we were neighbors for over a year right?" Devin asked.

"I guess. Why?" Jahda said.

"Well I thought we might have hooked up by now, you know." Devin smiled.

"Uhhh, no." Jahda said.

"One of those wrong flavored coffee things?" Devin said.

"One of those I don't like coffee things." Jahda said.

They both heard George scream and stood up.

James Dabner had always had a small bladder. He opened the tent to find a tree. As he stepped out the first stringer came out of the woods behind the tent and fell on him. He started to scream but as it fell, the stringer bit squarely down on his neck, cleanly into the vocal chords and ripped everything out. The next stringer fell into the open tent on the sleeping brothers. Rick awoke when George kicked him trying to fight off the thing that had just fallen on top of him. At one point it had been a woman. A large woman. Death had been a good diet plan because she had lost all her fat. Her skin lay in rotting folds with festering sores from rubbing together as she shuffled along. All that extra skin still added weight and George could not push her off. She bit down on his face several times while he kicked and screamed.

Rick and Henry managed to scramble away from the biting sack of skin but the next stringer bit into Henry's back as he crawled out of the tent. He yelled in pain. Rick pushed past him and managed to push the thing off of Henry. He knelt down to pull Henry away when the stringer stood. Rick saw his pistol at the tent door and grabbed it as the thing turned to face him. Rick could see the neck where it had been bitten. Its face was swollen and blue. The opaque eyes fell back on him and it started to come towards him. Rick raised the pistol and aimed at its head. He pulled the trigger. He missed. The thing fell on him and bit hard into his shoulder. Rick put the pistol to the things head and pulled the trigger again.

He shoved the corpse off him and stood. He looked around and saw James on the ground, his face frozen in a scream, as the stringer feasted on the contents of his abdomen. He raised the pistol to the back of its head and pulled the trigger. He looked in the tent. He placed the pistol on the back of the head of the stringer and pulled the trigger. George was dead. He looked at him and pulled the trigger again. He stood and looked down at Henry. He had been bitten several times across the back and was trying to stand. Rick didn't wait for him to get up. He pulled the trigger again. Devin and Jahda stood behind him watching. He turned around.

"I missed." Rick started. "He fell on me and I missed." He looked at his shoulder.

"Wait." Jahda said, reaching towards him.

"I won't miss this time." He put the barrel to his head.

"NO" Martin yelled.

Rick pulled the trigger. He didn't miss.

The gunshots had awoken the rest of the group. Hector and Maria stood outside the car holding their weapons. Ham locked herself in the truck. Martin had run over after he was sure Ham was safe. When he yelled Ham sat up and looked out of the back of the truck. She saw Rick put the gun to his own head and pull the trigger. She ducked back down. She rose up and looked the other way.

Hector and Maria had turned to the sound of the last shot. A stringer came from the other side of his car and fell on Hectors back, biting down as he did. Maria turned and screamed. She had a hammer and hit the stringer on the head. Pop. She tossed the hammer aside and knelt down holding Hectors head in her lap. He reached up and touched her cheek. His hand fell away. She reached into her back pocket and pulled out her small revolver. She leaned down and put the barrel against Hector's head and pulled the trigger. She looked up and saw Ham starring at her from the truck. She smiled with tears streaming down her face as she put the barrel against her temple and pulled the trigger. Ham screamed.

He heard her scream his name and ran. Martin opened the door of the truck and Ham fell into his arms sobbing. He hugged her tightly and lifted her out. She was almost a teenager now, but she cried like a baby in his arms. He turned and faced Hector and Maria. Hector was on the ground with his head resting in her lap, a trickle of blood crossing his forehead from the upturned temple. She lay to one side with her head resting against the tire of the car, eyes fixed on Hector. They were both gone. Devin and Jahda walked up to Martin.
"They're all gone. Rick, George, Henry, James, Hector and Maria. All gone." Devin said, shaking his head in disbelief.

They stood by the road for a long while....
"The next morning we loaded up in my truck and
started to make our way to South Springs." Martin said
to the wide-eyed Josh and Lori.

We are still Here

Tilly walked out of the saloon and down the middle of the road. Raj came out of one of the shacks lining the road. He saw the look on her face.

"Hey, hey. What's wrong?" Raj said, falling in beside her. She stopped.

When she turned and faced him, he could see the tears streaming down her face.

"I don't know. I..." she broke up. He took her hand and led her to the bench sitting in front of the shack behind her. He helped her sit down. She was still crying.

"What happened?" Raj asked.

"Nothing happened. I don't know how to explain." Tilly started.

"Explain what?" Raj asked again.

"I just said, I... leave me alone." Tilly said and stood.

"Wait, wait. I just want to find out..." Raj started, she interrupted.

"Find out what? Just find out how to leave me alone. That's what I need you to find out." Tilly said. She stood and walked away.

Raj sat on the bench watching her go. He started to stand but someone stepped between him and Tilly as she disappeared around the corner. It was Kate.

"Everything ok?" Kate asked.

"I don't know. She wouldn't say why she was upset. She just got mad at me." Raj said.

"Well it's been a hard few days." Kate said.

"I guess." Raj said, then his eyes widened, and he looked at Kate. "I mean yes. It has been an extremely hard few days and I am so sorry for your loss."

Kate just smiled and nodded. She reached out and touched his hand.

"Thank you, but it's been hard on us all. Including Tilly. Just give her little space right now." Kate said.

Raj nodded his head and went the other way to keep exploring the buildings for supplies. Kate joined the others at the picnic table. Scott had brought over an MRE for her. Amanda and Dottie joined them. Charlie and Jennifer grabbed a few water bottles and sat down at the picnic table with them. Ed stood in his doorway, watching until Charlie waved him over. The others eyed him, wondering if he was part of the team now.

"So, I guess this is breakfast." Charlie said, smiling as he tore open the heavy plastic bag.

"Guess so." Dottie said.

"My dad used to take these with us when we went camping." Scott said. He smiled briefly and turned to his mother. She was staring ahead, but he saw the corner of her mouth briefly turn upward. He reached out and touched her hand. She turned and looked at him, smiling broadly with misty eyes.

"I want you to know, your father was a hero. He saved all of us." Charlie said, looking at Scott.

"He was a hero to me before any of this, but thank you." Scott said.

Bridger and Evelyn joined the rest of them. The whole group, except for Tilly and Raj, was gathered around the picnic table.

"How is everyone doing this morning?" Bridger said, looking around the table.

"You're kidding right?" Amanda said.

"Actually no." Bridger said, turning to face her.

"How do you think we are doing? There are things out there that are trying to kill us and as far as we know this is all that is left in the world. They killed my husband, and Dottie's husband and Kate's husband and Janice and Jeremy and Clyde. Dead and gone. And I can't figure out why we don't just blow our brains out to end this misery." Amanda said, breaking down in sobs towards the end.

The rest of the group had slowly lowered their gaze and soaked in the words. They had all been thinking the same thing in one way or another.

"We have to live." Kate said.

"I know." Amanda said.

"I lost my husband several years ago. He drowned." Evelyn said, scanning her eyes over Amanda, Dottie and Kate. "The day I found out I wanted to die too. But I didn't. I couldn't. It wasn't my time yet."

"The Lord was talking to you." Dottie said.

"I don't know about that but maybe you're right." Evelyn said. "I just knew I still had something more ahead. And I still feel that way. Even after everything that has happened. I still feel like I, like we, have something more ahead."

"But is it something good?" Jennifer asked.

"We'll just have to be here to find out." Charlie said, reaching over and putting his arm around his daughter.

"So what now?" Scott asked. He had been listening to the conversation and knew his mother was right. They had to live. They had to figure out how.

"Well, I was hoping we could all talk about it." Bridger said.

"Let's talk then." Charlie said.

"Scott, could you go find Tilly and Raj, I want them to be here for this." Bridger asked.

"I'll go. I saw Raj just a moment ago. I know where they are." Kate said, rising.

"No. I'll go." Scott said, rising with her.

"It's ok. I'll go. I need to stretch my legs anyway." Kate said, patting Scott on the shoulder and stepping over the bench seat of the picnic table. She walked around the side of the saloon and started towards the other side of the compound.

"I'm going to get the radio." Scott said getting up from the table.

"I'm going to grab a few more bottles of water from the kitchen, does anyone want anything?" Evelyn said, rising.

"I could use a drink. A real drink." Charlie said.

"You know it's like seven in the morning right?" Bridger said.

"You know there are monsters roaming the woods right? If that doesn't deserve a drink, what does?" Amanda said surprising everyone.

"Good point." Evelyn said. She walked into the saloon and grabbed some water bottles. She reached under the bar on her way back out, snagging a bottle of vodka. It seemed breakfastier.

She put it down in the middle of the picnic table. They just sort of stared at it for a minute. Finally Ed reached over and broke the seal. They each took a swig from the bottle, except Jennifer and Dottie, and each made a grimace as they did. Most immediately regretting the moment of bravado. Amanda took two. She didn't grimace as much on the second go. Dottie looked over her glasses and wrinkled her nose at the bottle as Amanda set it back down on the table. Bridger could almost hear the harrumph.

"Ok. I guess we'll just save the rest of that for later." Evelyn said.

"The rest of what?" Scott said, walking back from retrieving the radio.

"Nothing. Don't worry about it. Have you heard anything on that since the other day?" Charlie asked.

"Not really." Scott said.

"What does that mean?" Charlie said.

"Well, I keep hearing something other than static but it isn't a voice talking. It's kind of weird and I only hear it now and then." Scott said.

"Alright, let's see if we can get it back." Charlie said.

"We could try the roof." Ed said, pointing above his head.

"Good. Just as soon as we're done here." Charlie said.

Kate stuck her head inside the next building. She had been in two others already and still no Raj or Tilly. She glanced inside and heard a muffled sob from other side of the room and looked in the corner. Tilly was sitting on the floor with her legs stretched out in front of her, back against the wall. One hand was holding her hair back, elbow resting against the windowsill next to her. She was picking at the wood of the sill with her fingernail. She stared out the window with tears rolling down her cheeks. Kate stood for a moment in the quiet of the room and looked at the girl. The sunlight came through the window in sharp lines and the shadows cut across her face. Her hair danced in and out of the light, at one moment bright red at other moments the color of blood. Her skin was pale but bright. She looked childlike and aged at the same time. Her face was awash with a torrent of emotion.

"Tilly?" Kate said quietly. "Are you ok, honey?"

Tilly turned her face towards Kate and grimaced.

"I don't know." Tilly said.

Kate walked over and sat down beside her.

"Why are you crying?" Kate asked softly.

"I blew up on Raj, right after I blew up on Bridger. I don't know why. I mean I know why, but I sit here now and think about it and I want to apologize. But when I think about doing that, what really comes to mind is to tell them to go fuck themselves. Then I get all confused again and start crying." Tilly said. "I think I've snapped."

"Listen, you don't have to answer me if you don't want too. I know we don't know each other that well and if you think it's none of my business, just tell me so. But I am trying to help and I care. All of us have been through a lot. Together." Kate said.

"Thank you. It's ok. I need to talk to someone. And I think it should be you."

"Ok. What did they do to make you blow up on them?" Kate asked.

"Raj just kept asking me what's wrong over and over and it just pissed me off more. I was still kind of raging from coming out of the bar, saloon or whatever the hell Bridger calls it."

"What happened in the saloon?" Kate asked.

"Well Bridger was in the kitchen grilling Evelyn about what happened between me and the asshole at the creek. And I grabbed a frying pan and threw it against the wall." Tilly said.

"Why did you do that?" Kate asked.

"Because that asshole had used it, his fucking eggs were still in it. It was like he was still there. And Bridger just wouldn't let it go. So fuck him too."

"But you know he wasn't there, right?" Kate said. "You know you don't have to be afraid of him any more."

"Afraid? I wasn't afraid of him. I put a shotgun in his mouth and pulled the trigger. I wasn't afraid of him at all." Tilly said, but the tears rolling down her cheeks betrayed her. She leaned forward placing her face in her hands.

Kate laid her hand across her back and rubbed between her shoulders, Tilly raised her head and Kate put her arms around her and pulled her close. She held her tightly. Tilly unleashed her tears onto Kate's shoulder. After a few minutes Tilly leaned back against the wall and stared out the window again.

"Thank you. I needed a shoulder just now." Tilly said.

"Your husband has one too." Kate said.

"I know. I need to apologize to him." Tilly said.

"Well let's go find him. Everybody is at the picnic table. We're trying to figure out what's next." Kate said.

"Trying to figure out what's next? What do you think should be next?" Tilly said.

"I don't know. I lost my husband. My son left me and I let him because I was scared I would have to watch him die too." Kate said.

"But he wasn't sick." Tilly observed.

"Not yet."

"But you think it's just a matter of time. For him. For all of us." Tilly said.

"I did yesterday. But today I wish he were back. I am going to cry every night for a while. I don't know what scares me more, having him here and watch him die or never knowing. I guess not knowing leaves me some hope. But I can't change the past. Neither can you. And the past can't hurt you. Not now. We are truly living for each day now. Like Amanda said just a few minutes ago, what happened yesterday is dead and gone." Kate said.

"Amanda said that?" Tilly asked.

"I think she is still like most of us, trying to make our brain believe what we thought was impossible. But she's right about one thing. We no longer have the luxury of reflection. It's time to learn, all over again, how to live." Kate said.

Tilly looked at Kate. Her hair was naturally brown but had been colored and highlighted to give her a dirty blond look, but Tilly could see some of the gray starting to show. The small crows feet around her eyes and the darkening circles under them made her looked tired but her eyes themselves burned resolute, like someone who has seen her own battles and walked out alive. She thought about what she would be feeling if she had seen Raj die and understood that this person in front of her had real strength. It wasn't the muscles on the outside that made Kate strong. It was the big muscle in her chest. And Tilly was beginning to see it.

"I don't understand." Tilly said. "I mean, everything that you've been through over the last few days, all the loss, how do you move on?"

"Oh, I haven't moved on. I will cry myself to sleep for a long time. But I will sleep. And I will wake. And we will live. We have too. That was my promise to JW. And that is my promise. To you." Kate smiled and took her hand.

Kate didn't have a daughter, she sometimes wished she did, but she knew she was a mother of boys and she loved that. But still. She fought the urge to push Tilly's hair back behind her ear, and if by some connection, Tilly did it herself. She smiled. Tilly smiled back.

"Let's go. We can talk again. Right now, we just keep moving forward." Kate said.

"I'm ready. Thank you." Tilly said, standing up and brushing herself off.

They walked out of the building, a two-room shack that a long time ago had held a different family enduring their own kind of apocalypse, and walked down the road to the other end of the compound. Raj came out of the last building on the left and saw Kate and Tilly walking ahead of him. He called out to them and they stopped. He watched Kate turn to Tilly and take her hands. She nodded at Tilly and then turned and kept walking towards the saloon. Tilly turned her head towards Raj and reached up and tugged on her lower lip. He knew that sign. She would do it when she wanted something. What she wanted he gladly gave. "Forgive me for being an asshole." She said.

He just nodded and put his arm around her. They walked towards the saloon with her head nestled against his shoulder, holding hands. She still had tears but now there was a smile under them.

Kate arrived at the picnic table just a few moments before Raj and Tilly. Bridger leaned against one of the support posts that held up the tin roof covering the table. He could see Kate's face and he swore he could see a slight smile on it as she sat down next to Scott. He glanced at Evelyn who turned her eyes from Kate to Bridger's and they nodded slightly to each other. He felt even better when he saw Tilly and Raj walking up holding hands. She still had rivers in her eyes but she was smiling too. She broke from Raj and walked straight up to Bridger.

"I'm sorry. I don't want to talk about it right now, but I'm sorry." She said. She turned to Evelyn standing a few feet away. "I'm sorry to you too."

"It's all good." Bridger said.

"No need to apologize." Evelyn said.

"Thanks." Tilly said. She turned and walked back over and sat down next to Raj.

Bridger looked around. Everyone realized the whole group was together now and as though the lights had flickered in a theater letting the audience know the play was about to start, everyone grew silent in anticipation of what was to come. Evelyn's eyes met Bridger's. He stepped forward from leaning on the outside wall of the saloon.

"Well, I am not really sure where to start, but folks we have some fences around us and we have a good bit of food and ammunition. We have as good of a ground floor as you could want in this situation. As far as what happened over the last few days, I think we all have our own thoughts on that and mine are probably like yours. We have had our knees taken out from under us and we have endured immeasurable loss. It sucks. It just sucks." Bridger said.

"That's an understatement." Dottie said, rolling her eyes.

"Yes, it is. Because no matter what word you use; devastating, terrifying, agonizing, horrifying, all those words would be an understatement." Evelyn chimed in, "What we saw, who we lost and what we had to do was all that and more. So saying it sucks works just as well."

Dottie looked back down at the picnic table. Amanda, already looking down, nodded at Evelyn's words. She reached over and squeezed Dottie's shoulder. Their eyes met, and they both took heavy breaths. Accepting the loss was the hardest part. Dottie nodded at Amanda and looked back down. Kate watched the interaction with Scott holding her hand on the table, softly squeezing it. They all took another moment to remember. Kate stood.

"Folks I don't know what to say except this. A month ago most of us didn't know each other. None of us expected or even imagined what would have happened to us over the past few weeks. We all had our things and our plans and our own lives. But that world is over. That life is over. We can't deny that any more. No matter what is left it is nothing like what was before. Today we have to find a way. A way to move forward. A way to go on. A way to live. My husband brought us out here to live. He made me promise him we would, and I intend to keep that promise. So now we all have each other. And that is all we have. Like Raj said that first night in the wide spot of the road we called home, we're still here."

Where the Roads

Don't Go

Martin walked out into the garage and looked up the driveway. He looked at the open garage door. He stuck his head back in the kitchen.

"Josh? It is Josh right?" Martin looked at the young man. Josh nodded. "Can you help me with this?"

"What's that?" Josh said, rising from his seat.

"This garage door, I think we should lower it. It would be safer." Martin said as they walked into the garage.

"Oh. Ok. Just push the button." Josh said.

"Huh?" Martin said.

"Yeah just push the button. It's got a battery backup in case of a power outage. We used it once to raise it right when we left but it should still have plenty of juice." Josh said.

"Ok, let's see." Martin said, pushing the button. The door whirred to life and lowered.

Everyone was still in the living room when Martin and Josh came back in. Even though it was his home, Josh felt out of place. These folks had been out in this and seen things Josh could only imagine. He felt both lucky and ashamed. He knew his father had done the right thing to keep them alive, but he felt like that they had run and hid instead of fighting back. He wanted to fight back.

"Lori and I need to leave." He said.

"Why?" Ham asked.

"Well, we came back to find her parents. We just stopped here to see." Josh said.

"See what?" Ham asked again.

"Just to see." Josh said, smiling at Ham.

"She asks a lot of questions." Martin said. "I do too. When was the last time you saw your parents honey?"

"The day before this all started, so maybe a month or so." Lori said, biting her lip.

"And you think they may still be here?" Martin asked a second question.

"I don't know, maybe." Lori said.

"Look, we're not asking for permission, we're not asking you to go, we're not asking anything. We are answering. She doesn't know where her parents are, that's a question. Well we're going to start answering our own questions. Not yours." Josh said, clearly agitated.

"You're right, Josh. But I am still going to ask mine. I just want to make sure that Lori here is on board with your plan. You do have a plan? I mean you're not just going to hop in your car and drive over there and knock on the door, are you?" Martin asked.

"Maybe. I don't see a problem with that." Josh said.

"Ok. So what happens when you have to run over a stringer and the car shuts off because the guts clogged up the intake, or one of the bones pierced the radiator? You got a back up for that? How about when you get there and by the time you get to the door the herd you attracted by driving down the road catches up to you and just when the door opens a out walks mom and dad stringer? Sorry Lori, but you have to know that could happen." Martin said.

"Hey, watch it." Josh said.

"No, you watch it. You want to be the man, fine, you're the man. And all those things are things you need to worry about, *man*. Including being smart enough to know that finding the answers to your questions will not be like a trip to the library." Martin continued. "She and you have come a long way already just to make it this far, but you said yourself you have not seen a lot of these things. We have. It's not all the same. Some are fresher than others." Martin said.

"Fresher?" Lori asked.

"Yeah, fresher." Devin continued. "The recently departed. The newbies. Stringers that have just, I don't know, turned is probably the best word. Those things can still move pretty good. Not really running but more like throwing themselves forward. Sometimes they do it so hard they lose their balance but they get up fast and just keep coming."

"Yeah but at least you see them coming. I hate the ones that can hardly move anymore. They just sit down in a chair or car or on a porch and just lay over. You think it's dead and gone until you walk past it and it reaches out and grabs your ass." Jahda added.

"Well, your ass is worth coming back for." Devin said smiling.

She just responded with her middle finger.

Martin looked back towards Josh.

"Son, the point is, we can and want to help. We just want to make sure we all know what we're getting into. There ain't much left in this world but to help other people anyway."

"I guess your right. We came here to do this and we are going to do this but it would be better if we could get some help. Will you help?" Josh said.

"Nope." Martin said. "I can't risk taking Ham on a search and rescue mission and I can't leave her here by herself because I am quite sure Jahda and Devin are going to offer to help you."

"Oh yeah." Devin said.

"Without a doubt, it'll be fun." Jahda added.

"So Ham and I will stay here and search these other houses for supplies until you get back." Martin said. "But let me offer you one more bit of advice."

"What's that?" Josh asked.

"Wait until tomorrow morning." Martin said.

"Why?" Josh said.

"Well that would give you the most daylight because when the sun goes down, these things become more aggressive. Not sure why, but I think during the day their eyes hurt or something. If you watch em, they all look down when the sun in up. I think they are shielding their eyes. At night they look ahead. During the day you can see them long before they see you but at night they can pick up your movement better because they aren't looking down. It's just a little thing but it might make a difference." Martin said.

"Plus it's creepy out in the dark." Ham added.

Martin finished the thought, "and if you left now, you wouldn't make it back by dark."

"What do you think?" Josh asked, looking at Lori.

"Tomorrow will be fine with me." Lori said.

"Ok. Let's find something to eat and get settled in for the night. The street has been pretty clear, and this house is already reinforced." Martin said, looking at the makeshift window barricades and then nodding at Josh. "So we should be good in here for the night. We just need to stay together and keep all the doors to the bedrooms closed."

"Why?" Lori asked.

"Stringers can't turn doorknobs." Ham said, looking into her backpack, grabbing a can.

She put the new can on the table next to the empty peach can. They had a few more hours until dark but the late November sky was heavily overcast and night would envelope the world without the courtesy of a sunset. The moon would stay hidden in the dark ink, its light reflecting back off the tops of the gray clouds. The day passed away with them skittering around the house, looking out windows and closing more doors. The quilts and blankets Josh and his family had spread around the house those first few nights had gone with them on the buses. Most now burnt and rotting in the woods. Josh pulled down the attic door and climbed up the ladder. He brought down a couple of boxes of old blankets and clothes his dad had put up there a long time ago. They made pallets out of the blankets and some of the clothes doubled as pillows. He also pulled out a box of winter coats that had gone out of fashion. That definitely didn't matter anymore. The nights had grown cold and the small stack of firewood outside the kitchen door wouldn't last. The walls kept the wind off, and the wind heralded the arrival of the coming winter with ferocity, whipping the empty limbs into a frenzy and blowing the leaves and paper around the cul-de-sac like a whirlwind. Looking outside the front window, Josh watched as the winds rearranged the flotsam of the apocalypse into new piles of finality. He turned back to the room.

"So you all knew each other? Before?" he asked.

Jahda was busy fluffing up the shirt she had wrapped inside the other shirt to make a pillow. Devin was pulling his boots off, absentmindedly sniffing each one. Martin stopped straightening the quilt in the corner and looked first at Josh, then at the others.

"Sort of." He began. "We lived in the same trailer park. Jahda and I lived next door to each other and Devin lived across the road. There were seven other families in our neighborhood. Most of us set out for Atlanta together, we lost some on the way there and then some once we got stopped. The rest you've heard already."

"Weird isn't it?" Lori asked.

"What's that?" Devin said looking up from fighting the urge to sniff his socks.

"Just that when this all happened we reached out to folks we didn't really know for help. I mean I didn't know Josh or his family, yet they kept me and a lot of others alive."

"I thought you two were the only ones left. You said that things happened in the woods." Jahda sang out.

"Oh, no. Things did happen. Josh's father died. Several others too. But not all of us. There are still about a dozen out there." Lori said.

"Out where?" Jahda asked.

"In the woods. They had to leave the spot where we were but I think they're still out there. They were going to some kind of compound." Lori said.

"Compound? What kind of compound?" Martin said as his interest in the conversation piqued.

"I'm not sure. Uncle Bridger, he's a friend of my dad's or was or is or I don't know, anyway, he scouted a place that we learned about because some creepy dude tried to attack us and got killed. He had built it. His buddy told us about it." Josh said.

"Got killed how?" Jahda asked.

"Well, the girl he attacked killed him. I'm sure it was in self defense." Josh said.

"Kind of." Lori said.

"What does that mean?" Martin said.

"Well I was there, and it was pretty much over. The asshole guy was trying to just leave and Tilly, that's the girl he attacked, she just pulled out her shotgun and killed him." Lori said.

"When you say attacked?" Jahda asked.

"You know, he *attacked* her." Lori said, glancing her eyes towards Ham. As though protecting her from hearing the word rape would somehow keep her from having dreams about monsters now. Martin caught the glance and appreciated it, nonetheless.

"Uh, ok." Jahda said. "I guess I can maybe see that."

"Well, what about this compound?" Martin said, drawing the conversation back.

"I don't know anything about it other than how to get there. Bridger told me where the turn off was from the main road and the rest was just a dirt road to the place. They said it had buildings, like old shacks or something, and a fence."

"Fence?" Martin said.

"Supposedly." Josh added.

They all bedded down together in the living room. It had been over a month since Josh had slept under his own roof. And the world had changed.

Honky Tonkin

Most of the others had already picked their building so Kate and Scott ended up separated by Evelyn. She offered to swap with one of them but Kate didn't want to ask her to move all her stuff, although her stuff consisted of one backpack, and a sleeping bag. Besides Scott was just as close as he had been in his bedroom on the other side of the house back home. The thought made an image of Josh leap into her mind. She hoped he had a safe place to sleep tonight. Scott had managed to get his gear put away and was standing outside his building watching the sky.

"So, you think we're gonna get some rain?" Charlie said as he walked up.

"I don't know. It's so strange you know?" Scott said.

"What's that?" Charlie asked.

"I never thought about the weather. I mean I thought about it but I never tried to figure out if it was going to rain or snow or whatever. I just let my weather app tell me how to dress." Scott chuckled.

"You and most of the free world." Charlie smiled.

"I'll see you in the morning." Scott said, walking back into his building.

Charlie walked down to the end of the compound and looked through the fence. He couldn't see very far into the trees. He wasn't sure if that was good or bad. He wanted to see the whole horizon, but he was afraid that if he could he would be overwhelmed with fear at what was walking off in the distance. The night swallowed them all once again.

Darkness had come hours ago but sleep still eluded her. Kate stood from the floor of her shack and grabbed her jacket. She slipped on her shoes and stepped outside into the cold night air. The sky had started to clear and the bright pale moon shone down like a beacon, illuminating the tops of the buildings and the trees outside the fence. She could see up and down the road as almost as clear as daylight. She knew Bridger or Raj or Tilly were somewhere out along the fence making the rounds. She wasn't scared or nervous but sleep just wouldn't come. Maybe she needed a nightcap. She wasn't a big drinker but on occasion she found that a drink sometimes helped her sleep. Usually it was just because she had gotten so worked up over something she needed to take the edge off. She would have to get three days past drunk to take this edge off. Hopefully one maybe two drinks would help her sleep though. Besides who cares. She made her way towards the saloon.

She opened the screen door and looked inside. The moon cast its light through the windows. She saw someone sitting at the bar with their back to the door. She could see the outline of hair falling down to the shoulders. It almost didn't surprise her. She approached the dark figure in the shadows without turning on the flashlight in her pocket.

"Amanda, honey can I join you?" Kate said with a smile on her face.

"Well you can join me but I ain't Amanda"

Kate stopped. She flipped on the flashlight. She saw the bottle of scotch sitting half empty on the bar and the glass sitting next to it. Her light landed on two bloodshot tear rimmed eyes surrounded by gray hair cascading down to her shoulders.

"Dottie?" Kate said, surprised.

"Yep. Dottie. I just wanted to come in here and..." she started.

"No explanations needed." Kate interrupted.

"Actually there is. I came in here because of you."
Dottie said.

"Me? What did I do?" Kate said.

"Not what you did. What you said. What you said about
our old life being over. I've said that myself a time or
two over the years. When I was young I was a wild
child. I swear. My hair was as red as Tilly's and I was
just as sassy. I guess that's why she gets on my nerves."
Dottie said, slightly losing focus both in her thoughts
and on Kate. "But that was my old life number one. The
day I married I put that life away."

"To Ray." Kate said.

"Hell no. To Pete Fairchild. And honey was he ever. He
was a pretty man. Stupid as dirt but pretty as a flower. I
got tired of him pretty quick, probably about as quick
as he got tired of me. We split, and I started drinking.
Not polite drinking. Drinking. Like my life depended
on it. And for a few years it did. Or so I thought. That's
when I met Ray. He was a honky tonker like me and we
always ended up closing down the bars slow dancing to
Conway Twitty. Another pretty man I might say.
Conway not Ray."

Kate was glad it was mostly dark because her
face had to be failing at masking her shock and
amusement at the story being told to her.

"Say, what brought you in here tonight? A drink?"
Dottie asked.

"Well" Kate said.

"Say no more. You like Scotch? Of course you like
Scotch" She said wobbling around the bar and slapping
another glass down on the counter. She left the pouring
to Kate.

"Anyway, as I was saying. What was I saying?" Dottie
looked slightly confused.

"Conway Twitty, a pretty man." Kate said, more than
slightly amused.

"Conway, Conway." A smile creased her lips. "Oh yeah, we closed them bars down for a few years. We moved in together, Ray and me, not me and Conway. Both of us had been married once, and that was the one thing we both swore off. Everything else was fair game. We lived a hard life between drinking and being broke all the time. Then one day Ray found Jesus."

"And you did too." Kate said.

"Oh hell no. I wasn't looking for his ass either. Jesus had to find me. Luckily he had Ray helping him look. After a while I saw Ray change from a hard drinking party man without a pot to piss in to a decent guy with a good job and more importantly he was satisfied with that. That was what got me. He was satisfied with his job, his Jesus and me. He just wanted me to be satisfied too. And for a long time I was. I was satisfied. But now I sit here drinking again and wonder if I was satisfied with life or was I just satisfied with Ray. Because now he's gone. And like you said. We're still here."

Kate put the glass to her lips and drank. The sharp sting on the back of her throat had the opposite effect of putting her to sleep. It burned going down her throat and the slight elevation in body temperature that accompanies a drink made her head sweat ever so slightly. The next moment or so the swimmy effect of the alcohol began to replace the burn in her stomach. She looked back at Dottie.

"I guess I meant we can figure out how to go on." Kate said.

"I know what you meant honey, I am just sitting here trying to figure out what I need to go on for." Dottie said as she looked back down at her now empty glass. She reached up and grabbed the bottle. She poured her and Kate another.

"No, no I just wanted one."

"Well, that's all I poured you." Dottie said

Kate smiled and took the second shot. She was pretty sure she would sleep now. Dottie swiveled on her stool to face Kate but the momentum of the stool swung half a turn to far and when she tried to stop she stumbled out. Kate reached out and grabbed her shoulder before she could topple all the way over. "I think maybe we should call it a night." Kate said as she helped Dottie straighten up.

Dottie stood straight and put her shoulders back. She took her hands a smoothed her hair back as best she could. It still had an Einstein quality about it in the light of the moon and Kate smiled just a little. She could feel the alcohol beginning to have a more pronounced effect on her and she didn't want to start laughing out loud.

"Sure. Call it a night." Dottie said.

"Which building is yours?" Kate said as they made their way back out onto the porch of the saloon. Dottie looked up and down the road a few times. From the saloon looking south you could see the road run past four buildings on either side. The last one on the right was the big barn they had spent the first night inside. The last building on the saloon side of the road was the Alamo, and it sat right across from the barn. The next two building were occupied, one by Raj and Tilly the other by Bridger. Dottie looked the other way. The other barn sat at the other end of the road, same side as the saloon, almost up against the fence. Kate knew she, Scott and Evelyn, occupied the three buildings between the saloon and the other barn. Dottie turned her head up and down the road another time.

"Not sure" Dottie said. "I think it's right there." She pointed directly across the road. They made their way across and Kate knocked on the door. No answer. She opened the door and turned on her flashlight. She could see the blanket on the floor and the picture on the box by the makeshift bed. Ray.

"Ok. Here let me help you." Kate said turning back to help Dottie down to the floor.

"We'll keep this between us." Kate said.

"Why?"

"Well I..." Kate started.

"Honey, I am almost seventy years old. I don't care what other people think. I really never have, but I especially don't now." Dottie said as she leaned back against the bundled up jacket she was using as a pillow. Kate helped take her shoes off and set them on the floor next to the blanket. Dottie was snoring almost immediately. Kate walked back outside.

"Someone have a rough night?" Tilly said from the shadows.

"Oh, you startled me." Kate said looking at Tilly emerge from the darkness between the buildings.

"Sorry. Just making my rounds. So what was that?" She said pointing her thumb at the door Kate just emerged from.

"Can I walk with you?" Kate asked.

"Sure" Tilly said.

They started down the road towards the other barn. Kate looked at Tilly as they walked. She carried a pump shotgun that she and Bridger had sawn the barrel down on. She also had a pistol on one hip and a large machete on the other. Her hair was tied back in a ponytail that stuck out of the hat she had on. A big blue Tarheel emblazoned on the front of an otherwise black baseball cap.

"Carolina fan?" Kate said pointing to her own head.

"I guess. Raj and I both did undergraduate there, and he did medical school at Duke. I don't know how much you know about that rivalry but it's intense. We decided to stick with Carolina but if Duke wins, we're still ok. We just don't tell anyone." Tilly said. "I don't guess anyone is left to care about that sort of thing now."

"When did Raj finish medical school?" Kate asked.

"Just this last summer." Tilly said. "He was supposed to start his residency this January in New Orleans. That's why we had gone down there. He wanted to see where he was going to work and we made it into our honeymoon that we never got to take."

"How long have you been married?"

"We got married his first year of medical school. We had waited since freshman year but we always knew we would get married. We met the first week of college and have been pretty much inseparable since." Tilly said.

"That's sweet." Kate said.

"So you gonna tell me who you were helping back there? Did Amanda tie one on?"

"Nope, I thought it was her too when I first walked into the saloon but it was Dottie." Kate said.

"Drinking?" Tilly asked

"Drunk."

"You're shitting me." Tilly said stopping and turning to face Kate.

"Nope. She told me she fell off the wagon that her and Ray had been on." Kate said.

"Oh, ok. I guess she is kind of entitled then. I just thought she had been an old bitch her whole life." Tilly said.

"Well you would be wrong. Apparently she has lived quite the colorful life."

"Well ain't that some shit?" Tilly said.

"Yes, and..." Kate started to talk but the rustle of the chain link to her left stopped her.

"You hear that?" Tilly said. "This way. Come on."

Tilly darted between the shacks and emerged in the open ground between the back of the shacks and the fence. In the moonlight she could see the shape against the fence. Kate came up beside her. Tilly raised her shotgun as they approached the thing against the fence.

"Hold on just a second there Annie Oakley." Bridger said walking along the fence in the darkness to their right.

Tilly inadvertently swung the shotgun in his direction. He ducked.

"Hey, don't shoot." Bridger said still ducking but closing the distance between him and them remarkably fast.

He stepped to the side of Tilly bringing his hand up with him and lifted the shotgun right out of her hands. She was so surprised her hands hung empty in the air for another second.

"Hi Katie, how are you tonight?" Bridger said. He turned his attention back to Tilly and handed the shotgun back to her. "I don't want you to shoot her. Sorry"

"Why not?" Tilly asked.

"Well for one, I don't want the sound. And for another, I want to watch her. I have been for almost an hour now." Bridger said.

"It's been at that fence for an hour?" Kate asked.

"Oh no. I saw her walking in the woods. It was just stumbling through the trees and all of a sudden stopped. It lifted its nose in the air and I could see it scenting like some kind of animal. It would sniff, look down, sniff again, look down, sniff again and the whole time slowly turning its body until it walked straight to where you see it now. She smelled us. The only thing that stopped her was that fence." Bridger said.

"I wonder how many more are wandering out there." Kate said.

"Well, we know this, if they get close enough to smell us we'll know." Tilly observed. "They'll be gathered on this fence."

"And since this is the only one I have seen tonight I don't think there are a lot of them out there. At least not close by." Bridger said. "But that could change if we fired off a shot. And like I said, I want to watch it for a while."

"Why?" Kate asked.

"Well, just to see if it tries to figure out how to get in or if it just stands there pushing against the fence. When Ed brought me here the first time, we found one like this. It had dug a trench with his feet because it just kept walking against the fence. Like the little engine that could." Bridger said leaning against the fence post watching it.

The thing on the other side watched them. All she wore was her shirt and shoes. The rest apparently lost on her journey to this place. The thin light of the moon gave her legs a bluish hue with pronounced dark purple veins. One of her thighs had been ripped open and the jagged gash above her knee had festered. The wound on her forearm was why she was the way she was. It was open and angry; puss and blood, black in the moonlight, oozed out down her hand. When she put her hand up on the fence it dripped from her fingertips. Her face was drawn and the skull beneath was outlined under the gaunt skin. Her eye sockets were sunken and black but her eyes protruded as though pushed from behind, pale cataracts covering her once blue eyes.

"She's starting to rot." Bridger said. He gazed down at her hand as it grasped at the fence.

Some of the stuff oozing out of her forearm splattered on Bridger's shirt as she slapped the fence. He wiped it with his finger and put it to his nose. They had not yet grown used to the smell of the infected. It had been the smell that had drawn JW out of the woods. The smell still wafted on the air but hadn't saturated the world yet, at least not their part of it. Bridger stepped back from the fence to avoid any more splatter. He wasn't sure if getting it on you was dangerous but he didn't think so.

"I wonder where it came from." Kate said. "I mean this is a person, or was. She was like us. Just trying to survive"

"Or she could be the first. She could be, what do they call it, patient zero." Tilly said.

"Unless she hopped a plane from Madagascar a month ago, I seriously doubt it." Bridger smirked.

"I know that smart ass, my point was she could have been wondering out here for a long time." Tilly said.

"Well at least you didn't throw anything at me." Bridger said.

He saw Tilly's expression in the moonlight. She lit up like a Christmas tree at first, flushed with anger. Then she looked at Kate and a wave of calm and even remorse swept over her face.

"I'm sorry about that. I shouldn't have acted that way earlier. It was just..." Tilly explained but Bridger stopped her.

"Tilly, stop right there. I'm sorry. I should have talked to you. I was wrong." Bridger said.

"I didn't say you weren't. You *should* have talked to me, but that still doesn't excuse what I did. I'm sorry, let's move on." Tilly said, holding out her hand.

"So we're good?" Bridger said taking her hand.

"Yep, we're good?" Tilly said, shaking his hand.

"Good. Now let's watch Tina." Bridge said.

"Tina?" Kate asked.

"Yeah, she looks like a Tina. So Tina." Bridger said.

Kate and Tilly looked at each other and then back at the thing clinging to the fence and burying its forehead so hard against it a trickle of blood had appeared above its eye. Tilly thought to herself that it looked more like a Gertrude but she held her tongue.

Waiting for the Day

To Come around

Bridger and Tilly leaned against the shack about twenty yards away in the shadows. Kate had gone back to bed, the alcohol finally having the intended effect. Raj had come on duty about two hours ago and was currently making his circuit around the fence. They hadn't seen any of the infected except for Tina. Tilly had conceded that upon further inspection she did indeed look more like a Tina than a Gertrude. Bridger was highly persuasive. It had calmed down since they had stepped out of its sight. They twice observed it stepping back from the fence slightly and scenting the air. The second time it did it, Tilly uttered a gasp under her breath. It opened its mouth slightly and took a few quick breaths and licked its lips. It then tilted its head back and breathed deeply through its nose. She could see the nostrils flair. Tilly didn't know if it was the dead skin of its nose or if the virus actually changed the muscle control of its face but the nostrils grew to almost twice normal size.

"That's creepy as shit." Tilly said to Bridger. He didn't disagree.

The thing at the fence dropped its head and jerked towards the sound of Tilly's voice. It began scanning with its opaque eyes looking for the source. It couldn't see them even though they were just a few yards away, until Bridger adjusted his feet and moved a little to his left. The thing smacked its head against the fence.

"See even Tina loves to watch me move." Bridger said.

"*Only* Tina loves to watch your old ass move." Tilly said without hesitation.

"I hate what happened, but I'm glad your back." Bridger said looking at her, smiling

"I didn't go anywhere but I get you." Tilly said turning her attention back to Tina.

"How long are we going to watch her?"

"Not much longer." Bridger said.

"Holy shit." Scott said walking between the buildings.

"Morning, kiddo." Bridger said, realizing the sky was starting to brighten a little with the approaching sunrise.

"What's going on?" Scott asked pointing to the thing at the fence.

"Oh, Tina? She's just hanging out with us this morning." Bridger said.

"Why?" Scott said.

"I guess she likes us." Bridger said.

"No. I mean why are you letting her 'hang out'? Why don't you just shoot her?" Scott said.

"We're not going to shoot her." Tilly said.

"What?" Scott said.

"We're not going to shoot her. Too loud."

"What are you going to do?" Scott asked.

"I don't know yet." Bridger said.

"You're not serious. What? Are you going make it a pet and call it Fido?" Scott said.

"No. Of course not. I intend to, uh, dispatch it. We don't risk the noise of a gunshot unless we have no other choice. Besides her name's Tina not Fido." Bridger said.

He reached his hand out and Tilly looked at him. He pointed to the machete on her hip. She handed it over to him.

"Where'd you get this?" Bridger said as he turned it over in his hand.

"It was in one of the shacks we checked. It looked like the gardening shed. Bunch of tools." Tilly said.

"Ok. Later today show me which one." Bridger said.

He stepped out of the shadow and approached the fence. The thing at the fence could fully see him now. The sun wasn't up yet, but the sky had turned orange in anticipation of its arrival. The thing began grabbing at the chain link with its hands and banging against it with its head. The mouth started a constant chomping. He walked up to the fence and raised the machete. He lined up the tip with one of its eyes and shoved forward. As soon as the blade slid through the eyeball and entered the depths of the socket, they heard the pop. The thing stopped moving and dropped to the ground.

"That sound is so weird." Scott said.

"Yeah, the sound. That's the weird part. Not the dead not dead part." Tilly said.

"Well that's weird too." Scott said, kneeling down to the ground to get a closer look at the crumpled thing on the other side of the fence.

"You wanna see her up close there Scotty boy?" Bridger asked. "Come with me. We need to drag her away from the fence and burn her. Grab Charlie and you two meet me at the back gate in ten minutes."

Scott stood and walked back between the buildings. The sun was just about up now and he could see Charlie walking with Jennifer. They were headed to the saloon.

"Hey Charlie, wait up." Scott called as he broke into a trot.

Fifteen minutes later they walked up to the back gate just as Bridger and Ed arrived.

"I thought I would ask Ed along too. Maybe give us a tour of the property so to speak." Bridger said.

Ed showed Scott and Charlie how the gate worked and they swung it shut leaving the pin out. Bridger tested it and he figured after watching Tina, the infected wouldn't be able to lift it and move at the same time. Or at least wouldn't be able to figure out how. They walked down the fence to where the infected lay. Scott stuck his foot out and rolled her over. The smell would have been no different if he had flipped over a deer that had been lying dead by the side of the road for a week. They all covered their noses. The smell of decay filled the body that just a few minutes ago was standing against the fence.

Charlie looked around the group, recognizing they were all surprised by how strong the smell was.

"This one smells worse than all those others. When Raj and I were burning them up the other day, we barely noticed the smell." Charlie said.

"I wonder why?" Scott asked.

"I don't know but we need to get this thing moved and burnt. And quickly." Bridger said.

"Where?" Charlie said.

Bridger replied. "Downwind."

They found a spot on the south side of a big tree that would block some of the wind; less they lose control of the pyre. Charlie had brought a small paint can filled with gasoline from the bus. They doused the body and threw some leaves and limbs on top. The body lit. The wind whipped, and they spent the rest of the morning making sure the fire didn't spread.

"Well, we are going to have to figure out a better way to do this." Charlie said as he tamped down a wayward ember.

"We need to dig a pit to do this." Ed said. "Like a trash pit, but bigger."

"I can't get over how much worse this one smelled." Charlie said.

"When I was watching it at the fence it smelled but it didn't seem any worse than the others we've seen. It was like as soon as it hit the ground the smell exploded." Bridger said.

"Maybe it died before the others." Scott said.

"I put a machete through its head. I know when it died." Bridger said.

"I meant the first time." Scott said.

"That's an interesting thought. I mean if it had been dead and rotting on the inside longer that would make sense. We really don't know shit about these things." Charlie said.

"We know they are dangerous. We know they will attack and we know they aren't really people anymore." Ed said.

"Do we really know that?" Charlie asked.

"Yeah, we do. We've seen the before and after. The after is not a person. Not even close." Bridger said.

"Still, it would be helpful to learn more about them, even if it's just to figure out their weaknesses." Charlie said.

"I don't disagree with you, but I am not about to start trying to take prisoners." Bridger said.

285

"Oh, me either. I just think we need to know more about them." Charlie said.

They started walking back towards the fence. Ed led them over to the creek side to show them the water wheel pump that brought fresh water from the creek. When Russell had cleared the land for his buildings, he had taken a bulldozer and just pushed all the trees down and shoved them all on one side of the compound. From that side of the compound you could see down the hillside until the berm created by the discarded tree stumps blocked the view of the creek itself. The land between the fence and the creek was littered with tree trunks and tree limbs haphazardly forgotten once the land had been cleared. They made their way through the pushovers. They struggled to find good footing over the broken and twisted limbs. They reached the creek. The water wheel pump was basically a hose attached to a wheel that had paddles on it. The paddles made the wheel spin in the current and the hose wound around the wheel gathering water as it spun. The hose was attached to a bearing the let it spin and the other side of the bearing was attached to a PVC pipe which led to a cistern inside the compound.

"Well that's some good old redneck engineering right there." Bridger said.

"Yeah, this works for now but we have to figure out something better. I don't trust our water supply to a piece of heater hose." Charlie said.

"Agreed." Bridger said.

They stood by the creek for a little while watching the water wheel turn. The temperature had climbed slightly but the cold wind still blew in their faces. They all saw the shape floating down the creek. The creek was about ten feet across and maybe four foot deep and the body would twist and turn as it bounced between the limbs overhanging the water. It came to rest against the water wheel, blocking the paddles. They stood and watched for another few minutes, hoping the body would dislodge itself.

"I guess we're gonna have to do it." Bridger said.

"I'll get it." Ed said as he pulled off his shoes and socks.

The water was cold but not as cold as it would get. The air was cold but not as cold as it would get. Ed still shivered against it as he pulled his pants off. He waded into the water naked except for his boxers. He looked back over his shoulder at the three other standing smiling at him as he cautiously tiptoed into the water.

"Go ahead Mr. I'll get it." Bridger said smiling.

Ed smiled. It felt good helping these folks. He could tell they were good people.

He made his way into the creek and reached out to try to yank the body free. As soon as he pulled on it, the first time it turned its head over. Ed fell back in the water. The rest of them stood about five feet away on the bank gawking.

"Is that thing still alive?" Scott asked, looking at the upturned body.

Ed scrambled back to the shore and stood with them looking at the thing. The face looked like a water skin from an old western, bloated and heavy with liquid. It raised its hands from the water and the skin peeled off as it moved its fingers. It bobbed a couple of times in the water then upended itself. The lower half was twisted and broken, with bones protruding from its legs. It bobbed again onto its back and slowly drifted down the creek. The last thing they could see was its face and nose, the mouth slowly chomping at the water filling it up. It disappeared.

"Yeah, we need to keep boiling the water." Ed said as he started getting dressed again.

Devin and Josh stood in the cul-de-sac looking up the hill. Jahda and Lori came out of the front door of Josh's house. They all gathered around the car.

"So we drive?" Lori asked.

Devin responded. "For a while. I think we should at least try. We can go slow and make sure we don't get hemmed in anywhere. Which way are we going?"

"Well I live near Arcadia Drive, oh sorry, you're not from here." Lori said.

"I spent some time here at school. Arcadia, that's past the college over by City Park." Devin said.

"Yep. That's cool." Lori said.

"What's cool?" Jahda asked.

"I don't know, it's just cool that he knows it." Lori said, unintentionally reminding everyone she was just over sixteen years old.

"Do you need us to bring you anything?" Devin said in a raised voice. He saw Ham and Martin standing outside the door watching them.

"Ice cream." Ham said.

"Just bring yourselves back." Martin said.

"We will. We'll be back by dark. That's a promise." Jahda said.

"I'm going to hold you to that." Martin said. He waved at them. He and Ham disappeared back inside. They could hear the deadbolt turn.

They each carried a sidearm and Lori had a shotgun. The rest of them carried some other type of weapon. Quieter weapons. Devin and Jahda each had a machete. Devin also a hammer hung from one of his belt loops and Jahda had a large hunting knife. Josh carried his own hunting knife and had grabbed a long hatchet he kept under the seat of his Jeep that was still parked in the driveway. They climbed in the car. Josh drove.

They drove by the Magix. The parking lot was empty. They turned and started towards the college and Josh took a side road that ran across the railroad tracks. They made it almost all the way around the school and drove by the football stadium. There were several cars in the parking lot and a few stringers wandering among them.

"Stop." Devin said.

"Why?" Josh asked.

"Well practice makes perfect. Plus I want to see the stadium." He said.

He stopped the car in the middle of the road. He was pretty sure he wasn't blocking traffic. And no cops left to give him a ticket. They got out of the car.

"Lori, you stay here." Josh said.

"Uh no. I am going too. I need to do this." Lori said.

"Well, ok but you're not taking that shotgun. Leave it in the car. If you get in trouble you run. Straight back here." Devin said. "Same for all of us. If you lose your weapon or anything goes slightly wrong, run. Don't wait. Run. We'll all get this done but we can be smart about it. Worst case, we get back in the car and keep going."

Josh opened the trunk of the car and pulled out a crowbar he had stashed in it before they left the woods. He gave the hatchet to Lori. They started across the parking lot towards the front of the store. The wind blew leaves and paper across the lot just off the ground, occasionally lifting it high in the air in a swirl. The stringers closest to them were all shuffling around looking at the ground; it wasn't until Devin tapped his machete against the light pole in the lot that the first one raised its head to see them. Devin motioned at Josh.

"Go ahead. Take that one."

Josh looked at the crowbar in his hand and flipped it a couple of times, trying to figure out the best way to use it. He decided to just swing away with it. He connected to the side of the stringers head and it caved in. The thing fell to the ground and Josh started towards the next one.

"Hold up. That one's not done." Jahda said.

"I bashed its head in. See?" Josh said turning to look down. The thing slowly started to turn over. Josh stepped back.

The thing rolled over and slowly sat up. One side of its head was deformed from the impact of the crowbar. One of its eyes had popped out of its socket and hung by the thinnest of membranes on its cheek. The other eye was frantically searching, but it too had lost any ability to see. Fluid streamed out from underneath it like bloody tears.

"It didn't pop." Jahda said, driving her machete into the hole left by the dislodged eye. Pop. "Unless it pops, it ain't dead"

Josh looked down at the thing on the ground and back up to Jahda.

"Gotta pop, ok got it." He turned to the next stringer.

It was a young girl wearing a white bathrobe. Her hair was matted, and the shoulder was covered in blood. The spot where her neck and shoulder came together was torn open and black. Her eyes were sunk in her head and it looked like she had chewed her own lips off. She was still trying to chew through her own cheek as she shuffled towards them. Josh swung the crowbar again. He connected with her forehead. It split open. Pop. The stringer fell to the ground. That was the closest two to them. The next group of three was on the other side of a van. They ducked down as they went around the side. Devin slowly raised his head as they came close to the front of the van. He looked through the driver's window and windshield to see where the stringers were. A face suddenly appeared in the window.

"Help me."

Devin almost fell over backwards. Jahda and Josh slowly backed away looking at the face in the window. Lori moved towards Devin keeping her eyes on the stringer she could see. The face in the van looked back over towards the stringers then back at them. He started to open the door to the van and before Devin could stop him he jumped out. He was wearing a pair of jogging pants but no shirt and no shoes. He stumbled towards them. The stringers were attracted by his movement and started coming around the van.

"Help me, you gotta help me." The man said. "Keep those things off me."

"What the hell man? What's going on?" Devin said.

"I don't think we have time to worry about that now." Jahda said as the stringers came around the van.

Two came from the back and three more were coming around the front. Devin turned and drove his machete through the first one. Pop. Lori swung her axe at the next one and hit it on the side of its head, lopping off its ear. The axe buried in the shoulder. She tried one time to pull it out but couldn't so she let it go. The thing fell towards her but she managed to back away as it fell to the ground. Josh brought the crowbar down on the back of its head, opening it up like a melon. Pop. Lori put her foot on the back of the thing on the ground and pried the axe loose.

"More. There's more." The man frantically pointed to the other three coming around the front of the van.

Devin looked back over his shoulder. He drew his eyebrows together and looked the stranger up and down again. He turned back towards the stringers and brought his machete through the chin of the next one. He released the handle and stepped back letting the stringer fall onto the ground. The impact drove the machete blade through the top of the things head. Pop. Devin flipped it over and pulled it back out. Jahda had driven the tip of her machete through the eye of the next one. The last one was wearing a jogging suit with an orange hat. Lori aimed for the hat. The axe found its home. Pop.

"Well shit." Devin turned and looked back. The stranger was gone.

"There he is. Oh shit. Stop him." Jahda said, but it was too late.

Devin pulled his pistol and aimed towards the car. He squeezed. He squeezed. He didn't fire. They watched the car drive away.

"Dammit" he said, holstering the gun.

"It gets worse." Josh said. "The shotgun."

"Shit" Devin said.

"Now what?" Jahda said.

They looked around. Devin stuck his head inside the van and turned the key. Click. There were a few other cars in the parking lot.

"We need to see if we can start one of these other cars." Josh said.

They walked across the lot to another car. It was locked. Devin took his hammer and smashed the window. They looked around; making sure the noise hadn't attracted any stringers. Nothing yet. Devin stuck his hand in and unlocked the door. He opened the door, half surprised some alarm didn't sound. He looked in the glove box and the center console. He looked over the visor and even under the floor mat. No keys.

"Next." He said.

"Wait, can't we hot-wire it?" Josh asked.

"Sure. Do you know how?" Devin asked.

"Well no but." Josh said.

"How about you Lori, can you hot wire a car? How about you Jahda, you steal cars in your pre-stringer life?" Devin asked. Josh knew when he was being mocked.

"Look, it was just a suggestion." Josh said lifting his middle finger.

"Well, this ain't the movies, but nice try." Devin said. "Since none of us were high end car thieves in the before time, we'll keep looking."

They started walking to the other end of the parking lot. Jahda looked towards the stadium. The tunnel she was looking down was one that allowed you to see part of the field. She stopped.

"Look, there are people inside the stadium." She was pointing down the tunnel.

On the field they could see what looked like several military tents. As they approached the gate to the tunnel, they stood and looked. There were people on the field moving around the tents.

"Hey." Lori called out.

"Shh." Jahda said.

All the people on the field were shuffling around looking down, in the familiar pattern they had all seen before. There were at least ten stringers walking around the small part of the field they could see.

"Look at that shit." Josh said as he pointed into the shadows behind the gate just to their left.

"What?" Devin said walking down the gate.

"That" Josh said. Devin could see a vehicle in the shadows behind the gate.

"What is it?" Devin said.

"That's Paulie's Truck." Josh said.

"We need that right now." Devin said.

"Ok. What the hell is a Paulie's Truck?" Jahda asked.

"Paulie the Pachyderm. The mascot. That's his truck. Well not really his, that is the one that he rides onto the field at the start of the game." Devin said.

"You have to be kidding me." Jahda said. "We are not going to drive around in some mascot's halftime ride."

"But we have to do this." Devin said.

Jahda Fields was twenty-four years old. The same age as Devin White. Although they both came from different backgrounds they arrived at the same station in life at the same place, The Commons of Willow Haven. A nice enough community for a trailer park with clean streets and well kept lots. Most of the residents were long-term owners. Living a more frugal life either by choice or by circumstances. Most were good folks and Devin lived in his grandmother's trailer. She had died the previous year.

Jahda had bought her place with her girlfriend several girlfriends ago. She decided to be single for a while before all this happened. She could see the sparkle in Devin's eye. She knew he needed her permission or something. She could never imagine anyone riding around in the big truck painted like an elephant that had a hose attached on its roof shaped like a trunk. But then again she could never have imagined the last month and half of her life either. They were going to do this. She knew it.

"How?" Jahda asked as she smiled at Josh and Devin.

"We have to get this gate open." Lori said.

"What about the stringers out there?" Jahda said as she pointed down the tunnel.

"If we can get inside, we can close that other gate." Josh said. He nodded towards the end of the tunnel. Just before it went out from the shadow of the tunnel there was another pedestrian gate.

Devin walked over to the lock and chain on the gate. He had the hammer, but he was afraid that the noise would draw the stringers from the field before they had a chance to get inside.

"I can squeeze in through this gate." Josh said. "I'll get inside and close that gate. Then we can get it open."

"Wait a minute. We don't know if the keys are even in the vehicle. And we already know we can't get it started without them." Lori said.

They all looked around at each other. She was right. They should keep going and look for something else.

"They are in it. We deserve this truck. And if they aren't we'll find them. I am not leaving without that truck." Josh said almost laughing.

"I'm in." Devin said. Jahda just shrugged her shoulders and smiled

We stood together, alone

The day rolled over into afternoon. Martin opened the front door and stepped out into the yard. Ham had fallen asleep on the couch. The house was insulated well against the cold air. He could see the wisp of clouds high above. Whatever warmth the sun brought through the clear sky was quickly stolen by the wind as it whipped through trees. This would be his sixty-fifth winter. He was pretty sure it would be like none he had ever experienced. He knew he and Ham were lucky to have Devin and Jahda with them. He prayed they still would be together after today. He looked up at the sky again.

"They'll be back Opa." He turned to the sound of her voice.

Ham stood in the doorway rubbing her eyes. She would be twelve soon but to Martin she would always be that little three-year-old running between the trees in the yard, trying to hide from him. Even now as she wiped the little sleep remaining out of her eyes, he could see the teenager she was fast becoming.

"I'm sure they will be Ham. But I still worry." Martin said.

"But they're smart. They'll be ok." Ham said.

"They're smart and they are capable but they're still just kids. At least they are to me. I hope they don't do anything stupid." Martin said as he looked back up at the sky.

Josh walked over to where the gate joined the brick wall of the tunnel. It was wide enough for him to squeeze through and he slipped inside the stadium. He slowly crept down the tunnel and squatted down just inside the shadows. He could see the whole field now. There were at least ten large tents set up and a large white trailer with a huge red cross painted on its side set up in the far end zone. Most of the stringers were at the other end of the field. There were hundreds, all milling around the white trailer. The dozen or so near this end hadn't noticed him, yet. He would have to leave the shadows to be able to close the gate. Not far but far enough. He slipped out into the light and stayed low as he crept towards the gate. He was trying to figure out what to secure the gate with when he saw the pin lying on the ground and felt his luck rise. He looked back at the others and nodded his head. He reached out and grabbed the gate. He pulled on it and it wouldn't move. For one brief second he thought he would have to retreat but then it came free. The sound of the gate rattled through the tunnel. He pulled it all the way to the stops. He looked up and saw that some of the stringers had turned towards the sound. He put the pin in and backed away from the gate as the first stringer arrived. It slammed into the gate but the pin held. Josh backed up. As soon as Devin saw the gate close he brought the hammer down on the lock. It took several swings but eventually it gave way. They slid the gate open.

"Uh, we probably need to hurry." Lori said as she looked at the crowd growing at the other end of the tunnel.

Josh ran over to the truck. It was unlocked, and he swung open the door. There were no keys in the ignition. Devin opened the passenger door and started looking in the glove box. Josh looked over the visor and under the mat. Nothing. They looked at each other across the center console. Josh opened it. Devin leaned forward and looked inside. He raised his eyes at Josh and smiled. He produced an elephant key ring with a remote and a key. He handed it to Josh. He put it in the ignition. Click. He tried again. Click.
"Nothing." Josh popped the hood.

Lori and Jahda were looking down the tunnel at the other gate. The noise Josh made closing it had attracted a few stringers. The noise the stringers made banging on the gate had drawn more. The gate was now blocking at least a dozen and more were gathering.
"Hey, you boys wanna quit playing? We are just about out of time." Jahda said nervously looking at the gate.

Devin and Josh met at the hood of the truck. Josh raised it up. Devin looked inside.
"The battery is disconnected." Devin said.

He grabbed the cable and began screwing in the side post. When the battery made contact the horn sounded. Except it wasn't a normal horn. This truck was the mascot truck. The horn sounded like an elephant trumpet. And it was loud. It sounded one time and stopped. Everyone froze. Jahda and Lori looked at Devin with wide eyes. Devin looked at Josh. Josh smiled. They all laughed. Then the gate collapsed.
"Oh shit." Devin said as he screwed in the side post as best he could.

Lori and Jahda ran to the back of the truck and jumped in. Josh turned the key as Devin climbed into the passengers seat. It cranked. He put it in reverse and hit the gas as the crowd came out their end of the tunnel. He slammed on the breaks, put it in drive and put his foot to the floor. He aimed it towards the open gate. He leveled three stringers; he could feel the wheel jerk in his hand as the tires passed over them. Lori and Jahda were holding on as best they could to the contraption that worked the hose. They saw the bodies on the ground as they passed over them. Two of them tried to stand again.

They roared out of the shadow of the stadium into the sun. Josh barely missed one of the light poles scattered throughout the parking lot. When they had made it across the lot Jahda banged on the roof of the truck. He stopped. Jahda and Lori jumped down from the bed of the truck. Josh and Devin got out and walk back to where they stood. They looked back at the stadium tunnel they had just escaped from. At first it was just a few but soon it was dozens of stringers, all wedging themselves through the open gate and pouring out into the parking lot.

"Did we just..." Jahda started.

"... let a stadium full of stringers out?" Devin finished.

"Yes, yes we did."

Charlie and Bridger stood at the fence looking back towards the creek. They couldn't quite see the water wheel but only because the creek sat lower than the land. They could see where the trees had been pushed over and could see the trees standing tall on the other side of the creek.

"You know, it would be nice to be able to see this far around the rest of the place." Charlie observed.

"I agree. What would also be nice is that if the rest of the place was as hard to get to as walking through that shit?" Bridger said, pointing to the pushed over trees.

They had walked through it yesterday both before and after the water wheel incident. The deadfall of limbs made it treacherous at best. Several times one of them had fallen, tripped up by the tangle of limbs. Mixed among all these were jagged arms of snapped limbs, just waiting for someone to have a wrong step.

"Too bad we don't have a bulldozer." Charlie said.

"Ain't it though? But Tilly said there was a tool shed. Maybe a chainsaw or two. Or at least another axe." Bridger said.

"You wanna cut this forest down with an axe?" Charlie asked.

"Not the whole thing, just a perimeter. Besides, all it takes is time and effort. And we got plenty of time." Bridger said.

"Well, let's go have a look." Charlie said. They walked over to the shack Tilly had pointed out yesterday and stepped inside.

There were several axes and even a two-man saw. There were also several gardening tools, hoes and shovels. Charlie moved a couple of heavy blankets and exposed a workbench. Sitting on top of the bench was a chainsaw. Charlie walked over to it and held it up in the light.

"Well, it's kind of small but I guess it will work. Besides it has to be easier that shoving that thing through a tree." Charlie said gesturing to the two-man saw on the wall.

"We'll use both. Let's go get something to eat." Bridger said.

They walked out of the shack and made their way down to the picnic table outside the saloon. Dottie and Kate were already there. Evelyn came out of the door carrying a couple of MRE's.

"Hey, let's get everyone together. I think I have an idea to make this place a little safer." Bridger said to Evelyn.

"Raj and Tilly are right behind me." She said as they came out of the saloon door.

"Where's Jennifer?" Charlie said.

"We're right here." Jennifer said as her and Scott walked up carrying a bucket of water from the cistern. They took it over to the big pot on the grill and poured it in so they could boil it.

"Where's Ed?" Bridger asked. Evelyn pointed up. The roof of the saloon was tall enough to see most of the fence. They had taken turns during the day keeping watch.

"Where's Amanda?" Bridger asked.

"Oh she said she was going to lie down earlier. I'll go get her." Jennifer said as she stood and walked towards the other end of the compound to get Amanda.

"Alright. Here's the plan. The trees are all pushed over on the west side of the fence. I think we should do that all the way around." Bridger said.

"Push them over with what?" Evelyn asked.

"Sorry, not push the others down. Cut them down. It was a pain in the ass trying to get through that stuff yesterday. If it's that hard for us to get through, how well do you think these things can navigate it?" Bridger said.

"Ok. I'm with you. But how are we going to do it?" Scott asked.

"We found a chainsaw and some axes. There is also a two-man saw we can use." Charlie said.

"Won't that take forever?" Dottie asked.

"We'll find out." Bridger said. "Look, this is just an idea. I think it happens to be worth the effort but that's why we're talking about it."

"So are we staying here?" Tilly asked.

"Huh?" Charlie said.

"That's really the question right? Bridger says it's worth the effort. Well it's only worth the effort if we stay here. So are we staying here?"

"I'm not sure we..." Bridger started.

"Look, if we stay that's fine. I like having a fence and a roof. *Well*, I like sitting in a hot bubble bath, listening to my playlist while eating chocolate but I'll settle for a fence and roof given our current situation. We just haven't talked about it since we got here. I know we've been busy and shit but maybe we should talk about what the big picture looks like."

Jennifer stuck her head into Amanda's shack. The building was divided by a wall between a front room and back room. The door was open between the two but she could see the makeshift bed against the wall in the front room.

"Knock knock." Jennifer said as she walked into the room.

She walked over to the bed. It was a couple of blankets with a sleeping bag on top. She knelt down beside it to look at the picture shoved between two of the boards in the wall. She lowered her head and looked up at it. It was a picture of Chris. She could imagine Amanda putting it there so when she woke up in the morning, or in the middle of the night, it would be the first thing she would see. Jennifer felt a tear well up in her eye. She raised her head back up and started to stand. Her hand slipped and moved the sleeping bag. She heard the distinct tinkling sound of a bottle roll from under it. She picked it up and looked at it. Vodka. It was almost empty. She briefly looked around and put the bottle to her lips. She wasn't really sure what her father's reaction to her drinking now would be but she knew what his reaction was before all this happened. He had caught her and Lori drinking beer in the garage one night and it had taken almost a month to let her even talk to Lori again. Their sleepover was the first time Lori had visited in almost a year. The vodka burned the back of her throat. She was pretty sure she wasn't going to be a vodka drinker. At least not straight vodka. She put the bottle back down. She saw something lying on the sleeping bag. She picked it up. It was a pill. She looked back down and saw a prescription bottle under the folds of the blanket the sleeping bag lay on. She picked it up and read it in the dim light of the room. Davis, Russell. Take one as needed for pain. She had to think a minute about who Russell Davis was. Then she remembered. This was his place, this compound. He was the one Tilly shot. She knitted her eyebrows together trying to figure out the mystery in front of her. She stood, still holding the bottle. She turned to exit into the front room to see if she could find Amanda. She raised her attention from the bottle long enough to see Amanda standing in the door of the front room. Or at least it had been Amanda.

Its face was bloated and blue. The tongue disgorged from the mouth and foam rolled out of its nose. The whites of its eyes were full of blood. Its eyes fell on Jennifer. The thing smelled her and lifted its head to absorb her scent. It began to chomp its teeth but the bloated tongue hindered the effort. She watched in horror as the thing methodically drove its teeth through its tongue until it finally bit it off. The thing then began chomping in earnest.

Jennifer's nose was overwhelmed with the smell of the things bowels, which had emptied into its pants when Amanda died. She tried to scream but instead had to fight back the vomit that rose in her throat. She fell backwards onto the sleeping bag as the thing reached out for her. Her hand fell on the bottle and she grabbed it as she scrambled towards the other corner. The thing reached for her leg and fell on the floor as Jennifer slid by. It grabbed her foot. Jennifer turned and brought the bottle down on top of its head as hard as she could. The bottle shattered, and the thing released its grip on her foot. Jennifer snatched her leg up and brought both her knees to her chest as the thing crawled towards her. It rose up on its knees and fell on her. Jennifer brought the broken end of the bottle up through the soft part of the things throat. She drove it as deep as she could, pushing as the thing continued falling on top of her. The bottle broke through the soft bottom of the skull just behind the nose. She had pushed it all the way through the things mouth and soft palate. Pop. It fell limp. She screamed.

Charlie had listened to what Tilly said. She was right. They needed to talk about a lot of things. He and Scott had spent a little time on the roof listening to odd things on the radio. They hadn't been able to explain it yet, and they hadn't mentioned to anyone else. This might be a good time to do that too. They heard the scream.

"Jennifer." Charlie muttered to himself.

Tilly and Raj both looked in the direction of the scream. Before they could move Bridger had already taken off running. Charlie was right behind him.

"Where, where?" Bridger yelled as he ran.

"There, to the left. That's Amanda's." Tilly pointed as she ran after them.

They all skidded to a stop as they saw the figure emerge from the shack. As she drove the bottle through the things neck, she had severed the arteries leading to the brain. The blood covered her from head to toe. She stood there starring at them. Charlie started towards her.

"Wait." Bridger said, reaching down and putting his hand on his pistol.

"Daddy" Jennifer said as she started crying.

Charlie ignored Bridger. He ran to his daughter. She fell into his arms sobbing.

"Are you hurt? Where's Amanda?" Charlie said as he checked his daughter over.

"She's in there. She was one of those things." She started sobbing again.

Bridger looked at Jennifer as he moved past her and went inside the shack. Tilly and Raj joined him. They could see a shape kneeling on the floor. Its hand were down by its side and from the angle they could see it looked like it was leaning forward on its face. They stepped around and could see the chin slightly off the floor with the neck of the bottle sticking out, the rest disappearing into its skull. Blood was everywhere. Bridger walked up and nudged the body over with the tip of his boot. It fell to one side and landed on its back.

"That's Amanda alright." Tilly said.

"What happened?" Raj asked.

Bridger reached down and picked up the pill bottle lying in the pool of blood. He couldn't read much of the blood soaked label, but he read the one word that mattered. Vicodin.

"She checked out." Bridger said holding the bottle up for Raj to see.

"Checked out?" Tilly said.

"Bought her own ticket, opted out. Whatever you want to call it. She killed herself." Bridger said.

He was visibly angry and walked past Raj and Tilly out the door. He walked straight past Charlie and Jennifer too. Evelyn, Kate, Dottie and Scott were standing right behind Charlie and Jennifer still trying to learn what happened. He walked right by them too. Ed stood on the roof and started to walk to the ladder to climb down and find out what was going on. He saw Bridger coming his way. He could see the look on his face. He decided he would sit back down and just keep watch. He didn't think Bridger looked like he was in a talking mood as he came closer. Bridger didn't stop until he was inside the saloon.

Tilly and Raj emerged from the shack. Charlie had managed to get Jennifer to sit down on one of the nearby benches. Dottie and Kate were gathered around them trying to comfort her and make sure she wasn't bitten. She wasn't. Evelyn and Scott walked over to Raj. "What happened?" Evelyn asked.

"Amanda killed herself. Took sleeping pills or something." Raj said. Evelyn's hand covered her mouth.

"Why is Jennifer covered in blood, what happened to her?" Scott asked.

"I guess she found her. She used a broken bottle to end it. There is blood everywhere but I think it all came from Amanda." Raj said.

"Now what?" Evelyn said.

"We'll need to burn the body." Tilly said.

"I'll help." Scott volunteered.

"We'll get started as soon as we know Jennifer is ok." Raj said.

"What happened to Bridger? He just stormed off?" Evelyn asked.

"I don't know. You'd have to ask him." Raj said.

"I think I will." Evelyn said. She stood and walked away from the group to the saloon.

Raj and Scott went back inside the shack. Raj walked around the body on the floor and grabbed one of the blankets. He threw it over his shoulder and nodded at Scott to grab her feet. Raj looked down at the bottle protruding from under her chin. Her mouth was open and he could see the bottle passing into the roof of her mouth. He stepped back slightly and felt something squish under his foot. He reached down and picked it up.

"What's that?" Scott asked.

"I think it's a tongue." Raj said as he tossed it onto the body. He reached down and grabbed her arms.

"Ready?" Raj asked.

"Go." Scott said.

They lifted her up. After a month living in the woods with less and less to eat, she weighed almost nothing. They carried her outside and lay her down on the ground. Dottie and Kate looked up as they exited the building. Jennifer buried her head into Charlie's shoulder and cried. Charlie looked back over long enough to see the thing on the ground. He saw the bottle sticking out of its chin. He didn't know his daughter was capable of doing that, but he was glad she was.

"My God." Dottie said. "Poor child."

Kate didn't know if Dottie was reacting to the body on the ground or the violence that Jennifer had to inflict to survive. She didn't think it mattered because the sentiment applied to both. She put her arm around Dottie as Raj spread the blanket over Amanda.

Under the Moon and

Under the Weather

Jahda and Devin sat on the tailgate of the truck. Josh was standing in the bed leaning against the hose reel. Lori sat in the cab watching back over her shoulder.

The crowds of stringers had streamed out of the tunnel and were wandering around the parking lot. Most were in a large group just outside of the gate slowly shuffling together. A few intrepid explorers had ventured out to the farther reaches of the lot. The stadium sat in a sort of geological bowl between three higher peaks. Even in this low-lying bowl, the lot rarely flooded because of an extensive waste water system underneath it designed to shepherd heavy rains to the nearby river. The natural slope of the lot and the surrounding landscaping helped contain the crowd a little, but they all knew this crowd was going to slowly disperse in every direction.

"Maybe not." Josh thought out loud.

"Huh?" Jahda turned as she shielded her eyes from the sun. It was starting to get a little lower in the sky and the temperature was starting to drop. The winter coats they had brought with them were still in the trunk of the car. And it was gone.

"I was just thinking. Maybe we can fix this." Josh said.

"Fix it how?" Devin said.

"Oh no, you two already did enough damage. We aren't fixing anything. We are driving back to Martin and Ham and moving on." Jahda said.

"But my parents." Lori said.

"Look honey, I don't want to upset you, but do you really think your parents are still waiting for you at home?" Jahda asked.

"I don't know. And the only way I will know is if we go there and check. Josh and I said we were going to do this and regardless of whatever else has happened we are still doing this." Lori said. "Right Josh?"

"Yep." Josh said.

"So if you want to start walking home, go ahead but we are taking this truck and driving to my house. Right now." Lori said. Jahda just threw up her arms and folded them across her chest. Devin smiled a little.

They stood there for another minute watching the crowd slowly expand around the parking lot. The terrain keeping them ever so subtly hemmed in. For now. Josh climbed into the cab of the truck and Devin jumped in the back with Jahda. He looked at Lori and smiled.

"Ready?" He said. She smiled.

Jahda and Devin sat down with their backs to the cab. She leaned over against him and he thought she was going to kiss his cheek. Instead she whispered in his ear.

"This isn't fun anymore."

"Yeah." He said.

They wound their way through the college. The landscaping and the grounds had always been meticulously kept. That was before the world stopped. They drove slowly down College Boulevard, the main street through campus, and on either side they could see everything in disarray.

They had to drive onto the sidewalk and even on to the grass in places where the road became clogged with abandoned cars. There were rotting corpses everywhere. Hanging from balconies, laying in the road and sticking through windshields. Some still moved but most didn't.   They could see stringers wandering between the buildings and Jahda kept watching to see if they were attracting followers behind them. So far she hadn't seen many.

"Down here at 10th take a right." Lori said to Josh.

"You live in Watercress?"

"Yeah."

"What are you rich or something?" Josh said.

"I don't know. I guess. We live in Watercress, if that makes you rich then yeah." Lori said.

"Yeah, it makes you rich."

"Does that matter?" Lori asked.

"Not anymore." Josh said.

"Would it have before?" Lori asked.

"Not to me."

They turned down the street.

"Third on the right." She said as they pulled through the gates of the community. They were open.

It was another quarter mile before Josh finally saw the third driveway but he couldn't see the house. It sat back behind the trees and the driveway disappeared into them. He stopped the truck.

"Are you sure you want to do this? I mean it could be bad." Josh said.

"I know. I almost expect it to be. I just have to know." Lori said.

"Ok."

He put the truck back in gear and pulled down the driveway. The house sat back from the trees a few yards and the lawn was spacious. They had not seen any stringers in the neighborhood as they drove through. They didn't see any now. The driveway led to a double garage. There was a turnout that made a circle in front of the steps leading up to the front door. They parked the truck in front of the garage. Josh and Lori got out.

Devin and Jahda jumped down from the back and joined them as they walked down the sidewalk to the front door. They kept looking through the windows as they passed but they didn't see anything moving inside the house. They climbed the steps to the front door and look in the sidelights. The house was still. Devin knocked on the front door several times. They waited. Nothing. He stood back and raised his foot.

"No. Don't. I've got the key." Lori said as she lifted the leather necklace from beneath her shirt. The key was tied to it.

"How did you keep up with that?" Josh asked.

"I've worn it around my neck most of my life" Lori said. She pulled the necklace off and inserted the key in the lock. It turned. She swung the door open. They stepped inside. Lori closed the door behind them.

"Mom. Dad" Lori called out softly.

"Which way?" Devin asked.

"We'll look upstairs first." Josh said.

"Oh we ain't splitting up." Jahda said.

"Why not?" Lori asked.

"I don't want to get shot because your Dad doesn't know you're with me." Jahda said.

"It won't happen. My Dad doesn't own a gun." Lori said.

"That you know of." Jahda said as her and Devin started towards the living room.

Josh and Lori walked up the stairs. The house stayed quiet. They couldn't hear anything, living or dead, moving around. They got to the top of the stairs and Lori motioned towards the end of the hallway. "That's my parents room."

They walked to the door and Josh knocked. Lori put her ear to the door but didn't hear anything. Josh opened the door. It was empty. They turned to the other bedroom. Lori put her ear to the door. Josh turned the knob and opened the door. It was Lori's room, and it was empty too.

Devin and Jahda walked through the living room and into the dining room. The place was really nice. Heavy wood furniture sat atop immaculate hard wood floors. All the rooms were large with tall ceilings. Jahda looked at Devin and raised her eyebrow. They walked into the kitchen. Again the place seemed neat and clean compared to most of the rest of the world. Jahda walked through another door into the mudroom. She admired the washer and dryer. It was a thing for her. Devin sat down at one of the stools at the serving bar. He looked down and saw a legal pad.

Dear Lori
I pray it is you reading this. I pray you are ok. I pray you are alive. We tried to find you. I want you to know that. We tried. We went to Jennifer's house. Wherever you are, we love you. We love you so much. We came back home and waited and waited. But your mother had an accident. She got bit. I tried to help her but there was nothing I could do. I kept her comfortable until the end. All she talked about was you. She loved you very much. After it was over I tried to end it. I couldn't. Not until it was too late. She bit me. I stopped the bleeding but I know what happens now. I love you.
Dad

"Whoa." Devin said out loud.

"What?" Jahda said walking over to see what he was reading. She read it too.

Devin had walked around to the other side of the kitchen while Jahda was reading. There was another door. He could see where something had been drug into the house and down the narrow hallway. The drag marks ended at the door. Jahda finished the note and was watching Devin. She stood and looked down the hallway, seeing the same marks he saw. Devin reached for the door started to open it but Lori and Josh came into the kitchen.

"Where does this door go?" Jahda asked.

"The basement. Well the stairs to the basement." Lori said.

"Ok. Listen. I need you to read this. We just found it." Devin said passing the yellow paper over to her.

Lori read the note. Josh read along with her and he felt her get weak in the knees.

"They came to Jennifer's. Oh god. Oh god." Lori said. "Oh daddy. Mom. Oh mom."

Josh put his arms around her, supporting her weight. She was sobbing and beating him on the chest.

"They came to Jennifer's. You took me away. You and your crazy father. You should have left me there." Lori pulled away.

"I'm sorry. How could we know? We were trying to help." Josh said.

"There's more." Jahda said as she nodded to the door.

Lori's hand shot to her mouth.

"No. No. They're not down there. Tell me they're not down there."

"I don't know. But I think they are." Devin said pointing to the drag marks on the floor.

"I can't. I can't." Lori said as she collapsed onto her bottom. Josh went down with her.

"I'm sorry." Josh said. She pushed his hand away.

"We'll go." Devin said as he looked at Jahda. She nodded.

They descended the stairs. Devin pulled out his flashlight. At the bottom of the stair was a door to the right. They knocked on the door and heard a rustling sound but nothing against the door. Jahda turned the knob and swung it open. The beam of Devin's light shone against the far wall. There was a body on the floor. It wasn't moving. Sitting in a chair on the other side of the body was someone. And it was moving. Devin and Jahda approached the person in the chair. It was a man, or had been. There was a plastic bag over its head and its arms and legs were tied to the chair. There was a rope around its neck that was tied to a water pipe that ran over its head. The light shone off the plastic, and the face appeared translucent.

"Why would he do that? He couldn't hang himself from that pipe." Jahda asked.

"I don't think he was trying to hang himself. Look." Devin said. "That's a slipknot. He tied it around his neck so that when he died and came back and tried to move, it would get tighter. He trapped himself."

Devin walked up to the thing. It jerked its head to the movement and continued fighting against the restraints, but he had done too good a job. Devin pulled out his machete and lined it up with the things eye. He drove it through the plastic. Pop.

They walked back up the stairs. Lori was still sitting on the ground and Josh was standing over her. Lori looked up at them.

"It's done." Devin said.

"They were down there?" Lori asked.

"Yes. Both of them." Jahda said.

"But your dad was brave. He rigged it so even if someone found him he couldn't hurt them. He was protecting others. I think he was trying to protect you." Devin said.

315

"Listen, it's going to be dark soon. I don't think we should try going back across town. If you don't mind, I think we should stay here tonight and head out in the morning." Jahda said as she looked at the setting sun.

"Yeah, that sounds like a good idea." Devin said.

"Lori?" Josh asked.

"That's fine. I'm not going back with you anyway." Lori said. Josh just looked at her and then turned and walked back out into the living room.

Devin and Jahda looked at each other and decided they would consider that a yes. They headed out of the kitchen to try to find some blankets. The night was going to be a cold one.

Martin stood outside Josh's house once again. The sun was setting over his shoulder and he walked to the center of the cul-de-sac. He turned and looked up the hill. It was just as empty as the last three times he checked. He walked back to the front door and looked back one more time before closing it behind him.

"They'll be back Opa." Ham said. "Won't they?"

"I hope so." He closed the door against the cold wind.

They walked back into the living room. Martin had brought in the last few logs by the back door and had a fire going in the fireplace. Ham was working on opening a can of chicken and another of fruit salad. He had never really been a fan of fruit salad but she loved the cherries. And the occasional peach but only if he would pick it out for her. He suffered through the pears and apricot for her. He would suffer a lot more. He would do whatever he could to keep her safe. He knew that he would have a better chance of keeping her safe with Devin and Jahda. They had all been through so much together. They had worked together to try to keep each other safe for so long now. He sat there in the quiet watching Ham dole out chicken onto a plate she found in the kitchen. She put one fork down in front of him and one fork down in front of her. He reached for it.

"Not yet." Ham admonished him. "I haven't finished setting the table yet." She placed a butter knife in front of him and then one in front of herself.

"Now." She said, smiling up at him.

He had no idea whether Devin and Jahda were safe. He didn't know if they were alive or dead. They said they would be back by dark. He could see the last light fading in the west. He wanted them to be here because he knew it helped keep Ham safe. But he didn't know where they were now. He didn't know how long the clock in his head was going to allow him to just sit here and wait on them to get back, but he knew it had started ticking.

Wait a little while

For the Hangman

Evelyn looked up at Ed as she walked towards the saloon.

"Everything ok out there?" Ed asked.

"Not really." Evelyn said as she walked up to the saloon. "Everything ok up there?"

"I haven't seen any deaduns if that's what you mean?" Ed said.

"Any what?" Evelyn asked.

"Deaduns. Sorry, let me translate my hick for you. Dead ones." Ed said smiling down at her.

Evelyn looked down at the ground smiling. She just shook her head and walked into the saloon.

She saw Bridger sitting at one of the tables. A bottle sat on it.

"I see you found the tequila." Evelyn said as she lifted the bottle.

"I did." Bridger said, taking the bottle and pouring some more into his glass.

She reached behind the bar and grabbed a glass for herself. She poured a shot and raised it to him.

"Here's to not having to explain" Evelyn said.

Bridger raised his glassed but knitted his eyebrows.

"Explain what?" Bridger said.

"Why you stormed off and ran in here and started drinking." Evelyn said. She drank. He didn't.

"Why? You really want to know why?" Bridger turned to Evelyn.

"Ok." Evelyn said.

"Ok. Fine. You know what JW and I did before this? Way before this?" Bridger asked.

"I know you were in the Army together. That's all Kate ever said." Evelyn said.

"We were. We served together in the big ashtray. Iraq and then Afghanistan. We were on a team together. Our job was to BDA after airstrikes and clean up the loose ends. You know what that is?" Bridger asked.

"Not really" Evelyn said.

"We went in after the target had been blown all to hell to make sure we blew the right thing to hell. If the bombs missed, our job was to try to blow the right thing to hell. Do you know what happens to humans when you drop thousands of pounds of ordinance on their heads?" Bridger asked.

"I can't imagine it's good." Evelyn said.

"Hmmph. It ain't." Bridger looked back over his glass and lost himself in thought for a second. She imagined he was looking at something in his mind that she would never want to see.

"Well after a while that kind of work can get to you. That's part of why most of us end up getting out. It's not the job. The job is the job. You do what you have to do to make sure your side wins. But sometimes you see a face, or a hand or a small toy and the things you did quit being about the job. You question whether or not you can stand in front of God and justify it." Bridger said. "A lot of us have had a hard time with that. I did. I got through it but a lot of guys couldn't. I would have folks call me after I got on TV and say 'Hey this brother is hurting, can you help?' and I would. I would help talk guys down who wanted to end it all. I would get them into some treatment and then just when we all thought they were getting better, you'd get a call that they found them dead."

"That must have been hard." Evelyn said.

"It was. So I stopped helping." Bridger said.

"Why?" Evelyn said.

"Because I quit caring. I mean I still cared about them but I started seeing the devastation they left behind. The families torn apart, the children left without a father and I got angry. I started asking how someone could be so selfish to think their suffering justifies inflicting suffering on others. Then I got cynical. If you want so bad to be dead, take the time to get your affairs in order so your dumbass doesn't screw up everyone else's life. Pay your bills, set up a college fund for your kids. Don't just be a selfish fuck." Bridger said.

"Kind of harsh isn't it?" Evelyn said.

"Yeah, it was. But I think I had to be that harsh in my mind." Bridger said.

"Why?"

"To mask the guilt I felt for abandoning them." Bridger said. "But this is different now."

"How so?" Evelyn asked.

"I'll save it for everyone, because everyone needs to hear this." Bridger said as he downed the shot of tequila and slammed the glass down on the table.

Raj and Scott had carried Amanda over to the gate. The rest of them gathered together and followed them as they carried her down the road and into the woods. The place they used yesterday would have to work since they hadn't had time to dig a pit yet. None of them thought they would need one so soon. Especially not for one of their own. Bridger and Evelyn came out of the saloon just as Charlie was closing the gate behind them. Jennifer turned from Charlie and went back inside the gate.
"If you don't think you can come, I understand." Charlie said.
"No. It's not that. I need to get something." Jennifer said as she walked back towards Amanda's shack.

She walked through the door and went into the back room and looked around. She could see the blood on the floor and gingerly stepped over it. She knelt down by the sleeping bag and grabbed the picture sticking out from between the boards. She walked back out of the cabin to where her father was waiting for her. She held up the picture.
"She would want this." She said.

Charlie reached out his hand and brushed the hair out of her eyes. He smiled at her as he swung the gate back shut. He saw Bridger and Evelyn walking from the saloon.
"I'll get it" Bridger said as he jogged up. "We're coming too."

Raj and Scott lay Amanda down while they gathered some limbs and leaves to help the body burn. Everyone joined in the effort. The wind had died down as the sun started to set in the sky. When they had gathered enough, they gently set Amanda down on the pyre. The wind gusted as they did, blowing the blanket off her face. Everyone could see the bottle sticking out of her chin. They all looked over at Jennifer. She walked up and took the blanket. As she lay the picture of Chris on her chest, she brought Amanda's hands up and placed them on top of it. Jennifer stood back and spread the blanket back over Amanda's face again. Charlie brought the paint can and poured gasoline on top of everything. Everyone stood silently watching, each shivering a little as the sun fell in the sky. "So." Charlie took a step back. He pulled a piece of cloth out of his pocket and wrapped it around a stick. He doused it with a little gasoline.

"Listen up folks." Bridger stepped forward. "Before we say goodbye to Amanda, I want everyone to hear this. Amanda left because she wanted to. She left the way she did because she was too scared to face what was outside the fence. Understandable. And some of you might feel the same way. That's understandable too. Let me say this. If you think you want to follow Amanda down that path, talk to someone. We are all here for each other. Talk to everyone. Maybe you can see a different way. But if you've talked and talked and you're still sure you want to go the Amanda way, come talk to me. I won't stop you. I'll give you the gun. Because if you want to follow Amanda you are not going to put the rest of us in danger by taking pills or slitting your wrists or whatever else you come up with. No, you are going to put a bullet in your brain so someone else doesn't have too. Now, someone want to pray or something?"

Ed sat on top of the saloon. The air was cold and still in the fading light. He rearranged the blanket that was thrown over the nylon hunting chair he was sitting on. He pulled the collar of his coat up around his neck and pulled the knit cap he wore a little lower on his ears. His breath formed a fog in front of his mouth. A slight breeze gently carried it away. He could see the thin line of smoke rising over the trees. The same slight breeze sheered it off as it climbed above the tree line reminding him of the smoke stacks from the mill back home. Night fell.

The Dead of Night
By SB Poe

Marionette Zombie Series
Book 4

The Last Goodbye

Josh leaned against the doorframe as he looked into the bedroom. Pictures adorned the mirror over the white wicker vanity table. A dog. A group of girls, including Lori and Jennifer, at some concert stared back from another. Several stuffed animals peered from the closet. Lori was lying on the bed with her back to the door.

She'd barely spoken to any of them since Devin and Jahda told her what they found in the basement. The pantry had yielded up the few things left to eat, and the others sat at the dining table eating a small meal of tuna fish and peanut butter but Lori didn't join them. She had not moved from the kitchen floor. She leaned against the dishwasher looking at the stairs to the basement. Josh tried to talk to her, but she just kept staring straight ahead. Then she announced she was going to bed and walked up to her room. Josh followed a little while later.

"Lori, I know you're not asleep." Josh said "Come on. I'm sorry. We didn't know. There was no way any of us could have known."

"We didn't have to leave." Lori said, rolling over and looking at him.

"You're right. We didn't have to. But think about it, Jennifer's house was surrounded when we got there. How long would you have been able to hold off that crowd? Do you think you would have survived long enough for your parents to come?" Josh knew his argument was solid, he also knew that if he had a chance to see his father again, he would do anything.

"They came. They came, and I wasn't there. And I wasn't there because of you." Lori said.

"Ok. Fine. What are you going to do now?" Josh asked. "Stay here?"

"It's my home." Lori said.

"No it's just a house now. Four walls and a roof. Just like mine." Josh said. "Lori, listen to me, you need to stay with us. You need to stay with me."

"Why?" Lori said.

"I... I... need you. I need you with me." Josh said.

"I don't care what you need. I need my mother and father and you kept me from them." Lori said.

"But staying with them now isn't an option. I know you're upset, I know how it feels to lose someone close." Josh said.

"You had the chance to say goodbye." Lori said.

Josh just stood and looked at her. He knew he couldn't win this argument.

"You're right. I'm sorry. We'll be downstairs. Goodnight." Josh said. He turned and walked down the stairs.

Jahda and Devin had found a few blankets in one of the closets and spread them out on the floor. Devin grabbed a pillow off the big couch and threw it down too.

"I'll take the floor, you take the couch." He said to Jahda.

"Well ain't you the gentleman. You can bet your ass I'll take advantage of that." She said as she flopped down on the couch. Josh walked into the living room.

"How's she doing?" Jahda asked.

"I don't know. I guess she's ok, but she's pretty pissed at me." Josh said.

"She's not pissed at you man. She's just a little broken right now, and she needs someone to blame. You didn't do anything wrong. Hell from the stories you've told us it sounds like y'all did most everything right." Devin said.

"He's right. She'll see that. She'll snap back. Just let your girlfriend sleep for now." Jahda said.

"I really hope you're right." Josh said. "But she's not my girlfriend."

"You're kidding right?" Jahda said.

"Nope. I mean we kissed once but nothing serious." Josh said.

"Well brother, the way you and her look at each other, it's serious. Even if y'all don't know it yet." Jahda said. "Go to sleep."

Josh grabbed one of the blankets and curled up on an overstuffed recliner. They had been going so hard today that within a few minutes they were all asleep. They had barricaded the doors with furniture and the windows were high enough off the ground that they were pretty sure a stringer couldn't get to them. Besides, since they had gotten here they hadn't seen any stringers at all. Well except for the two in the basement.

Lori lay in her bed looking out of the window. She cried into the same pillow she had cried into when her dog, Sir Pemberton, died last year. She looked back out of the window at the tree limbs she used to climb when she was not much younger. She thought about the dream she had the other night before they crossed the bridge. She cried some more. Finally she cried herself to sleep.

She woke to starlight. It was still night. She sat up and put her feet on the floor. The air was cold and she could see her breath. She thought of her mother and father two floors below her. A lump formed in her throat. Sleep had cleared her mind a little and some of the shock had gone away. She knew that she had probably overreacted to Josh, and she was going to fix that but right now she needed to have her own chance to say goodbye. The house was quiet and dark but she knew her way around, why wouldn't she, it was her home. She made her way down the stairs and looked back down the open hallway. She could see someone asleep on the recliner so she tiptoed into the kitchen.

She went down the stairs. She stood at the door to the basement for a long while. Finally she opened it up and turned on her flashlight. She could see a shape in the chair and another on the floor. She could smell the rot on them but she had to do this. She walked up to the shape on the floor and shined the light. Her mother had been gone for a while now and her skin had turned black and bloated. She recognized the necklace she wore. A single silver cross with the inscription, 'Oh Lord in the darkness, Lead me home'.

She reached down and took the chain off. She turned to her father. He was still tied to the chair and she couldn't see his face through the plastic. She reached up and undid the rope holding his neck. His head flopped forward and for a brief moment she thought he was still alive. She jumped back and almost screamed.

It was in that moment that she knew Josh had been right. She was more afraid he was undead than sad that he was gone. She knew he had been gone a long time now. And no amount of anger was going to change that. She pulled the plastic off his head and looked at his face. She sat down on the floor next to them.

"Mom, Dad, I love you. I am alive. I'm sorry I wasn't there when you came but I don't know if I would be here now if I had been. I came looking for you too. And I found you. I love you both so much. Thank you for everything you gave me."

She sat on the floor and cried for a while. When she finished, she reached over and pulled her father's watch off his wrist. It was something she had given him on one of his birthdays when she was little. Her mother picked it out and had it engraved. "The Best Daddy a little girl could have. Love LOLO". She strapped it on her wrist and stood.

"I love you both. Goodbye." She turned and went out the door, closing it behind her.

She looked up to the top of the stairs and could see some light. The sun was starting to rise. She got to the top of the stairs and walked into the living room. She saw Josh still asleep in the recliner. She knelt down beside him and brushed his hair out of his eyes. They opened.

"I'm sorry." She said.

He reached out and ran his hand through her hair and pulled her to his lips. She kissed him back.

"I'm sorry too. We should have come back sooner." Josh said.

"I don't think it would have mattered. I think this is what was supposed to happen. I need to believe that." Lori said.

Jahda had awoken when Lori had first come down the stairs but she didn't say anything. She lay there until she saw Lori come back out of the kitchen. She watched the moment the two of them shared with a silent smile. She wanted to jump up and say 'See, told ya so' but she restrained herself. She gave them another minute and then she rolled over and yawned loudly.

"Ohhh, that was a good sleep right there." She said, announcing that she was awake. She turned and looked at the two of them and then at Devin on the floor. He was still flat of his back snoring hard. She sat up and kicked his feet.

"Wake up bitch." She said. She rolled her feet up under her and sat up higher on the couch. She looked out the window to see the sun rise.

"Oh shit." She said as she quickly ducked back down. "Wake up Devin. Wake up right now." She said as she kicked his feet in earnest. "Get down" She motioned to Lori and Josh as she slid off the couch onto the floor.

"What, what?" Devin said as he sat up on the floor.

"SHHHH" Jahda said.

"What?" Devin said in a harsh whisper.

"Outside. Slowly. Look outside." Jahda said.

They all slowly looked over the couch. The sun hadn't crossed over the horizon yet but the world was already brightening as it marched towards the sky. The grayness was giving over to whiteness and the outside world came into view. It was full of stringers. Sometime during the night a large crowd had gathered on the yard and it was still there wondering around. Some were right next to the window, their heads passing across the bottoms. Josh turned and looked out of the only other window he could see right now, the one in the mudroom door. He could see more stringers on that side of the house too.

"Shit." Devin said.

"What do we do?" Lori asked.

"Can we get to the truck?" Josh asked.

Devin crawled over to the other side of the living room and looked down the hallway to the front door. He could see that several stringers had made their way up the steps and were now milling around the porch right outside the door. Through the sidelights it looked like the porch was full.

"Not that way." Devin said as he crawled back.

"We can't get through them?" Josh asked.

"Too many." Devin said.

"So we're stuck. Until they leave." Lori said.

"They won't leave. I promise you the ones by the house have already smelled us. That's why they are so close. They won't leave as long as they can smell us. And we can't change our smell." Jahda said.

"So what are you saying?" Josh asked.

"I'm saying that either we figure out a way out of here or this is where we will spend the rest of our short short lives. Once they figure out we are on the other side of that door, they'll get inside." Jahda said.

"I thought they couldn't open doors." Lori said.

"Yeah, but if enough of them are pushing against it, it's going to collapse. If they get inside, we are toast." Devin said.

"Ok, look, really quietly we need to get upstairs. If they do get in, they'll have a harder time finding us. But if they see us moving, it could set them off. So really slow and really quiet." Jahda said.

They all crept as best they could to the stairs and quietly made their way up. They went into Lori's room and looked out of the window onto the back yard. What had been an empty lawn twelve hours ago was now full of stringers. They went across the hall to her parent's room and looked out of the window into the front yard. It was just as bad. Jahda looked down at the truck sitting in front of the garage. She had an idea.

"Lori, is there a room that has a window that we can get out onto the roof of the garage?" Jahda asked.

"Yeah, my bathroom window looks out over the garage. I used to climb out there sometimes." Lori said as she began to understand part of the plan.

"Ok. So we can get out and get to the truck."

"Yeah, but we won't make it into the truck. There are a bunch of stringers around it. They probably smell us on it too." Devin said.

"They'll leave." Jahda said.

"Why would they do that?" Josh asked.

"Because I am going to open the front door." Jahda said.

Devin and Josh stood at the top of the stairs. Jahda was standing one step down. She looked down the hallway and could see shapes moving around the porch through the sidelights. She looked back up at Devin and Josh. Lori stood by the window in the bathroom waiting to do her part. She kept her eyes on the stringers around the truck.

"Ok folks, everyone ready?" She asked.

"I guess." Devin said. He had his pistol in his hand.

"Yeah, let's get this done." Josh said. He had his out pistol too, an old army issue M9 from his father.

Jahda looked back down the stairs and then back up at them.

"Make sure you don't shoot me when I come by." Jahda said smiling at Devin.

"Not a chance." He said smiling back.

She crept down the stairs and looked at the front door. She knew she had to move the chair out of the way to open the door but she hoped the sound and movement of her doing it would help with the plan. She turned back one more time.

"Well, here goes nothing." She said as she walked down the last few stairs.

She reached the chair and started to grab the back. She looked out of the windows beside the door. They had seen her. The ones she could see were all turning and their mouths had started their methodical chomping. She didn't spend too much time watching as she dragged the chair away from the door. She could hear them on the other side, banging and scrapping. She heard the sound of glass breaking and looked into the living room. A stringer put its head through one of the windows. It impaled its throat onto the broken glass and was stuck. It was hanging over the sill, black blood pouring onto the floor, mouth still chomping. She heard the door start to crack.

"Ok it's time." She yelled up to them.

The time for quiet was over. She stood in the middle of the foyer and reached for the door. She turned the deadbolt and the latch lock. She took a deep breath and reached for the door handle. She turned it in her hand and pulled the door open. The stringer on the other side of the door was surprised at first and just stared blankly at her. And then the others behind it began falling into the open space pushing the first one aside. The first one across the threshold was a woman. Her hair had burnt off along with most of the soft parts of her face. Her hands were a mixture of fingers and bones. Some of the fingers still had skin and muscle but some didn't. They just hung between the others even when she reached out, because there was no tendon to straighten them.

Jahda shot her just over the right eye. The noise of the gun in the house was loud. Even louder than she had anticipated but noise was what she needed now.

"COME ON YOU FUCKERS. COME GET YA SOME DARK MEAT." She yelled as she fired into the crowd cramming through the door.

She heard more glass breaking. Devin and Josh had come to the bottom of the stairs and could see into the kitchen. Stringers had started breaking the glass on the mudroom door. They could see them squeezing through. The jagged glass ripped into skin, slicing deep, but the stringer ignored it and kept crawling through. "We're running out of time." Devin said. He yelled back up the stairs. "LORI, TALK TO ME."

"Not yet." She called down.

"Shit, this isn't working." Devin said.

Jahda was still standing in the foyer firing at faces as they appeared. She had almost blocked the door with bodies.

"COME ON. COME GET US." She yelled again.

"COME ON. COME ON YOU DEAD MOTHER FUCKERS." Devin yelled too.

Jahda started to back up towards the stairs as more of them came over the dam of the dead at the front door. Devin and Josh stood on the first few stairs waiting for her to get to them. She fired a few more times and backed up to them. The smell of gunpowder and rot filled the house.

"Ok. Now we just have to hold them off until we can go." Jahda said turning to Devin and Josh.

They all aimed their pistols at the crowd filing through the door. They heard more glass breaking. They knew they were trying to come in from all sides now. They could see into the kitchen and the first one through the window was still hanging as the other piled against the door. They were pushing against the things lower back and legs while his arms and shoulders doubled over the broken window of the door. They were squeezing him like a tube of toothpaste and most of the rot inside was coming out his mouth and nose.

They stood about halfway up the stairs randomly firing at the stringers coming closest to them. The living room looked like a cocktail party of the dead. Each of them stumbling and falling over the bodies Josh, Devin and Jahda were stacking up on the floor with each round they fired. They nervously eyed the top of the stairs listening for Lori.

"They're gone. They're gone. Let's go." Lori finally called out.

Devin ran to the top of the stairs and into Lori's bathroom. He helped her open the window, and she climbed out onto the roof.

"IT'S OPEN. LETS GO." Devin yelled back to Josh and Jahda.

Jahda turned and headed up the stairs. Josh backed up still firing at the bottom of the stairs as more and more began trying to climb over the pile of dead. He fired one final round and turned and ran. The stringers began climbing the stairs. He ran into the bathroom as Jahda was going out of the window. He climbed out behind her. Devin had already jumped down on the ground and was helping Lori and Jahda off the roof. He walked down to the edge and looked down. He stepped off and hit the ground hard.

"You ok?" Devin said reaching down a hand.

"I guess. Let's go." Josh said. He stood and ran to the driver's door. He looked back at the house.

They had managed to lure all the stringers outside of the house inside. He could see through the windows. The house was full. He could see some in the upstairs windows too.

"Let's go Josh." Jahda said from the back of the truck.

"Yep." He climbed into the truck and started it up.

Jahda looked at the house as they drove away. The stringers had started to find their way back out of the door, chasing the scent. She sat down against the back of the truck cab and smiled.

"Why you got that big old shit eatin grin on your face?" Devin said as he looked at her.

"It worked." Was all she said, she kept smiling.

Where the cold wind blows

Bridger made his way behind the Alamo and started towards the south end of the compound. The sun would be up soon and he could already see the stars to the east fading away as the light of the local star engulfed them. He had studied military strategies and tactics from Sun Tzu to Tecumseh. Attacks come at sunrise in order to have a pitched battle all day. Bridger knew that was from eras long gone because modern warfare didn't care about the sun. He had spent most of his time training at night. Most of the operations he had been a part of had happened at night. The time for protracted daylight battles had long passed before Bridger had ever took up arms. Never the less, he still always liked being on shift at this time of day. Just in case.

He walked along the fence. He looked through the trees but couldn't see anything moving. He came to the east side and looked at the swath of pushover they had traversed to the creek. He knew they had to make the other sides of the compound as easily observable. He wasn't sure how enthusiastic the others would be to follow his suggestions after his harshness to them about Amanda. He had not slept easy as he replayed the words in his mind that night. He looked down at the ground and shrugged his shoulders. He sighed deeply. He pulled his knit cap off and ran his hand across his head. The smooth baldness had given way to uneven stubble.

"You have a rough night?" Tilly said as she came between two of the buildings.

"Not really. Just a long one." Bridger said as he straightened himself up.

"Well, go grab some coffee. I think Evelyn has some water boiling." Tilly said as she motioned her head towards the saloon.

"Sounds good. You got this?" Bridger said.

"Yeah, Raj is coming to join me in a minute and we'll make the rounds for a while." Tilly said.

Bridger looked at her. She was dressed in jeans and a surplus camo winter coat with a fur-lined hood. It wasn't cold enough yet for her to have it drawn up over her head. She had on a baseball cap and her red hair was pulled back in a ponytail. She had a pistol on one hip and a machete on the other. He thought about the first time he met her, her head sticking out of the window of her crushed car. They had both came face to face with this together on the side of the road that day. It seemed like a lifetime ago. Several lifetimes.

"What do you think about this?" Bridger asked.

"About what?" Tilly asked as she looked around.

"All of it. The way things are now." Bridger said.

She turned and looked at him. She was slightly confused, and a little taken aback. They had been almost side by side since the day that truck crashed down on her. Even as she was dealing with what happened with the asshole, Bridger hadn't asked her much at all.

"Are you serious?" Tilly asked.

"Yeah. I mean, I'm just trying to get some perspective." Bridger said.

"Perspective? Ok. Here's my perspective. We're alive. A couple of months ago we all were living lives we thought mattered, and they did. Then. Kate was right. Hell that asshole that tried to, you know...." She looked up at Bridger, he nodded. "Even that asshole was right. New world, new rules. The real bitch of it is that we don't know the rules. We're having to make 'em up as we go. And right now the only rule I got is to stay alive. All of us." She said.

"You think this is the best way to stay alive? This place?" Bridger asked.

"Sure. For now at least. We have food, we're pretty isolated and we don't see many deaduns." Tilly said.

"Any what? Deaduns?" Bridger said.

"Yeah, I heard Ed say it." Tilly laughed a little.

"Deaduns. Hmm" Bridger smiled. "I think I'll go and get that coffee now." He turned to walk away and stopped and turned back. "I want you to know something."

"What's that?" Tilly said.

"That day, the first day, when I found the wreck. I am glad it was you and Raj in that car." Bridger said.

"Why's that?" Tilly asked.

"I just am." Bridger smiled. He turned and slung his rifle over his back. He waved back over his shoulder. "See ya."

Tilly watched him walked away.

"That was weird." She said to herself. Raj walked out from between Kate and Evelyn's sheds.

"Hey, ready?" Raj said.

"Sure." Tilly said.

She turned to meet him and took one of the shotguns from him. They turned and walked down the fence together. Bridger walked to the saloon. The grill was going and Bridger saw an old percolator coffee pot sitting on the grates. He could smell the coffee. Evelyn walked out the back door of the saloon.

"Where'd you find that?" Bridger asked, pointing at the coffee pot.

"Oh, it was under one of the cabinets in the kitchen. I pulled everything out this morning just to see what we had as far as cookware goes." Evelyn said, as she held up a cast-iron skillet.

"Nice." Bridger said. "Whatcha cooking?"

"I don't cook. I organize. Sorry. But I thought you could whip up one of your good tasting MRE breakfasts for everyone. You said you knew how." Evelyn said.

"I did indeed." Bridger said. "We'll have to find the right MRE's. But I'll make it simple. Since we mostly have old surplus, we'll just need to grab the sliced ham, potatoes-au gratin, and some of the little hot sauce bottles. Come on."

Bridger walked by her and went in the back door to the kitchen. She sat the skillet down on the picnic table and followed him back inside. He paused inside the door to set his rifle down and Evelyn didn't see him until she ran into him. Bridger was off balance and fell back against the stove. He caught her as she fell against him. He looked at her face. In the early morning light he could all the lines of life around her eyes. Her hair was starting to gray in places. Her eyes were a pale blue. She looked up at him. He stood up straight and stepped back. They both laughed a little.

"Well, next time I'll not stop in the doorway." Bridger said.

"Yeah that's probably a good idea." Evelyn said as she wiped her hand back over her hair. "Ok. Let's get to it."

They walked into the kitchen and went over to the stack of MRE's in the corner. He reached up and pulled one of the cases off. They went through several boxes and found the right bags. He tore them open and dumped all the contents onto a table.

"So we just need the one thing out of these bags? What about all the other stuff? There's a lot of food in these things." Evelyn said.

"Yeah. They're designed with a lot of calories. We can survive on these for a while." Bridger said.

"We have the rice and beans too." Evelyn said.

"Is that what you want to do?" He asked.

"What?" Evelyn asked.

"Survive? Here?" Bridger said.

"I guess. I mean what choice to we have?" Evelyn asked. Bridger raised his eyebrow.

"Hold up. Yes I want to survive. I don't know what choice we have about leaving here. That's all I meant. Don't hand me your pistol." Evelyn said. She smiled.

Bridger realized what she meant and looked down.

"That was kind of rough, wasn't it?" Bridger said. "I mean, what I said. That was a little too much."

"No. It wasn't. It needed to be said. I think everyone needed to hear it. Like you told me yourself, things are different now. New rules." Evelyn said.

"Tilly said the same thing just a few minutes ago. New rules." Bridger said.

"She's right."

"Yeah, she also said that we are making them up as we go. She said the first rule is stay alive." Bridger said.

"Good first rule." Evelyn said.

"Agreed." Bridger said. "Alright. Let's get this going." She turned and looked at all the contents left on the table.

"What about this?" Evelyn said.

"Well you said you organize, so organize." He said as he walked out the back door. She smiled.

Kate stood in her room and looked down. She had her sleeping bag spread out on the floor along with a couple of blankets. She didn't have to get dressed because she had slept in her clothes. She decided she would go one more day in these jeans and then they would have to be washed. The colder it had gotten the less they had cared to do laundry. Besides, they all stunk. She fantasized about her shower. She pictured it in her mind, letting the water wash over her and warm her up. Suddenly an image of JW stepping into the shower with her sprang into her mind. She opened her eyes and looked down. A single tear rolled down her cheek.

"Good morning Mom." Scott said as he walked into the shack.

She turned to face him and wiped her eyes.

"Everything ok?" He asked.

"Yep. Just, you know, momma stuff." She said.

"Ok." Scott said, shrugging his shoulders. "I'm going to find some breakfast, you wanna come?"

"Sure, I'll be out in a second." She said.

Scott walked back outside. She turned her head back to the floor and took a deep breath. She closed her eyes again and briefly saw a flash of JW's face before the memory faded again. She took another deep breath and opened her eyes again.

"Let's go." She said, mainly to herself, and she walked out the door to meet Scott.

They walked over towards the saloon. Charlie and Jennifer were sitting on one of the benches on the front porch. Dottie walked out of her shack directly across from the saloon as Kate and Scott approached. They all stopped.

"Good morning." Kate said to everyone.

"Morning Kate. You too Scott." Charlie said.

"Everything ok, Charlie?" Kate asked.

"My daughter is still with me, so yeah. But yesterday was rough." Charlie said.

"How are you doing Jen honey?" Dottie asked.

She smiled but the tremble of her lips betrayed her stoicism. Dottie walked over and sat down beside her. She put her arm around her and hugged her.

"It's ok sweetie. It's all over now." Dottie said as she patted her shoulder.

"Yesterday is over, but what about tomorrow? Something else could happen tomorrow." Jennifer said.

"I know honey. I know you had a terrible thing happen. You had to do something hard to stay alive. But you did it. You stayed alive. You fought for it. You earned today. And now that you earned it, you wanna spend your time frettin over it? Come on honey, you're alive. I'm alive. Hell, we are all alive today. Tomorrow and yesterday don't matter a flitter if you're not alive today. You earned today. You should try to remember that." Dottie said as she patted Jennifer on the knee.

Jennifer wiped the tears from her eyes. She looked up at Dottie. Her hair was almost white. The lines on her face traced around her mouth and down towards her chin. When she spoke the whole surface of her face moved. The wrinkles gathered and retreated together as though conducted by the motions of the lines around her mouth. Her eyes were green and bright. Jennifer looked at them.

"I'll try." Jennifer said.

She did actually feel a little better. They all stood and made their way to the picnic table behind the saloon. They found Bridger standing over the grill stirring something in a cast-iron skillet. And they smelled coffee.

"That smells like breakfast." Charlie said as they sat down at the table.

"Just an old standby." Bridger said as he spooned the concoction onto each plate.

Dottie bowed her head.

"Dear Lord" She started. Everyone else heard her and lowered their eyes. "Thank you for this day. Thank you for this food. Thank you for this new family you have given us to help us through these crazy days. Amen"

"Amen" Bridger said.

They sat together and ate breakfast. Evelyn sat next to Kate and Scott. Charlie and Jennifer sat across from them with Dottie by their side. Bridger stood by the grill spooning the food into his mouth. He sat the plate down when he saw Raj and Tilly cross between two of the buildings.

"Hey, y'all come get something to eat. You too Ed." Bridger said as he looked up to the roof. Ed looked down and stood.

The whole group was gathered together eating. It had been over two months now since the first reports echoed the outbreak of the Marionette virus.

"Listen folks. Since we're all here, I guess we should talk about things." Bridger started. "I don't know how y'all feel but I think we should stay right here and make this place better."

"Is anyone talking about leaving?" Evelyn asked.

"Well no, but I just wanted say my peace." Bridger said.

"What other choice do we really have?" Dottie said.

"Well, we really don't know what things are like outside. None of us have been out there." Jennifer said.

"That boy and girl went out." Ed said.

"That boy and girl had names, Josh and Lori." Jennifer said.

"Well, Josh and Lori ain't come back." Ed said.

Bridger shot a glance at Kate. She winced at Ed's words.

"That don't mean nothing." Bridger said.

"Well it means the world outside is fucked." Ed said.

"How so?" Charlie asked.

"Well if everything was all cool, I would hope the boy would have come back for his momma by now." Ed said, nodding towards Kate.

"That doesn't mean anything happened to them." Scott said.

"Never said it did. I just mean that they didn't find anything other than what we already seen. Just more deaduns." Ed said.

"So we stay here." Kate said. "What do we need to do to make this place *better* Bridger?"

"Oh and by the way, he'll come back." Kate turned and said to Ed.

"I'm sure he will. No disrespect meant." Ed said.

Bridger told everyone his idea. They would work in two teams of four. Three cutters and one lookout. Each team would work one day on, one day off. Tilly and Raj would cover night watch. The teams would be Scott, Charlie and Kate with Jennifer on lookout. Ed, Evelyn and Bridger with Dottie on lookout. Everyone would be armed.

"So when do we get started?" Charlie asked.

"I thought we would all walk out there together this afternoon so everyone could get an idea of what we're trying to do. We can start tomorrow. As long as everyone agrees." Bridger said.

"Won't it take a long time to do what you want to do?" Dottie asked.

"Best to get started right away then." Bridger smiled at her.

Road of Bones

Fire had ravaged some of the neighborhoods. Burnt framing jutted upward, black against the overcast sky. The truck made its way through the abandoned streets. The wind carried the coldest air of the season. The clouds were sagging heavy and low, full of moisture that was still deciding between rain and snow. Some streets brought cars piled on top of each other, a testament to the panic that unfolded. As they navigated the town, it had an eerie ancient feel, as if frozen in time. Except this menagerie had moving parts. Everywhere they looked, scattered among the wreckage, walking down the streets and wandering through the yards, stringers. Probably letting a couple of thousand out of the stadium wasn't the best idea. Jahda and Devin sat in the bed of the truck with their backs against the cab. Josh and Lori were in the front. Josh turned left and stopped. He knocked on the back glass. Devin turned around so he could hear.

"Look." Josh said.

He was pointing down the street. Devin and Jahda both stood and looked over the cab of the truck.

"What?" Jahda said.

"The car. The one on the left. That's our car." Josh said.

Sitting halfway up on the curb in front of an electronics store was Janice's car. The trunk and both passenger side doors were open. They all hopped out of the truck.

"So are you wanting to get it back or something?" Devin asked.

"Not really, but I would like to know what the hell that guys deal was." Josh said.

"The crazy dude who stole it? Hard pass on that one. I hope I never see him again." Devin said.

"I guess you're right. Let's see if he left anything." Josh said.

They walked over to the car. Jahda looked up and down the street. Josh looked in the passenger door. Nothing. He looked in the back seat. Nothing. They walked to the back of the car to look in the trunk. The shotgun was lying on the ground next to the car. There were several empty shotgun shells lying on the ground too. They all looked into the trunk. There was a stringer with half its head missing curled up inside. Black blood was splattered against the open trunk lid.

"Looks like he took this one out. But why leave the gun?" Josh asked as he looked at the stringer.

"I guess he ran out of ammo and decided to run." Jahda said.

"Or maybe he had another gun and left that one because he didn't need it." A voice came from behind them.

Jahda turned but the sound of the shotgun being racked made her freeze. The others had yet to start turning. They all raised their hands. Jahda had turned enough that she could see the man standing behind them. She raised her hands too. She could see he had managed to find some clothes. And shoes.

"Oh shit. It's you. You're the folks from the stadium." The man chuckled "Damn shit luck, huh? At least for you, I mean. As for me, it works out great."

"Why? Why you doing this?" Devin said over his shoulder.

"Take a look around man, this is the way things are now. Survival of the fittest and all that." He said.

"More like survival of the sneakiest." Lori said.

"Whatever keeps you alive, hon.?" He said.

"Don't call me hon. My name is Lori." She snapped back.

"Ok calm down kitten. I mean Lori. Lori, my name is Grayson." Grayson said.

"I don't give a shit what your name is." Lori said.

Josh glanced at Devin. He nodded at the pistol in his waistband. Devin eyes grew a little wider, but he nodded.

"I am damn glad you guys showed up when you did at the stadium, and I am damn glad you showed up today." Grayson said continuing to chuckle. "Nice truck you brought me."

Josh suddenly reached over and shoved Lori into Devin. They both fell to the ground. Grayson was briefly distracted as Josh wheeled around and quickly drew his pistol.

"Hey, hey don't shoot. It's not even loaded. Shit." Grayson said as he dropped the shotgun.

He turned and ran down the sidewalk as fast as he could. Josh stood there, with his pistol in his hand, watching him run away. He didn't shoot.

"If we ever see that crazy son of a bitch again we'll just shoot him. Anyone object?" Jahda said.

"Sounds good to me." Devin said.

Jahda reached down and picked up both shotguns. Empty. Devin took one from her and they all climbed back in the truck. They were a few more miles from the entrance to Josh's neighborhood and the cul-de-sac. They made their way there as rapidly as they could. It still took almost an hour of diverting around wrecks and small crowds of stringers.

The night that stood sentry outside the window had retreated a few hours ago. By the calendar in his head it was somewhere around January. They missed Christmas, no one had noticed. The sky brightened and the afternoon winds came in gusts. Empty limbs whipped violently one moment and sat silently still the next. Martin stood by the boarded-up window watching the three stringers that had managed to work their way through the woods. They were now aimlessly wandering in the yard next door. It was more than he had seen since they found this place. He turned to Ham.

"There's more." He said.

"How many?" Ham asked.

"More. Not too many yet, but more." He said.

"Do we have to leave? What about Jahda and Devin?" She asked.

"Listen, I don't know where they are and I don't know what happened to them. Maybe they will come back but there are more stringers starting to show up. We don't have to leave right now but we need to start to get ready. We can get some things loaded up." Martin said.

"Loaded in what? Your truck broke. That's why we walked here." Ham said.

He looked at her. For barely twelve she had a good understanding of the situation, even parts of it that Martin had spent the better part of an hour trying to figure out.

"That boy, Josh, that's his jeep sitting in the garage. The key is in it." Martin said. "Once we are loaded up, we'll be ready to go. Ok?" Martin said.

"Ok. Where are we going to go?" Ham asked.

"I don't know." Martin said.

"That doesn't sound like much of a plan." Ham said.

"What did you say?" Martin turned to her, surprised.

"Nothing." She retreated.

"No really, what did you say?" Martin said. He softened as he realized he had seen her grow up faster in the last few months than the last few years.

"It's not really a plan. Just driving off with no where to go." Ham raised her chin as she spoke more confidently.

"You know what? You're right." Martin said. Ham beamed. "We should make a proper plan."

He was glad she had started thinking at least one step ahead. He smiled.

"Let's get the map. We'll fix a little bite to eat and make a plan." Martin said.

Ham took some plates out of the cabinet and sat them on the table. Martin unfolded the map and brought a candle over. Ham opened a can of sausages and put a few on each plate. They sat down and she gave thanks. Ham sat on her knees in the chair so she could lean over the map. Martin sat half on the table, holding the candle high above his head. Ham started looking at the map.

"Where are we Papi?" Ham looked up and asked.

Martin pointed to the spot on the map. She put her finger next to his. She started tracing different roads.

"Which road did we get here on?" Ham asked. He pointed again.

She traced it all the way back to a little town called Spivey's Hamlet. She reached into Martin's shirt pocket and pulled out his pen. She drew a sad face over the town.

"Why did you do that?" Martin asked.

"That's where we lost the Dabners and Hector and Maria. I remember the name of the town. I thought it sounded nice. I was wrong." Ham said matter of fact.

Martin stood for a while watching her. It had not dawned on him, until that very moment, that all these things he had seen, she had seen too. Somewhere in his mind he had convinced himself that he had kept her safe. That was a lie. He had kept her alive, but he hadn't kept her safe. She had seen unimaginable horror and lost friends in the process. She had been forced, on two occasions, to shoot stringers. And even though they weren't people, still. And here she was, drawing a frowny face on a map and moving on. He realized something else too. There was a truck pulling up to the curb.

"Ham, be still." He said.

She looked up from the map at his face. He was staring over her shoulder. She turned.

"Well I'll be." Martin said. "It's them."

Martin watched through the opening in the boards covering the front window as Josh and Jahda stepped out of the truck and met the infected in the yard next door. Devin and Lori came around the other side as Jahda was pulling her machete from the eye socket of the last stringer. Martin opened the door.

"Welcome back." Martin said.

"We was going to leave you." Ham said.

"Really?" Jahda asked.

"Yep, I was looking at the map." Ham said as she pushed passed Martin.

She jumped into Jahda's arms, surprising Jahda and Martin, and gave her a hug.

"Glad we didn't leave?" She asked.

"I sure am." Jahda said, returning the hug.

Martin stepped aside so Jahda and Ham could go inside. He stepped back when Devin and Josh approached.

"Nice truck." Martin said as he nodded towards the odd vehicle parked at the curb.

"Thanks. It's a loaner." Devin said.

"We saw the stadium. It was neat." Josh said. He smiled at Devin.

"Yeah, neat." Devin said chuckling.

"Uh huh." Martin said as he stepped aside again.

Devin and Josh walked inside the door. Martin took another look at the truck. He looked at the three bodies lying in the yard next door. The wind picked up again and a few leaves scuttled low across the cul-de-sac, raspy against the asphalt, like the death rattle of the world. He stepped inside and closed the door.

Don't Leave Today

Everyone stood against the fence looking towards the creek. They couldn't see all the way to the water wheel slowly churning about a hundred yards away but they could see a lot. Bridger stood between them and the creek.

"Look folks. See how far we can see? That helps us. But more than that, these pushovers are a bitch to walk through. Anything or anyone trying to get close to us will have a hard time doing it. I know it is a lot of work but I think we need to do it." Bridger said.

"How?" Dottie asked.

"We have some axes and saws." Bridger said. "We have a small chainsaw too, but I don't think we should use it. Too loud."

"Lot of trees." Jennifer said.

"We don't have to cut them all down. Just some." Bridger said.

"We can start with the smaller ones and go from there." Charlie said.

"Seems like it's settled then." Evelyn said. Everyone nodded, some more enthusiastically than others.

"Great. First group starts tomorrow." Bridger said. "Me, Evelyn, Ed and Dottie."

Bridger followed behind as the group made their way back inside the fence. He had overheard a few complaints but for the most part everyone seemed to be on board. He caught up with Raj and Tilly who were walking just behind the others.

"Hey listen, I know I didn't ask first but I assume you two are okay with pulling night watch?" Bridger asked.

"Sure. I get it. You're just trying to set me and Raj up." Tilly said smiling.

"Well you two would make a great couple." Bridger said. Raj smiled then seriousness returned to his face.

"How long do you think this will take? To do what you want to do." Raj asked.

"Well at least a couple of weeks. Maybe more. It will probably take longer just because we don't need to be in a big hurry." Bridger said.

"If we don't need to be in a hurry why do it at all? If it will make us safer shouldn't we do it as quickly as possible?" Raj asked.

"It will make us safer, but that is just part of it." He continued. "The other part is boredom."

"Boredom?" Raj asked.

"Yeah, boredom. We need to stay busy. We all have a lot of shit on our minds and most of it we can't do a damn thing about, instead of sitting around brooding over that shit we need to stay busy. Plus it makes us safer." Bridger finished.

"Dude, did you just say brooding?" Tilly smiled. They all did. Bridger walked on ahead.

"Why so many questions? Tilly asked Raj.

"I don't know. I just want to know what the plan is, just to know." He said half smiling.

"Are you ok?" Tilly asked, knowing he wasn't but hoping he wouldn't say so. She had sensed him trying to navigate her emotions.

"Sure. Are you?" Raj asked.

"Sure. All good." They kept walking; both lying and knowing the other one did too.

She took a few more steps and stopped. She stood there watching as he took a few more until he realized she was no longer beside him. He stopped and turned.

"Raj listen, we should talk." Tilly said and immediately regretted it. Not because she didn't want to talk but because it sounded like the start of her standard junior high school break up speech.

"Talk? Now? You know we are outside the fence right?" Raj asked.

"I know and maybe not right this second but we need to talk." She said, but he called her bluff.

"No. You want to talk and I want to listen so you talk and I'll listen. And keep an eye out." Raj said and smiled.

"Ok. Here goes." She started nervously. "I'm trying. I want you to know that. I really want things to be ok with us, I do, and I think they will be soon. Please just don't be angry or disappointed with me. I don't know what I would do if I.."

"Angry? Disappointed? Is that what you think?" He interrupted. "No, no, no. I am not angry or disappointed or anything else. I am confused."

"Confused?" She asked as she drew her eyebrows quizzically together.

"Yes confused. I love you and want to be there for you but at the same time I feel as though me being near you would somehow make you uncomfortable. And then the other day you flinched when I touched you." He said.

"I'm sorry about that." She said.

"No, you should not be. It is a completely understandable if not expected reaction. I am just unsure how to proceed." He half smiled.

"You know one of the things I love about you?" She asked as she stepped closer to him and took his hands in hers.

"What's that?" Raj smiled wider.

"This." She hugged him tight as the gulf between them closed.

They walked, hand in hand, behind the others. As they approached the gate Kate stopped and turned. She smiled at them. Raj turned and set the gatepost inside the hole and they all walked towards the saloon as the sun set over their shoulders.

The trees swirled in the wind, dancing to their own music. Charlie stepped outside his shack shivering against the morning air. He carried his sleeping bag draped over his shoulders as he stepped onto the path. The ground, almost constantly mud, normally would give a soft squish but this morning it was a distinctive crunch. He looked up and down the track that served as their main roadway. The frozen moisture on the ground sparkled like individual diamonds even in the dim light of the overcast morning. He turned to see his daughter come out of the shack next door. She was bundled up in her blanket as well. They smiled at each other.

"Wow. It's cold this morning." Charlie said.

Living as they had for the last few months had allowed their bodies to acclimate. They had adjusted as the temperature had fallen for the most part. This morning was markedly different.

"I'm FRE-E-ZING." She said smiling back.

"Let's go over to the saloon and see if we can get that fire going." Charlie said.

They put their bedding away and started walking towards the saloon. As they came around the corner they saw Dottie walking over too. Charlie and Jennifer grabbed a few of the split logs by the picnic table and walked inside the saloon. Kate and Scott soon joined them as they warmed up the potbelly stove. The room became warmer almost instantly. Evelyn emerged from the kitchen with the percolator and soon the room was full of the smell of coffee. Kate and Scott passed out MRE's. Raj and Tilly came inside as the coffee was being poured.

"Lord almighty it's cold out there." Tilly said as she stamped her feet just inside the door.

"It started dropping sometime after midnight. The wind started as the sun came up." Raj said as he set down the shotgun against the wall by the door.

Ed and Bridger came in next. They had gone to the shed to grab the axes and saws. They sat them down outside against the picnic table and walked into the saloon.

"Damn y'all, the hawks out this morning." Bridger said.

"The what?" Jennifer asked.

"The hawk." Scott said. "It means it's cold and windy. My dad used to say it. It was some kind of army thing I think. Right?"

"Well not really but that's how your Dad knew it, for sure." Bridger said. "Anyway folks I think we probably need to wait a bit before heading out. Let the sun get up good."

"Y'all are still going out there today? In this cold?" Jennifer asked.

Bridger looked at Evelyn and Ed. His eyebrows knitted when he cast his eyes on Dottie.

"Don't look at me like that. I'll out work all of you and twice on Sunday's" Dottie said as she lifted her middle finger at Bridger. The room erupted in laughter.

They broke bread together and spent time under the warm glow of the stove. As the sun climbed towards what would be its lowly winter zenith Charlie stepped outside.

"Well you know what they say? If you don't like the weather in the south just wait a bit, it'll change." He said as he swung the door open and stepped into a bright sunny sky.

The day was still cold, but the sun had managed to break out of its cloudy jail. The winter air still kept the ground crunchy under his feet for the most part but there were a few muddy spots to navigate now. As they walked outside, they could see the subtle steam rising off of the thawing frost. Bridger and Ed walked over to the picnic table and grabbed the axes and saw.

"Well, I guess we can get started." Bridger said.

Raj walked over and handed the shotgun to Dottie. "You'll want this." He said.

She took the shotgun and slung it over her shoulder. Ed and Bridger had the tools. Evelyn came out of the saloon slinging a backpack over her shoulder. "I've got a couple of MRE's and some water. Do we need anything else?" She asked.

"Nope. Let's get started." Bridger said.

"Listen. Do y'all mind if I tag along for a while today?" Charlie asked.

"Not at all. Why?" Bridger said.

"Just to kind of get a feel for what we're trying to do." Charlie said.

"I'll come too." Jennifer said.

"No, no. You stay here. Help Kate and Scott. I just want to help get it started. We'll go out together tomorrow." Charlie said.

She shrugged her shoulders and turned to Kate.

"Come on Jennifer, we'll find something to do." Kate said as she wrapped her arm around her shoulders. She looked back and waved at Charlie as they walked towards the gate.

Charlie reached over and relieved Bridger of one of the axes he was carrying. They walked out the gate. Ed set the post back, and they started down the muddy track.

"We'll just head down about hundred yards or so and then start." Bridger said.

They got to a spot that Bridger decided would be a good place to begin. They all took their axes and went to work. Dottie stood on the road watching. After about thirty minutes they all stopped and looked at each other. Everyone was drawing heavy breaths, some more than others. Ed leaned on his axe.

"Damn. This sucks." Ed said.

The four of them started swinging again but with a little less vigor. The adrenaline rush of starting had waned rapidly. They worked taking a few breaks for the next few hours. They managed to cut down several smaller trees and Bridger managed one larger tree. They had felled them in more or less the same direction. Bridger wanted to keep the road clear.

"Another break?" Bridger asked as the small tree he was working on fell to the ground.

"Sure." Evelyn said. She took another few swings and left the axe buried in the tree.

They had worked a steady pace and looking around they could tell a difference.

"You know, I wasn't sure about the benefit of doing this but I gotta admit, even with this bit we've done I can see what you are talking about." Charlie said as he looked at Bridger, the breath steaming from his mouth in gushes.

"It's a lot of work but I think it's worth it." Bridger said.

"I agree. I think I am going to head back now. I get what needs to be done. I'll make sure we stay on track tomorrow with Kate and Scott." Charlie said. He stood.

"Great. We'll see you this evening." Bridger said.

Charlie turned and started walking back towards the compound. He looked back over his shoulder and could see the others grabbing their axes and heading back into the woods. He turned back towards the compound. He got about halfway up the road and stopped. He glanced back partially over his other shoulder and slowly brought his head back. There. He stepped forward a half step. Between the trees he could see something. He tilted his head left and right. Finally he started walking towards it. About twenty yards into the woods on the opposite side of the road he could see a girl. A young girl. In a dress. He slowly approached her.

"Hey, you ok?" Charlie said, as he got closer. There was no response from the girl.

She stood in the shadow of a big oak tree. As he got closer, he could see she was not ok. He saw the cuts and tears on her legs and the dried blood on her arms and hands. The dress was covered in mud and blood and her skin had the gray pallor of the others he had seen. She was a deadun, but she was motionless. She looked dead. Deader.

Charlie stood looking at her. He was only a few feet away and yet this thing still had not moved. He bent forwards and looked up at her eyes. The lids were closed. He couldn't see her chest rise and fall but he wasn't sure it would. Did these things breathe? He had told Bridger they didn't know shit about these things. He thought briefly about trying to somehow restrain it so they could learn something about them but then an image from some movie flashed in his mind. A mad scientist dissection. He dismissed it from his mind with a quick smile and turned his attention back to the thing in front of him.

He considered that he should turn back and get some of the others and looked around. It was just him and this thing. He unsheathed his knife and turned it over in his hand and raised it above his head like Norman Bates. He drove it down to the top of the things head. The blade glanced off the hard bone of its skull and Charlie slightly lost his balance. The things eyes suddenly opened as he leaned towards it trying to regain his footing. He felt the sharp pain in his shoulder as the thing bit into his flesh. His eyes grew wide, and he screamed. He hammered the knife into the side of the things head rapidly. Pop. The thing went limp. He dropped the knife and covered the wound with his hand. He could feel the blood soaking through his clothes. He knew. He stumbled back out towards the road.

Bridger and Evelyn both heard the scream. Ed turned and started leaping over the fallen trees towards the sound. Dottie started back towards the road with Bridger and Evelyn. They all stepped out onto the muddy track as Charlie stepped out just up the road. They could see blood on the hand covering his shoulder. They ran to him.

"What happened?" Bridger asked.

"Bit. I saw one. It was asleep or frozen or something. I walked right up to her and..." Charlie trailed off, trying to remember what went wrong.

"Let me see." Evelyn said.

"It's no use. I felt it." Charlie said.

"Let's get you back and let Raj take a look." Evelyn said.

"Oh shit. Jennifer. How am I going to tell Jennifer? How..." Charlie started.

"Hey, hey. Calm down. I don't know but I do know she'll need you to be calm. Right now." Evelyn said.

"You're right." Charlie said. "Shit." He nodded but Evelyn could see the weight heavy on his shoulders.

They all walked with Charlie back to the gate. Ed opened it up and they all walked through.

"Let's go to the saloon." Bridger said.

Charlie walked with Evelyn's arm wrapped over his shoulder. Bridger, Dottie and Ed followed closely behind. They walked up onto the porch of the saloon and in through the door.

"Ed, go find Raj. Tell him bring the first aid kit." Bridger said. Ed nodded and ducked back out the door.

Kate was in the kitchen and heard them come through the door. She came around the corner and saw Charlie slumped in a chair with Evelyn in the chair next to him helping him take off his jacket.

"What happened?" Kate said as she came in the room.

"Charlie. He thinks he got bit." Evelyn said looking in Charlie's eyes.

"Ed went to get Raj." Bridger said as he took his own jacket off.

"Where's Jennifer?" Charlie turned his eyes towards Kate and asked.

"Her and Scott went to see if there were any more blankets on the bus. I'll go get her." Kate said.

"Not yet. Please. Just... not yet" Charlie said.

"Ok." Kate said as she glanced at Bridger. He walked over to the bar and grabbed a bottle. He poured a shot into a glass and handed it to Charlie. He drank it down.

Evelyn managed to get Charlie's jacket off and unbuttoned his shirt. He pulled it off his good shoulder, and she helped him pull it off the other one. He had a t-shirt on and it was covered in blood. They could see the small tears in the material.

"Let's let Raj take that off." Evelyn said.

Charlie nodded at her as he raised the neck of his shirt to look underneath. He grimaced as he did, not from pain. He looked back up at Evelyn and lowered his shirt back down. She stood. Her eyes met Bridger's. They both had the same look. What now?

Raj came through the door with the first aid kit and stepped in front of Charlie.

"Ok. Charlie. Tell me what happened?" Raj said.

Charlie started recounted the story. Raj cut away the t-shirt, the whole time nodding and giving the "uh huh, mmm, ok" sounds meant to reassure the patient during the examination. Raj cleaned the shoulder with alcohol and wiped the blood away from around it. He finally stepped back from in front of him long enough for Bridger, Kate and Evelyn to see the wound. On Charlie's left shoulder, just under the collarbone, was an oval pattern of several small punctures. It was almost an exact replica of the wound on the top of JW's foot. Kate put her hand over her mouth and the tears rolled down her cheeks. Bridger, Dottie and Evelyn just looked down. Charlie kept staring at the wound, tears rolling down his cheeks too.

"I'm sorry." Raj said. He tore open a gauze pad and covered the wound. He taped it down and gave Charlie a couple of pads and a roll of tape out of the kit.

"Save them. For someone who may need them later." Charlie said.

"I'll leave them. It is up to you whether you use them or not." Raj said. He stood and stepped back.

"I think I need to see my daughter now." Charlie said. He stood. Bridger quickly stepped forward between Charlie and the others.

"Oh no now. You just sit right back down. We'll get her." Bridger said. He turned to Kate. "Kate, do you mind?"

"I'll get her Charlie. You just rest." Kate said, wiping the tears off her cheek. She walked back into the kitchen and out the back door.

"Thank you." Charlie said as Kate exited. He turned to Bridger. "I get it. This is what needs to happen. You can't let me go get her. I understand."

Bridger nodded. He turned to Raj.

"Raj, can you and Dottie sit with him a while? I need to do something." Bridger said.

"Sure." Raj said.

"Evelyn, can you come with me?" Bridger asked, he looked at her and she recognized that he really wasn't asking. She nodded, and they walked back out the front door and out near the picnic table. Once they got a few yards away Evelyn turned to Bridger.

"You want to tell me what the plan is now?" Evelyn asked.

"I'm not sure but I know this, the clock is ticking." Bridger started. "From the time JW said he got bit until the time he became one of those things was about twenty-four hours. Give or take a couple. Right when this started I saw a man die in his bed and he turned within minutes. My guess is that it happens pretty quickly after death but it takes a little while for the bite to kill you. But that's just a guess."

"Well, one thing we know for sure you're right about. The clock is ticking." Evelyn said.

"We have to get him isolated and under guard. Like right now." Bridger said. "He knows that has to happen. He said as much."

"Where?" Evelyn asked.

"I guess the shack he's already in. We need to move him there as quickly as we can." Bridger said. She nodded in agreement.

They walked back inside the saloon. Charlie was sitting up a little straighter in the chair. He was anticipating the arrival of Jennifer and he wanted to make sure he looked as strong as he could. For her. They all heard the back door of the kitchen swing open and Charlie turned to look back over his shoulder as Jennifer came around the corner. His eyes met hers. They filled with tears. She rushed over to him and knelt down beside him. She saw the covered wound.

"Daddy. No. No. No." She said, her voice devolving into harsh sobs. She leaned her head towards him and he pulled her close. He stroked the top of her head.

"It's ok. It's going to be ok." He said. "You'll be ok."

She kept sobbing, and he looked up at the others. They all made their way out of the saloon to give them a moment of privacy. All except Bridger. Charlie looked up at him and nodded. Bridger stepped back a little and found a seat at a table across the room. He watched as they hugged and cried and cried and hugged. He gave them a wide berth. After the tears had subsided, and they had a chance to begin to come to terms with it, he stood.

"Charlie, we need to talk." Bridger said.

"Ok." Charlie said, looking up from his daughter.

"We need to move you." Bridger said as Jennifer's eyes climbed up to his. "You need to be somewhere comfortable."

"And secure." Charlie said, understanding what Bridger was saying.

"That too." Bridger said as he looked at Jennifer.

Bridger watched as Charlie stood. Jennifer backed away from him as he picked his coat up from the back of the chair. He ran his good arm through the sleeve and she helped drape it over his other shoulder.

"Thank you, honey. Go ahead. I'll be out in a minute."
Charlie said. She walked out of the saloon. He looked
up at Bridger.
"Ok. Where to?" Charlie asked.
"Back to your shack." Bridger said.
"Listen, I am not one to complain, but since it's
probably the place I'm going to die in, can we call it a
hut or something. Just don't want my final place to be
some shack in the woods. Hut sounds more romantic."
Charlie smiled.
"Sure. Let's go to your hut." Bridger smiled back. They
headed out the door.

Another road

Night descended on the cul-de-sac. Jahda and
Ham slept on the couch. Devin slept on the floor. Josh
came out of his room without waking Lori and stepped
into the bathroom. It was fetid. They used the shower
and sink as an all purpose urinals and the toilet for
serious needs. They could flush it by filling it with water
but that was in limited supply. Most of the time they
went in the backyard. But nighttime was different. Josh
leaned into the shower and tilted his head back.
"Aaahh" He said as the pressure on his bladder
decreased.
"Wait a few years, you'll be doing that five times a
night." Martin said from behind him.

Josh jerked halfway around, a steady stream painting the wall and splattering back on his hands. He cut it off, eyes wide and turned back.

"Damn, you scared the shit out of me." Josh said.

"Nah, just the piss." Martin said, nodding towards the fluid now running down the wall.

They both laughed. Josh stepped out and Martin stepped in and relieved himself. He turned to Josh.

"Listen, since everyone is asleep, I wanted to talk to you. Just you and me." Martin said.

"Ok. What about?" Josh said. Martin turned and zipped up his pants. They walked to the kitchen.

"The place you came from. The place in the woods. The compound." Martin said.

"Well I never actually made it to the compound but sure. What do you want to know?" Josh asked.

"How far?" Martin asked.

"About 75 miles."

"And you know the way?"

"Most of it. Bridger told me how to get to the compound from my families place. So yeah, I know the way." Josh said.

"Bridger, he's in charge?"

"I don't know if in charge is the right word. He knew my Dad. They were in the army together. He and my Dad kind of took charge to get us out but I don't think anyone is *in* charge."

"How many people are there?" Martin asked. Josh tilted his head a little. Martin could tell he was counting.

"There's my brother, my mom, Bridger, Ms. Collins, Charlie and Jennifer, Raj and Tilly, that Ed guy, Dottie and Amanda so eleven. Yep, eleven." Josh said.

"And you know these people?" Martin asked.

"I guess. Jennifer is Lori's friend and Charlie is her father. Amanda was with them. She lost her husband just before I left. Raj and Tilly came with Uncle Bridger. Ed was already there but Bridger trusts him. Ms. Collins was our next-door neighbor." Josh said nodding towards the street.

"And Dottie?" Martin asked.

"Oh she's a straight laced church lady. Her husband didn't make it. You'd probably like her. She's old too." Josh said smiling.

Martin smiled. He probably deserved that for making Josh piss all over himself. Martin reached into his pocket and produced his lighter. He lit the candle, and it illuminated the map he had spread across the table earlier.

"Where?" Martin asked.

Josh looked at the map and found Hwy 44. He traced it back towards South Springs until he found a cross road he knew by name near the lake. He reversed his finger north and followed it until it came to another crossroads. This was where that fireworks stand is, he thought to himself. He turned east and traced another few miles. He stopped.

"Here, right here." Josh said. Martin looked down.

"There's nothing there." Martin said.

"That's kind of the point, right?" Josh asked.

"I guess so." Martin said. He patted Josh on the back.

"Go back to sleep. I'll keep watch." Martin said.

"Nah, I'm good. Always was kind of an early riser. The morning all this started, when it got to Atlanta, I got up and left to go fishing so early that my mother almost panicked trying to find me." Josh said smiling. It seemed so long ago now.

"I was up early that morning too. Before all this, I was a security guard at Ham's school. It was a good job. I had retired a year earlier from Caloosa County Sheriff's office and I enjoyed being around the kids. Anyway, I got up like I always did, around four and turned on the TV. The first thing I heard was Atlanta and since we lived right by the Georgia line, my ears perked up. I had been following most of the news the day before but it still seemed like something overseas and far away. Atlanta was right outside." He continued. "The local emergency broadcasts started coming across the scanner I kept in the kitchen. I woke Ham up and we started packing. Jahda knocked on the door a few hours later. Her and Maria, I told you about Maria and Hector right?" Martin looked at Josh.

Josh nodded.

"Her and Maria came over to see if we wanted to go with them." Martin said.

"Where?" Josh asked.

"To the speedway. There was going to be a big shelter set up and everyone was going there." Martin said.

"I thought you said you went to the big shelter south of Atlanta." Josh said.

"We did. The speedway got taken over as a military staging area. They were going to marshal a force to go back into Atlanta. It never happened. But making all the civilians travel halfway across Georgia sure did." Martin said, the anger rising in his voice. It was the first time Josh had seen Martin seem angry. He continued. "Anyway, things went the way they did for a reason I guess."

"So you're thinking about asking them if they want to try for the compound aren't you?" Josh said, changing the subject back to the beginning.

"Yeah, I am. What would you say?" Martin asked.

"Well, Lori and I came back to South Springs to get some answers. I think we got them. I think I would like to see my mother again. And Lori would probably like to see her friend. So if that's what you want to do, I guess we would be in." Josh said.

"In what?" Ham said as she walked into the kitchen. She sleepily rubbed the corner of her eye. Martin and Josh looked up at her and then back at each other. Josh started to speak but Martin spoke first.

"Ham, you know how you said I had a terrible plan." Martin said, turning to her.

"Yeah."

"I think I have a better one now." He smiled.

Bridger had sat in the corner watching after helping Charlie to his hut. Jennifer had sat down on the bed and softly sang for her father. Bridger eyes drifted. He felt himself dozing off. The room grew quiet except for the soft sound of Jennifer's song. His eyes closed. He felt himself drift away. He bolted upright in the chair. The sun was gone. It was the dead of night. His eyes started darting around the room. They had not adjusted to the dark yet and he couldn't wait. He reached down and toggled the flashlight on his rifle and brought it up. It landed on Charlie's face. He smiled.

"How you feeling Charlie?" Bridger asked.

"Surprisingly good. She fell asleep right after you did. I can't sleep. Or maybe I can and I just don't want to." Charlie said.

"Why not? You need to rest." Bridger said.

Charlie laughed out loud. He waved his hand at Bridger.

"Not laughing at you. I just thought about that old "I'll get all the rest I need when I'm dead" trope of tough guys and druggies. Except now I kinda get it. I don't want to miss anything. It's weird. My whole life I seemed to be waiting for it to get started. Even when we had Jennifer I still felt like I was waiting on the starters pistol to let me know when to go. I thought there would be some magical moment when I would hear a bell telling me 'Ok, now pay attention to the things around you because this is why you're here.' Then her mother died, and I started trying to listen for the bell telling me it was time to get off this ride. Now I just want to watch her. I don't want to leave her. Will you promise me something?" Charlie asked.

"What's that?" Bridger asked.

"Promise me, when I'm gone, y'all will look after her." Charlie said.

"Of course." Bridger said.

Charlie smiled and leaned his head back against the wall. He closed his eyes. Bridger kept his open.

When the sun broke above the horizon, the light filtering through the trees glanced sharply off of the metal roof of the saloon and directly into Evelyn's eyes as she made her way across the compound. She passed the saloon without stopping and walked down to the next-to-last shack on the left. She knocked on the door. Bridger opened it up.

"So how is he?" Evelyn asked.

"See for yourself." Bridger said as he stepped aside.

Evelyn didn't know what to expect. She had seen them put JW into the back of the SUV and he was in pretty bad shape. That was only a few hours after he had been bitten. Besides Bridger, only Kate and her boys had seen him right at the end. She had not expected to see what she saw now.

Charlie was sitting up with his feet off the cot. Jennifer was sitting in the chair next to him. They were laughing.

"Oh hey Evelyn." Charlie said.

"Hey Charlie, how you doing?" Evelyn asked.

"Well, I get another morning with my daughter. That's pretty good." Charlie said.

"It sure is." Evelyn said. She turned and quizzically looked at Bridger. He just shrugged. They both stepped outside.

"I don't get it." Evelyn started.

"I don't either. Maybe it just takes longer with some folks." Bridger said.

"Well, at least they get a little more time together." Evelyn said.

"Yeah, this is going to be hard on her." Bridger said.

"Especially since the only other person she knows is gone too." Evelyn said.

"Yeah, he told me about her mother." Bridger said.

"I was talking about Lori." Evelyn said. "What happened to her mother?"

"He said she died. Before all this."

"That sucks." Evelyn said.

"Yep. Listen if you could go and get Raj I would appreciate it. He can stay with him for a little while and check him over." Bridger said.

"What are you going to do?" Evelyn asked.

"Just get a little rest." Bridger said.

Evelyn walked back towards the other end of the compound and saw Raj and Tilly coming out of their building. She broke into a jog and caught up with them.

"Morning y'all two." Evelyn said.

"Good morning Evelyn. What is the hurry?" Raj asked.

"It's Charlie." Evelyn said. Raj and Tilly's eyes grew wide.

"No, no. Not that. He seems fine. That's why I came to get you. Bridger would like for you to come sit with Charlie for a bit and check him over." Evelyn said.

"Sure. Let's go." Raj said. He and Tilly turned with Evelyn and walked back towards Charlie's.

Raj ducked inside the saloon briefly to retrieve the first aid kit. He met them back outside, and they went to Charlie's. Evelyn walked up to the door and knocked. Jennifer opened it. Bridger nodded at them as they came through the door and stood. He gathered his jacket off the back of the chair.

"Charlie, I'll see you later. Ok?" Bridger said.

"Oh yeah, but no hurry." Charlie said. He smiled at the others in the room, proud of his gallows humor.

Tilly took the chair Bridger had been sitting in. Raj sat down on the bed next to Charlie. Jennifer sat back down in her chair. Evelyn walked out the door with Bridger. Bridger glanced at Tilly and gave her the 'You know what to do if you have to' look. Tilly nodded at him.

"So Charlie, how are you feeling?" Bridger heard Raj start as he closed the door behind him.

Bridger started walking towards the other end of the compound. Evelyn fell in with him as he walked by his own shack.

"I thought you were going to get some rest." Evelyn asked.

"I am. I just want to make a quick walk around the outside to make sure we don't have any more of these things lurking." Bridger said.

"I'll go with you." Evelyn said.

Bridger looked at her and began to object. He had not known Evelyn Collins for long but he knew her long enough to know that it wasn't really up for debate. He smiled at her. They approached the gate and Bridger looked back over his shoulder at the top of the saloon. He waved. Ed waved back. They stepped out of the compound. Bridger walked back down the road to where they had been cutting the trees down. He retrieved the axes they had dropped.

They turned and walked back to where they met Charlie in the road and Bridger went into the woods the way Charlie had come from. Evelyn followed. He navigated a few yards before he could see a flash of color through the trees. He went to it and lying on the ground was the deadun. It was a young girl. Or had been. He knelt down beside it and looked at the wound in the side of its head where Charlie's knife had found home. He reached down and rolled the body over. Finally he took his knife and slowly plunged it into the things belly. He drew it out and smelled the blackness oozing down the tip. He winced. He wiped the blade on the things dress before sheathing it. He stood and wiped his hands on his pants.

"So, you find what you're looking for?" Evelyn asked.

"I guess." Bridger said. "Let's go."

They walked for a few more minutes and Bridger made a cursory attempt to act like he was doing what he told her he was doing but Evelyn wasn't buying it.

"You know, we can just go back inside. You don't have to pretend like the only reason you came out here wasn't to check on that deadun." Evelyn said.

"I just, I don't know, wanted to make sure." Bridger said.

"Make sure of what?" Evelyn asked.

"I don't know, make sure he was bitten by.."

"Bit by what? A deadun? Did you think he got bit by someone out for a walk in the woods?" Evelyn asked.
"I don't know. I mean he hasn't turned yet, and I was hoping maybe it was some mistake. That he really wasn't infected. That he was going to live. We've just had so much dying. I was hoping... I don't know" Bridger said.
"But he is infected. And he is going to die. I think we know that." Evelyn said.
"Yeah." Bridger said.

They walked back into the compound and Bridger went to his shack to get a few minutes rest. Evelyn went into the saloon where she found Kate, Scott and Dottie sitting at one of the tables.
"This seat taken?" Evelyn asked as she sat down.
"How's he doing?" Kate asked.
"Oh, he'll be fine after he gets some rest." Evelyn said.
"Charlie will be fine?" Kate asked surprised.
"Oh. I thought you meant Bridger. Sorry. But actually when we left Charlie an hour or so ago he was in good spirits and looked pretty good too." Evelyn said.
"But it's been almost a day now. How is that possible?" Kate asked.
"I don't know. But like Charlie himself said the other day, 'we don't know shit about these things'" Evelyn said.

Footprints

Josh stood in the garage and looked inside his jeep. Lying in the back seat floorboard was a box of ammunition that his father had given him. Josh had forgot to put it in his backpack. He held the box in his hand and thought about that day. He had seen his father's reaction to the images on Scott's computer. He remembered thinking about the fear in his eyes. He remembered thinking his father was overreacting. He remembered thinking a lot of things. And how wrong he had been. Now he knew that the fear in his father's eyes wasn't misplaced, it was honest. He should have known it. He had never seen his father afraid of anything. Not really. He could feel his cheeks getting wet. He missed him so much now.

"Whatcha got there?" Martin said as he walked through the door from the kitchen.

"Oh just a box of ammo. I dropped it here by mistake when we left." Josh said as he hurriedly wiped his eyes.

"The others are in. They think somewhere away from everything is a good move. Are you sure we can get there?" Martin said.

Here it was. The chips were on the table. Josh knew that his answer would determine what the next move was. Just a few months ago he would have haphazardly answered and moved on. Maybe it was the fact he was just lost in memory of his father or maybe he had grown up just a little, but whatever it was he measured his words. Probably for the first time in his life.

"I know the way. I know what it was like when Lori and I came back here. But I have no idea what the road is like now. I don't know why it would be worse than before but I can't make any guarantees." Josh said.

Martin nodded at him. For the last hour or so he had been talking with Jahda and Devin about doing this. At the end they all agreed.

"Ok. I think we should go. We can spend the rest of today rummaging around the neighborhood for supplies. I would hate to show up empty handed." Martin said chuckling.

An hour or so later Jahda, Devin and Josh stepped through the front door. Martin closed it behind them. They climbed into the truck. Josh turned to Devin.

"So we slow roll all the way out and see what follows?" Josh asked.

"Yeah, like we talked about. Just see what shows up. We can work our way back." Devin said.

"So I should use the horn?" Josh said smiling and raising his eyebrows mockingly.

"If you do, I will shoot you myself." Jahda said. Devin laughed.

He put the truck in gear and they climbed the hill crossing over into the neighborhood. The day started out warmer than the day before but the clouds began rolling in as they slowly made their way through the neighborhood. They watched the road in front of them and Josh would check the mirrors to see if anything crossed behind.

"There's one." Jahda said.

She pointed at a stringer walking across the lawn just ahead of them to the left. They stopped and watched. It acted odd. Its gait was stilted and stiff. It was looking straight down and each step seemed increasingly harder than the last.

"Looks like an old Frankenstein movie." Josh said.

"Looks more like the Wizard of Oz tin man before he got his oil." Jahda said.

They slowly rolled on. They made it all the way to the end and slowly turned around. They started back through the neighborhood. When they got to Charlie and Jennifer's house they stopped.

"We're starting here?" Devin said.

"Yeah. The folks who lived here don't live here any more. You'll meet them when we get where we're going. We can see what they left." Josh said.

"Works for me." Devin said. They climbed out of the truck. Josh took the keys and put them in his pocket.

They walked down the driveway and across the yard. Devin and Jahda both stopped to notice the lumps in the yard. What had once been infected corpses were now just disorganized piles of bones wrapped in strands of rotted ligaments and tattered clothing. A large black spot of decay marked the surrounding ground.

"Lori was in here?" Devin asked.

"Yeah, her and a few others. It was a pretty intense day." Josh said.

"Looks like it." Jahda said as they stepped over the last few piles.

The front door was standing open and Josh tried to remember if it was open the last time he was here. He couldn't. Jahda stepped in front of him and tapped her machete against the open door. They waited. She tapped again. No sound came from within the house. They stepped inside. They found a bit of food but Josh spent his time looking through the closets gathering clothes and blankets.

"We'll need this I think. Not sure what they found at the compound but most of the stuff we brought with us was lost in the fire at our first campsite." Josh said.

"I'll help" Devin said, and they loaded up all they could find in the back of the truck.

They moved down the street going from one house to the next. They only encountered two other stringers. One was trapped between a bookcase and a wall and the other had fallen into an empty swimming pool and couldn't get out. Devin took care of the one behind the bookcase. They left the one in the pool.

They came from between the houses and started walking back to the truck. Jahda looked towards the street and stopped.

They ducked down behind an abandoned car. They watched as a woman slowly made her way across the lawn and towards the street. She would take a few steps and stop. Ever so slightly she would tilt her head one way and then another before moving on. She repeated the process a few times until she reached the sidewalk. They watched as she reached up and opened the mailbox. She retrieved a package.

"Hey." Devin stood and called out.

The woman turned to the sound of his voice and froze. Then she hurriedly ran back the way she came. She turned in the doorway of the house, looked at them and slammed the door shut.

"What the hell?" Devin asked as he started towards the house. Jahda reached out and grabbed his arm.

"Leave her. Just leave her. It doesn't matter. Let's go home." Jahda said.

They walked back to the truck. The bed was almost full. Mainly clothes and blankets but they found a lot of food too. Devin had found several walkie-talkies and a pair of binoculars from one house and Jahda found several more handguns in some of the cars parked in driveways. They siphoned gas from them into two metal gas cans they found in a backyard shed. They also found three axes, two hatchets and a half dozen machetes. It had been a good haul.

Back in the cul-de-sac Martin, Ham and Lori stood in front of the house next door. It once belonged to the Menendez's, but they never came home. Lori looked in through the window. She could see into the living room and partially into the kitchen. She tapped on the glass and waited. After a few minutes she repeated the process a little louder.

"I don't see anything." She said as she stepped away.

"Ok." Martin said as he put the crowbar against the doorframe.

He wedged it into the space between the striker and the latch. As he pried against the door, the sound of splintering wood filled their ears. Lori briefly looked back inside the window. Nothing moved. Ham watched the road behind them. Nothing moved there either except for the leaves. The door finally gave up the fight and swung open. They stepped inside.

The air was stale. The house had been untouched for months and their movement stirred the settled dust. Martin closed the door behind them and grabbed a chair from the dining room to prop against it. They made their way into the kitchen. Ham looked at the pictures adorning the hallway wall. She stopped in front of one showing an older couple, a younger couple and two children. They were all wearing mouse ears in front of a big castle.

"I went there once. When I was little. Didn't I Papi?" Ham said as she looked at the picture. "I like the duck more."

Lori smiled down at her. She had always liked the duck too.

"Yep. We went for your fifth birthday. That was fun because you were too little to ride most of the rides. And I was too old." He smiled at her. "But we did get to meet some princesses and one duck."

"They weren't real princesses." Ham said looking at Lori. "But they were nice."

They went through the house and found an almost fully stocked cupboard and lots of clothes. They took it all. Martin found several duffle bags full of gym clothes. He tossed those out and filled the bags with food. He went into the garage and found several rolls of duct tape and a toolbox. Lori found the storage closet in the spare bedroom and took several boxes of batteries and candles. Martin stepped back outside and pulled the garden cart they found outside of Evelyn's house into the living room. They stacked the duffle bags on top. They had already been inside the other houses. They were empty. They rolled the cart inside Josh's house. They loaded all the duffle bags into the back of the jeep in the garage.

"Now what?" Ham asked.

"We wait for them to get back. Once they are here, we eat and try to get some sleep. We'll leave first thing in the morning." Martin said.

"Can we eat now?" Ham asked. "We found lots of food."

"That food probably has to last us a while." Martin said. "But I don't see the harm in a little snack." He reached into the back of the jeep and retrieved a box.

"I found these. They supposedly last forever." He said as he handed each of them a Twinkie.

Ham's eyes lit up. They sat down at the kitchen table. Ham devoured hers in two bites. Lori took a bite of hers. She had never been a fan but after a few months of whatever they could scrape out of a can, the sugary softness of processed preservatives tasted divine. She smiled as she leaned back in the chair. For a moment the reality of life faded away. The soft candle glow illuminated Martin and Ham's faces. She could see the old man in the little girls eyes. She thought about how her mother always told her she had her father's eyes. A single tear unconsciously rolled down her cheek. She wiped it away and took another bite. The world was not going to rob her of this tiny little moment of joy. Things happened for a reason. Out of all this misery she had found new friends. Real friends. They didn't have to help her but they did. She smiled. She took the last bite.

A short time later they heard the truck slowly pulling into the driveway. Martin looked out of the window and Lori went to the front door. She opened it as they came onto the porch. Devin and Jahda walked in first followed by Josh. He paused when he got to her. She smiled up at him and kissed him briefly on the lips. He smiled back. As they walked through the door Josh turned and looked back out at the cul-de-sac. The wind had turned hard out of the north and came in sharp gusts. Above the street, Josh saw broken limbs hanging from long neglected power lines. As Josh bundled his shoulders up against his neck and turned to go inside the house, the first drops of rain started to fall. The temperature started falling with it.

Cold as the Dead

Bridger sat up on his cot. He looked through the window and figured he had been asleep about two hours. He cleared his throat. It took the apocalypse to finally quit smoking, but he sure missed that wake up stick. He stood and slung the rifle over his shoulder. It never left his side now. He remembered days long past when the wind whipped as it did now except it carried heat and sand instead of cold and rain. The desert nights introduced him to scorpions and dung beetles. He and JW used to catch them and have bug battles. Most of the time they just crawled around each other but sometimes they would fight. It was something to do. Boredom dulls. It was a lesson JW taught him without knowing it. JW had always kept the guys busy, so they didn't have a lot of time to worry about things out of their control. Like girlfriends and wives back home. Whatever happened there had to wait. And worrying about something you couldn't control was the hallmark of boredom. It had been just one of many things JW taught him.

He opened the door and looked around at the other shacks. Huts, he reminded himself. His mind turned to Charlie. Neither Raj nor Tilly had come to wake him so he assumed they hadn't needed him yet. Or they took care of Charlie themselves. He doubted that. He knew he would be the one. He had been the one for JW and he had offered, less than tactfully, to be the one for all of them. He thought about those last few minutes with JW. The wind came in a heavy gust and peppered him with tiny pinpricks of water. Sleet. He knew that sometime soon he would have to take his knife and drive it into the base of Charlie's skull. He can still see the pain in Kate's face every time he looks at her. All he can see around him is pain now. Pain and terror. As he walks out into the now frozen track, he wonders if that's all that's left. JW didn't teach him the answer to that.

"Did you have a good nap?" Evelyn asked as he approached the saloon, snapping him out of his thoughts.

She was standing just inside the door. As he began to answer the sky opened up and heavy sleet started to fall. He trotted to the open door, and she stepped back to let him in. The heat from the stove hit him in the face as he crossed the threshold.

"I should have slept in here. It's getting cold as shit out there." Bridger said as he stamped his boots on the floor.

As his eyes adjusted to the dimness of the room, he saw Kate and Dottie sitting at one table with Scott and Ed sitting together at the bar. Kate stood and walked over to Bridger.

"Have you been back to see him?" Kate asked.

"No. I haven't. I was on my way over now. Has Raj or Tilly said anything?" Bridger asked.

"Well, Tilly came in here about a half an hour ago." Kate said.

"What did she say?" Bridger asked.

"She grabbed an MRE and said Charlie was hungry."

"Hungry? Charlie? Are you sure?" Bridger asked as he knitted his eyebrows together.

"That's what she said. What's going on Bridger? Is Charlie bit or not?" Kate asked a little more passionately.

"He's bit. And he was bitten by a deadun. An infected. I checked." Bridger said.

"I saw it too." Evelyn added.

"Then how can he be hungry? Something's wrong." Kate said.

"Wrong? He's still alive. What's wrong with that?" Bridger asked.

"That's not what I meant. It's just that JW went..." She stopped. She could feel the lump rising in her throat. Her mind was whirling.

"I know. But I don't know what else to tell you. I'll go check on him now and let you know if something changes." Bridger said.

"I didn't mean it the way it sounded." Kate blurted out.

"It's ok." Evelyn said. The two of them went back to the table to sit with Dottie.

Bridger turned and walked out the door. He was anxious to see if Charlie was actually hungry. He was sure that they had misunderstood. Tilly had most likely grabbed the MRE for Jennifer and was just kidding in her own little smart assed way. Bridger thought to himself that he should say something to her but winced at the thought of her retort. He decided to just leave it alone.

He knocked on the door. He turned to look back at the sleet falling now and thought he saw a flake or two of snow. The door opened behind him and he turned. His eyes met Jennifer's.

"I'll go get a couple of water bottles Dad." She was laughing off a joke as she opened the door. "I'll be right back." She smiled at Bridger as she stepped out. Bridger smiled back and stepped inside. Tilly was seated in the corner under the window. She had some book she found flopped open and appeared deep in concentration. Raj was seated in the chair next to the bed. Bridger's eyes fell on Charlie. He was on the bed, sitting up and eating.

"How you feeling Charlie?" Bridger asked.

Charlie just shrugged his shoulders. Raj turned and looked at Bridger and smiled. He had the look of a doctor encountering something totally new. A horrified yet fascinated look of intrigue.

"I guess I feel fine. Considering." Charlie said. Then he turned to Raj. "What do you say Raj? How am I feeling?"

"Well, your temperature seems slightly elevated but other than that you seem fine." Raj said as though he couldn't believe his own words.

"There ya go." Charlie said.

Bridger tried to mask his confusion but failed. Tilly raised her eyes from the book she wasn't really reading and noticed the look of uncertainty that crossed his brow.

"That's great." Bridger said.

He could hear the same skepticism in his own voice that he heard in Kate's just a few minutes earlier.

"I can't really explain it." Raj said finally. "But it is possible..." He paused.

"What's possible Raj?" Bridger slowly asked.

Raj looked around uncertain. Since he had come into Charlie's room a few hours ago he had been having one nagging idea. He hadn't allowed himself to form it into a complete thought much less words. He looked at Charlie and the words came, anyway.

"Listen. I know this may seem crazy." Raj started. "And let me say before I start, infectious diseases were definitely not my forte in medical school but I did have to study them. If this thing that has happened, these walking dead, if it is an infectious disease it would make sense."

"What would make sense?" Tilly chimed in.

"Charlie. Charlie would make sense." Raj said.

"How so?" Bridger asked.

"Yeah, how so?" Charlie asked. Everyone looked at him. "I'm right here guys, I am kind of interested in how this story goes." They smiled.

"I learned about a place called Yambuku. In the seventies it had people survive long before they knew what they were even dealing with. They survived because they just did. For some unknown reason they were immune and we still don't know why." Raj said.

"Immune to what?" Bridger asked.

"Ebola." Raj said.

Bridger didn't know the history of Ebola. He didn't want to know it. Enough time spent in West Africa doing various things for God and country had given him a healthy fear of the tiniest of microbes and Ebola was the most vicious of all the vicious fuckers crawling around that shithole.

"They still don't know why. It didn't appear genetic because parents were immune but children weren't. They all drank the same water and ate the same food. It was as though they were just randomly lucky." Raj continued.

"And you think that applies here? To Charlie?" Bridger finally asked. "You think Charlie is randomly lucky?"

"I think it may be possible." Raj said.

"Ok. Back up. You think it may be possible that he is what? Immune? From Marionette?" Tilly said, standing as she spoke.

"I think it's possible. Let me show you something." Raj said, and he leaned towards Charlie. "Do you mind?" Raj asked Charlie as he reached for the bandage. Charlie let him remove it.

"Look. His wound. It's actually starting to heal. Some of the bruising is beginning to turn color which indicates healthy blood flow" Raj spoke as though demonstrating to interns during rounds. "The tissue doesn't appear necrotic and the punctures themselves don't exhibit any foul odor."

Bridger stood wide-eyed looking at the wound. As Raj removed the bandage he had expected to see the same gaping maw that enveloped JW's foot at the end. Instead what he saw looked like it did two days ago. A bite. Nothing more. Charlie looked at him and smiled. At the end, JW looked dead long before he died. Charlie looked alive.

"From what we all saw this isn't what happens when you get bit." Raj said. "He hasn't had any of the other symptoms we've seen either."

"Maybe it just takes longer." Bridger said, repeating his own words.

"I thought about that and maybe it's true but I don't think so in Charlie's case." Raj said.

"Why not?" Tilly asked.

"Even if it took longer, there would still be some deterioration of his condition. Look at him. He seems to be as healthy as before and the wound is healing." Raj said as he turned to Charlie.

Bridger stood with his back to the door. His mind was racing at the information he was being given. Instinct kicked in and he started to analyze what he knew. Charlie was bitten by a deadun. For sure. He isn't getting worse. Maybe. His thoughts were interrupted by Charlie's voice.

"Listen folks. I really like what Raj is saying and it would be really great news, for me especially, but let's get serious for a minute. I got bit. I ain't dead yet and maybe I won't die but are you willing to take that chance? I'm not. I like spending time with my daughter but I wouldn't do it without one of you here to make sure, if something happens, that my daughter would be safe. So let's not get stupid." Charlie said.

Tilly sat back down in the chair by the window. The gray sky darkened as the sun slid below the milky curtain of clouds that had hidden it most of the day. Raj helped reapply the bandage covering Charlie's wound.

"Ok. Nothing changes for now." Bridger said. "I am going to get something to eat and then I will be back."

He stood and pulled his coat back on. As he slung the rifle over his shoulder, the door opened and Jennifer walked back inside. The others looked at her. She noticed their faces.

"What? Do I have a booger or something?" Jennifer said, wiping the tip of her nose.

Bridger walked out the door to the sound of laughter and closed it behind him. He made his way back over to the saloon and walked inside, greeted by the warmth of the stove and the attention of the room. He could feel all the eyes fall upon him and it took all of his strength to not repeat Jennifer's comment. A smile crossed his lips at the thought. He walked over to the stove and grabbed the percolator. He poured a cup and sat down at the larger table with Kate, Evelyn and Dottie. Ed and Scott turned around at the bar.

"I don't know what to tell you." Bridger started.
"Jennifer just told us she thought he was doing better.
Is she right?" Kate asked.
"She is. He is. Doing better." Bridger said. "And that's
not just me. Raj says that medically he looks like he is
getting better. Or at least not getting worse."
"How?" Scott asked.
"Like I said, I don't know what to tell you. Raj says he
thinks that maybe Charlie is immune. Maybe he is."
Bridger said. "I don't know. All I know is what I saw. He
looks ok."
"So now what?" Evelyn asked.
"Charlie said we shouldn't take any chances. We keep
him under guard for now." Bridger said.
"I'm sorry. Did you just say he was immune?" Kate said.
"I said it was possible."
"Is it?" Kate asked.
She looked around the room. No one answered.

Fly away little bird

Martin sat at the kitchen table. The moon slowly wedged a single beam between the boards covering the window over his right shoulder. It raced across the room faster than he could ever hope to see and trapped millions of tiny flecks of dust in its grasp only to let them slowly slip away. He registered their slow descent and waited. He heard the distinct creek of the floorboard. He had expected Josh to round the corner from the hallway. Instead he saw Lori. She smiled at him as he hovered over the candle on the table.

"I couldn't sleep. It's weird. I think I am actually a little excited about leaving." She said as she grabbed a water bottle and sat down at the table with him.

He stood and grabbed a spoon from the drawer and slid the jar of peanut butter over to her. She dipped the spoon.

"Excited?" Martin asked.

"Yeah. Like I said it's weird. Since this whole thing started, I have been scared all the time. I was scared since before Josh and his family got us out and I have been scared ever since." She said.

"And now."

"Oh I'm still scared. But the last few days with Josh and with all of you has been different. Finding my parents was bad."

"I'm sorry about that." Martin said.

"It's ok. I'm ok. But everything else has been crazy. A good crazy. We fought back. We figured things out. It was..."

"Crazy?"

"It made me not as scared." She said. "And that's why I am kind of excited."

Martin leaned back in the chair and smiled. The moonbeam winked out as it fell behind the clouds again.

"You know, I am kind of excited too. We have been going for a long time." He leaned forward in the chair again and folded his hands together on the table. "Ever since the whole thing fell apart out on the interstate, we've just been running. A wide spot in the road here, an abandoned convenience store there, just places we end up, not anywhere we were going."

"Is that how you ended up here?" She asked.

"It was. We had had a hard day or two and just wandered this way. We just kind of headed west after Atlanta and this place was just next on the way." He said.

"On the way where?"

"That's just it. We weren't on the way anywhere. Now we are." He said.

"And that's why you're excited?" She asked.

"That and I always enjoy meeting new folks." Martin smiled.

The conversation at the kitchen table first drew the attention of Jahda followed shortly after by Ham. They joined Martin and Lori at the table and each spooned out some peanut butter.

"I wish we had some bread." Ham said as she put the spoon in her mouth. "You think we'll have bread again?"

Jahda sat back in the chair and looked at her. Her first instinct was to laugh at the absurdity but a brief moment of realism made her hesitate. She realized the answer wasn't an absolute.

"I think so. I think we'll get this figured out. Someone will. I bet there are people out there right now working hard to make sure that we beat this thing. This isn't the end." Jahda said.

"Geez, I just asked for some bread." Ham said giggling.

The others smiled. Jahda laughed. Josh came into the room and sat down next to Lori. Devin rolled over on the couch and sat up.

"I guess we need to get everything ready. It's almost time to go." Martin said.

"All the blankets and clothing are in the bed of the truck along with all the other supplies except the food. We put most of it in the back of the jeep. We just need to load up our own gear and we'll be ready." Jahda said.

"Well let's get going." Devin said standing and clapping his hands.

Within a few minutes they had each gathered their own backpacks together and were busy checking their various weapons. Jahda tied down one machete to her pack and looped another through her belt. She carried a pistol and made sure it was loaded. The others followed suit. Martin tied the quiver for his bat around Ham's pack and slid her rifle into it. He slipped the bat into the back seat of the jeep.

"Is everything ready?" Martin turned and asked as they all gathered in the garage.

"The truck and jeep both have plenty of gas and we have almost twenty gallons in cans in the truck. We've got everything loaded." Josh said.

"I've got one of the walkie's and Jahda has one so we can stay in touch." Lori said.

"I've got the killer tunes." Devin said as he strummed his air guitar. They all looked at him. "No seriously, I found some CD's." He pulled a disk from his backpack. Ham giggled at him.

"That's great Devin. Since we have the music covered, I think it's time we get going." Martin said to the others.

Josh turned and pressed the button. The garage door whirred to life one last time. The panels of the door climbed the track and settled above the jeep. The open door ushered in a blast of cold air and the moonlight spilled through. Martin stepped out into the driveway.

"SNOW!!!" Ham squealed.

"Sorry honey. It's ice. Mostly." He walked down the driveway a little but it didn't seem frozen over.

Josh walked over to the truck and reached inside to crank it up. It came to life. Jahda had already started the jeep.

"Let's go." Josh said as he and Lori slid into the truck.

Martin and Ham climbed into the back seat and Devin took shotgun. Jahda closed the driver's door. She flashed her lights at Josh and pulled out of the driveway. She looked in the rearview mirror at the open garage door and the bay window. She lowered her eyes and looked at Ham. She smiled.

The headlights of the truck swept across the cul-de-sac as Josh pointed the nose up the hill. He hesitated only briefly. He was old enough to remember where they lived before here and remembered when they moved in. The boxes and boxes they had to empty and put away. The bonfire his father had to get rid of the boxes. He looked in the rearview mirror at the house, illuminated in the red glow of the taillights, as it slowly crept away from him. The steady beat of the windshield wipers fighting against the thin sheen of ice on the glass brought his eyes forward again. They climbed the hill and set off towards the intersection at the entrance to the neighborhood.

Evelyn came out of the kitchen just as the water began to boil in the percolator. The sky was still spewing ice from time to time and the temperature had gotten increasingly colder. Most everyone had gone to bed last night after the discussion with Bridger but Evelyn suspected most were like her and unable to sleep for long. She replayed what Bridger had said while she stoked the coals from last nights fire in the stove. As soon as she poured the black liquid into her cup, she heard the door open behind her. She turned.
"Morning Kate." She said.
"Good morning Evelyn." She said as she stamped her feet and drug herself over and sat down at the table by the bar.
"Coffee?" Evelyn asked.
"Sure."
Evelyn took the cup she had just poured and sat it down in front of Kate. She retrieved another cup from the back of the bar and poured it for herself. She sat down.
"Sleep well?"

Kate just shrugged and pulled the cup to her lips. She paused.

"Did you?"

"Not really." Evelyn admitted.

"Do you think it's really possible?" Kate said.

"I don't know. But I'll say this, Bridger does." Evelyn said.

"Evelyn, I love Bridger, I've known him a long time. He and JW went back a long way. He knew things about my husband that I will never know. I trust him. But just because he believes it, it doesn't make it so." Kate said.

"No it doesn't but it could still be true." Evelyn said.

"You know what I find funny?"

"What's that?"

"I find it funny that we, me included, have all managed to wrap our minds around the fact that when people die, they don't stay dead. We accept that. And yet we are complete skeptics to the possibility that someone could be immune." Evelyn said.

"Well its kind of easy to accept when you watch it happen. We have all seen people come back so we believe." Kate said.

"And how many more days does Charlie have to stay alive before we believe?" Evelyn asked.

"I don't know." Kate said and brought the cup to her lips as she turned her gaze to the window and the graying sky.

The door swung open again and Scott walked inside and sat at the bar followed shortly by Ed. Within a few minutes Dottie also arrived. She sat at the table with Evelyn and Kate. Finally Dottie spoke up.

"I listened to y'all last night. I heard what that Bridger fella said. I prayed on it."

"Yeah, what did God have to say about it?" Ed asked.

Dottie shot him a glance but continued.

"I believe if Jesus could bring Lazarus back from all the way dead, keeping old Charlie alive should be a piece of cake." She concluded.

"He couldn't keep my Dad alive." Scott said under his breath as he sat at the bar. He glanced around but nobody heard him.

The door swung open again and Raj stepped inside with Tilly behind him. She reached up and pulled the hood down on her coat and stomped her feet. Raj pulled his knit cap off his head. They walked over to the table and sat down.

"Well?" Evelyn said.

"Well what?" Tilly asked.

"Bridger told us what you said about Charlie." Kate said.

"Oh. Ok. What did he tell you?" Raj asked.

"That you think Charlie is immune." Ed said.

"Possibly. Maybe a little more than possibly. Likely." Raj said.

"Why?" Evelyn asked.

"Why what?"

"Why do you think it's likely?" Evelyn asked.

"Well several things but the most obvious is that he is still alive." Raj said.

"But you don't know for sure." Dottie said.

"I know for sure that it has been almost three days since he was bitten. But no I don't know for sure that he is immune. I don't think we could ever know for sure. Him being alive is a pretty good indicator though." Raj said.

Bridger looked down from the brightening sky he had been viewing from the window in the corner of the room. Jennifer slept on the cot with her sleeping bag pulled over her head. Charlie lay on the floor with several blankets under him and over him. The night air was frigid, and they both wore several layers of clothes while they slept. Bridger sat under a blanket on the chair with his rifle resting against the wall beside him. He steadily but quietly stamped his feet inside his boots to keep his toes warm. The knit cap was pulled low over his ears and the collar of his jacket was up around his mouth. Only his eyes and nose were visible, and each breath billowed from under his collar like a smoke stack. He stood and looked out the window again. He could see a faint glow from behind the windows in the saloon. He could imagine the warmth of the stove. Just the thought made his temperature rise slightly. He turned back to the inside of the room and looked at his roommates. They were sleeping comfortably enough for now. He knelt down next to Charlie. He could hear him snoring softly.

"Fuck it." He said to himself.

He stood and walked to the door. As he swung it open, he could see the first light starting to break through the trees. The ground was white. He stepped out and his boots crunched beneath him. It felt like ice but there were a couple of inches of snow on top of it. He turned and walked towards the saloon. It seemed like a lifetime ago that he steered his car down the street to JW's house. They had acted and reacted and the entire time they had managed to stay half a step ahead of death. But they had been losing almost every step of the way. Even when they got lucky, it came with a cost. And not once in the entire hell that had become their life had they had one moment that felt like they were doing anything other than marking time until death arrived. He knew death would come for them all but maybe not for Charlie, at least not today. He smiled a little.

They all turned as the door opened. Bridger ducked his head as he came inside and when he turned all eyes fell on him. Again he thought about what Jennifer said last night and again the smile crept across his face. He tried to stop it but it was just too damn funny. He stepped forward.

"Where is Charlie and Jennifer?" Evelyn asked.

"Sleeping." Bridger said.

"And you left them?"

"Just to get a cup of coffee." Bridger said and walked over to the stove.

"So you think Raj is right?" Kate asked.

"Huh?"

"You think Raj is right. You think Charlie is immune."

"What makes you say that Kate?" Evelyn asked.

"Because she knows I wouldn't leave them alone for a second if I thought he wasn't." Bridger conceded.

For a brief moment everyone took a breath and let the words wash over them. The moment was broken as Jennifer's scream pierced the morning sky. Bridger turned but felt his stomach sinking as he did. As a result Tilly made it out the door first, but she paused on the porch of the saloon. Bridger came after her and almost knocked her down. He paused too. The others piled outside as Jennifer ran around the other side of the hut. As they watched Charlie emerged on the side opposite her. As he did, he became aware of the crowd watching from the porch. He stopped and turned to face them. As he raised his hand, a snowball hit him square in the side of the head.

"Now we're even." Jennifer said as she emerged from the other side of the shack.

She turned to look where Charlie was staring. She waved at them. They all waved back.

Seventy Miles or so

They stopped as they came to the bridge by the elementary school. Jahda pulled the jeep alongside the truck and Martin rolled down his window.

"Let me check." Martin said as he opened the door.

Josh hadn't thought about it. Martin had lived in the south his whole life. He knew about the occasional black ice and the once in a lifetime events that cripple the area occasionally. This wasn't that bad. But it was cold enough for the bridge to maybe freeze. And if you have ever slid sideways across a frozen bridge, especially one over water, you tend to be more cautious.

He stepped to the front of the jeep and took a few steps out onto the bridge. The roadway felt normal. He took a few more steps and waved for Jahda to pull up. She did. He climbed back in the jeep.

"Nice and slow." Martin said. He got on the walkie. "Josh. It feels fine but go slow. Just follow us and when we get on the other side you can pull around." He said.

"Sounds good."

They crept across the bridge. Lori looked over the side at the river below. The water looked almost black. The wind formed whitecaps in spots as it swept across the surface. The wind bounced the overhanging branches in and out of the water like a zealots baptism. She could see shapes against the shore. It took her a minute to see them for what they were. Bodies. She didn't look away.

Jahda steered the jeep around the last vehicle on the bridge and they slowed down so Josh could pass by. Martin rolled down his window again.

"Let's make sure we get there. No reason to drive crazy. Especially in this weather." Martin said. "So how far from here?"

"About seventy miles or so. It shouldn't take too long. Even in this weather." Josh said.

He pulled the truck around and started down the road. As they crept northward, the temperature crept lower. The slightly decreasing latitude also signaled an increase in moisture. At first the snow looked wind blown and was sporadic. The farther they traveled the more often it came and the heavier it got. The headlights failed to cast a glow much more than a few yards ahead. As the sun crept upward behind the clouds, they were able to go a little faster but not much. He saw the County Line Gas station ahead through the almost steady snow. It had closed a few years ago after the owner got shot in a robbery. Josh knew it meant they were almost to the lake, and the lake marked the halfway point to where they were going. Everything looked white. The clouds covered the sky, and the snow covered the road. They were moving slowly but steadily. Josh straightened up a little in the seat and realized he had been hunched over the steering wheel the whole time. His back creaked, and he flexed his fingers. He relaxed just a little.

Suddenly he felt the road disappear. What a moment ago felt like asphalt under the vehicle instantly felt like glass. The nose of the truck started to drift to the right, and he put his foot on the brake. The simultaneous move of braking and turning the wheel had a violent effect. The truck whip lashed around and slammed hard against something. It came up on two wheels and rammed back down, stopping completely. From behind Jahda had seen the taillights of the truck suddenly whip sideways. She slammed on the brakes and stopped the jeep. They watched as the truck spun and hit against the concrete guardrail and stopped.
"Are you okay?" Josh asked.
"Yeah. That sucked. What happened?" Lori asked.
"Yeah this one is on me." He said. He reached over and grabbed the walkie.

Martin stood beside the sign that read 'Lake Spring Bridge' with the walkie in his hand. He heard Josh's voice through the speaker.

"We're ok. I forgot about this one." Josh said.

Josh opened the door. Lori tried to open hers but it was up against the guardrail. She slid over to Josh's side. She stepped down out of the truck and slipped. Josh tried to grab her and they lost their footing. They landed in a heap. They both laughed. They were about twenty yards down the bridge over the lake.

"How's the truck?" Josh heard Martin say on the walkie.

He looked back the way they had come and saw them standing through the fog that had grown thicker as they had approached the lake.

"It's still running. But I don't know if I can move it off the bridge. It's pretty much ice." Josh said. "Hold on"

Lori and Josh climbed back in the truck. He gave it some gas and heard the wheels spinning. He hit the four-wheel-drive button. He heard additional wheels spinning when he gave it some gas but they still didn't move.

"Yeah, I don't think it's moving." Josh said into the walkie.

Martin grimaced a little.

"Ok. Sit tight." Martin said. He turned to Jahda. "Any suggestions?"

"We can try to pull him off with some rope." She said.

"Yeah, I don't think we have that much rope. He's a pretty good ways down the bridge."

"Where's the rope?" Jahda asked.

"On the truck." Martin said.

"Ok. Wait here." Jahda said as she climbed out of the jeep.

"Wait, where are you going?" Martin asked.

"I'm going to get them off the bridge." Jahda said smiling.

She reached back into the jeep and grabbed the floor mat from her side.

"Can you hand me that?" She said pointing at Devin's side. He handed the floor mat from under his feet.

They watched as she took the floor mats and threw one down on the ice, stepped on it. Set the next one down stepped on it. Retrieved the first one and placed it in front of the one she was standing on. They watched as she repeated the process all the to the truck. Josh watched her coming.

"Tell him to get the rope." He heard Martin say over the walkie in Lori's hand.

He reached into the bed of the truck and pulled out the rope they had found hanging in one of the garages. It was a little heavier than clothesline but not much. And they didn't have much. Jahda arrived as he pulled it out.

"Great. Let's cut it in half." She said.

"That's not going to make it twice as long." Josh said.

Jahda looked at him and raised one eyebrow.

"No shit Sherlock. Watch." She said.

She took the rope and cut it roughly in half. She took one length of the rope and handed it to Josh. She knelt down by the rear tire. She looped one end of the rope through the wheel opening and back around the tire. She repeated that several times moving to the next opening in the wheel after about three passes. Josh caught on to what she was doing and started to make his way around to the other side.

"No." She said. "Do the front. It's four-wheel-drive right? You'll want to have a little steering too."

He hadn't thought of that. Besides, he was pretty sure he couldn't have gotten to the other side, it was up against the guardrail. It took them about ten minutes to finish looping the rope around the tires.

"Alright. Let's see if this works." Jahda said. Josh climbed into the drivers seat and Jahda climbed into the bed of the truck.

He eased it into reverse and gently pressed the gas. He could feel the wheels starting to slip but with each slip the rope got just a bit of traction.

"A little more gas." Jahda said from behind him.

He touched the pedal. The wheels started spinning faster, but the traction increased enough that the truck started to move. He let off the gas.

"No, you'll need to just stay on it. Keep the wheels spinning." She said.

"You wanna do it." Josh said.

"You want me too?" Jahda said right back.

"Nah, I got it." He said.

He pressed the pedal again and got the truck moving. It felt strange to have just enough traction to barely move while hearing the engine go several thousand RPM's above normal. It reminded Josh of being in a flat bottom aluminum boat during a heavy wind. They were just along for the ride. He could steer just enough to keep from turning sideways but not from running into the guardrail three more times as they bounced back towards the jeep. Finally the rear tires made contact with the part of the bridge that had earth and not air under it.

"Yay" Ham said from the back seat as the truck cleared the bridge.

"Nice" Devin said.

Martin walked over to the truck and looked at the roped looped around the tires. He shook his head.

"Where'd you learn that?" Martin said.

"My grandfather. It's a long story, and it's too cold to stand here and tell it right now." Jahda said.

"Well we're not getting across that bridge. At least not right now." Martin said.

"You think the weather will be better tomorrow?" Lori asked.

"It's still Alabama, the weather might get better today. I don't remember too many times bridges stayed iced over for long. Sky just needs to clear up, sun come out for a bit and we'll be on our way."

"In the meantime?" Lori asked.

"We could go back to the county line. That store back there closed before all this happened. It should be ok." Josh said.

"Let's go." Martin said.

A few minutes later they pulled on either side of the defunct gas island. Some of the rope had worn through during the short ride back and was making a steady thump thump against the side when they stopped. Josh climbed out of the truck and cut the rope free.

Devin and Jahda walked up to the door of the old store. She swung it open and stepped inside. She tapped against the doorframe and heard the heavy rasp of dead lungs. The stringer stood at the back of the dimly lit room. She stepped sideways as it slowly came down the aisle of empty shelves. Devin stepped the other way and started down the other aisle. He paused and looked down. Another one sat on the floor with its back against an empty shelf. Half of its face was torn away, and it had a crowbar sticking from its chest. When it turned and tried to stand Devin could see that it had been sitting for so long the skin on its back had fused against the shelf and tore away as it tried to move. He quickly stepped over to it and drove his machete through its eye. Pop. He looked back towards Jahda.

She watched the thing coming towards her. Its clothing was falling apart. She could see the large stain on the front of its shirt with the bullet hole in the center of its chest. She steadied her balance and brought the tip of her blade up. When the thing stepped in range, she drove it forward. Pop. It went down. She walked around it slowly. The others came through the door.

"Everything ok?" Martin asked.

"Yeah, just two. They been here a while, I think." Devin said.

Jahda walked to the back of the store. The door to the walk-in freezer was closed. She grabbed the handle and popped the locked. It swung open. It took her a moment to process what she saw. The stringer on the floor was trying to reach out to her, but it was so emaciated that it could barely raise its head. One hand slowly crept forward and stopped. She stepped towards it and realized that this had once been a child about Ham's age. She paused.

She raised the machete above the things temple.

"Have peace." She said as she drove the tip through the side of its head. Pop.

They made a fire in the old steel drink cooler by the counter. They moved all the stringers together in the freezer and closed the door. They pulled the jeep and truck right up to the doors to keep them blocked. They slept between the aisles. The sky cleared as they slept. When they woke the sun was creeping over the trees. The lake began the morning holding the cold close to the surface but soon lost the battle to the sun. Vapor rose from the water like sprites' reaching for heaven and the morning was soon blanketed in an ethereal fog. Josh stood looking through the window of the store. He had left without knowing if he would ever see his family again. For the first time he began to wonder if they were still there.

Look over the Hill

Kate leaned against the counter in the kitchen looking at the cup in her hand. Evelyn came through the door and smiled at her.

"Do you believe it now?" She asked.

"I don't know." Kate started.

"Is it that you don't believe it or that you don't want to believe it?"

"What the hell is that supposed to mean?" Kate asked. She was surprised to feel anger start to rise inside her.

"Kate I know losing JW..." Evelyn started.

"Fuck you." Kate said. "None of you would be here right now without JW."

Evelyn paused and looked at her. She started again.

"Kate I know losing JW was hard. It was hard for all of us because of what you just said. He got us here. I also know it was infinitely harder for you."

Kate looked at her. She felt everything she had felt since JW died rise up inside her.

"It's not fair. I hate myself for saying it but it's not. Why should Charlie get to be the one who lives? Why does he get to keep going when my husband didn't?"

"It's not fair Kate. It really isn't. But good people died before this happened too. My husband died a long time ago." Evelyn said. "None of that was fair but there is nothing we can do to change it. We just can't. And even that's not fair."

"Ok fine. So Charlie is immune or whatever, what the hell does that matter to me? It doesn't bring my husband back, and it doesn't change the fact that my son is out there somewhere. Maybe." She choked up on the last.

"I know." Evelyn said.

Evelyn turned and went back through the other door into the saloon. Dottie sat at one of the tables along with Ed. Scott had sat back down at the bar. Evelyn patted him on the forearm as she walked by. She kept going back outside. Raj and Tilly were sitting at the picnic table watching Charlie and Jennifer walking up and down the track. The sun was out and even though it was still cold, the snow had stopped falling and everything was starting to melt. Snowy Alabama days never lasted long. Bridger sat at one end of the porch watching the track of road between the buildings slowly turn into mud. Evelyn walked up and sat down next to him. He smiled at her.

"So I guess he's going to be ok?" Evelyn asked.

"Raj thinks so." Bridger said.

He turned and looked at her. She raised her eyebrows. He knew she wasn't satisfied with his answer. It dawned on him that he wasn't quite sure how he knew that but he knew it, anyway.

"I think so too." He said. She smiled.

They stood and walked back over to the picnic table where Raj and Tilly were sitting.

"What are they doing in there?" Tilly asked nodding towards the saloon door.

"Same as out here I guess." Evelyn said.

"A serious what the fuck moment, huh?"

"I guess." Evelyn said.

"They just keep walking back and forth. Are we sure they both haven't turned?" Tilly asked with a smile on her face.

"Pretty sure." Raj said. "I am a doctor."

"Yes you are." Tilly said and leaned against to him.

"Ok doc, what now?" Bridger asked. "What comes next?"

"Treat him for the bite wound and monitor his recovery." Raj said.

"How close should we monitor 'his recovery'?" Bridger raised one eyebrow as he asked.

"Look at him." Raj said and nodded at Charlie. He and Jennifer were turning back around from the far gate and walking back towards them. "He's going to be fine."

"It truly is a miracle." Dottie said from over their shoulder. She had managed to come out of the door without any of them hearing her. Bridger was impressed.

"We got more coffee going if y'all want some. It's too cold out here for me." Dottie said.

She walked back inside. Raj and Tilly stood and followed her.

"You going?" Evelyn asked.

"In a minute." Bridger said.

"What's bothering you?"

"What do you mean?"

"Just a feeling. Do you not think Raj is right?"

"It's not that." Bridger said.

"So there is something?" She smiled.

"It's nothing, really. I have been playing this out in my head. Charlie being immune and all that."

"And."

"And I think its great news for Charlie and Jennifer."

"But" Evelyn seemed a little exasperated trying to draw this out of Bridger.

"But that's it. It's great news for Charlie and Jennifer. It doesn't change anything else. It doesn't make the world go back to the way it was. It doesn't bring anyone we lost back, and it doesn't keep us any safer than before. I guess what I am trying to say is that if Charlie is immune, it really doesn't mean a damn thing."

The sun had burned off most of the fog but the ground was still covered in white. The road was still icy in spots but was mostly a black ribbon stretching into the distance. They traveled slightly faster. Josh could see the bright red fireworks sign ahead although it didn't seem quite as bright now. He slowed as they took the fork to the left. He thought he saw smoke coming from the woods behind the old post office. He glanced at the fireworks stand and noticed the door was hanging on the hinges. When he turned his eyes back to the road in front of him he realized that this was the last stretch. They had about five or six miles to go and they would be there. But what would they find? He unconsciously slowed down a little. They approached the spot he knew. The half painted post and the little dirt road to the left. He knew about a hundred yards into the woods was the creek and the gate. Past that about a quarter mile was a wide spot in the road and what's left of a burnt out bus, some long dead stringers and memories. He was home. He slowed down more.

"Something wrong." He heard the voice come over the walkie. He took it from Lori.

"Nah. We're almost there. I have to kind of feel my way from here because I am just going by what Bridger told me." Josh said.

"Take your time." Martin said.

Josh slowed to less than ten miles per hour. It was almost a crawl. He remembered the directions. Around three miles total, around two bends and halfway around a third there would be a dirt road on the left. Just a wide spot through the woods. He rolled his window down. The cold air shot in but the heater on the truck worked just fine. He looked at the woods to his left. The uncommon white highlighted the empty blackness of the trees. All the limbs sagged under the newfound weight of the snow and ice.

"Whoa." Lori said as she placed her hand on the dash.

Josh whipped his head around to her and followed her gaze back through the front windshield. He tapped the breaks and steered to his right slightly off the road. He looked back out the open window as he passed the pile of bones and clothes in the middle of the road.

"What happened here?" Lori asked.

"Looks like someone put down a bunch of stringers." Josh said. They drove by.

He began around the last bend and started looking. Just like Bridger said there was a wide spot between the trees. He turned in.

"Are we here?" Martin asked over the walkie.

"I think so. He said it was way back in the woods though so I guess we'll see." Josh said.

They followed the path back into the woods. The trees lining either side clearly marked the road but the track itself was still hidden beneath the surface snow. The truck dipped slightly as it found mud. He felt the tires spin as he pressed on the gas to get through the slick spot. Jahda saw him start to spin and stopped in case he needed to reverse. She watched him and saw the ruts left behind the truck.

"I think I am going to go just a little to the left. I don't want to get in his ruts." Jahda said. She pulled a little to the left of the tracks Josh left and started after him. She heard a loud pop and stopped.

"Hold on Josh. Something happened." Martin said as Jahda stepped out of the jeep. She walked to the front and knelt down beside the tires. She stood up and kicked it.

"What happened?" Martin said as he stood on the other side.

"Blown tire. Looks like we ran over a small stump. It looks like something cut it off. It sure looks sharp." She stood and kicked the tire again.

"Beavers probably." Martin said as he stepped out of the jeep.

Jennifer came up to Bridger and Evelyn as they stood on the porch. They didn't see Charlie with her.

"Is everything ok?" Evelyn asked.

"My dad needs you. He wants you to come to the gate." Jennifer said looking at Bridger.

He turned his head and looked down towards the gate. Charlie was standing in the middle of the track looking his way and waving both hands like ground control at an airport. Bridger started towards him. Jennifer and Evelyn fell in behind him.

"What is wrong?" Evelyn asked.

"I don't know. He just kept asking if I could hear something, which I couldn't, and then he sent me for him." She said nodding at Bridger. They got to Charlie.

"What's going on?" Bridger asked.

"I heard something. It sounded like a car." Charlie said.

They all paused and listened. Each of them started looking slightly higher and higher in the sky, as though you hear through your nostrils. Finally Bridger looked down slightly.

"I don't hear anything."

"Me either." Charlie conceded.

"What did you hear? Specifically." Evelyn asked.

"It sounded like a car or a truck. In the distance back towards the road. Maybe even on the road. But it slowly got closer and just when I sent Jennifer to get you I heard a shot or pop or something. And then it stopped. But I swear I heard it." Charlie said.

"Ok. So I'll hang out and see what's up. Y'all go back to the saloon and warm up." Bridger said. "Evelyn?"

"Yes."

"Can you get me those binoculars?" Bridger said.

Charlie and Jennifer started back to the saloon.

"Yep." Evelyn said.

"Get Tilly and Raj too." Bridger nodded. She nodded back.

"Well shit." Devin said as he came around from the other side. "We got a jack?"

"I think the ground is too soft to jack it up?" Martin said.

Josh and Lori had walked back to see if they could help. They couldn't.

"We can try to change it. We can put something under the jack. An axe handle or something." Jahda said.

"Josh, how far to where we're going?" Martin asked.

"Honestly I don't know but it can't be too far." Josh said.

"Let's do this for now. Let's just all pile in the back of the truck. We can go a little farther and if we don't find it we come back and get this done. Then we can figure out what to do next. But if we do find it, we can come back and get this on a little warmer day. I don't think it's going anywhere." Martin said.

"Now that's a good plan Papi." Ham said.

They grabbed their backpacks and climbed in the back of the truck and they started off again. Josh felt another slick spot under the wheels. He added gas, the engine revved, and they slid through. He also found two rather large puddles that weren't frozen or snow covered. They were just mud. He slow rolled into the first one and almost let it come to a stop. He had to shower on the gas harder than he wanted to get out the other side. The next one he came to he gave it gas the whole way through. As he topped a hill, he looked down the track and could see what looked like a fence across the road. It was still several hundred yards away.

Bridger stood at the gate trying to mark the sound. As soon as Evelyn was out of sight he started hearing what Charlie heard. It was definitely a vehicle. He could hear the engine rise and fall. Tilly came beside him and handed him the binoculars. Raj and Evelyn stood on the other side. They all heard the sound. Bridger knew it was about to top the hill in front of them. He put the binoculars to his eyes.

"Go get the others." Bridger said as he looked. "Now."

Tilly turned and walked back towards the saloon. Bridger put the binoculars back to his eyes. Bridger handed the binoculars to Evelyn, and she looked up the hill and saw a truck slowly coming towards them.

"Someone's coming, Bridger wants everyone at the gate." Tilly said as she burst through the door. They all looked at her stunned by her entrance. She straightened up and looked around.

"What did you say?" Scott asked.

"I said there is someone coming. We heard a vehicle coming down the road and he sent me to get everyone." Tilly said.

"So y'all heard it too." Charlie asked.

"Yes, Charlie. We did. So once again, if everyone could just get to the fucking gate. Now. Please?" She turned and walked out of the door.

Scott and Ed stood along with Charlie and Jennifer and followed her. Dottie sat down at the table and looked up at Kate.

"Someone needs to pray hard for that girl." Dottie said.

Kate smiled at her and walked out of the door. She paused on the porch and looked down the road. She could see the others gathered in front of the gate. There was a truck stopped on the other side. She saw Bridger swinging the gatepost out of its hole and watched the others back away so the truck could pull inside. She stood watching as the truck pulled in. She saw four people, one of them a child, jump from the back of the truck. Then she saw the driver get out. She took off running.

The only child

For a hundred miles

Kate hugged Josh again. She couldn't stop smiling. The tears rolled down her cheeks freely. She wouldn't let go. Even when she wasn't hugging she tried to touch him. To make sure it was real. Scott watched her after hugging his brother a few times himself. Jennifer and Lori were standing with Devin. Jahda and Ham stood by Martin who was spending a few moments retelling of the stranded vehicle they left just down the road to Bridger.

"We'll get it whenever y'all want but don't worry about the food. We got plenty for now." Evelyn said.

Kate and Josh walked over to the others. Lori saw Josh and joined him. Josh took a moment to introduce his new friends to his family.

"Mom, Scott this is Martin." He turned to Martin. "I can't believe this but I don't know your last name."

"Hauk." Martin said. As he shook hands with Scott and accepted a hug from Kate, Josh turned to introduce them to the smallest member of the group.

"This is Ham." He paused and instantly got the joke. "Hauk."

"Katie is my real name but I don't like it." Ham said.

"Hi Ham. My name is Kate" Kate said as she bent down to shake her hand. Ham looked slightly embarrassed. Then Kate smiled at her.

They all stood by the gate talking for another half hour. Josh told them of what he found at the house, besides his new friends. Devin told the story of the visit to Lori's parents. Jennifer comforted Lori as she shed tears during the telling. As the story unfolded Bridger nodded towards Jahda when Devin described the escape plan.

Josh stood just outside the group gathered around listening to Devin. He looked to his right and saw Charlie listening. He looked around at the rest of the group.

"So Charlie." He said as he turned and looked up the track. He could see the smaller buildings lined up on either side. They were old but standing. He could see two larger buildings at the far end with the bus parked between them. And he saw the barn just to his left. "Is this place as good as it looks?"

"It is. We have a decent water source. Some good supplies and we don't get bothered a lot." Charlie said.

"You're going to have to tell me all about what's happened since I left. By the way where's Amanda?" Josh asked as he looked over the group again.

Charlie straightened his back. His expression bounced between regretful and quizzical. Finally he shuffled his feet below him and absentmindedly rubbed the healing wound under his shirt.

"Yeah. There's a lot we have to tell you about." Charlie said.

The Journal of Cameron Day

Oct 17

NJFD8- Ohio- predicts OSU wins football champ. Ha ha ha

LN8UN VK LI-6161 Comet watch in Australia – cool!!!!!

Oct 19

K5JN4 VK GL – 8116 Virus in Madagascar. Rabies?

7GHN6 KK *8- Medical conference call ??

Oct 20

LN8UN VK LI-6161 AUS Rabies outbreak Same as Madagascar ??

UNI88 – Rabies outbreak Somalia ???

NN79M – Rabies outbreak Iraq ???

WTF is happening with all this rabies?

Oct 21

Spain.

Radio Log

JRD2S 10/19 5995 VK 30 Ohio – Large Railhead MIL VEH Columbus RR Yard

Oct 23

NJF3D 7095. VK 30 NY – Military cordon erected NYU Hospital

Thing is spreading across the whole country. Named Marionette. Time to hit grocery store.

Oct 24

Caravan of sorts came flying by the post office. Two buses and a couple of cars being led by a big SUV. They looked like they were in a hurry. The buses were from South Springs Schools. They drove north. Most folks I had seen at once in days.

Oct 28

The military bombed Atlanta, Baltimore and Kansas City. The radio chatter said all the cities and towns are falling. They also said the military action did little to slow it down. I heard a guy talking from Atlanta. He was stuck in a radio station downtown. He had managed to get the generator of the building running again and stayed on the air until

Oct 29

Sorry. Couldn't finish yesterday. I need to process this. I don't know what to think. Is all this real? Did they really destroy these places? Is this really happening?

Oct 31
FTF3D 3395. Maritime contact
Not doing to well today. I am still listening to the chatter on the radio. It isn't getting any better. Last night I was able to pick up a transmission from some Navy ship trying to make port in Greenland. The port wouldn't let them come into the harbor because they hadn't been cleared as infection free. Sounded like Greenland was infection free. Then I lost the signal.

Nov 4

Never did get the Greenland signal back but I listened to a couple of kids talking to each other last night. One of them was from Ohio and the other was in California. Ohio said that they were stuck in a farmhouse but they had a generator and plenty to eat. California was somewhere outside of San Francisco and was in a garage with his sister. They were trying to find their way to Washington State and found the radio. They had hoped to reach some local help. Ohio was obviously not local but he did try to help. He explained to them what he called the "zombie rules". I wrote them down.

1. Kill the head
2. Don't get bit
3. If you get bit you will turn into one.
4. If you die you will turn into one.
5. Run or die

He said that if you hit them in the head there will be popping sound. That's how you know you got it. He called them poppers.

Ohio's signal faded out. I never found it again.

Nov 9

I listened to a replay of the VP statement that was being played on some loop from New Mexico. Just over and over again.

Nov 11

Today was a big day. I had a visitor. His name was Toles. I can't remember his first name. Some initials I think. JR? JW? Anyway he came looking for the smell that started the other day. He said his group was camped on the Watson place. We talked about the things had been going on. He had seen it up close. By the time he left I had too. It's all real. That night the woods to the north lit up in flames. It came from the direction my visitor went. I don't think I want to go check on him.

New day

I lost track of the date. I think it is the first of December but I can't really tell how that matters any more. It's cold.

The radio is silent. I need to clean the panels again. Or maybe there's no one left.

New day

I am just going to just label everything new day from now on. Food is going to be running out in another week or so. I may not be able to hide much longer.

New Day

Decided to venture out today. The first time I have gone farther than the post office in months it seems. Should have paid attention to the car battery a little more. Walked the two miles over to the Holman farm. I found the Holmans in the barn. Found a horse in the pasture. The horse lives in the post office now. I left the Holmans where I found them.

New Day

Well today is the day the food probably runs out.

New Day

It's been two days of living on the can of tuna fish I found in my old lunchbox. I either have to leave to find food or sit here and starve. Decisions decisions.

The Marionette Zombie Series
Season 2
Includes Series Books 5-8
By SB Poe

Printed in Great Britain
by Amazon

18946949R00243